HOLLYWOOD *dirt*

ALESSANDRA TORRE

Hollywood Dirt

by

Alessandra Torre

ISBN-13: 978-1-940941-71-4

Editor: Madison Seidler
Proofreader: Perla Calas
Front Cover Design: Hang Le
Cover Image: Shutterstock
Formatting: Erik Gevers

This book is dedicated to strong Southern women everywhere, most notably the beautiful and intelligent Tricia Crouch.
Thank you for everything.

This book is set in a real town, with references to real persons. When those names are mentioned, they are used in a fictional manner and should be taken as such.

INTRODUCTION

Southern women are unique; there is no disputing that. We are women born of conflict, our pasts littered with battles and chaos, self-preservation, and protection. We've run plantations during wars, served Union soldiers tea before watching them burn our homes, hidden slaves from prosecution, and endured centuries of watching and learning from our men's mistakes. It is not easy to survive life in the South. It is even more difficult to do it with a smile on your face.

We have held these states together, held our dignity and graciousness, held our head high when it was smeared with blood and soot.

We are strong. We are Southern. We have secrets and lives you will never imagine.

Welcome to Quincy.
Population: 7,800
Average Household Income: We'll never tell.
Secrets: Plenty

The town of Quincy, Georgia was once the wealthiest town in the United States. Home to over 67 Coca-Cola millionaires, each original share is now worth ten million dollars, making this small town of Southern Belles one very lucrative place. Yet, you don't see Bentleys and butlers as you drive through. You see a small town—its plantation mansions gracious and well-tended, keeping with the simple Southern traditions that have existed for centuries. Smile. Treat your neighbor as yourself. Be gracious. Keep your secrets close and your enemies closer.

And from the beginning, Cole Masten was my enemy.

CHAPTER 1

Hollywood doesn't mix well with dirt roads. They don't understand how we work. Don't understand the intricate system of rules that we live by. They think that because we talk slowly, we are stupid. They think that the word 'y'all' is an indication of poor grammar. They think their Mercedes makes them a better person, when—to us—it's just an indication of low self-esteem.

The cavalry arrived on a Sunday afternoon in August. Semis followed by limos, work trucks and buses trailed by matching sedans. Catering trucks—as if we didn't have restaurants in Quincy. Some more semis. The scent of our camellias competed with their exhaust, the huff of diesel bringing with it the scent of pretension and importance. Brakes squealed and everyone in the tri-county area heard it. Even the pecan trees straightened in interest.

A Sunday. Only Yankees would think *that* was an appropriate time to thrust themselves into our lives. Sunday, the Lord's Day. A day spent in the pews at church. Under live oaks eating brunch with our friends and families. Napping through the afternoon hours, front-porch visiting time at dusk. Evening was for quality time with your family. Sunday wasn't a day for upheaval. Sunday wasn't a day for work.

We were at the First Baptist Church when the word hit. A whispered stream of excitement down the long line of the table, scooting by and hopping over cornbread, dumplings, pecan pie, and broccoli casserole. Kelli Beth Barry was the one who passed the news to me, her red hair coming dangerously close to some marshmallowy sweet potato during the relay. "They're here," she said ominously, the excited glow in her blue eyes not matching the dark tones of her message.

I didn't have to ask who 'they' were. Quincy had been waiting for this day for seven months. Ever since the first hint reached Caroline Settles, assistant to Mayor Frazier, who received a phone call on a Monday morning from Envision Entertainment. She had transferred the call to the mayor's office, picked up her box of Red Hots, and settled into the chair outside of his door. Chewed her way through half the box before scooting to her feet and back to her desk, her round butt hitting the seat just in time for the mayor to walk out, his chest puffed, spectacles on, a notepad in hand that she knew good and well only contained doodles.

"Caroline," the man drawled with some level of importance, "I just got a call from some folks in California. They want to film a movie in Quincy. Now we're just in preliminary talks but—" he looked over his spectacles with a degree of sternness and dramatics, "this needs to stay within the walls of this office."

It was a laughable statement, Mayor Frazier knowing what would happen the minute he turned back to his office. In small towns, there are two types of secrets: the kind that we pull together as a mini-nation to protect, and the juicy. The juicy things don't stay quiet. They aren't meant to. They are a small town's sole source of entertainment, the morsels of fat that keep us all healthy. Those secrets are our currency and little is as valuable as a first person, no-one-else-knows-this testimony. Within five minutes, Caroline called her sister from the mayor's personal bathroom, settled in on a padded toilet seat where she breathlessly recounted every word she'd heard through the closed door:

"They said 'plantation'—like *Gone with the Wind…*"
"I heard the name Claudia Van. Do you think *the* Claudia Van is coming to Quincy?"
"He mentioned August, but I don't know if that's this August or next."

The gossip circle had just enough information to run wild, and speculation and false assumptions spread like the lice epidemic of '92. Everyone thought they knew something, and every day a new piece of information was offered up like manna to our starving social lives.

I got lucky. I nabbed a front row seat to the action and became Interesting to a town that had firmly blacklisted my name three years earlier. Interesting was the first step toward Valued, something that Mama and I hadn't been able to accomplish in our twenty-four years in Quincy. It wasn't a status I particularly cared about, but it was something I was intelligent enough not to turn up my nose at.

The movie was the most exciting thing that had ever happened, and the town counted down to the arrival with breathless anticipation.

Hollywood. Glamour. Studios. Celebrities, the most important of whom was Cole Masten.

Cole Masten. The man women think about in the dark of night. When their husbands are snoring, or—in my case—when mothers are sleeping. Quite possibly the most beautiful man to grace Hollywood in the last decade. Tall and strong, with a build that looks perfect in a suit but reveals the muscles of his body when he strips down. Dark brown hair, enough of it to dig your hands in and grab, but short enough to look polished. Green eyes that own you the minute he smiles. A smile that causes you to forget the words out of his mouth because it draws your body into such a state of hopeless need that thought becomes irrelevant. Cole Masten was the epitome of walking sex and had every woman in town drooling over his arrival.

Every woman but me, that is. I couldn't be. For one, he was an ass. All cocky attitude and no manners to speak of. For two, he was—for the next four months—my boss. Everyone's boss. Cole Masten wasn't just the star of this movie. He was sinking his own money into the production, bankrolling the entire operation. It was Cole who read the little Southern novel that no one had ever heard of. The novel about our town, the novel that exposed the plantation homes and work trucks for what they were: camouflage. The camouflage of secret billionaires.

That's right. Our quiet town of seven thousand residents holds more than Southern manners and prize-winning fried chicken recipes. We also hold discretion, the biggest indication of which lies in our bank's coffers and buried in our backyards' dirt. Stacked in freezers and attic eaves.

Cash. Lots and lots of it. In our small town, we have forty-five millionaires and three billionaires. That's a rough guess, the best estimate our whispered calculations can attest to. It may be more. It all depends on how stupid or smart the generations have been with their Coca-Cola stock. That's where it all came from. *Coke.* Say the word Pepsi in this town, you best watch your back on the way out.

So Cole found out Quincy's wealthy little secret. Was fascinated by it, by our little town of such little pretense. And so he assembled a team. Hired a writer. Stayed out of the tabloids long enough to build a three-hour movie around a seventy-two page book. And now… thirteen months after Caroline Settles started the buzz, they had arrived. Hollywood. A day early. I told them to arrive on Monday, told them all of the things wrong with a Sunday arrival. I watched the madness and wondered how many other hiccups awaited us.

I followed the crowd onto the church's lawn, watched Main Street become invaded, men hopping from buses and trucks, a swarm of shouting and pointing as everyone ran in different directions that seemed to make no sense. I smiled. I couldn't help it. This expensive fat bully, pushing its way in on a Sunday. Thinking they were in control. Thinking that this was suddenly their town.

They had no idea what they had just walked into.

SIX MONTHS EARLIER

CHAPTER 2

My mother was a beauty queen. Miss Arkansas 1983. She had me in '87, the circumstances which I haven't been privy to and haven't really cared about. I have vague recollections of my father—a large man, one who smoked cigars and lived in a big house with shiny floors. One who yelled and hit and shook me when I cried. The day after my seventh birthday, Mama woke me up in the middle of the night and we ran. Took his car, a big sedan with leather seats and a Garth Brooks cassette tape that we listened to all the way to Georgia, the only break coming with the whirring of the rewind. Those are my last memories of my prior life. Garth Brooks, leather seats, and my mother crying. I had lain across the back seat, her coat over my body, and tried to understand her tears. Tried to understand why she was doing something if it made her so upset.

We left the car in some town along the way. Drove it 'til it shuddered, then abandoned it and walked, a magazine gripped tightly in my mother's hand. I snuck peeks at it while we moved, tried to focus on the cover, which swung with each swing of her hand. When a man stopped, offered us a ride to the bus stop, his hands lifting me into the back seat, I got a better glimpse, my body stuffed against hers, our suitcase crowding beside us on the seat. The headline read: COCA-COLA MILLIONAIRES. And there, on the front, holding out a glass bottle of Coke, was a bald man, his smile beaming.

Eventually, I met that bald man. Johnny Quitman. He hired my mother as a teller in his bank, a position she still holds to this day. He was one of Quincy's third generations of millionaires, a newbie who still got in early enough to hit it big, hence his enthusiastic cover grin.

For a while, when pondering our late-night escape to this tiny town and the worn magazine clutched in my mother's grip, I thought she was looking for a new husband and hoped to move here and snag one of the rich men mentioned in the article. But she never did. Never even tried. Best I could tell, we moved to town, she settled into work, and never flirted with another man again. Maybe her love for my father was too great to overcome. Or maybe she just needed a safe haven to grow old and die. That was all she seemed to be doing. Waiting to die. A sad end for such a beautiful woman.

I sat on the porch, hot air floating under the edge of my skirt, my bare feet propped on the railing, and watched her. On her knees, a towel down to protect her light slacks, she dug at the roots of an azalea bush, the sweat on her arms glistening in the afternoon sun, a big hat shielding her face from me. She and I were alone in this house, the fireflies more active than our souls. I sat in the heat and watched her work. Contemplated offering her lemonade, though she'd already turned me down twice.

I would not be my mother. I wanted, in some way, to live my life.

CHAPTER 3

"In Hollywood a marriage is a success if it outlasts milk."
~ Rita Rudner

Cole Masten walked slowly down the length of the car, an ice-blue Ferrari, his sunglasses tilted off his face enough to hide his features but give him uninterrupted sight.

"It's a beautiful car," the salesman before him twittered, making an unnecessary hand gesture that encompassed the car in one pretentious gesture.

Of course it was. For three hundred thousand dollars, it should be. He tilted a head at the suit who stood to the left of the car, giving him a quick nod. Justin, his assistant, stepped forward. "He'll take it. I can handle the paperwork and payment. If we can just give Mr. Masten the keys…?"

Cole caught the keychain mid-air and slid behind the wheel, the dealership staff scurrying to unlock the large glass doors that made up the right side of the building. Through the glass, along the street, stood the crowds of people. Of women. Of worship. He clenched his jaw and tapped an impatient beat on the gearshift, waiting. The crowd undulated, hands waving, bodies jumping, a living, breathing thing, one that could love as easily as it could hate. When the glass parted, Cole revved the engine and slowly pulled forward, his glasses back in place, nodding to the crowd and smiling that trademark smile, the one he'd perfected a decade earlier.

Smiled.
Waved.
Nodded at one girl in the front who collapsed against the arms of her friends.

Let the flashes pop. The occasion documented, his foot gentle on the gas until he completed the turn onto the asphalt and could floor it.

He'd spent twelve years in this business—should be used to it. Should be appreciative of it. The lights, the attention… it meant that he was still hot, that his publicists and agents were still doing their job. That the ever-present beast was getting fed and wanting more. That he had a little more time before he was forgotten. That didn't mean he liked it. The invasion. The act.

He took his aggression out on the car, taking the curves of the Hollywood Hills faster than necessary, the Italian car handling the challenge, the back end only skidding a second before gripping the asphalt and tearing off. By the time he came to a stop at the gates of his compound, his heart was beating hard, his mouth stretched in a wide grin. This is what he needed. The risk. The rush. The danger. She'd like it, too. They were cut from the same cloth; one of the things that made them work. He left the car idling in front of the house, and jogged up the steps, his hands in his pockets, a trio of housekeepers passing him, their polite murmurs following up the stairs.

Three years. He'd lived here three years and was still treated like an object. By his staff, by his team. By, at times, his wife. He stepped into the house and saw her, through the back window, at the pool.

A photo shoot. He groaned, wanting some alone time with her, to give her the car, a moment without assistants and cameras, a moment that wasn't going to happen right now. She stood on a rock he had never seen, one brought into their pool area, her spectacular body on full display under the lights, the suit sheer enough that her nipples were visible, their dark buds causing his eyes to sharpen, to take in every photographer present. All men, one of them laughing into her ear as he spread oil across her shoulders. Her eyes met his across the distance, too far for him to read them, the only indication was her chin coming up slightly, and he raised a hand, a smile crossing her face.

Five weeks together—that was all they had. Then she would be headed to Africa, and he would head to New York. The story of their marriage. Bits of time stolen between lives apart.

Maybe he'd drive some more. Burn off some steam. Because right now, for whatever reason, he was angry. Maybe it was the fact that, after half a year apart, he'd come home to find his wife on display. When all he'd wanted, all he'd been waiting for, was to throw her against the wall and thrust out every latent need and desire he'd had for the last six months. Remind himself of how she tasted. How she moaned. How he could make her moan. Without others around. In an empty house, with no one to watch him reunite. He flung open the front door and jogged back down the steps toward her new car.

CHAPTER 4

Someone knocked on our door. I lifted my head from my book and stared at the front door, its clean white surface giving no hint of the mystery behind it. *A knock.*

The sound occurred again, causing me to sit up, setting *Odd Thomas* aside, my curiosity growing. In a town as small as Quincy, one where we didn't lock our doors, a town where there were no strangers, there were two types of visitors:

1. The type of which is considered family, a close friend who could waltz into a house without introduction. I didn't have any of those anymore.

2. The type of which an introductory, I'm-calling-to-ask-if-I-can-stop-in was required. There were no pop-ins, no swing-bys, no unknown knocks on doors. That was rude. Unacceptable.

I'd been well trained in the social etiquette; we all had. There were rules in the South for a reason—we didn't spend the last two hundred years cultivating our society for nothing. I untangled my way from my blanket and moved to the door, pushing aside the lace curtain and staring into the face of a stranger. A smiling, waving energetically, as if he isn't popping by unannounced, stranger. Fairly handsome, actually. Perfect skin, white teeth, a brilliant blue polo tight enough on his upper body to show some gym-grown masculinity. I opened the door.

"May I help you?"

"God I hope so." At the words, my libido returned to its pit of despair, every syllable on the man's tongue drenched in an over-affected gay man's lilt, his slouch against the doorframe filled with such dramatic despair that I almost laughed. "*Please* tell me you are the owner of this fabulous estate."

Ha. Funny. I was wearing Keds, the toe cracked from too many cycles in the wash. The watch on my wrist was one that included plastic as its main ingredient, and I was standing in the doorway of the former slave quarters of the Anna Holden plantation. This guy was hilarious. "Nope," I drawled, crossing my arms. "Why?"

He had the ridiculous reaction of looking perturbed, like it wasn't my business. As if he hadn't knocked on my door and interrupted my reading. "Do you have the number of the owner?"

I shook my head. "I'm not handing out the Holdens' number to a stranger. What do you want with them?"

"I'm not really at liberty to discuss." He sniffed.

I shrugged. I wasn't going to sit here and beg the man. He wanted to be all secretive, fine. "Good luck." I smiled politely and shut the door, interrupting my view of his agitated face. The Holdens were in Tennessee for the next two months. He could pound his manicured hand on every door to their mansion or he could come back with a side of information. The choice was his.

It took three days for the pretty boy to return. I saw him coming the second time, his seersucker suit moving gingerly down the dirt path to our cottage. I looked up from my place in the rocker and gestured to the empty one beside me. "Feel free to take a seat, Mr. Payne. It's hot out."

It *was* hot. The type of humid heat that saps your energy within minutes. The type of heat that brings out crocodiles and snakes—the evil creatures. Everyone with any sense is indoors. Yet, here were Bennington Payne and I, under the eaves of my rented porch, the fan beating a furious tune, creating a waft of hot air just bearable enough to keep me in place. I reached down, dug in the ice bucket at my feet and pulled out a beer. Held it out to him, my own stuck in between my thighs.

He didn't argue, didn't give me any sass, just grabbed the beer, took one dubious look at my free rocking chair, then plopped down, twisting the lid off and flashing me a grateful smile. "How'd you know my name?" he asked, delicately wiping his mouth after downing half of the Bud Light.

I rocked back, my hair pulled up and secured by my head. "The way you've been stomping around? The cows in Thomas County know your name by now." I laughed against the mouth of my beer, tipping it back as I glanced sideways at the man. "You can take off that jacket, you know. It's not earning you anything other than sweat."

He turned to me, his face studying mine as if I held another sentence inside. Getting none, he set down his beer and pulled off the jacket, folding it over carefully before leaning back in the chair, the jacket protected in a neat package on his lap. It was a smart move. Local police can read crime scene actions just by following the drags and prints in the pollen. It's our curse of the South. That, and mosquitos and snakes and flying cockroaches and the hundred other minute contributions that scare off Northerners.

"Is that why I've been so unsuccessful?" he asked. "Because I'm, as you so politely put it, stomping around?"

"It's two-fold," I said bluntly. "You're stomping around, *and* you're not telling anyone why. No one likes that. We are a private town. We don't really welcome strangers. Not your type of strangers. We welcome honeymooners, vacationers, tourists. You're here for something else, and that makes everyone very suspicious."

He sat in silence for a moment, finishing the rest of his beer with one long draw. "I was instructed to be discreet," he finally said.

I laughed. "Were you instructed to be successful? 'Cause you can't be both."

The sun moved a little lower, to the place where it peeks through the trees and glares on the front porch, the moment of day when I typically pack up and head back inside. I reached over, snagging his empty bottle and dropped it with mine into the bucket, standing and stretching before him. I stuck out a hand. "Summer Jenkins."

"Bennington Payne. My friends call me Ben. And, at the moment, you're looking like the only friend I have here."

"Let's not label the relationship just yet." I smiled. "Come on in. I've got to put supper on."

"It's just unnatural, a girl that age being unmarried. Especially as pretty as she is."

"Well, what do you expect? You know what happened with Scott Thompson. Summer hasn't had so much as a breakfast date since then."

CHAPTER 5

Mama and I lived in the former slave quarters of what was once the largest plantation in the South. I acted as caretaker of the plantation, making sure the groundskeeper kept the grass at two inches or less, kept the pecans picked, and the house spotless. The Holdens spent five months a year at this home, the other seven months hopping between a Blue Ridge cabin and a California home. They were an oddity in Quincy, one of the rare families that took periodic leave of our city limits. I'd heard the snide comments, seen the sniffs of disapproval when their seats sat empty at Easter Service. It was ridiculous. The whole town was ridiculous. A bunch of rich folks squatting on their money until they died. Everyone silently tallying up each other's millions when no one really knew who had what. The core group had all started the same: forty-three initial Coca-Cola investors put in two thousand dollars each in 1934. On that one day, in that one moment, they were all equal. Over the next twenty years, with stock sales, purchases, reinvestments, marriages, divorces, and bad decisions, some networths sky-rocketed, some became paupers.

Now, it's a guessing game of who's richer than whom. It doesn't really matter. It's all more than any one generation will ever be able to spend.

Six years ago I accepted care of the Holden estate in return for free board and five hundred bucks a month—a very fair trade for a job that takes around ten hours a week. Mother moved into the cottage's second bedroom and covered the groceries and household items. Yes, I was a twenty-nine year old woman who lived with her mother. One who didn't do drugs, party, or have sex. I read books, drank the occasional beer on a hot afternoon, and did the *Times* crossword puzzle on Sunday afternoons. I hadn't attended college, I wasn't particularly gorgeous, and I often forgot to shave my legs. On the upside, I could cook some mean dumplings and bring myself to orgasm within five minutes. Not at the same time, mind you. I wasn't *that* talented.

And, right then, with whatever Bennington Payne had up his sleeve, I was his best bet. Even if I wasn't one of the elite. Even if I was a Quincy outcast.

CHAPTER 6

I pulled a chicken from the fridge and placed it in the sink, running water over it to finish its thaw. Turning to Bennington, I caught his study of our home. "Like what you see?"

"It's very homey," he said brightly, taking a seat on one of the dining chairs.

I hid my smirk with a turn back to the sink. "Spill, Bennington. What do you need in Quincy?" I yanked open the freezer door, grabbing bags of vegetables.

There was a last moment of hesitation before he spoke, his words suddenly quick on their tumble out, the feminine lilt masked by a briskness that spoke of a big city. "I'm from Envision Entertainment. I'm a location scout. I need to procure spots for—"

"The movie," I finished, setting aside the chicken and filling a large pot, proud of myself for having at least one piece of information.

"Yes." He looked surprised. "How'd you—"

"We've all known since the day the mayor was called," I said dryly. "You might as well have put up a billboard on 301."

"So then there shouldn't be a problem," he said eagerly. "If everyone knows a movie's coming, then I'll just approach the plantations—"

I cut off his enthusiastic response with a quick shake of my head. "No one's gonna let you film at their home."

That stopped him, his face turning an interesting shade of gray that clashed with his blond highlights. "Why not?"

"Why would they?"

"Money? Fame? Bragging rights?"

I laughed. "First, no one in Quincy needs money—present company excluded, of course. And even if they *did* need money—which they don't—they aren't going to broadcast it by allowing your film crews to take over their plantation." I ticked off the first point on my fingers.

"Second, this is the old South. Fame isn't a good thing. Neither are bragging rights. The more you brag, the more flash you show—that's a sign of weakness, of insecurity. You can tell the truly wealthy from their confidence, their grace. People here don't show their wealth, they hide it. They covet it."

The man stared at me as if I spoke Greek. "But all the mansions," he sputtered. "The big gates, the diamonds…" His eyes darted around my humble abode as if my threadbare space would hold some proof as to his point.

"All old wealth," I said, waving a hand dismissively. "Purchases made back when they were cotton farmers with new money. Back when Coke went big and the whole town celebrated their wealth together. That was almost a hundred years ago. Two generations back. Have you seen any new construction in town? Rolls Royces with air conditioning and satellite radio?" I waited, turning off the water and setting the pot on the stove.

"So what do I do? I need a mansion. Preferably two. Fifteen other locations to shoot at!" His voice squeaking, he dug a shaky hand in his pocket and pulled out a bottle of medication, his panic attack occurring without a single wrinkle in his forehead. I looked in fascination and fought the urge to poke it and see if it moved.

"It would seem…" I said slowly, snagging a glass and filling it with water, "that you need a local source. Someone who Quincy knows and trusts. Someone who can target the landholders who would be amendable. Someone to handle negotiations with the local vendors, hotels, and city officials."

"But that's my job," he protested weakly, accepting the glass of water, his throat bulging as he gulped it down.

"And what are they paying you for that?" I leaned back and crossed my arms, staring down Ben in hopes he'd break. I hadn't really expected him to break. I'd expected him to brush off his girly suit and ignore the question. But I was wrong and I fought to keep the surprise from my face when he answered.

"A hundred and twenty," he said primly, crossing his legs and straightening the fabric of his pleats, as if he were regaining some semblance of composure by spilling his guts.

"Thousand?" I shouldn't have even asked; it was a stupid question with an obvious answer. He wasn't sitting at my scratched table for the price of a vacuum cleaner.

"Yes. But that's for five months of my time. Negotiations, red tape management, the—"

"I'll do it for twenty-five, cash." I stepped forward and held out my hand, my face set, poker-stare in full force.

"Fifteen," he countered, already rising to his feet and eyeing my outstretched palm.

"Twenty." I glared. "Remember, I'm the only hope you have."

He reached out with a smile and shook my hand, his grip firmer than I expected. "Deal."

I squeezed his hand and flashed my own smile back at him. *But, between me and you? I'd have done it for five hundred bucks.*

CHAPTER 7

Ben was staying at the Wilson Inn, a mistake, but one I didn't blame him for making. Quincy has two major lodging options: the Wilson Inn, a three-star motel, and the Budget Inn, a place my cockroaches would turn their noses up at. What lies below the internet's radar are our bed-and-breakfasts, seven of them in the square-mile radius of Quincy proper. I told him to pack up and booked him a room at the Raine House, the nicest of our B&Bs. We set a date for eight the next morning at the coffee shop on Myrtle Way. I told him to bring cash and I'd bring names.

The next morning, over a cracked linoleum table, I added a little Southern into Ben in the form of grits and gravy. And he added five thousand dollars' worth of Hollywood into me with crisp green bills. We worked for four hours, ending the meeting with a clear game plan and a schedule for the next week. He drove off in his rental car, and I started calling names on our list.

It wasn't an easy sell. Say my name in Quincy and a typical upper-crust face will curl in distaste. Try to then wrangle a favor out of them and you might as well be digging into rock with a plastic fork. But I knew my place. I rolled over and played weak. I groveled and kissed wrinkled buttocks and made sure they felt superior. And I got Ben four appointments out of twenty calls made. I hung up the phone a few hours later with a tired smile, happy with the outcome. It was more than I had hoped for out of Quincy. Maybe three years has been long enough, maybe the mud on my face was starting to wear off.

Or maybe, between the movie and the cash, some Quincy residents were willing, for just one quick moment, to overlook my sins.

CHAPTER 8

"Mr. Masten, tell us about your wife."

"I'm pretty sure you're familiar with her." He smiled, and the woman blushed. She crossed, then re-crossed her legs.

"When did you know that Nadia Smith was *it* for you?"

"We met on the set of *Ocean Bodies*. Nadia was Bikini Babe Number 3 or something like that." He laughed.

"And you were Cole Masten."

"Yeah. I walked into my trailer one day and she was stretched out on the bed in a string bikini. I think that was probably when I knew. When I saw this gorgeous brunette, without a shred of self-doubt, lying on that bed as if she belonged there. She's gonna kill me for telling this story."

"And that was it?"

"Tracy, you've seen my wife. I didn't really have a chance."

"You've now been married almost five years, which, in Hollywood, is quite a feat. What would you tell our readers is your best advice for a successful marriage?"

"That's a tough one. I think a lot of elements make for a successful marriage. But if I had to pick one, I think honesty is crucial. Nadia and I have no secrets between us. We've always said, it's better to just get things out in the open and deal with them, no matter the consequences."

"I think that's great. Thank you for your time, Mr. Masten. And good luck on *The Fortune Bottle*."

"Thank you, Tracy. Always great to see you."

CHAPTER 9

Mama and I had a routine, our life a well-oiled machine that worked. Nights I cooked dinner, she did the dishes and cleaned up. On the weekends, we cooked together. Most of our social life revolved around cooking, growing, or eating food. But that was life, especially for a woman, in the South. Other women might take offense to that, but I *liked* to cook. And I *loved* to eat. And nobody made food that compared with what came out of your own garden and kitchen.

I get that living with Mama wasn't exactly the sexiest concept around. I knew that some people found it odd. But we'd always gotten along, and given our limited incomes, we'd needed the financial assistance of each other.

Mama had grown quiet since I'd gotten the job with Ben. I hadn't told her about the money yet, but I could feel the wings of my freedom flexing, pushing on the bones of my shoulders.

I needed to tell her about the money.
I needed to tell her about my plan, not that one had been formulated yet.
I needed to tell her that I was going to leave.
She needed to know that, soon, she would be alone.

I could hear her moving in her room, heard the scrape of a hanger on the rod, her floor creaking. It was a good time to tell her, as good a time as any. I folded down the corner of the page I was reading and closed the paperback, before setting it on the table.

Her door was open, and I leaned against the doorframe and watched her, her hair damp and in rollers, her nightgown sticking to her legs, her feet pale, toes that no one but me ever saw painted dark red. She glanced at me when she turned to the bed, the laundry half-sorted, her hands digging through the pile and pulling out socks.

"The movie," I started. "You know… my job with Ben."

"Yes?" She paired two socks with quick efficiency and rolled them.

"I'll get a lot of money from it. Enough to—"

"Leave town." She set down the roll of socks and looked up at me.

"Yes." Leave *her.* That was really what the root of this problem was, and I tried to find the words to explain…

"Don't worry about me." She stepped around the bed and toward me. "That's what you're doing right? Feeling guilty?"

"You could come," I offered. "There's not anything here—"

"Summer." She stopped me, putting a firm hand on my arm. "Let's go sit on the porch."

We turned off the front porch light in an attempt to ward off mosquitoes, the moon beaming at us across hundreds of neat cotton plants. *I will miss our porch.* I thought about that as I settled into one of its rockers, the tension leaving my shoulders in the first push of my foot on the railing. It was hot as Hades outside, the battle against mosquitoes a constant fight, but still. There was something about the absolute solitude that I loved. It grounded me, calmed any anxiety in my bones.

"Quincy was a great place for you to grow up, Summer." The words floated over from her rocker, the creak of her chair moving her shadow back and forth beside me. "The people here are good. I know sometimes, with the way you've been treated, that it's hard to see that, but—"

"I know." I spoke quietly, and the words came out clogged. I cleared my throat and spoke louder. "They are." I meant it. I'd never really know anywhere else, but I understood, deep in my bones, the beauty of the town, of the people who lived there. Even with the hatred toward me, the disdain I could feel in their looks, this town still loved me because I was one of its own. A bastard child, yes. A non-native, sure. But there wasn't a person in our county who wouldn't stop to help me if I broke down on the side of the road. Not a soul who wouldn't pray for me in church if I fell sick. If Mama lost her job tomorrow, our fridge would be stocked with casseroles and our mailbox filled with donations. I didn't think there were a lot of places in this country like that. I thought it took a town of a certain size, of a certain mindset, to be that way.

"It was a great place to grow up," she repeated. "But you are a woman now. And you need to find your own place. I know that. I wouldn't be a good mother if I tried to hold you back. I'm just sorry that I couldn't, financially, put you on this path sooner."

"I could have left before, Mama. Plenty of times." And I could have. I could have gotten a job in Tallahassee. Or taken advantage of the Hope Scholarship and gone to Valdosta State or Georgia Southern. Gotten student loans and been on my merry way. I didn't really know why I didn't. It just never felt right. And my desire to leave Quincy wasn't ever strong enough to prompt action. Then Scott and I started dating, and any thoughts of leaving were discarded. Funny how love could spin your life in an entirely new direction before you even realized what had happened. And when you did realize, you didn't care because the love was bigger than you and your wants.

Our love had been bigger than me. That's what had made its crash so devastating.

"Where will you go?" Mama's voice was calm, as if I hadn't just taken her world and broken it in two.

"I don't know." It was the truth. I had no idea where I'd go. "Do you want to come?"

I felt her hand find mine, her grip strong and loving. "No sweetie. But you will always have a home here, and with me. Let that give you the confidence to take risks."

It was a sweet sentiment. I continued to hold her hand, our rockers moving in sync and tried to figure out how much, out of the twenty thousand, I could spare and how long that small amount would last her.

CHAPTER 10

"Assuming a role is like putting on another life and trying it on for size. You spend four months in that life and sometimes pieces of it stick."
~ Nadia Smith

Cole Masten settled into the seat of his Bentley and picked up his cell. Dialed his wife's number and pressed a button, sending the call through the bluetooth. He listened to the phone ring through the speakers and pulled out of Santa Monica Airport, heading north on Centinela Avenue toward home. The time spent in New York had been hell. Half promotional, half productive—at least he'd made some headway on *The Fortune Bottle*. For the first time since he'd started in this business, he felt excited by something. Maybe it was the risk of his money in the pot. Maybe it was the thought of total control—of the cast, the direction, the marketing. Total control was a rarity in Hollywood, a rarity that had cost him financially. But it would all pay off, with interest, when it hit the box office. This movie would be huge, he knew it, had felt it ever since he'd first heard of the sleepy town full of millionaires.

Nadia's voicemail came on, and he ended the call, weaving in between slower cars as he drew closer to home. If she weren't home, she would be soon. He'd managed to finish a day early, to give them at least one extra day together before he left for Georgia. Only six weeks until filming started. He turned up the radio, tapping his fingers against the steering wheel as he downshifted and passed a semi. He'd send the staff away as soon as he got there to give them some privacy.

The sky was dark by the time he wound up their tight, curving street and pressed the button, opening the gate. He saw her Ferrari parked in the garage and smiled. Jerked his car into park and hopped out, his fingers itching to touch her skin, inhale her scent, push her down on the bed. He walked up the side path, the stone uneven beneath his shoes, the landscape lighting illuminating the tall palms in dramatic fashion as he moved to the back door.

When he walked in the house, it was quiet and dark. He stopped in the kitchen, emptying his pockets onto the counter and pulling off his jacket. There was a note to Nadia on the large marble island, one from Betty, the house manager. He glanced at it, then lifted his head, the sound of the shower starting above him.

Skipping the elevator, he jogged up the stairs, a smile on his face when he reached the second floor. It was the strange voice that stopped his smile, the laugh that was distinctly masculine, and he opened the door slowly, the light from the hall spilling into the dim bedroom, the lit bathroom illuminating in clear fashion the end of his marriage.

Nadia's hands were on the counter. He had always loved her hands. Delicate fingers, she had played piano as a child. They were very dexterous. That night, her polish was a deep brown. The nails had coordinated with the tan granite that they dug into.

Nadia's head was tilted down, her mouth open in an O of pleasure, the man's head at her neck, saying something against her hair. Her feet were bare and spread, pushed up on her toes, a position that pushed out her beautiful ass. The man's hands gripped that ass.

"I love your ass," Cole whispered, his mouth nipping at the skin.
"Of course you do," she giggled, rolling onto her back, destroying his view.
"I hereby claim it as mine."
She propped up on her elbows. "Uh uh uh. That ass belongs to my future husband."
"Then let me own it."
She tilted her head at him, a question in her smile.
"Be my wife, Nadia. Let me worship at the shrine of you until I die."
"Now, Mr. Masten, how can I possibly say no to that?"

The man pushed his hips forward, and he heard her gasp. Saw the flex of her arms as she pushed back against him.

Cole stepped into the bedroom, his head pounding, his chest tight. The sounds of his feet on the carpet were thunderous, yet the couple didn't turn, his wife didn't hear, didn't notice. Maybe because she was too busy moaning, her head lifting and falling back against his shoulder, one of her beautiful hands leaving the counter and reaching out to the mirror, bracing against it.

"Tell me you'll never leave me," Cole whispered the words against her neck as he kissed the skin there.
"Never?" Her eyes opened wide in mock indecision. "Never is a very long time, Mr. Masten."
"Tell me you'll always be honest with me. Tell me you won't ever leave without letting me fix whatever issue first." He lifted off her neck and hovered over her face.
She pushed against him with a laugh. "Silly man, we won't ever have issues. I am an issue-less woman."
"Every couple has issues, Nadia."
"Not us," she whispered, her legs parting beneath him, her smooth legs wrapping around his waist and pulling him tighter.
"Never?"
"Never."

He didn't know how the elephant got in his hand, its ceramic body heavy as it looked up at him with a peaceful expression. It was a Buddhist piece, something Nadia brought back from India, their decorator finding 'the perfect display post' for it, one that sat to the right of the bathroom entrance. But he recognized, when he closed his hands around it, the fury that pushed hard through his veins. Fury he hadn't felt in a long time. Not since he was a teenager with out-of-control hormones. Now, as a grown man, Cole stepped from the dim room into the lit bathroom with the elephant in hand, both hands, because for a peaceful animal the thing was heavy. Not too heavy to distract him from the words of the man, a disgusting proclamation of emotion. Not too heavy to drown out the response of his wife, saying the three words that were to be sacred only to them, forever and ever. He felt the thin string of control break as he swung the elephant hard, from left to right, hitting the shoulder…
"Tell me you won't ever leave."
and then colliding with the head…
"Never."
of the stranger fucking his wife.

The man crumpled to Cole's marble floor, and Nadia's scream was so loud it hurt.

CHAPTER 11

I was in church when the news hit. My toes were pushing against the tight fit of my heels, my eyes on the back of Mrs. Coulston's head. She had a mole on the back of her neck. A light brown mole. It was horrifically ugly, yet I couldn't take my eyes away. Couldn't concentrate on the sermon, which was probably for the best since this was the time of year that it was all about tithing and financial duties to the church. This time of year always made my skin crawl, my opinion of Pastor Dinkon drop, my goodwill to the church faltering in one half-guilty, half-irritated step. I understood that money was needed, to pay the utility bill, to resurface our church's parking lot. But *my* money wasn't needed. Not when Bill Francis had donated five million to this little church just three years ago. Not when we were constantly having bake sales and pancake breakfasts and a hundred other things. Fifty dollars out of my monthly five hundred was a drop in the ocean of the church's coffers.

Beside me, in my new Nine West purse—a *Fortune Bottle* splurge—my hand groped, moving past tissues and pens before I finally found my goal: a peppermint. My fingers closed on the plastic-wrapped mint. I had to unzip it further to slide my hand out and Mama stiffened, turning and shooting me a look of disapproval. I withdrew the mint from the red leather and carefully pulled on its plastic twisted end. The process sounded loud, and I held my breath as I eased the candy out, Pastor Dinkon's guiltfest sermon continuing, uninterrupted. We were about twenty minutes in, which was about halfway, and I popped it in my mouth, returning my eyes to the mole. She really shouldn't wear an updo. Then again, I tried to remember the last time I saw Mrs. Coulston with her hair down and came up blank. I guess, at her age, women didn't really wear their hair down, some unspoken rule—the same rule that made most women her age go short. I was glad she hadn't hacked it all off and gone the updo route instead; her hair really did look beautiful—dark black and silver strands twisting perfectly up and pinned. The mole was really the only problem. Surely she could get it removed. Frozen off or something. The thought suddenly struck me that she might not even know it was there. It *was* on the back of her neck. I had the sudden, horrible desire to touch her shoulder. Gently, just a *nudge*. Nudge at her and point. Bring her Sunday morning attention to it.

A horrible idea. I sat on my hands just to make sure it didn't happen.

There was a commotion three rows up. A shifting, leaning, shuffling. Mayor Frazier was trying to get out of his row. In the middle of the *sermon*. I watched with fascination as he dipped and weaved, his mouth making regretful motions, his face tight. I elbowed Mama, but she was already watching. Everyone was, a general shift of disapproval at the distraction. Typical Quincy. I knew I wasn't the only one bored; I knew the disapproving hums were actually *happy* for some action, something to poke their minds before they headed in the direction of a nap.

When Mayor Frazier's shoes finally hit the middle aisle's floor, their black shiny selves moved. Quick, important steps, his hand wrapped tight around his cell phone, and I suddenly realized that this was about more than just an urgent need to urinate. This was something else, something that made his eyes light up, his cell phone at the ready, his feet all but jogging to the exit. When he passed our row, his eyes darted to me, and there was a moment of connection, a moment where I realized that this was about The Movie.

Something had happened. And suddenly, my interest in Mrs. Coulston's mole and notifying her of its existence was gone. In that moment, with twenty minutes left in the sermon and a sea of bodies on either side of me, I wanted only one thing: to hop over the aisle and follow him.

I didn't, of course. For one, Mama's hand settled on my arm and squeezed. A warning squeeze, one that said *I know what you're thinking* and *Don't you dare*, all at one time. For two, I wasn't a barbarian. I did have some form of self-control, some respect for our God Almighty and for Pastor Dinkon, even if that day's sermon was a load of fundraising crap.

I sat there, my nails biting into my panty-hosed knee, my toes pushing against the front of my shoes, and waited. All through the sermon. The offering. All through three songs of worship. Through the closing, and then, with the crowd rising as one polite mass, I grabbed my purse and bolted out, my eyes frantic for the mayor.

"That Bobbi Jo girl never did anything to nobody. And now she's in an insane asylum after what Summer Jenkins did."

"An asylum? I thought Bobbi Jo was up in Athens. Dating a doctor up there."

"Nope. She's in an asylum. Doped up on drugs all the time. That's why no one's heard from her. Her mama made up that Athens story to save face. But Summer's the one who should be locked up. That's my opinion."

CHAPTER 12

IS CODIA FINISHED?

Associated Press. Los Angeles, California.

Police and emergency personnel were called to the Hollywood Hills West home of Cole Masten and Nadia Smith Saturday night at approximately 7 PM. Shortly after their arrival, an ambulance departed, heading to Hollywood Presbyterian Medical Center where Jordan Frett was admitted into ICU, his head wrapped in blood-soaked cloths. There were no arrests made as of press time, but police stayed at the Masten residence until almost midnight, photographers clogging the narrow street leading to their home. "Paparazzi were so thick we couldn't get through," Hollywood Hills resident Dana Meterrezi said. "It was a crowd of cameras and people, all converged on the Mastens' gate, some trying to crawl up the fence. I saw the police arresting three of them, just in the ten minutes it took me to get through." A total of eleven paparazzi were arrested and charged with trespassing and unlawful entry.

Rumors have ripped through Hollywood, both parties' representation declining to comment. The only quote we could get was from Jordan Frett himself, who said from his hospital bed, "Nadia Smith is an incredible woman." Frett is the director of Smith's current project, a romantic comedy set in South Africa. Why Frett was at the Mastens' home is unknown.

The Mastens have been married for five years.

CHAPTER 13

"Is this bad?" I leaned against the countertop and looked at Ben, whose expression was pale and tight, his fingers a blur over his laptop, my puny internet service already cursed into oblivion an hour earlier. "I mean, I know this is bad, but *how* bad is this?"

"Gargantuanly bad."

I broke open a boiled peanut and popped the nut in my mouth. Thank God my check had already cleared. I mean, not all of it. The studio still owed Ben a quarter of his paycheck, so Ben still owed me five grand, but I was sitting on a fatter bank account than I'd ever seen so if *The Fortune Bottle* went up in flames, it didn't make too much difference to me. I tossed the shell into a Solo cup and watched Ben, a man who seemed awfully stressed considering he had also received the bulk of his monies. "Why do *you* care if *The Fortune Bottle* crashes?"

He looked up. "*The Fortune Bottle* isn't crashing. Movies don't fall apart over *this*." He waved his hands to encompass whatever *this* was.

Another peanut followed the first into my mouth, the resulting chew squirting in beautiful salty goodness. "Then what's the problem?"

"The problem is Codia. Cole and Nadia are the glue that holds our picture perfect world together. The glittery ideal that we all strive to become. They are at the center of our world and the forefront of the public's eye. They buy each other extravagant gifts, have ridiculously hot sex, and vacation on yachts in St. Barths. Codia *can't* fall apart, they *can't* get divorced, they can't even squabble over dinner reservations! And they certainly can't have Cole attempt murder on Nadia's lover!" His voice squeaked, and I saw, for the first time in four-and-a-half months, a break in the perfect landscape that was his forehead.

I pointed a finger in wonder. "I think you have a wrinkle."

"What?"

"On your forehead. When you were just yammering on about Cadia. Your forehead actually moved."

"Codia. Not Cadia. Codia." His chair shot away from the table, my internet performance forgotten, his smooth-soled shoes heading to the bathroom in search of a mirror.

"Whateveria," I mumbled, stepping to the fridge to grab the sweet tea. I refilled my own and then poured him a glass, setting it down with purpose next to his energy drink. I didn't care if it happened the last day of his visit. The man would, eventually, drink my sweet tea and love it. Ben stepped from the bathroom, his hand on his forehead, his face irritated. I waited until he sat down before I spoke.

"I got a call from the sheriff."

Aww… the cute little wrinkle reappeared. "About?" he asked anxiously.

"Cole Masten. Jeff's worried he's violent. Doesn't want him in our town. He's gotten some calls from voters."

"Voters?" The wrinkle deepened, and I fought back a smile.

"It's an elected position. Being sheriff, I mean. Votes are everything, especially in an election year."

"Which, I assume, this is."

"Yep."

"Of course it is." He groaned. "Of all the things I worried about, Cole Masten's risk to townsfolk was never one of them."

"The sheriff's not as worried about our townsfolk's safety as…" I shifted against the counter and found a new position.

"As what?" His hand closed around the tea glass, and I mentally urged him on.

"Well." I shrugged. "This is a carry state. We value our personal safety. I think he's a little concerned your Californian Golden Boy is going to get himself shot."

The glass of tea froze halfway to his lips. He coughed out a laugh, then smiled cautiously. "You're kidding."

"I am definitely not kidding."

"You can't shoot Cole Masten. No one is *shooting* Cole Masten." He stood as if he was going to defend Cole himself, the base of the tea glass hitting the table, a splash of it coming out. Well damn.

"Well, sure. As long as he isn't running around hurting people. But you might want to have a chat with him. Let him know these country bumpkins are armed."

"Nobody just 'has a chat' with Cole. He has layers of people to go through for that."

"Well, then." I waved my hand. "Tell all those people."

Ben stared at me for a long moment, a twitch in his jaw jumping.

"You want dinner?" I finally asked. "I'm making fried catfish."

"Yes." The word was out of his lips before I even named the meal. I turned back to the fridge, the furious tempo of his fingers against keys resuming. The poor man. I swore, at the way he scrambled for food, I didn't think, prior to Quincy, he'd ever been properly fed.

CHAPTER 14

When you spend half a decade of your life with someone, the ending should occur in a personal fashion. Face to face, hand in hand. Words spoken out of lips kissed, tears shed on seen cheeks. It shouldn't be easy; it should be painful and honest; it should take hours instead of minutes; it should involve yells and cries and discussions, but it should be substantial. A moment thought over and worked out. Not the casual and simple act of a stranger handing over a legal envelope.

Cole was in the downstairs gym when it came, on his back, his arms straining upward, his third set almost done when the door opened. He stared at the ceiling, and worked through the remaining reps, his breath huffing out on each upward press, his mind thinking through what he would say, and how he would say it. The apology, that was what he was stuck on. Was an apology required when he injured someone who she was fucking? It wasn't just the fucking that was the problem. Fucking wasn't allowed, but it was understandable, the animalistic need of one body to couple with another, a million years of survival instincts pushing through veins eager to procreate. The issue was that this hadn't been just fucking. This had been a relationship, an affair. Cole had heard her tell that prick that she *loved* him. That was the problem. And a hundred sets weren't fixing the problem. He racked the barbell and sat up. Looked right, his bare chest heaving, he was surprised to see a man in the doorway. Not Nadia after all. All that deliberation over what to say, for nothing.

"What?" he called out, his voice echoing slightly in the big space.

"I'm with Benford, Casters, and Sunnerberg, Mr. Masten." Way too many names stacked in one short sentence. Cole wiped his forehead warily and saw his assistant standing behind the man, his face tight.

"And?"

"I'm just dropping this off." He held out a crisp white folder, COLE MASTEN stamped on the front as if born that way, the folder thick enough to contain a hundred headaches. A lawsuit. Probably from that prick director. He was surprised it had taken this long. It'd been almost four days since that night. He nodded to Justin, and his assistant sprang forward.

"I'll take it."

"We'll just need your signature of acceptance, Mr. Masten," the stranger said.

Cole held out a hand and accepted the clipboard and pen, his hand damp when it gripped the instrument, his signature sloppy across the bottom of the receipt. He held it out, ignoring the man's words of thanks. Leaning back on the bench, his hands wrapping around the iron, his palms bit into the grip.

"Aren't you going to open it?" Justin spoke from the doorway.

He didn't lift his head, didn't look away from the ceiling. "Let Tony handle it. Settle with the prick."

"It's from Nadia."

That caused his head to lift, and he ducked out from under the bar, his eyes meeting Justin's. "The package?" Reality didn't come in a sudden burst of understanding; it was a slow dawn. *Not a lawsuit. If not a lawsuit then…* "No." He shook his head. "No."

"I haven't opened it, but…"

"She's just mad. Embarrassed. Hell, I don't know how cheating wives feel. But she wouldn't have…" He pushed to his feet, grabbing the envelope out of Justin's hands, his fingers ripping at the seal, pulling out the thick stack of documents, stapled together at the top, the court's stamp already present, crooked in its imprint, as if this life changing document hadn't been worth a straight stamp. Jesus, the paps would have it by now, the news, his agent… he flipped the first page over. "Has Owen called yet?" Owen Phiss, his publicist. Also Nadia's publicist. Christ, how intertwined could two lives be? He thrust the papers at Justin and stepped away, his hands clenching into fists, his mind trying to sort through too many emotions at once, the wave of them competing for the narrow channel that was his sanity.

"Call Tony. Get him that." Tony Fragetti, his attorney. An entertainment attorney, not necessarily the strongest card right now. Yet Tony—like everything else in this house, in this life—was also Nadia's. "Stop." Justin paused, his cell phone out, and looked up. "Wait." Cole walked to the wall and put his palms on the surface, his fingers pushing into the padded wall covering, and he wondered, if he punched it, what would break. He let out a long, controlled breath.

"Don't do anything." When the words finally came, they had purpose and direction, and he pushed off the wall and walked to the door, grabbing his water bottle off the floor and finishing it off. "I'm going to find Nadia."

CHAPTER 15

Yes, for a girl like me, twenty thousand dollars was a lot. The most money I had ever seen. Enough for a ticket out of this town, enough to get my own place far from here, in a city that didn't crown a Peanut Princess every August. Twenty thousand was enough for me to buy a reliable car, some clothes with new tags on them, an education. But after careful financial calculations done, it wasn't enough, not to properly set up Mama in a new place, one with a rent payment and deposit. I stood in the kitchen and watched her iron and wondered if I could really leave her. Pack my bags and kiss her cheek goodbye. Wondered how much of her support was a farce, and how much was real.

I needed more out of Hollywood. As much as I could get. I grabbed my keys off the ring and a Cherry Coke from the fridge. "I'm running into town," I called to her. "Gonna track down Ben. I'll be back later."

She waved, a smile crossing her face, her eyes darting back to the tricky collar of the shirt before her.

Ben and I were almost done. The spots had all been picked, fields cleared for set construction, the old Piggly Wiggly parking lot rented for the trailers. Quincy didn't have enough lodging, the crew and cast booking up every hotel room in the surrounding five cities—Tallahassee only forty-five minutes away. But forty-five minutes, according to Ben, was too far, so the Piggly Wiggly lot was now a mini-city, RVs and trailers stacked so close together it looked like a refugee camp, if a refugee camp had million-dollar RVs. It was hilarious. It was entertaining. And it was exciting. Really exciting. I had shook hands next to Ben, examined shooting schedules and saw budgets, rent figures and payouts of sums that made my jaw drop. It was a world I had never known, never expected to know, but was suddenly in the middle of, stubbornly stuck to Ben's side like a tick that wouldn't give up. And he didn't try to pull me away. He needed my connections as much as I needed the excitement. We prepped and prepared for August, and I anticipated it with fevered excitement and also dreaded its arrival because that meant our work would be done, and I would once again be an outsider, my nose pressed against the glass, watching the ball with no ticket to attend.

There were five weeks left. I needed a ticket. It was time to lean on Ben.

He opened the door in a bathrobe; the sash pulled tight, my eyes went to the monogrammed design on his breast before giggling.

"Shut up," he intoned, spinning on a heel and moving into the room, taking a seat at the desk, my hand carefully swinging the door shut behind me. Ethel Raine owns the Raine House, a matriarch who considers powerful sneezes as noise disruptions worthy of eviction.

"I just find it amusing that—when packing for Quincy—you thought elegant loungewear was needed." I smirked, launching myself on his meticulously made bed.

"And I thought the rule of the South was to call first," he pointed out, raising a carefully plucked brow at me.

"Well, you singlehandedly ruined that tradition," I said, picking out one of his pillows and stuffing it behind my head. "I didn't want you to be alone in your offensive sea of faux pas."

"How gracious of you," he drawled in his best Southern imitation.

"It's true, I am a lady." I dipped my head. "Speaking of which, how is local casting going?"

He took the abrupt topic change in stride. "Already spent your cash?"

I shrugged, rolling on my side. "Just wanting more of it."

"A company out of Atlanta is casting the filler parts. Grabbing authentic country bumpkins from up there."

I made a face at him. "I should have clarified. I need a job, not a role."

"Do you have any experience? With lighting, camera work, costumes?" He groaned when I shook my head. "Didn't you work on a school play at least?"

"Nope." I rolled to a sitting position. "Keep thinking."

"Let me call Eileen Kahl this afternoon, once California gets up and moving. See what she has."

"Who's she?"

"The AD. Assistant Director," he added, at my blank look. "But it's probably too late in the game, Summer."

"I'll fetch coffee, do laundry, *anything*," I drawled, kicking my feet out from the bed.

"I'm gonna remember that when you call me, bitching about picking up Cole Masten's used underwear."

I wrinkled my nose at him. "Okay. Forget the laundry position. Though…" I said thoughtfully. "I bet a Cole Masten *authentic* used brief would fetch a hundred bucks on eBay. I could start a side business: The Cole Masten Gently-Used Underwear Store. Free shipping on all orders!" I imitated Ben's sparkly hands, and he raised his eyebrows primly at me, as if he was uber sophisticated and above all of my adolescent activities.

"Oh *please*." I rolled my eyes. "You know you'll miss me in Vancouver." I hated to bring it up, had avoided thinking about Ben leaving, the writing on the wall beginning to taint our time together. We were almost done. He'd have no need to stay once filming began. I remembered our initial meeting, the conversation in our kitchen. Five months of his time, he had said. Five months that was almost up.

He surprised me by coming over and hugging me, his grip surprisingly strong. "Promise me that you'll bathe daily. And wash your face. And use that Dior mascara that I gave you."

I pushed him off with a laugh. "I've got five more weeks with you. Plenty of time for you to compile a better list of guilty promises to swear me to."

He smiled and tightened the cinch of his robe. "Want to hit Jimmy's for lunch?"

I stood. "Sure. I'll go and grab us a table. Let you get…" I waved a hand at his outfit. "Dressed."

He mocked my hand wave. "Done."

I tossed my Cherry Coke in the trash and left. I would miss Ben. I would miss our job. I would miss the excitement and energy of Something New and Different. I didn't want to go back to a life where my most exciting moments were when the next Baldacci novel released.

I jogged down the staircase and smiled at Ethel Raine, a woman who had warmed tremendously to me after Ben and I reserved every room in her B&B for the next five months. The rooms here would be for the Directors, Assistant Directors, Producers, and Production Manager and Designers—the key people who deserved more than a bunk bed but didn't deserve an entire house like Cole Masten and Minka Price, for which we've rented out the Kirklands' and Wilsons' homes. Minka Price—if she didn't succeed in backing out of the project—was bringing her family, so she got the more 'comfortable' of the two homes. We had prepared/hoped/squealed for Cole Masten to bring Nadia Smith but, from the latest issue of *STAR*, I no longer expected that to happen. They were as done as our Waffle King after the Cow Incident of '97.

"Is it normal?" I asked Ben, biting into one of Jimmy's subs. The secret to a successful Jimmy's experience is to befriend his wife, Jill. I coughed over a first cigarette with Jill, decorated the homecoming float next to her, lent and borrowed tampons in times of distress. I was in, no questions asked. Ben… it took him a few months of properly coached ass-kissing and attention-giving. Now, at the last leg of his stay, he got the best cuts, could call in an order on his way, and was allowed to sit at one of the window tables. Fancy stuff.

"Is what normal?" Ben responded, loudly sucking on his sweet tea's straw. Yes, sweet tea. I had actually converted him into a human being.

"A star trying to quit a movie this late in the game. We start filming in less than a month—doesn't it seem like…" My sentence trailed off in the face of an overdramatic amount of shushing coming from Ben. He glanced around furtively as if the CIA was trying to listen in.

"Not here," he hissed.

I took my own loud suck of straw, shaking the ice in the cup as I did so, frustrated. But Ben was right. Everyone in Quincy was straining their delicate ears to get every bit of information they could about the movie. You wouldn't believe the stupid things I was overhearing:

"Did you know that Minka dyes her hair blonde? She's a natural redhead… that's what Emma Statton said, and she might be hired to do makeup."

"I heard the movie's big scene at the end involves an explosion, and the Miller plantation is going to be blown up. Trace Beenson ordered the dynamite yesterday for it. Four tons of TNT."

"I just heard from my sister's dentist that Cole Masten and his wife are swingers. The Kirklands' place is gonna be like that Playboy Mansion up in California. Johnny said Mr. Masten's requested to have a stripper pole installed."

There was so much bullshit flying around that our flies were confused. Every once in a while, I'd hear something with a grain of truth in it, but it was rare. *The Fortune Bottle* was the most exciting thing that had ever happened to any of us. And I—I was seeing a little of my black curtain of disgrace lifted. Random girls had been calling up 'just to chat' and 'God, we've missed you.' Ghosts of my past wanting to reconnect, their hidden motivations clear. This town had grown up and forgotten me, my actions from three years ago putting me firmly in the We Don't Know Her pile. Summer Jenkins, voted Most Friendly, class of 2005? That girl got buried after high school. When the 'smart kids' went off to college, when the farm boys moved into the family business, when the cheerleaders and Home Ec princesses got married and had babies, I floated, lost in the wind of this town. When I scored Scott Thompson, my stock had shot way up. When it fell, I landed in the town's bad graces and stayed there, a small piece of Quincy that got looked over. Sure, everyone had always acted friendly, chatted with me in line at the IGA, asked about Mama, complimented my baked beans at Sunday church dinner, but any calls, any friendships, any social engagements had petered off years ago and stopped completely after the Disaster of 2012.

Until the movie.

I didn't want friendships born out of curiosity and gossip hoarders. It was too late for Quincy and me to rekindle our flame.

I wanted out.

CHAPTER 16

"In Hollywood, an equitable divorce settlement means each party getting fifty percent of publicity."
~ Lauren Bacall

Cole found Nadia at The Peninsula. Not a gigantic sleuthing job, as it was her hotel of choice. They had stayed there during the kitchen renovation, after late shoots, Emmy parties, and during moves. He could have found her four days ago, but he'd had wounds to lick and was afraid he couldn't see her face without screaming into it. Now, there was no other choice. He wouldn't talk through lawyers, not when their relationship was at stake.

Could he get over this? That was the question he had struggled with since Saturday night. There had been rumors since… well, there had always been rumors. But it was Hollywood. Hell, the tabloids had posted false stories of his 'affairs' for the last five years. So he'd ignored anything that had been said about Nadia. But now, with the proof of infidelity stuck in his mind, everything came to the surface. The AD in Madrid. That surfer on the Pitt movie. The bodyguard who quit last year. How many more had there been? And how many had been legitimate and not just gossip?

He jerked his car to a stop, nodding curtly to the valet, his feet not slowing, his mouth not smiling, everything focused on getting inside and to her room.

"Cole." When she spoke, the world stopped. Just as it had six years ago, on the set of *Ocean Bodies*, when she'd been a nobody, and he'd been the world's biggest somebody, yet still distracted by just her whisper of his name. Cole stopped short, turning to see her standing in the lobby, her hair in a ponytail, tight leggings on with tennis shoes, a fitted tank damp against her chest. Her fingers busy screwing on a bottled water's cap. *She'd been working out.* The thought struck him as offensive. She should be curled into a ball of sorrow in a big fluffy bed, her knees tucked to her chest, face red, tissues piled up. The room next door should call to complain about the wailing, her assistant should be hovering nearby with alcohol and chocolates, none of which should be able to calm the hysteria. Her cheeks shouldn't be glowing, her chest shouldn't be damp, she shouldn't be fine. He looked at her, she looked at him, and the lobby fell silent.

"I got the papers." It was all he could think to say.

She swallowed, and the delicate lines of her throat grew tight. She'd had a neck procedure done two years ago, had the doctor pull the skin tighter. Depending on the position she slept in, he could sometimes see the scars. Minute scars, ones you wouldn't even see if you didn't know where to look. Her next husband wouldn't know where to look. Wouldn't know that she'd miscarried twice and was allergic to shellfish. *Her new husband.* Was he already thinking that way? Was this fight already lost? She straightened. "Let's go somewhere more private."

Off The Peninsula's lobby were two conference rooms. They stepped into the second, Cole pulling one of the heavy doors closed, the room dark and empty. With the door shut, the light was gone, and they stood, a few feet away from each other, and said nothing. Another time, another place, they would have been clawing at each other, his hands lifting her up on one of the tables, her hands yanking at her dress, his tie, his belt. But now, with everything between them, they just stood in the dark.

"I'm sorry, Cole." Her voice floated from the outline that was her darkness, and slowly she took shape, her eyes on him, her teeth showing white as she bit at her bottom lip.

He blinked, the words unexpected from a woman who had made a career out of not apologizing for a damn thing. "You should have called, not…" he waved a hand in frustration. "Not gotten lawyers involved."

"It's over. We… we're over."

"No," he hissed the words and stepped forward, flinching when she stepped back. "I—" he shut off his next sentence before it crawled out and died. *I decide when we are finished. I should be the one making decisions, choosing our fate.* That's what he had started to say. Stupid words, stupid sentences. Especially when dealing with a woman like her.

"I don't love you anymore." She looked down, a silver piece on her ponytail holder bobbing in the darkness. "I don't know if I ever really did. Love you, I mean. I think I just loved the idea of you, of COLE MASTEN. But now..."

"We're equals," he said darkly. And equals didn't come complete with the clouded judgment of stardust. It was her Academy nomination, that was what probably did it, changed them. She had been so busy since then, hardly ever home, hardly ever in the mood.

"Yes." She lifted her head. "I'm sorry."

He closed his eyes and said nothing. Stepped back and turned away, needing space, needing distance, wanting a do-over on this entire conversation, relationship, life.

"And it's not personal." She was talking again, saying things, and he tried to refocus, tried to find his wife and her words and understand them. "It will just be simpler with the paperwork if we have the attorneys handle it."

"Prenup." He spat out the word. They'd been through that battle after engagement, the fight continuing right up to the week before the wedding. Everything had been clearly and simply laid out in a hundred-page document.

"I'm not supporting *The Fortune Bottle* unless I own half of it." There it was. The familiar edge in her voice that a man could jump off.

"What?"

"Jesus, Cole, didn't you at least read the agreement?" In the dark, her arms waved like dragon flaps.

"Enlighten me."

"Our prenup stated that we each walked with what we started with, plus any earnings that accrued during our marriage, minus any joint assets."

"I'm glad you are so familiar with it." How long had she been planning this?

"We are petitioning that *The Fortune Bottle* is a joint asset."

"But it's not." This was stupid. *The Fortune Bottle* was a book *he* had read, an option *he* had purchased from *his* accounts, the ten million in preproduction costs paid for out of those same accounts. No one would consider it a joint asset. Still, there was a twist in his stomach.

"I think it is. And Tony agrees with me." Tony. So, in this division, she had claimed the attorney. Great.

The prenup had put joint assets in a category of its own, one where a mediation session would determine who gets what. The issue was that Nadia knew what a successful film brought in. They had sat in the actors' chairs for so long, watching the big money go to the studios. Now, with *The Fortune Bottle*, everything would be different. A budget of sixty million, revenue of six hundred million… *that* was where the real money lay. And now, with his heart breaking before her, it was what she wanted to discuss. How quickly she had moved off her apology. Similar to how quickly she had moved off their marriage.

He stepped back, turning, twisting the doorknob, and moved into the light of the lobby, brightened tenfold by the snaps of a hundred paparazzi flashes.

He elbowed through the crowd, hotel security appearing and pushing him ahead. Nadia liked cameras, let her deal with them. When he got to the front, his car was waiting, and he ducked in, slamming the door behind him.

The leather shifter hot against his hand, he jerked into drive and onto the crowded street, his fingers quick on his phone. Damn Los Angeles traffic. He needed an open road, something to open up this car on, preferably one that ended in a cliff.

"Hey."

"Justin, I need a divorce attorney. One with teeth. Find that guy who just got Michael Jordan's ex everything."

"Just a second." He could hear the click of keys, the sound of productivity, and his stress lessened by a degree. Then there was the blare of a horn, Cole swerved to avoid an asshole, and felt the stress chalk back up. Maybe he'd go to Georgia early. Get the hell outta this town, get away from Nadia, away from everything. Talk to some people who, for once, didn't have sticks up their asses.

Justin came back on the line. "Good news is, I found him. Bad news is, he lives out of the country and his site says he's not taking on clients. Oh… Wait." There was the furious sound of taps. "I see a Florida office number. Let me call them and see what I can do."

"Get him. I don't care how much money you throw at him, just do it. I want to talk to him today."

"I'll send you his contact now, and I'll have him call you by the end of the day."

"Let him know we'll fly him out here. Tomorrow if possible."

"I'll try." An odd response from a man who could do anything. "I'm sending the contact now, but don't call the office 'til I speak to them."

"Thanks." He saw an opening to his turn and took it, the car jumping into action, the blare of a horn sounding as he wedged the exotic car in between two vehicles.

"Meet me at the house." Cole ended the call and opened Justin's text, seeing the contact card.

Brad DeLuca. DeLuca Law Firm.

The attorney. He saved the contact and then tossed the phone onto the passenger seat, swerving into the far lane and flooring the gas.

CHAPTER 17

Quincy sat in rocking chairs, on front porches freshly painted, and watched the train wreck of Codia occur. It was beautiful in its disaster, a full explosion decorated with high-def photos, a hundred a week, all spelling out Hollywood Doom in spectacular fashion. I munched on pecan brittle and flipped through the pages of *STAR*, saw the argument of Cole and Nadia in their driveway, her face striking in its anger, his hands strong and powerful as he spread them in the air and shouted. I poured pancake batter and heard, from the living room TV, the moment that Cole moved into a hotel and Nadia took full control of their ginormous home. I watched Cole's attorney, a handsome man, his features tight in concentration, discuss the intricacies of intellectual property, while painting my toes on our worn living room sofa.

I couldn't, from our tiny little cottage in the cotton field, understand why any woman would cheat on Cole Masten. How greedy could a woman be?

"They're talking about pushing filming back." Ben stood on my front porch, his shoulder slumped against the door frame, his cell phone hanging limply from his hand. It'd been ten days since the head crack heard 'round Hollywood.

"What?" I swung the door open wider and waved him in.

"I had to drive all the way over here; my cell isn't working. Thank God I checked email."

"That storm last night," I murmured, helping his dramatic self to a chair before he went full queen and collapsed. "Cell service is always hell after a storm."

It wasn't exactly the storm's fault as much as it was Ned Beternum, who let his goats graze the field he leased to Verizon. Even though the cell giant had threatened legal action several times. Even though his goats loved to chew the juicy wires that magnetized the thing. Heavy rains typically flooded his west acreage, so Ned would move them into the higher field, giving us all weak service until Verizon flew someone in to fix things. We, as a town, didn't really care. We'd survived without cell phones for thousands of years, didn't much use them anyway. That was what home phones were for. And if you weren't home, that was what answering machines were for. No need to fix a system that wasn't broken. Who wanted to be available twenty-four hours a day?

"September," Ben wheezed, his hand reaching out, and I grabbed my iced tea from the coffee table and passed it to him. "That's what they are saying now."

"September." I tried to see the reason for Ben's agony. "That's good, right? Gives us an extra month."

"Yeah. Peachy. You'll have more free time to crack peanuts and crochet mittens." I hid a smile. "Delays in filming are *bad*, Summer. Ominous. Expensive."

"Wait a minute." I frowned. "That's not what you said earlier." I adopted a deeper, yet feminine voice. "The Fortune Bottle isn't crashing, Summer. Movies don't fall apart over *this*." I mimicked his dramatic hand gestures, and he stared at me, a grimace on his pretty little face.

"Was that supposed to be me?"

"Yes."

He finished a sip of tea and wiped at his brow with a monogrammed handkerchief. "Please don't ever do that again."

I snorted… but I swear it was ladylike. "Ditto."

He sipped more tea, and I sat on the couch, my bare feet tucked underneath my butt. There was a companionable silence as I relaxed back against the cloth, my eyes closing.

"At least they aren't talking about the girls."

I cracked an eye open. "What?"

"Cole's fucking his way through half of Hollywood right now. I haven't seen that hit newsstands yet." The gossip was delivered in a hushed voice, Ben's hands happily clapping as if he might be the next stop on the Cole Masten Penis Train.

"Is that newsworthy?" I didn't know that a newly single actor screwing would be any big surprise to anyone.

"Is any of *this* newsworthy?" He leaned forward and picked up the closest magazine, an *OK!* that I bought because it was a dollar cheaper than the others. "Kelli Gifford shares her punch recipe!" he read off the cover in an excited fashion, then tossed it back down. "It's all crap, and yes, a detailed accounting of Cole Masten's bedroom activities would certainly be newsworthy. His publicists must be working overtime."

Ben had a point. I'd certainly pay three bucks to read about Masten's actions in the sack. Hell, with my level of sexual inactivity, I'd pay three bucks to read about Ben's actions in the sack. Or even Ned Beternum's goats. Or… well, I think you get the picture. It'd been a long time. Nobody since Scott. Three long years.

My pity party was interrupted by the clink of ice in Ben's drink. He looked down at the glass, and I stood up to get him a refill. Opening the fridge, I pushed any thoughts of Cole Masten and sex out of my mind.

CHAPTER 18

9:27 AM. The redhead knelt on the bed over Cole's face, her legs trembling on either side of his head, her smooth thighs cool against his skin. She panted his name, her fingers in his hair, pulling then releasing, a string of motions she wasn't even aware of doing.

"I can't," she gasped, one hand reaching wildly back and grabbing at the flat plane of his stomach, her body bucking against his mouth. He held her in place, his mouth devouring, tongue fluttering against her clit, all of his focus on getting her up and over this mountain.

Well, *almost* all focus. He closed his eyes for a moment, holding off his own orgasm, the mouth on his cock, talented, and he moved one hand off the redhead, reaching down and threading his fingers through the hair of the blonde, her movements never stopping, never slowing—a perfect blowjob.

The redhead was close, his mouth soaked with her juices, her taste everywhere, the sweetness of a woman. She fought him, her mouth begging, wanting more but unable to handle it until the moment that she broke, her guttural cry loud and long, his fingers biting into her skin as he held her down, his mouth carrying her through, stretching it out gently before she rolled off his face, her body twitching against the bed as he propped himself up, his hand pulling at the hair of the blonde, pulling her off his cock and up to his mouth.

She tasted like masculinity and he kissed her hard, then pushed her away, rolling to the side of the bed and standing, his cock at attention, ready for more. He pulled open the bedside table drawer and grabbed at the pile of condoms, pulling one out and sticking the foil piece in his mouth, tearing it open with his teeth. "On your knees," he ordered, their bodies scrambling into place, and he felt, in the moment before he knelt back on the mattress, his hand gripping at the first arched ass, a stab of loneliness. Loneliness. A new emotion that was growing increasingly familiar. Two women before him now, the prior night spent with their legs entangled with his, their hands on his skin, and he'd laid there, in the dark, and never felt so alone.

He pulled the girl backward and onto his cock. Listened to her moan and tried to find validation in the sound.

"You're late." Brad DeLuca barked the words, hanging up a call and tossing his cell onto the white linen tablecloth, the iPhone hitting a glass stem with a loud crack.

"Sorry. Business to attend to." Cole sat down, a waiter appearing, fresh water set out with lemon.

"Bullshit."

"What?" Cole looked up.

"Pussy isn't business, and this, right now, is the most important thing in your life, so when we make an appointment, keep it." DeLuca leaned forward on the table and stared at his client.

He'd been trying to get DeLuca to LA for two weeks and a lecture was the first thing out of the man's mouth? Cole stared at the man warily, an eyebrow raised. "You work for me, you know that, right?"

When the attorney laughed, it was a low chuckle, one born out of confidence and experience, and one with absolutely no trace of humor in it. The man stood, a grin on his face, and pulled a card from an inner pocket of his suit. "Here." He set the business card down before Cole, one finger tapping at the white surface. "This is Leonard McCort. He'll put up with your bullshit and cover your ass in court."

Cole felt a moment of panic. "But, you're the best." Justin had confirmed it, vetted DeLuca, already had confidentiality paperwork signed, retainers paid, a suite at the Chateau Marmont booked. Not to mention the phone calls, filed responses already in play. The man couldn't waltz out *now*.

"Exactly." DeLuca said the word like that was *it*, like Cole Masten wasn't the biggest thing to happen to Hollywood since CGI, like he would just walk away and leave Cole with some second-rate asshole.

"I've paid your advance," Cole sputtered.

The man looked at him like he was an idiot. "I'll refund it." It was, in retrospect, a fairly idiotic statement.

"Just… Just sit down for a second. Please." The word was disgusting as it came out, rank with misuse, and he felt irritation in the midst of his panic. But it was the panic that drove this train, panic that pushed every retort out of his mind and left him broken and desperate, in front of this man.

The attorney didn't sit; he stayed in place, his eyebrows raised, and waited.

"I'm sorry I'm late." He risked a glance at his watch. Twenty-two minutes. This dick was giving him hell for twenty-two measly minutes.

It took DeLuca a quarter hour to get over Cole's tardiness, but finally the attorney was re-seated, had downed an omelet, and the conversation had moved on to the matter at hand.

"You've lived your life as a celebrity for a long time, but in the courtroom, against your wife?" DeLuca tapped the table. "You're equals to each other. You're nothing to the judge. You're normal." He leaned back, and Cole looked away. *Normal.* The word was painful as it crawled in his ears.

"If I'm going to represent you, you have to know that life as you know it is over. You are not a bachelor yet, not until this divorce is final. You are my bitch, and I will say if and who you fuck, what you say to whom, and when and how you work. If you want to keep this movie as yours, you will leave this shithole of a city and go to Georgia. You will keep your dick clean and pretty-boy head down and do your job… nothing else. I've buried five of your fucks since Sunday, and my team doesn't have time for the popularity contest your dick has entered. Before you break a paparazzi's neck or barge into the hospital and finish that director off, let me do *my* job. We are going to return you to being Hollywood's Golden Boy and remind everyone of who the slut in this relationship was. You listen to me, and I promise you that I will keep *The Fortune Bottle* yours—along with any other shared asset you want."

"Just the movie," Cole said quietly, his eyes on the table. "She can keep the rest."

"I need you to commit to my terms."

Cole shrugged. "Yeah. Whatever."

"No drugs."

"I don't do drugs." He winced at an early memory of Nadia, a line of coke down her back, his nose dipping to hit between each thrust into her. A stupid combination, sex and coke. Neither of them able to feel much, their highs better than anything going on between their bodies. In the early days of their relationship, the drugs had been something that bonded them. But they'd both grown up. Gotten smarter. Stopped doing a lot of things, come to think of it, together.

"Well don't start. And no drinking. A beer or two is fine, but I can't have you drunk."

"That's fine." He rubbed his neck. "Anything else?"

"No sex. No relationships. No women. No men." The man didn't smile; he just leaned forward and stared at Cole.

No sex. That was probably for the best, his stream of fucking doing absolutely nothing to help his psyche. *No relationships.* Even less of a problem. After Nadia, he couldn't imagine ever walking down that path again. *No men.* The easiest rule of them all. He looked up and met the man's stare. "Agreed."

Deluca held the eye contact long enough to be satisfied, then nodded and glanced at his watch, his wedding ring glinting out against tan skin and strong hands. "Then let's go."

"Go?" He looked up at the man, who was now standing, peeling a couple of bills off and dropping them on the white tablecloth. "Where?" He had a massage scheduled—had planned for Brenda the Masseuse to work off the hours of sex with her hands before he took her from behind, bent over the massage table. It'd be another fuck, another attempt to replace a hundred memories of Nadia. Eventually, those memories would be buried. Eventually, he'd be able to push inside a woman and not hear Nadia's moan in his mind. Maybe he'd have to cancel the massage, but he wasn't going anywhere with this man. He had zero interest in going to another meeting, another lecture surely planned, this one with publicists and more suits in attendance. He stayed in place in his seat. "Where?" he repeated stubbornly.

"Quincy." The attorney smiled, and Cole felt off-balance by the change, the man's answer taking a second longer to compute. *Quincy*?

"Right now?" He stayed in his seat, thought of a hundred good reasons to stay in Los Angeles right now. But his question was ignored, the attorney striding through the crowded tables, his shoulders wide and strong in his custom suit. The man could be a damn bodyguard, with his build and intimidation.

Cole sighed and grabbed his cell phone, rising from the table with a sigh.

It looked like, for the immediate future, his new role was as Brad DeLuca's bitch. A role he'd never played, a role he already hated.

CHAPTER 19

I'd had a variety of jobs since my graduation from Quincy High. Fresh out, my new diploma stuffed in a drawer, it was Davis Video Rental. That was in the early Cole Masten days, when he was a twenty-five year old playing sexy high school quarterbacks who dated the nerdy girl and made her popular. I spent my days alphabetizing titles, catching sticky-fingered teens and watching movies on the twenty-seven inch mounted in the store's upper corner. Each night, I'd bring home a couple of titles and watch more. By the time I'd worked through the entire Comedy and Drama section, Horror and Classic, I put in my notice. Life was too short for Sci-Fi or Western.

After Davis Rental, I drove down to Tallahassee. Applied at a handful of restaurants and bars, striking out until I found a Moe's with a flirtatious manager who hired me on the spot. I struggled a little there. It wasn't the restaurant or the stoners I worked with. It was the students, each ding of the door bringing in a fresh wave of individuals who were *doing* something, *going* somewhere. Each new face was a subtle point to the invisible sign on my chest that said UNDERACHIEVER in big bubbly letters. Prior to that job, my lack of continuing education, my lack of a life plan… it had never bothered me. I didn't apply to colleges because I wasn't really interested in them, didn't have a childhood dream of leaving Quincy to become a marine biologist or whatever it was that high-schoolers were supposed to want. I liked to read and watch movies. I loved to cook and work in the garden. Before that job in Tallahassee, there didn't seem to be anything wrong with those simple pleasures. But for some reason, with that job, those students… I felt like less of a person each day that I walked in those double doors. And then one day, sitting in the parking lot before my shift, I couldn't do it anymore. I just started up my truck and drove back home.

After that, I stuck to the county limits. Got the Holden job and moved in, grew roots through my soles and into the plantation's dirt. I blocked out the images of smiling student faces and focused on the simple things I loved. And slowly but surely, the happiness creeped back in. And around that time, Scott Thompson started coming by. Once he won my heart, there wasn't much thought about plans or college or Life Outside of Quincy. Love did that to you. Sucked you in and blurred out everything else.

It was after Scott that I started thinking about leaving. It wasn't so much that life in Quincy felt inadequate, and it wasn't the shame that I'd felt at Moe's. It was more that, after my experience with him, I wanted something different. I wanted to be someone different, someone without scorn, someone without a past.

Someone with a future.

CHAPTER 20

Justin Hitchins got the call when on Sunset Boulevard, leaving The Coffee Bean with a double espresso, one wheat bagel with light cream cheese, and a container of sliced strawberries. He stopped his step into the crowded street, moving back two paces, until he was safely out of harm's way, in between two parallel-parked cars. He reached for his cell, almost dropped everything, then glanced around, carefully depositing the espresso on the hood of the black Mercedes to his right. Digging in his pocket, he answered the cell a moment before it went to voicemail.

"Morning."

"This guy's a fucking lunatic," Cole Masten hissed, his voice at whisper level.

"He's what you wanted. Did you see the dossier I emailed over with his list of cases? He's never lost—"

"We're on the jet right now, Justin." There was a muffled bump across the line. "He wants me to go to Quincy *now*, to get out of LA. And call the production company—we're keeping the original timeline, no delays on filming."

Not an entirely bad plan, seeing the path his employer's life had taken recently, but Justin swallowed that opinion in light of more pressing issues. "You're going to the airport right *now*?" He would need to call the scout, see if Cole's house was ready for occupancy, see if their local restaurants had a list of approved meals, see if… his mind jumped hurdles, moved through crowds, and had a minor panic attack all in the three seconds it took Cole Masten to respond.

"Yes, right now. I told you… insane."

"Why are you whispering?" The Cole he knew—had worked for over thirteen years—stood straight and ordered. He hadn't ever heard a whisper out of the man unless it was printed in a script.

"You meet the guy and tell me you aren't going to hide in a plane restroom and whisper when you complain about him."

Justin smiled at the visual. "Okay, when are you landing?"

He didn't hear the response. It was drowned out by a loud horn, typical in Los Angeles, the accompanying screech of tires another norm. He turned his head, saw the Range Rover swerve, saw the blur of bright white and Xenon headlights slam into the back of the black Mercedes and realized, several moments too late, what was about to happen.

The Range Rover slammed the parked Mercedes forward, not far, but enough to collide with the minivan parked before it, Justin Hitchins a soft cushion in between the two vehicles.

The espresso sloshed up and out in the air, his cell flew from his hand, and Justin Hitchins' world went black.

CHAPTER 21

The call went dead in Cole's hand. He glanced down at the cell, the plane dipping, his hand bracing the wall for support, and cursed. Damn service. He pocketed the phone and opened the door, stepping out into the jet's short hall, a bedroom to the left, seating to the right. In one of the chairs, Brad DeLuca spoke into a phone. Apparently his service worked just fine at forty thousand feet.

He stepped forward, settling into a chair across from the attorney. Justin would handle it, would have everything ready by the time they touched down. Maybe it wouldn't be so bad. He was just thinking about coming down to Quincy and escaping the madness of Hollywood. Maybe he needed the kick in the ass to get him there. He felt better already, every minute putting more distance between him and Nadia. Felt better with this freak of nature next to him. The man was terrifying, but he was in his corner, fighting for him. He would rip out the throat of Nadia's puny lawsuit and eat it for breakfast. Cole relaxed against the back of the seat.

"Have you called Quincy?" Brad DeLuca spoke from beside him, and Cole swiveled his seat to face the man.

"My assistant is handling it. They'll be ready for us."

"I'm not staying, just dropping you off. I've got to get back home." The man glanced at his watch. "I'll call you when I land tonight. Pick up the phone. We'll game plan then, and I'll have a response filed with Nadia's team by the morning."

"Okay." He flipped his cell against his leg and looked at the man. "This all you do? Divorces?"

DeLuca nodded. "That's it."

"Dismal job. Ripping apart marriages."

The man grinned. "That depends. For me, my divorce was the best thing that ever happened. I lost a mistake and ended up marrying my soulmate. You can waste your life away, tied to the wrong spouse. Divorce can right at least one of our wrongs."

Cole laughed. "So you're Replacement Cupid? Steering husbands away from one mistake and on to their next?"

The man smiled. "One day you'll thank me."

Cole looked away. "It's Nadia Smith. Not many women can hold a candle to that."

"Stop thinking of her as Nadia Smith. She's not a shrine you pray to; she's a woman. I love my wife more than life itself, but she has flaws. If Nadia and you were perfect together, she wouldn't have fucked another guy and served you divorce papers. You *will* move on from this. You *will* be stronger after this."

It sounded like a crock of shit. A brutal crock of shit. It'd been a long time since anyone, other than Justin or Nadia, spoke to him without carefully selected undertones. Cole shifted in his seat and wished they'd gone by his house first. He'd have liked to shower and change, grab some clothes. No matter. First thing, upon landing, he'd find something else to wear, just to tide him over until Justin arrived. His assistant knew what to do, would catch a flight in with a month's worth of outfits. He pulled at the collar of his shirt and rolled his neck. Maybe he'd have Justin get him a massage in Quincy. Better yet, book a full day tomorrow at a spa.

DeLuca got on the phone, and Cole reclined back in his seat, closing his eyes and trying to push the thought of Nadia from his mind. She'd looked beautiful, standing in the hotel. Beautiful and unaffected. He hadn't expected that. It hurt, even more than the papers, even more than what he'd seen in their bathroom. It made it all worse than just an affair or a fight or cheating. It meant that Nadia could walk away from their years together without hesitation. He'd looked through the divorce paperwork. It was too detailed, too tight, to be thrown together in the last week. She had been planning this. *That* was what made his chest tight. And what made his head hurt was how oblivious he'd been to the entire thing. How disconnected had they been that he hadn't seen any signs? That he'd thought they were great when they'd been on the brink of disaster?

And then for Nadia to bring up *The Fortune Bottle*. In the moment when they should have been discussing their love, their relationship, their lives—his *movie* was what she brought up, what she cared about, *fought* for. He suddenly remembered scattered comments from Nadia about the movie, her request to be an executive producer, her transfer of funds last month "just moving stuff around." He groaned and leaned forward, holding his head in his hands.

"Hey." DeLuca looked up from his phone. "Stop stressing."

"I'm thinking back on the last few months… I think she's been setting me up for this."

"It's my job to worry now. It's your job to stay in Quincy, follow my rules, and make a movie that kicks ass."

"Okay." Cole leaned back and huffed out a breath.

He could do that. Sitting back and letting others take care of things, have them worry about things, those were things he was used to. He could lick his wounds in Quincy, avoid temptation, and make a movie.

Easy.

CHAPTER 22

The moment that all hell broke loose, I was in my bathing suit, my butt resting in four inches of cold water, my feet propped up on the edge of the bright blue kiddie pool.

"You're going to burn." Ben made the comment from underneath three layers of sunblock, one cowboy hat, and linen pants.

"No, I'm not."

"Yes, you are," he said with the grave sincerity of a eulogy. "I watched you. You didn't put on any sunscreen."

"I never wear sunscreen." I scooped up some water and drizzled it over my thighs.

"You do realize that the sun is literally aging you right before my eyes."

"You do realize that this is Georgia and not the Wild West and that you look absolutely ridiculous in a cowboy hat, right?" I flicked my hand at him and water sprayed, his pale body squirming away, his metal folding chair tipping sideways on the grass. I laughed, dipping both hands in the water and taking advantage of his struggle to stand, getting him as wet as possible from my position in the pool.

"Stop!" he shrieked, his bare feet finally gripping onto the grass and standing.

I laughed. "Fine, pretty boy. No more splashing." I held up my hands in peace and smirked as he picked up the overturned chair and moved it to a safer place.

We were in the front yard of my house, in the shade of the big live oak; yet, even submerged in water, it was still hot. The Holdens had a pool, a big giant thing behind their house. With them in Tennessee, we could have swum there, but that just didn't feel right. I had done it once or twice in the last six years but had looked over my shoulder the entire time, worried that the Holdens would magically transport two thousand miles and catch me. The kiddie pool worked just fine for me, and it didn't come with a side of trepidation.

From the back porch, we heard Ben's phone ring, loud and shrill in the quiet afternoon. He craned his neck back at it and sighed heavily.

"Just let it go," I urged. "It's Saturday. No emergencies to deal with."

Like I knew he would, he hefted out of the chair and ran toward it.

Thank God he had.

CHAPTER 23

The first oddity, when the jet touched down on the dusty runway, was that there was no one there. Well, there was someone there. One lone airport employee who stood on the tarmac and gawked, his hands tucked in his front pocket, his mouth doing everything but offering to help with their bags. Granted, they didn't have any bags. But this man didn't know that. DeLuca stepped off the plane, shook the man's hand, and introduced himself. Cole followed suit, the man's eyes widening underneath a decade of dirt and sun. "You're that movie star," he said in surprise.

Cole nodded and flashed a smile. He couldn't help it; it had become, since entering this business, so ingrained, so automatic, that it was as if he had no control of it. But there were no cameras here, no screaming crowds of fans, no need to display a megawatt smile to this country bumpkin. DeLuca looked at him strangely.

"So… ah… what are you guys doing in Quincy? Got engine trouble?" The man glanced at the gleaming aircraft, one that had barely had the runway clearance to land on their strip.

"No. Has my assistant not called?" Cole dug in his pocket for his phone. No texts from Justin. Strange. Normally, after this link of time, he'd have an itinerary, hotel confirmations, the name of his driver. He held up the phone. Two bars of service. Pressed the power button and hit restart. Damn Verizon.

"Uh, nobody's called us," the man said slowly, glancing toward the dimly lit building. *Us.* So maybe there'd been more than just him guiding their giant death trap safely to the ground. Reassuring.

"Has my car arrived?" A question he knew the answer to, even as it fell from his lips. Behind the man was a large gravel lot holding only two vehicles. Neither one looked capable of air conditioning, much less a private driver. Where was security? Justin had had hours of flight time to prepare. This shouldn't have been difficult, and he should have, at the very least, texted Cole an update. So many mistakes, from an assistant who didn't make mistakes, and Cole felt the first flick of worry uncoil in his stomach. He dialed Justin's number and held the phone to his ear, DeLuca's phone sounded, the man turning away.

It rang eleven times. After four, he was irritated. After seven, he grew worried. When the man's voicemail finally picked up, he was panicked. He didn't leave a voicemail, just hung up the phone and locked it. From behind him, DeLuca rejoined them, his big hand falling heavily on Cole's shoulder. "Bad news," the attorney said. "Your assistant has been in an accident. TMZ posted the news an hour ago. He's alive, but pretty beat up."

Another crack in a sinking ship. And Justin… Justin was his glue, the constant, the only friend who Cole could name with ease. *He's alive… but pretty beat up*. Cole took a deep breath and ran his hands over his face. "Okay. Let's head back."

"No." The order in the man's voice caught him by surprise.

"I need to see him—in the hospital; he's been with me for years," Cole protested. Thirteen years, to be precise. Two more than the dead ringtones in his ear. A long time. Before Nadia, before the trio of Oscars, before his fame hit ridiculous heights. He needed to go to him. He should leave this dust-filled sauna and return to his city of clean hands, cool air and luxury. What kind of city had an airport like this?

Not city. He corrected himself. Town. That had been the draw of it all. A sleepy town, filled to the brim with millionaires. Come to think of it, they probably didn't even *have* a spa. The tightness in his back grew worse.

"You're not going anywhere. The LA hospital is going to be a zoo filled with paps waiting to see that pretty face of yours. You'll turn the whole thing into a circus, and he's not awake right now anyway, isn't going to be able to talk to you for a while."

"What happened?"

"He was the side effect of a car accident. Was on foot and got pinned between two cars." DeLuca's voice softened.

Cole looked away, his eyes running into the airport handler, who still stood there, his head tilted, catching every word. He let out a loud breath. DeLuca was right. Going to the hospital would be a disaster. He'd send flowers, maybe a strippergram, would have Justi—his brain hiccupped on the realization that his right hand was suddenly *gone*, the man who did everything, greased all joints, made all arrangements. *Gone.* In a hospital three thousand miles away with his focus on his own life, no longer on Cole's. He staggered a little in place, DeLuca's hand reaching out and gripping his shoulder, holding him up.

Ten minutes later, they were in a borrowed truck, rattling away from the airport.

Cole held up a hand against the sun, which blared in at an uncomfortable angle. The window was open, the dirty, hot air sweeping in and over him, and he reached to raise it, chuckling a little at the foreign feel of an actual window crank in his hand.

DeLuca held the phone away from his mouth. "I'm tracking down the local Envision contact now." They rounded a tight turn, and Cole gripped the handle firmly, looking around for a seatbelt. Nothing.

"Bennington Payne?" DeLuca barked into the phone. "Where are you *right* now?"

CHAPTER 24

When Ben answered the phone, I relaxed my arms, lying fully back in the kiddie pool, my head propped up against the edge, a folded towel acting as a pillow.

Ben's linen pants wandered my way, his cell against his ear, the other hand pressed against his free ear, as if he were in a rock concert and not the middle of nowhere. He was probably getting poor reception. I closed one eye and half-squinted his way, the nosy half of me eavesdropping.

"Ummm… Quincy?" He said the city as if it was a question.

"I'm sorry, who is this?"

I opened both eyes when he did the frantic snapping waving thing at me. I sat up and raised my eyebrows, waiting for more.

"Yes sir. But… now? I thought that—okay. Yes sir." I wondered how many 'yes sirs' this conversation was going to involve. Wondered how I was supposed to piece any of this together when all I had were half sentences full of Ben stammering.

"What's your address?" That question was aimed at me, a loud whisper further soundproofed by his hand atop the receiver.

I told him, this change in the conversation certainly taking a turn toward Interesting. Ben repeated it into the phone, then—with a final 'yes sir'—ended the call.

I didn't think a man could be paler than my sweet vampire, but oh… oh… one can. I watched his face lose all color, the push of his cell into his pants pocket a fumbling, awkward movement.

"What's happening?" I demanded, making the effort to stand, my bathing suit leaking thin streams down my legs.

He swallowed, his Adam's apple bobbing dramatically. He looked at me, my worn black bathing suit, then down at the kiddie pool, as if some answer lay in its bright blue depths, then back at the house, his rental car parked at an odd angle underneath the dogwood tree, then back at me.

"Cole Masten is here."

"Where?" Here was a very particular location. And I knew, for a fact, that he wasn't *here* here. Yet, with an almost sinking certainty, my address just blindly passed over, I suddenly realized that *here* here was an eminent possibility, and I stepped out of the kiddie pool quickly, crossing the dry grass, until I stood right in front of Ben.

"Where?" I repeated with enough aggression for him to start.

"In Quincy. Just left the airport. That was his attorney. He wanted to know where I was, is bringing Cole here now, said something about his assistant being in the hospital." The words came out in a mad rush, as if they wouldn't be true if spoken fast enough, and I stepped back a step just to get away from their stench. "How far away is the airport?"

I closed my eyes, tried to think. "Five. Maybe ten minutes. Holy shit." I glanced back down at my bathing suit, thought about my house, the dirty dishes in the sink, my tampon box on top of the toilet, the remnants of Ben's and my mani-pedi party still on the coffee table, mail scattered on the table… this was bad. I took off running, the white-linen-panted gay close on my water-pruned heels.

"See, the Thompson family is one of the original forty-three. That was really the root of the problem. Summer is a sweet girl and all, but she just doesn't have the family background, the rearing to handle difficult times with grace. That was the problem. You know the girl has no father. That should tell you something right there."

"Marilyn, she has a father. He lives in Connecticut, that's what Betty Anne says. He has some flesh-eating disorder where he can't be around other people. That's why they moved here."

"That has got to be the most idiotic thing you have ever said. No, she doesn't have a father. He ran off when Francis was pregnant with Summer; that's the real story."

CHAPTER 25

It turned out that the window didn't roll all the way up. It was broken. Which was just as well since it was too hot to be in a truck with no air conditioning and no airflow. Brad DeLuca chuckled; Cole rolled the window back down, and took the phone that Brad passed him.

"The guy said he's at 4 Darrow Lane. Do me a favor and look it up on my GPS."

Cole opened the maps app and found the address. "It's two miles away. Keep straight for a bit."

The attorney nodded, and they continued on for a moment in silence, Cole spreading his feet and bracing out against the rock of the truck.

"I haven't driven a truck in years." Brad commented. "I've missed the stick."

Cole laughed. "Yeah. I miss my Ferrari's stick right now." Maybe they could trailer it over. The truck hit a large pothole, and his hands found the dash and held on. Maybe not. His car wouldn't last its first trip down a dirt road. He glanced over at the man, his fierce profile different in the light of the afternoon sun, his strong hands loose and relaxed on the wheel, his body as comfortable in the old truck as it had been at the Beverly Hills restaurant. Maybe DeLuca wasn't such an asshole. Maybe he was exactly what Cole needed—someone who wouldn't kiss his ass—someone who would give it to him straight, without the expensive bullshit that everyone in Hollywood sprinkled on their gluten-free parfaits every morning.

His optimism was punished with DeLuca's next words. "I told that guy at the airport that I'd have his truck back in an hour. So I'm just dropping you off with this guy. His name is Bennington—he's the location scout for the movie so he should know his way around town and be able to get you settled." The sun shifted behind a cloud, and the outside world grew a little darker.

Cole glanced toward the sky. "Bennington?" he repeated.

"Yeah. Bennington Payne. I didn't pick the guy's name."

Cole smiled, glancing down at the phone when it chimed. "Turn right here." They eased around the bend, and Cole glanced back at the road they'd just left. They hadn't passed another car since they left the airport. It felt strange after a lifetime in LA, a city where rush hour stretched twenty hours a day, and cars became second houses. He'd been to remote locations before, had filmed a samurai film in the Netherlands, had spent two months in Alaska, but this was the first time he had really felt the openness, the quietness, the solitude of a place. Maybe it was because the divorce papers and Justin's accident were so recent, the two key parts of his life, of his armor, breaking off at once, his skin underneath raw and delicate. He watched the fields go by, perfect row after row of uninterrupted green and white. The phone buzzed in his hand, and he pointed to the right, to the large plantation house, ivory columns stretching up three stories, the wide front porch complete with a half dozen rockers, the ensemble framed by a chorus of hundred-year oaks. "That's it."

"What's wrong with you?" Ben watched me in confusion, one perfect brow arched high as I tore through the house, a laundry basket in hand, scooping everything off every surface, my feet slapping at the floor, my damn bathing suit riding up my crack. The tampons, can't forget those. I rushed into the bathroom, the yellow box dumped in, along with half of the contents of our medicine cabinet. Tonight would be fun, Mama screaming for Preparation H while I fished the remote control out of the loaded-to-the-brim basket.

"Shh!" I hissed at Ben, going through a mental checklist of the things I had time to do versus what was critical.

"He's not going to come inside." I heard Ben's sentence through the fog of self-preservation and skidded to a stop, the laundry basket bouncing, a roll of toilet paper popping out and tumbling down the hall 'til it came to a stop alongside Ben's foot.

"What?"

"They're just coming by to pick me up. They probably won't even get out of the car."

Of course. I took my first actual breath in. That made perfect sense. Why would they come in? They probably won't come to a complete stop—will just roll by and pop open the door, yelling and waving for Ben like he was chasing a train. I set down the laundry basket on the kitchen counter and glanced down at my bathing suit. "Okay. Great. I'm gonna change."

There was a loud knock on the door, and my eyes flicked to his in panic.

CHAPTER 26

"Are you sure this is the right place?" The porch board under Cole's left heel was soft, and he shifted his weight onto the other foot, his eyes taking in the embroidered curtain covering the window. Inside, there was the murmur of voices, the shuffle of steps.

"Yes," DeLuca said shortly, glancing at his watch for the umpteenth time. "This is it."

They had bypassed the main home and pulled up to a tinier version with two vehicles parked in front—an old Chevy truck and a Ford sedan with Oklahoma plates. The car was probably the scout's—a rental. The truck… well, who knew what hillbilly would be--

The door swung open, a tall blonde standing there, Cole's eyes dropping past her face and landing on her swimsuit—a faded black one-piece with jean shorts hastily buttoned as he watched. Her hair was wild and long, as were her tan legs, stretching down forever and ending in pink toe nail polish. Nadia would laugh at that polish, would snicker under her breath and mutter 'juvenile' or 'white trash.' She'd also raise her brows at the tan, her hand frantic in her bag for some sunscreen, the reminder to apply taken seriously, all while texting her assistant to book her next spray tan.

"Is Bennington here?" Brad rested a hand on the doorframe, his arm blocking Cole's view of her chest but Cole saw the flick of her eyes from his to the attorney's, saw the slight drop of her mouth as she looked up into DeLuca's face. Something inside of him twisted in an ugly manner. The girl had a damn movie star on her front porch and had looked away. He turned away, resting his hands on the worn wood of the porch's railing and coughed out a laugh at the state his fragile ego had become. Wow. How low had he fallen that a strange girl couldn't look at another man without him caring? DeLuca was a handsome guy; anybody could see that. Plus, he had the alpha male type testosterone that made women crawl over each other to his side. It was natural for the girl to look at him, for her attention to divert from Cole, especially when he had asked her a question. But still. Three Oscars in his storage unit. Her gaze could have at least lingered.

He turned back to the door, leaning against the railing and crossing his arms, waiting for this round of introductions to pass so they could get to the hotel and he could take a shower. The location scout had appeared, replacing the blonde at the door. Too bad. She'd been better to look at. The scout was hyper, his head bobbing rapidly, his hands occasionally joining in—the combination of gestures and head nods making Cole's head hurt.

Someone had said something to him. DeLuca's head was turned, both sets of eyes on him, expecting some sort of an answer. Cole lifted his chin, straightening off the railing. "I'm sorry, what?"

"It turns out there aren't a lot of lodging options in Quincy but Bennington—"

"It's Ben," the man interrupted, practically fawning forward. Behind him, in the doorway, the girl reappeared, a baggy white T-shirt now pulled over her swimsuit, her wild hair contained in a ponytail. Her eyes met his, and he smiled, the Cole Masten smile that unlocked every door. She didn't smile back. *Shit.* Everything was falling to hell, including his smile. He made a mental note to have Justin—to have someone—make him a dentist appointment. To practice in the mirror this evening and make sure that everything was working right. Maybe it was her. Maybe she was gay.

"Right," DeLuca continued. "Ben says the lodging accommodations in town are fairly limited—that the closest town with any real hotels is Tallahassee—"

Cole's ears perked up at this, his arms dropping from his chest. A college town. Bars. Sexy ass coeds who would beam up to him like his word was God's. Maybe that would give the ego boost that, right now, seemed to be needed.

"—but I told him that wouldn't work. That you needed to be in

Quincy." DeLuca smirked at him like he knew what he was thinking.

Oh, right. The rules. Cole slapped a mosquito on his neck in response, feeling a drop of sweat run down his back. "Not to ruin this delightful party," he waved at another insect, "but could we move this inside? To the air conditioning?"

Bennington and the girl exchanged a quick look, then the girl smiled sweetly. "Certainly. Can I get y'all anything to drink? Some sweet tea, perhaps?"

CHAPTER 27

It only took eight minutes for my hero worship of Cole Masten to nose dive into a sea of dislike. His looks weren't the problem; if anything, the man leaning against my railing was even *better* looking than on a movie screen. I studied him when he turned around, when he gripped the railing and looked out on the Holdens' farm. And I saw a bit of pain—in the hunch of his shoulders, in the chew of his cheek, some torture in the eyes that had turned back around and met mine. I thought then, my hand resting on the doorknob, looking out on the front porch that held two of the sexiest men I had ever seen, that there was something *there*, in him, something whole and raw and beautiful.

Now, I know what I saw. I know what that something was. It was asshole, pure and simple. It was spoiled rotten—I get what I want because I deserve it, you are beneath me—asshole. I've experienced men like him before. Carl Hanson grew up on the same dirt I did, attended Quincy High just like me, danced with me at the Homecoming Dance, and rode dirt bikes with me in the summer. Then he graduated. Went to New York after UGA. Found out what Daddy's money could buy him, found out what life outside our county line was like, and came back a few Christmases later. Looked so far down his nose at me I could see the specks of cocaine in his nostril. He palmed my ass like he owned it at the church winter social, and I punched him smack in the nose. Broke the knuckle of my index finger doing so, but it was worth it. Mr. Hanson paid my hospital bill. Came over and had tea with Mama and me and delivered a pile of apologies for the asshole that his son had become.

I had nine more knuckles and a well-healed tenth. If Cole Masten planned on following up his visual examination of my body with any action, I'd let him know how hard girls in the South could punch.

The start of my dislike began with his request to come inside. It was rude of him, the action a personal dig at my faux pas of not inviting them inside. One rude action pointing out another rude action did not cancel each other out; it just bought you an extra ticket to the Dickhead Show.

I should have invited them in; I know that. It was hot as blazes outside, the sun just low enough in the sky for the mosquitoes to journey out, the scent of fresh humans luring them closer. But the house was a mess, and Ben had *promised* me they wouldn't come in. It was the only thing that had allowed me to open my front door with any composure. Because sure, I was in my bathing suit and some cut off shorts, but at least they wouldn't know that my house was messy. That my bathroom trash had not been emptied. That the Honey O's box from that morning was still sitting opened on my kitchen counter. All was salvageable until the pretty boy had to go and gripe about wanting to come in. *So* rude.

Cole Masten's second strike came three minutes later, the men awkwardly standing in my living room while I flew around like a crazy woman attempting to get drinks.

I watched Cole from the corner of my eye, in deep discussion with his attorney, and noted the delicate white skin—skin that would bake in our sun. Each summer we literally fried an egg on the pavement. Just one egg, a local one from a local chicken, the egg carried and presented with great ceremony by our mayor. The frying was done on the previous summer's hottest day of the year, and it was always an event, time taken out of everyone's non-busy schedule to bring potluck items and huddle around the Smith Bank & Trust parking lot to stare at one of Mama Gentry's sad little eggs. Sometimes they fried quickly; other times it was unseasonably reasonable and only a few bubbles of excitement were produced. So yeah, eggs fried in our sun. His California pale skin would crinkle up like crispy bacon. I contemplated, while opening cabinets and searching for glasses, my damp suit getting itchy, offering him sunscreen, a friendly Welcome to Quincy gift. I hadn't. Instead, yanking open the dishwasher, I made a side bet with myself that the next time I saw him, he'd look like a lobster.

"I need to run," the first man said regretfully, tilting his head toward the door. "Got a truck to return and a plane to catch. My wife will have my head if I don't make it home in time for dinner."

He left the group and walked toward me, my hands stalling in their reach into the dishwasher. I set down the glass in my hand and shook the hand he offered. "Thank you so much for your hospitality. I'm afraid I didn't catch your name."

"Summer," I managed. "Summer Jenkins. Can I fix you a tea for the road?"

He chuckled. "No, but thank you. I appreciate the offer."

Wife. That was what he'd said. His *wife* would be upset if he didn't make it home. Not much of a surprise, all the good ones were taken. And he'd had manners too. I left the kitchen and opened the front door for him, waving goodbye, my smile dropping when I shut the door behind him and noticed the dust on the door's window. *Great.* Disasters at every turn. I suddenly thought of Mama, and I glanced at the oven clock. Four PM. Still an hour and a half until she got home from work. Plenty of time to get Cole and Ben out of here and clean up, get a casserole in the oven. Maybe one of those Stouffer ones. Carla at the IGA promised me they tasted homemade, but we'd be able to tell. You couldn't fake authenticity, not in these parts.

I returned to the kitchen, Ben's phone to his ear, Cole Masten looking dubiously at my couch like he wasn't sure it was fit to sit on. I cracked the ice in its tray and plucked out a few cubes, dropping them in his glass. Ben could fend for himself, his Tervis still sitting half-full somewhere in this wreck of a house. "Tea?" I called out.

The man turned away from my couch and eyed me. "Sparkling water, please."

That right there was the second strike. I smiled, the expression born more of spite than of sweet. But in the South, our smiles are our weapons and only a native knows a snarl from sincerity. "I'm afraid I don't have sparkling water." You are not a man, I thought. A man doesn't drink sparkling water; he chugs tap water from a hose after changing his oil.

"Still is fine." He turned away from me and took a careful seat on the couch. I turned back to the sink, my eye roll hidden. *Still is fine.* Oh, it'd be still. Still in my tap, the same place it was this morning. I twisted the faucet's knob and filled the glass. Turned it off and carried the glass over, moving a coaster and setting it down. I raised my eyebrows at Ben who was still on the phone, his hand making some sort of *justaminute* motion so I sat down on the recliner. Glancing over, I saw Cole Masten study the glass before taking a sip.

"How was your flight in?" I asked.

The man looked at me when I asked the question, his eyes traveling over my legs as he swallowed the first sip of water, then took a larger one. It was a shame, really, to have that much beauty. God could have divided up his thick eyelashes, strong features, hazel eyes, and delicious mouth among three men, therefore giving more women a chance at happiness. Instead, Cole Masten hit the jackpot. A jackpot that was tipping back his glass, taking his time with his answer, his delicious neck exposed, his mouth cupping the glass, a hint of his tongue…

God. I shifted in my seat and pulled at the neck of my shirt, looking away. Suddenly wished, more than anything, he and Ben would hurry up and leave. Let me have my house back, let me have a half hour or two of peace and quiet before my mother arrived home. It was a desire that made absolutely no sense. Every red-blooded American woman would claw my eyes out to be that close to HIM. Maybe it was the small town country in me—the same stupidity that had me saying 'no thanks' to college applications and to finding a 'real job.' Maybe it was the fact that I was raised to believe that 'real men' had manners, and weren't picky, and didn't wear aftershave that attracted mosquitoes.

Ben hung up the phone and, in the next minute, Cole Masten got his third strike.

CHAPTER 28

This might just be the worst two weeks of Cole Masten's life.

Losing Nadia. *The Fortune Bottle* at risk. Justin's accident. Going with Brad DeLuca to Quincy. A horrible decision. What was he thinking? It would have been okay if Justin had been here, getting him settled, arranging his schedule, keeping Cole the right balance of busy and relaxed. Justin would have been dealing with this scout, keeping Cole's hands clean, keeping him from sitting on some stranger's couch and sipping her water. What had she asked? Oh, right. About his flight.

He took a sip of water to avoid answering the question. Such an innocent question, pointless small talk. God, when had he last made small talk? Or polite chit-chat? Or anything that didn't involve "Yes, Mr. Masten" or "Of course, Mr. Masten" or "Absolutely, whatever you want, Mr. Masten." Small talk was for a different breed of people—people with time to burn and relationships to build. He hadn't needed to build relationships, not for a very long time. He'd had Nadia and Justin. He'd had an agent, manager, and publicist. All requirements covered, nothing further needed.

He swallowed the water and wondered how many of those relationships, given recent events, were in jeopardy. Nadia had been the queen of small talk, of relationship building. She'd been the one who sent liquor on birthdays or steaks on anniversaries. She'd been the one to write thank yous after dinner parties, who remembered things like kids' names and health issues. Maybe if he hadn't had Nadia, he'd have made more of an effort. But he hadn't needed to; she was that arm of the unit that was them, she was…

Jesus. He stood quickly, setting his glass down on the table, and moved to the window, the location scout saying something. He didn't listen; he rubbed at his face. He had to get his shit together. He had to stop thinking of everything wrong in his life. Maybe he needed a life coach. He dropped his hands and turned to the man, who had started speaking. "Start over," he interrupted. "I wasn't listening."

The man—Wennifer? What the fuck was his name?—stopped talking, then started again, his eyes darting to the girl as he spoke. "Wait." Cole held up his hand and turned to the girl, whose hands were reaching out, moving his glass onto a coaster. "Who are you? I mean, no offense, but *why* are you involved in this?"

Her eyes flashed and he, despite himself, liked it. Liked the fire in her spirit. Wished that Nadia had had more of that. Nadia's fire was reserved for maids who didn't show up on time, for contracts that didn't give her points, for YSL when her dress for the Oscars didn't fit properly in the chest. She'd rarely shared that fire with him. He'd always overlooked that, or seen it as a benefit. Now it just seemed like another red flag he'd missed.

"She's been helping me." The blonde's mouth shut when the talent scout spoke, her glare shooting to him as she untangled her long legs and stood up, her face level with his chin, tilted up so that he could see full force the impact of her stare.

That was another thing that people rarely did. Looked him square in the face. People glanced away, looked down, nodded a lot. Fans were the exception, their hands and eyes reaching out incessantly, eye contact the golden ticket they all coveted.

This woman's eyes did not covet his, they burned holes through his shell and found their way to his soul, pushing into every dark and insecure corner and finding them all disappointing. She stood toe-to-toe with him and growled out her retort. "You're standing in my living room, sucking up my air conditioner, drinking my *still* water. That's why I'm here, Mr. Masten. And I'm not *involved* in anything. Ben is my friend, he was here when your attorney called and bulldozed y'all's way into our pool party."

She was authentic Quincy, and he had to appreciate that, wished—for a moment—that Don Waschoniz, *The Fortune Bottle*'s director, was there to capture this moment, this spirit. She said "y'all", and it didn't sound forced, didn't sound cheesy or contrived. It sounded sweet and dignified, her fire almost cute in its venom. He was Cole Masten, for God's sake! She should be yanking down her bathing suit and bending over, not putting her hands on her hips and standing up to him. She'd be a perfect Ida—the female lead—a Coca-Cola secretary who strikes it rich alongside the rest of the investors. There wouldn't even be acting involved; she just had to roll through makeup, stand on her mark, and speak the lines. He grinned for the first time in days, and she took a step back, her eyes narrowing. Ooh… a mean look. That translated even better. All Southern fight and attitude. If she could recreate that scowl and use it on the recipe scene, it'd be a slam-dunk.

"Get out."

He laughed at her faint accent—not like the one that their extras had attempted—God those had sucked. They hadn't known it; they had passed through their Californian ears just fine, but now he knew.

"I mean it." She pointed to the door, her mouth set in a hard line. "Get out, or I swear to God I'll shoot you."

The talent scout moved nervously between them, patting Cole's shoulder frantically, like a pat would accomplish anything. "She means it," he whispered loudly. "She has guns in her coat closet."

Cole took a step back, his eyes on her. "What was your name again?" he asked.

She growled in response, and he laughed again, letting the tiny gay man push him out the open door and into the summer heat.

Perfect. She'd be perfect.

Now, he just had to call Envision. Give Price exactly what she'd been begging for—a release from the contract. One problem solved in his first fifteen minutes in this town. DeLuca had been right to bring him here. On the ground, here in Quincy, he could get done the things that needed to get done. He could dig his hands in and distract his mind from everything Nadia.

The press wouldn't love the loss—they would have to spin it the right way, to work with Minka on an exit strategy and PR campaign. And they might lose out on a few box office points, but his name alone would bring in the fans. And the blonde and her authenticity would be worth it. She was exactly what the movie needed.

CHAPTER 29

I realized the error of my ways as soon as the door slammed shut behind Cole Masten's broad shoulders. I shouldn't have lost my temper, should have behaved like a good little Southern girl and smiled politely. Cursed him to hell and beyond in my mind while showing every pearly white in my mouth. Showing emotion was something that should be done behind closed doors. Raw emotion was weakness, and I knew better than to show weakness, especially when dealing with a stranger.

I don't know what came over me. The man and money behind *The Fortune Bottle*, and I had kicked him out into the heat because I didn't like him asking who I was. It had been a perfectly reasonable question, even if it had been worded and voiced inappropriately. He was a stranger, a Yankee. He couldn't be expected to know all of the rules that govern our Southern Society. And let's jump straight to the meat of it—Cole Masten could ask any question any way he wanted. The twenty thousand in my bank account was from his pocket; he was the conductor on the Get Out Of Quincy train. It didn't matter if I didn't like him. It didn't matter if the Actual Real Life Cole Masten disappointed every fantasy I had stashed in my fantasy bank. He was an actor. It was his job to be different than he actually was.

I sank onto the couch and rested my head back. The damn thing now smelled of him, some exotic scent I would need to Febreze out. Well, there went my chance to get any type of job on the set. Not that Ben had had much luck with Eileen WhatsHerFace. I'd heard his half of the conversation with the AD. It hadn't been great for my self-esteem. I really didn't have a lot of brag-worthy talents. 'Making delicious carrot cake' and 'a sparkling sense of humor' didn't really seem like Top 10 Qualities Desired on a Movie Set. *Damn.* I kicked out a foot and rested it on the coffee table. Looked at the ring of moisture caused by Cole's glass and frowned. Leaned forward and wiped it away. He'd left his water. I could be a dear and bring it out to him. Apologize for my outburst and invite them back in.

Nah. Ben had a car. They could get in it, crank the A/C, and head into town. Ben was probably on the phone with Mrs. Kirkland. Her house would be close to ready, their RV already delivered, big plans in place to road-trip around the country on Envision Entertainment's dime. Cole Masten moving in a month early shouldn't be much of an issue.

I blew out a frustrated breath. What the hell would he do here for a month?

CHAPTER 30

"There's only a month before we start filming. It's impossible." The clipped tones of the director came through a burst of static and Cole glanced at the cell, cursing at the low number of bars.

"Nothing's impossible. You know Minka is dying to get out of this movie. Let's call her agent, make them think we are rolling over, and get something out of it. Maybe a cameo. Or cash. Or I don't care. But this girl is *perfect*, I'm telling you. Right now, get your ass on a plane and over here."

"You're an actor, Cole. You know everyone can't do this. The last thing I want is to stick a wooden face on the screen."

His hand grappled for the seat's controls, sliding the chair all the way back and attempting to stretch out his legs a little. "That's the beauty of it, Don. She won't have to act at all. She just has to be herself. Aniston has made a freakin' career out of it; this girl just has to do it for one movie."

"No. I'm not doing it. I'm not throwing this entire movie in the can just because some wanna-be starlet sucked your dick in a corn field."

"Cotton field, Don." Cole grinned. "Didn't you read the book? I know I sent you the book."

"WHATEVER!" the man exploded. "I'm not doing it."

"I'm not in love; the girl blew me off. But she was Georgian as hell in doing it. Pure freakin' Southern Charm. Be at the Santa Monica airport in an hour, I'll have a jet waiting. Meet the girl, and you can tell me tomorrow to go to hell and fly back home. It's twenty-four hours, Don. And you know this Price thing isn't going away. She smells Oscar on that Clooney piece and is creaming for it."

There was a long pause, and Cole watched as they slowed, a tractor ahead of them, a man perched atop two huge wheels.

"I'm somewhere. Give me an hour and a half… and make it Van Nuys. I want to see this girl tonight, I don't care how late it is when I arrive, and then I'm flying back. My kid has some awards ceremony thing in the morning."

Cole smiled. "It's done. Call me when you land."

There was a grumble, and the call ended. Cole slammed a hand on the dash in celebration, the loud sound making the man beside him jump. "What was your name again?" Cole asked.

"Bennington. Ben," he amended.

"Ben, pull the car over. I'm gonna drive."

Ben obeyed, the sedan bumping as it rolled over the tall grass. By the time he put the car into park and opened his door, Cole was there, larger than life, the afternoon sun haloing him as Ben looked up and stepped out.

"Thanks," Cole said, settling his long legs into the car, Ben jogging over to the passenger side, half afraid the man would pull off and leave him behind.

When Cole hit the gas, the wheel yanked left, the car slid a little in its U-turn, and Ben gripped the handle.

"Sir, the… uh. Town is back there."

"We're going back to the girl. What's her name?"

"Summer. Is she… uh… is she the one you were just talking about on the phone?" There was a bit of shrillness in the man's voice, a highness that didn't really fit, and he glanced over, his hand tightening on the steering wheel as they took a curve fast. The car had some pickup. Surprising.

"Yes. Something wrong?"

"You're wanting to cast her? As an *actress*?" The man's face was almost white, and Cole glanced at his hand, holding the center console tight, his knuckles almost bleached from the grip. He couldn't tell if the man was scared of his driving or the prospect of Summer as an—

Summer. A terrible name. Was Ethel or June already taken? Summers should be reserved for thirteen year old girls with braces on their teeth. He slowed down a little, brought the speedometer needle under sixty and watched the man's shoulders relax a little.

"Yes," Cole answered the question, his foot shifting to the brake as he looked for the turn.

"An extra?"

He chuckled. "No."

"Not… I mean you mentioned Minka…" The man—Ben was it?—swallowed hard and pointed right. "That's the street."

Cole applied the brakes, the cheap car skidding to a stop instead of turning. He shifted the car into park and turned to face the man. "What's wrong? Spit it out."

"Nothing." The man's hands moved nervously in the limited space between them, his gaze flitting to Cole's eyes, then down, then back up, the entire production a little nauseating. Literally nauseating. Cole grabbed his arms, stilling the movement. "Stop that. Talk."

"Summer… she's not an actress. No background in film. I asked her already. Tried to get her a job."

Cole shrugged. "And?"

"And…" Ben looked away. "She can be a little headstrong."

The corner of Cole's mouth turned up and he smiled. "Yeah. I got that."

"Maybe you should let me bring it up to her. I don't think…" He twisted his mouth, and if Cole could open his lips and drag the words out of him, he would. Instead, he waited.

"I don't think she likes you very much." The words rushed out of the man quickly, and he gripped his seatbelt as he said them, his eyes jumping to the side.

For the first time since Nadia left him, Cole laughed. Not long, just a few beats in time, but he felt a pinch of something tight relax, felt a bit of himself come back. *I don't think she likes you very much.*

"Good," he said, shifting the car back into drive and turning down the dirt road. "That's a good thing."

CHAPTER 31

"The only reason I'm in Hollywood is that I don't have the moral courage to refuse the money."
~ Marlon Brando

I was in my bedroom, fishing items out of the laundry basket, when the knock came, the crack of the door heard, then Ben's voice. "Summer?"

I stepped out of the bedroom and into the hall, my steps hesitant until I saw that it was just him. "Hey," I said.

"Hey," he repeated.

We looked at each other for a long moment, then burst out laughing.

"So tell me," I said, my butt on the back porch, my feet in flip-flops on the top step, the lines of the wood against my bare thighs. "How badly did I screw things up?"

I cradled a Miller Lite in my hands, Ben's colder than mine; I had grabbed the fridge door the minute Ben's car left the yard.

"Pretty bad," Ben laughed, pausing in his sip to straighten up, his index finger pointed straight out, a furious look on his face. "Get OOUUUUTTT!" he mimicked, and I covered my face, laughing.

"Pretty bad," I agreed, finishing the remainder of the beer and setting it down on the porch. "Did I at least look kick ass?"

"In your baggy tee, grandma bathing suit and ripped shorts?" he grimaced. "Oh yeah. Totally kick ass."

There was a quiet moment as he took a sip, and I swatted a mosquito, crickets starting their cadence from across the field.

"He wants you to star in the movie," Ben finally said, his eyes on the field, his hands joined together around his beer.

"What?" I stared at him, willed his eyes to meet mine, a joke on the edge of my lips. But when he turned his head to me, when his eyes met mine, I saw the sincerity in them. Saw a bit of something else, too. Sadness? Worry?

"Are you serious?" I demanded, jumping off the porch and standing before him, my hands on my hips. "Bennington…" I searched for his last name.

"Payne," he supplied.

"Bennington Payne, are you yanking my leg?"

"I'm not." He tilted back his beer and took a long pull of it, a line of condensation running down its stem. "He does. Wants you to take *Minka Price's* place. Thinks you're *perfect.* Authentic." The word 'perfect' was enhanced by a gesture of the jazz hands variety.

I had to sit down, could feel the growing crescendo of the crickets closing in on me, the evening heat suddenly too much. I'd been hoping, three days earlier, for a job delivering donuts on set, brewing coffee, running copies. Now… *Minka Price's* role? Mrs. Holden would be crushed. She had made plans to come back during filming, her heart set on meeting the actress in the grocery store, or the gas station, or on an evening walk, her pen and notepad conveniently nearby for an autograph and *Oh, do you mind a photo?* I sat on the closest step and tried to process this.

"It's a no-brainer, Summer," Ben said quietly. "No one gets an opportunity like this. Girls in Los Angeles screw, kidnap, and kill for something like this."

I smiled at the image, a hundred big-breasted bottle blondes in different compromising positions, hands outstretched for a role that seemed undeservingly before me. I couldn't act, had never tried. Hadn't taken drama in high school or participated in church plays. And now… to take Minka Price's place? Town would have a field day, whispers flying at a furious pace, the gossip mill twisting my good fortune into something ridiculous, that much was certain. I'd be famous. Not Price famous but still. I hung my head between my knees and took in a deep breath. I didn't want to be famous.

"It'd be a ticket to the show…" Ben said soft and teasingly. A ticket to the show. Yes, being in the movie would put me in the middle of the action, would show me everything that I'd been worried about missing and then some. It would be very exciting. I'd seen the budgets, seen the amount of money—Cole Masten's money—being poured into a production that would trump any event in Quincy's history. A sudden thought hit, the first one that should have come to mind earlier. "How much does it pay?"

Ben shrugged. "No idea. But you could ask Cole."

Cole. Oh yes. The man I had banished from my home. I twisted my mouth. "Where is he?"

"In the car. I made him wait there."

I laughed. "Oh really. You *made* him wait?"

He smiled ruefully. "He might have offered."

"How kind of him," I muttered. A lead role, it had to pay a lot. Enough to set up Mama and properly escape Quincy. More than enough. I glanced back at the field and wondered what I was still thinking about.

"Okay," I turned back to Ben. "Let's ask Cole."

CHAPTER 32

Cole had never had a mother. The official industry story, printed a hundred different times, in different ways, was that a drunk driver killed his mother when he was young. It's amazing that, after eighteen years in the spotlight, the truth never came out.

The truth was, his mother had been the drunk. She'd always been a drunk. Not a stumbling around, unwashed hair drunk who got kicked out of bars in the middle of the afternoon. No, she was more of a dignified, mimosas at breakfast, cocktails at lunch, wine with cheese as a snack, fall asleep before dinner drunk. He had very few memories of her. She was always in bed by the time he got home from school and was never up before he left. He'd been twelve when it had happened. It was a Sunday, when the maids were off, when the house was quiet. He'd been playing in the front yard, a baseball in the air, tossed up by his own hand, the other posed to catch it, when her car had pulled down the drive. He hadn't caught the ball. Instead he had stared, her white convertible zipping down the drive, the red top of it up, the glare on the windshield making it impossible to see inside. When the gate at the end of their drive opened, there was a squeal of tires, and then her white car was gone.

He hadn't known, staring after the car, that it had been her driving. He had only known, reaching down to pick up the missed ball, that something felt wrong.

His mother had never slowed when approaching the stop sign. If she saw the minivan approaching, she didn't react. The minivan's driver—a forty-two year old divorcee with two children strapped into backseat car seats—saw her, her foot jamming on the brakes, the vehicle skidding to a stop a second too late, clipping the back end of his mother's Jaguar V12. The bump sent the convertible into a spin that was stopped by the brick corner of a Starbucks. One couple at an outside table dove out of the way and survived with only abrasions. The minivan divorcee and her two children had whiplash and temper tantrums. His mother had a cerebral fracture. She might have survived that except for the spark that hit the broken fuel line, causing an explosion heard three blocks away. An explosion. Lucky for her. Lucky for his father. No autopsy. No blood tests. The Masten name and reputation stayed intact.

Had his mother lived, she would have been nothing like the sunny burst of nurturing that knocked politely on his window.

Cole jumped at the noise, scowling as he looked away from his phone and up through the car's window. A woman stood there, mid-fifties, her mouth stretched into a smile, her fingers wiggling in a wave. He tried not to grimace and rolled down the window.

"You must be Cole Masten." The woman smiled, a relaxed, natural gesture that was nothing like the forced politeness of her daughter. And that was who this no doubt was. Summer Jenkins's mother. Their similarities lay in the lines of their features, the light hazel of their eyes, the golden brown of their hair. This woman's was cut shorter and curled. Cole liked it better long, better for twisting up in his hand and pulling. Better for… he shifted in his seat and reached for the handle. Opened the door and stood, feeling better as he looked down at her instead of up.

"How'd you know?" He smiled politely, feigning humility. Fans liked that—the *aw shucks I'm nobody* shtick.

She held up a cell phone, a flip one, one with actual buttons instead of a touch screen. "My daughter left me a voicemail." She tilted her blonde coiffed head as if it helped her to remember. "She said, 'Don't come home. Cole Masten is here.'" She opened her purse and dropped in the phone. "Nothing to make a mother come home quicker than to tell her to stay away."

There was a moment of silence, and he shifted into a new position against the side of the car. So, she lived with her mother. *That* was something you didn't see in LA.

The woman eyed him, her gaze shifting over his clothes, and he wondered if any evidence from last night was present. "How do you know Summer?" the question was a polite one, voiced in light tones, but there was a trap in the words, a danger in the vowels.

He spoke cautiously. "I just met her today." The woman said nothing, and his mouth moved in a search to fill the silence. "A few hours ago. I came here to meet Ben."

"Do you work on the movies also?" Her hand wrapped around the strap of her purse, and she pulled it higher up on her shoulder.

He studied her. Tried to see a joke in her question. "Yes. I'm an actor." An Academy Award winning actor. An actor *Time Magazine* just put on their cover. She smiled as if it was a cute little job. "That's nice. I'm Francis Jenkins. Summer's mother." She let go of the purse's strap and stuck out her hand.

"Cole." He shook her hand, and her grip was firm and strong. Funny. He'd always imagined Southern women to be meek and mild, to avoid eye contact and to yield to their male counterparts. Between Summer and her mother, that image was being reworked.

"Why are you out here, in Ben's car?"

He tucked his hands into the front pockets of his pants. "Giving him and Summer a chance to talk. She may have kicked me out of the house." He grinned sheepishly, and the woman laughed.

"You'll forgive my daughter. She's intent on leaving me grandchildless. You were probably too tempting to that goal." She winked, and it was his turn to laugh. This woman was nothing like his mother. Nothing like Nadia's mother—a stuffy blue-blood who showed prize Greyhounds and fluently spoke three languages. He felt the slip of her hand through his arm, and she gripped it tightly. "Be a dear and help me inside."

"Yes, ma'am." He tried the Southern moniker on for size, and the woman laughed again.

"An *actor*, you say? We need to work on your Southern drawl."

They climbed the steps, the front door swinging open before their feet hit the top. Summer paused, her face surprised. "Mama. You're home early. And I see you ignored my voicemail."

"Oh, you called?" the woman said mildly. "I must have missed that."

Cole bit the inside of his cheek to hold back a smile, the older woman squeezing his arm before she released it. Summer kissed her mother on the cheek and waited until she passed inside, Ben's greeting to Francis faint through the screen door. When Summer looked to Cole, her eyes held him in place, his body leaning against the porch's railing just so his legs wouldn't go weak. The front door fully shut and then it was just them and the setting sun and the whistling crickets.

"Did Ben talk to you about the part?" He shouldn't have started with that; he should have made small talk about the weather, or politics.

She nodded. "He did."

"And?" God, this was stupid. Any other blonde in LA would be on her knees unzipping his jeans for this role.

"And I'm curious about the compensation."

The compensation. *That* was unexpected. He coughed back a laugh. The porch floorboards were weak, the house tiny, the truck parked under the tree had rust spots eating through its side. Her whole life could be bought with one bottle of wine from his cellar. He scratched at his neck and met her eyes. They flashed at him, and he composed himself, dropping the grin. "What would you like for compensation?"

"I don't know." She crossed her arms in front of her chest, and he mourned the loss of view. "I don't know what is fair. That's why I'm asking you."

"And you trust me to be fair," he said slowly. Los Angeles would chew up and spit out this girl before she even found her way to an agent's door. Don't trust anyone. That was the first rule of Hollywood. He learned that from his first agent, when he was modeling, and the first go-see came up. "Don't trust anyone," Martine Swint had snarled, leaning over her desk and pointing one long red fingertip in his direction. "People in Hollywood will build you up just so that they can rob you blind. You gotta be an asshole to not be assholed. Don't ever forget that." And he never had.

"I'm asking you for your honest opinion about what a major role in a movie of this size, for someone with my experience, is worth." She raised her chin.

He took the asshole route. Losing Minka was manna to *The Fortune Bottle*'s budget, and this slice of Southern Belle was the gift that just kept giving. "A hundred thousand. Your name has negative box office weight; we'll have to spend a fortune just to get you camera ready, and the filming will take three, four months of your life. That's being a bit generous, but hey," he flashed the smile that fixed everything, "I like you, Summer. I think you'd be a good fit."

She didn't move, didn't blink, just stared at him, her eyes narrowing slightly. She had freckles, a light smattering of them across her nose and cheeks. He hadn't seen freckles in years. Freckles were avoided by sunscreen, concealed by makeup, or lasered off by a plastic surgeon, the records of which would be eventually leaked to the press and made out into something more.

He shifted and she still stared. Maybe he could give her one-fifty. Hell, he could give her five hundred thousand. That was what she was really worth; that was really the minimum for a film this size, with their budget. But if they could get her cheap, then he could pad the film budget, have an allowance for the overages that always came. This was strange, her saying nothing. Maybe it was a Southern thing. California girls wouldn't shut up—their mouths moved like a biting teeth toy wound all the way up.

"Don't do that."

"What?" He straightened off the porch railing.

"That smile thing. It's creepy."

He stopped smiling. "Ten million Americans would disagree with you."

"Then ten million Americans are idiots."

He said nothing, but decided, right then, that he didn't much care for this girl. As Ida, her attitude would be perfect—the secretary known for standing up to Coca-Cola executives. But personally, he had enough shit to deal with. A diva as a costar wasn't something he needed. "Are you interested or not?"

"I'm not."

His foot stopped halfway back in its step off the top step. "You're not," he repeated.

"It's not enough money. I'm worth more."

"The toe of your shoe is held together with duct tape," he pointed out, and she smiled. *Smiled.* A sweet, sunny smile that was betrayed completely by her eyes, golden knives which could cut through a weaker man's gut and drag his entrails out for the buzzards.

"How much money I have is not indicative of my worth. If it was, then I would be the lesser individual on this porch."

"You're saying you're not the lesser individual." *That I am.* Of all the insults hurled at him, his worth had never been insulted. Then again, in Hollywood, worth was dollars and cents and power. Here, in this conversation, on this porch, they seemed to be talking about something else.

"Out of the two of us, only one of us is being an ass right now."

"So you don't want the role."

"Not for that amount."

He stepped back, turning away from her and taking the steps off the porch.

"Goodbye, Mr. Masten," she called from the porch, and he turned his head to watch her, her shoulder leaning against one of the porch posts, her arms still crossed over her chest. "That's what we say, in the South, when one person leaves. It's called a valediction."

"What is it called when one person makes a huge mistake?" he called out, opening the driver's door to the Taurus.

"Easy," she said, pushing off the post and stepping to the front door. "That's called life."

CHAPTER 33

I walked into a heated discussion, Mama and Ben facing off across the dining table, the topic of conversation—apparently—gay marriage. Ben was of the opinion, obviously, that it was A-Okay, and Mama… well… Mama's from the South. If a marriage doesn't have a penis, virginal vagina, and a preacher, it doesn't count. I, myself, am of the opinion that two people should be able to do what they want, assuming that action doesn't hurt anyone else. I walked to the couch and decided not to voice my opinion, should the wrath of anyone turn to me.

"Ben." He ignored me, talking fast, his fingers counting off a list of inalienable rights.

"Ben!" This time, his head popped toward me. "That asshole is waiting for you outside."

"Summer!" Mama chided.

"Now?" Ben asked, moving to the door. "Did you—"

"No," I interrupted.

"Did she what?" Mama asked.

I groaned, Ben gasped at my idiocy, and from outside there was the long blare of a horn. Ben waved a goodbye and scampered for the door. I closed my eyes and felt the couch sink next to me. Opening one eye, I saw my mother, her head settling back on the couch pillow, mimicking my pose.

"Bad day?" she asked quietly after a long moment of rest.

I could only nod.

"He's very handsome."

"Yeah."

There was a long stretch of silence, and I pulled at my sweaty T-shirt. It had been too hot on that porch, with both the bathing suit and shirt on.

"What do you want for dinner?"

"I was going to put that Stouffer's lasagna in. Give it a try. Carla says it tastes homemade."

Mama sighed. "We already out of that cabbage and sausage?"

"Yeah. Ben and I ate that for lunch."

She didn't say anything else for a while. I guess the idea of pre-created and frozen lasagna appealed to Mama about as much as it appealed to me.

"Do you want to talk about it?" she asked.

"No. Not yet."

"He's very handsome." The repetition didn't make the observation any less obvious.

"I know, Mama."

We didn't say anything else, and I drifted off to sleep there on the couch, waking once when she covered me with a blanket and a second time when the kitchen timer went off, the room smelling of cheese and meat sauce.

The lasagna ended up not being half bad. After eating, we stuck our dishes in the sink and moved out to the porch, a pint of strawberry ice cream passed between us, the porch light off to deter mosquitoes, the summer heat leaving us alone for a brief moment.

Mama went in first, kissing me on the cheek and patting my shoulder. I stayed out, my feet gently pushing against the porch, rocking the chair. It was a gamble, turning down the role that Cole Masten had offered. A hundred thousand dollars was more than I would ever have the opportunity to earn. But it wasn't the money that had been the issue. It had been the respect. Cole Masten had no respect for me, for this town, for our way of life. I could smell it on his skin, read it on his handsome face, in the tone of his voice.

When I stood up, the ice cream pint empty in hand, I stretched, my back popping, my eyes to the north, to the Kirklands' big, two-story home with one light on upstairs. Soon, Cole Masten would be there. Ben had gotten him a room at the Raine House for four or five nights, until the Kirklands were able to get out and let Cole in. It'd be odd to have him just a quarter-mile away. To see him come and go. For him to see my comings and goings. Not that he'd be watching.

I turned to the door and decided not to second-guess my decision any more. It was done. As we said in these parts, that egg had been laid. It couldn't be put back in the chicken now.

CHAPTER 34

"She's an idiot." Cole hit the steering with his hand, then reached for the shift knob, correcting himself when he realized he wasn't in his car. Instead, he gunned the gas, the Taurus barely changing speed.

"Careful," Ben cautioned. "Cops are everywhere in town."

Cole ignored him, tightening his grip on the steering wheel. "An idiot," he repeated. This was a disaster. He wondered how far out Don's flight was. Wished for Justin for the tenth time. Justin would have had a backup plan, Don's flight itinerary, a dinner reservation set, the wait staff already prepped for Cole's arrival. As if on cue, his stomach growled.

"You eaten?" Ben asked.

"No." He should have eaten on the flight. Scarfed down one of the three options that the leggy blonde waitress had proposed. She'd wanted him. All but fucked him with her eyes. But he'd felt DeLuca's eyes on him, definitely heard the warning that the man had voiced as soon as the blonde had waltzed into the back, her hand trailing across his shoulder. "Don't even think about," DeLuca had barked. "Three months," he'd said. "Give me three months, then you can screw porn stars into oblivion."

Three months. Crazy to think that this might all be over by then. A lifetime together so easily torn apart and broken down into line items and billable hours. He had nodded at DeLuca like it was nothing.

"There's a restaurant right next door to the bed and breakfast. We can grab something to eat there."

"A bed and breakfast? That's where I'm staying?" He glanced over at Ben.

"Just temporarily," Ben hurried. "It's the nicest place in town. The Kirk—the home we have reserved for you will be available at the end of the week. We just weren't expecting you this early."

"Yeah," Cole said shortly. "Me either." He slowed, turning down the street Ben pointed out. Before them, Quincy stretched out, in all her beauty, the lights of Main Street twinkling at them through the dusk.

A thousand miles west and three thousand miles above Oklahoma, Don Waschoniz sipped a Crown and Coke and shifted in his seat, his overactive bladder making its presence known. He reclined his seat a little and closed his eyes, determined to get a little sleep before landing.

CHAPTER 35

A quarter past eleven o'clock that night, my phone rang. I muted the television, and picked up my cell. "It's late," I whispered at Ben.

"I know, but I know how anal you are about calling before I come."

"Before you—" I yanked back the covers. "When? Why? I swear to—" I stopped talking, catching a glimpse of myself in the dresser mirror. My face was pink, my eyes alive, body tense with anticipation. I stopped my death threat. "Talk," I finally spit out, and my voice sounded the way it should: irritated and in control.

The background of the call changed, and there was suddenly static and road noise. "Summer," Cole Masten's voice spoke, arrogance and order in every syllable. "I'm picking up Don Waschoniz, *The Fortune Bottle*'s director, in twenty minutes from this pisshole you call an airport. Then we're headed to you. Meet us outside in thirty. If you can sell him on your sweet demeanor, then you can have the role and name your damn price. If not, then tell me now, and we'll set up auditions on every corner of Quincy, and you can watch the excitement from your front porch. It's up to you, babe."

"Five hundred thousand." Any posturing had left my voice, and it was just him and me, with only the road noise between us, as I waited for his response. "That's what I want, and I'll do it."

The engine noise faded, the roll of tires still keeping me informed of their progress. "Fine," Cole said, his voice sharp. "Five hundred thousand."

Ben was suddenly back, his voice hushed. "Bye, Summer."

I hung up the phone and stared across the bedroom at my reflection. Then I lay back against the bed and silently screamed my excitement to a quiet and empty room.

Five. Hundred. Thousand. I was terrified to say the giant sum aloud, my earlier bluff called in his quiet steps off my porch. But I had won. He had taken it, and I was in. Assuming the director liked me. I sat up with a jerk. This fight still hadn't been won. Not yet.

I pushed off the bed and stood.

CHAPTER 36

By the time they picked up Don Waschoniz (ten minutes late), gauged his mood (irritable), got him convenience store coffee because this town didn't have a Starbucks (big mistake), Cole's stress was at an all-time high, centered mostly on the enigma that was Summer Jenkins. She had accepted the role, but would Don like her? And would her attitude scare off the director?

He glanced away from the road, at his cell. He had insisted on driving, had informed Ben that he'd be, from that point on, the one to drive. He was sick of being ferried around like a delicate star. And here, in the country, real sweat actually damp against his shirt, he was beginning to remember what it felt like to be an actual man, not just Hollywood's version of one.

They rounded a curve, and the headlights picked up deer eyes—ten or more sets of them. He cursed and applied the brakes. The car skidded to a stop, and Ben's hand braced against the dash in an unnecessary, dramatic fashion.

Cole looked out the window, at the dark stretch of nothing before him. He realized, as a baby deer bounded over the ditch and across the field, that he hadn't thought of Nadia in hours. Refreshing.

He looked back at the road. Waited for one last slowpoke, and then gunned the car into drive, their turn just up ahead.

When she opened the door, the scent of apples wafted out. Apples and cinnamon and sugar. Cole stood before her, blocking the doorway from the other men, and inhaled. "Is that...?"

"Apple cobbler," she said with a smile. A smile. A second knock to the unstable foundation on which he stood. "I didn't have time to make pie. I hope it's all right." She moved to the side, and he stepped in, turning to see her greet Ben with a hug and shake Don Waschoniz's hand. A smile. First time he'd seen a natural one of those cross her face. It was a beautiful look on her, her cheeks flushed, hair down. She had on jean shorts with a flannel long-sleeve shirt, the sleeves rolled up, the shirt's first three buttons undone, showing a hint of cleavage. Her feet were bare on the sparkling linoleum floor, and he glanced around the house. It was perfect—every couch cushion in perfect place, a lit candle on the dining room table, the countertops wiped clean, one dish atop the oven, covered in a white embroidered cloth. His stomach growled, and he stepped closer, lifting the edge of the cloth. A wisp of heat floated over his face, and his stomach growled in response. He felt a pang of something, deep inside, a hole he hadn't known existed, and he dropped the cloth, stepping away, turning back to the small living space. A home, that was what this was. Had he ever had one? The nineteen thousand square foot mansion in Malibu, the New York apartment where he and Nadia had fucked like rabbits, the house in Hawaii… all shells. Empty shells of sex and ambition. He felt her move toward him, felt a soft touch of her hand. "I invited the boys to the porch," she said. "Would you like to join them? I'll cut some cobbler and serve it out there."

"The porch?" He didn't want to leave this space, felt rooted on this cheap floor, by the warmth of the dessert, his legs sluggish to move.

She misunderstood. "I lit a citronella candle out there. The bugs will stay away." Her voice was so different, so gentle and sweet. Is that what a half a million bought him? A sexified Betty Crocker?

He jabbed to see what lay beneath the skin. "I don't really like *cobbler*." He let disdain drip into the word, and his heart warmed when her eyes sharpened.

"You'll eat it and like it, Mr. Masten," she said in an entirely new version of sweet, one with dark fingers that ran along his skin and dug into the weak spots. He grinned and leaned forward, putting his mouth against her ear, watching her stiffen at the movement. "Ah… there's my girl." Another thing she didn't like. She put her hand on his chest and pushed, and he didn't yield, instead covering her hand with his.

She yanked back the hand like it was burned. Stepped back and turned away, to the fridge, opening it and reaching down, his eyes catching on the arch of her back, the long stretch of her legs.

"Coming?" Don Waschoniz's voice came from behind him.

"Yeah," Cole muttered and didn't look back, didn't watch her straighten, didn't hear the door to the freezer as it was yanked open, the vanilla bean ice cream pulled out.

Don and Ben took rockers, and Cole sat on the top step, his back to the door. He didn't want to see her come out, didn't want to see the cozy house framing her. He felt unsteady, like everything he had known, everything he'd had control of, was unraveling. He needed something to be constant, needed *something* to be in order.

"She seems nice," Don Waschoniz spoke from behind him, and he turned his head enough to see the man in his peripheral vision. *Nice.* Not the word he'd originally had in mind to describe Summer Jenkins.

"She's an incredible cook," Ben said. "Her—"

"We don't care about her cooking, Ben," Cole interrupted tersely.

"Don't be a dick," Don said easily. "We're about to eat some of it, and I haven't eaten since the Houston airport."

Cole stood, the change in position necessary since this was apparently going to be a Hollywood jerk-off session. He leaned against the porch column and stared out, the flickering candle casting everyone's face in a pale orange hue. "What's taking her so long?" he grumbled. They didn't need to be fed. They needed Don to look at her face, listen to her talk, see her from different angles and heights. She needed to be the bitchy woman he had met six hours ago, not this *other* person. She stepped onto the porch, two plates in hand, and he turned his venom on her. "We're short on time, Summer."

She glared at him and turned to the two men, passing them each a plate. "Sorry to stick y'all out here, but Mama's sleeping. She has to be up early, and I thought this could give us a place to talk." She turned to Cole. "Would you like a plate? Inside you mentioned not liking cobbler…" She blinked wide, innocent eyes at him, and he wanted to, right then, grab her shoulders, and push her against the wall. Put his mouth on her sassy one and—Jesus. He stepped back and almost fell down the steps.

"No," he snapped, and she smiled again. Her smiles were blood in the water, his demise the closely lurking shark. He looked away, and she sat down in the free seat.

"Summer," Don spoke through a mouthful of food. "Can you stand over here? Where I can see you? It's important that I see your face."

"Certainly." She moved past him, and he smelled a scent other than pie. Vanilla maybe. She took a position like Cole's, against a different post, her new spot squarely in front of him, and he shifted. Looked away and wondered how long this whole thing would take. Maybe this was a mistake. Five hundred thousand on a nobody? It was ten percent of what Price had committed to, but still… it was too much for this girl. Don Waschoniz leaned forward, set his plate on the ground, and stood.

"The character we are looking for is a thirty-one year old divorced woman. How old are you?"

"Twenty-nine."

"Turn your head to the left. Say something."

"Like what?" She giggled, and he saw a dimple pop up in her cheek. *Jesus.* How close did Waschoniz need to stand? He was practically touching her, his hands now moving aside her hair to peer at her neck. That didn't matter; no one was asking fuckin' Kristin Stewart to see her neck. "The brown fox jumps over the lazy dog," she drawled, and he laughed.

"No. Tell me about the cobbler. Tell me how you make it."

"Cobbler?" She laughed again and Don crouched down, looking up at her. "Well… I would have made pie. Pie, in this area, is much more popular. But pie takes a good hour longer than cobbler and so—" Every time she said 'pie'—the word more Southern than the others—a pulse jumped in Cole's dick.

"Look at me now. Follow me when I move." Don stepped toward Cole, and her eyes went that way, a breath of time stalling when her eyes met his, before they were back on Don, and she was speaking again.

"—so I pulled out what I had in the fridge. Cobbler is pretty basic." She blushed, and he heard a soft exhale on Don's part. "It's really just apples, which I had. Honeycrisp or Granny Smith are the best, but these are Pippin apples. So… uh… apples, sugar, lemon juice, uh… butter, of course, and flour, cinnamon, some ground nutmeg and vanilla extract. I'd already done that prep, I was going to put apples on our pancakes in the morning." Every word out of her mouth was freakin' silk, and Cole would have bet a thousand bucks, right then, that even Ben had a hard on. Forget *The Fortune Bottle*. This woman could have a career in food porn.

Don stood on a chair and motioned her closer. "I need to see some fire in you, Summer. Can you get angry for me? Give me some edge, some attitude?" Her mouth parted, and Cole stilled, watching, waiting for the moment that she turned her head to him. But she didn't. She just looked up at him, and Cole tensed when he heard her speak. "Why do you need to know what goes into my apple cobbler, Mr. Waschoniz? Is my homemade dessert not good enough for you?" She pulled at his shirt, and the director stumbled off the chair, his eyes on her, her face strong and words quick, each vowel a stab out at Don. Even Cole, standing three safe feet away, felt violated. "Don't come into my house and insult my cooking. Not if you want to walk out of here with both testicles and that pretty California smile intact. I will poison your tea and—"

"Okay, okay." Don laughed, stepping back, a little unsteady on his feet, his hand reaching back and grabbing the rocking chair for support. "You can do scary. I get it."

Summer laughed, and the tension on the porch lifted, carried off by a chorus of crickets and frog calls. Cole turned his head and listened. If it was a clip, he'd tell the sound director to turn down the audio, would tell him that nature's soundtrack wasn't that loud. But here, on the ground, it was. Incredible.

"Hey City Boy," Summer called out, her hand holding open the door, the other two men already inside. "You coming?"

He looked at her, and she looked at him and there was a moment of truce.

CHAPTER 37

"I didn't believe it, thought you were on freaking tilt, but damn, she's *perfect.*" Don Waschoniz crowed from the back seat, his hands hammering the back of Cole's seat with enthusiasm.

Cole shifted uncomfortably in his seat. "Well, not perfect."

"Are you kidding me? God fucking squeezed Ida Pinkerton out of a test tube and into that girl's mother. Or sorry, *mama.*" He laughed like a hyena and pounded the seat again, Cole's shoulders lifting from the impact. "Fucking perfect!"

In a town like Quincy, a blind man could have a sense of direction. Cole turned right and then, two miles later, left. Pulled into the empty lot of the airport, pleased with himself, and parked. Before them, the jet sat, fat and expensive, on the tired runway. Beside it, in worn coveralls, a man excitedly waved.

"What's that guy's name?" Cole looked at Ben, pointing to the man.

"Wallace. Summer calls him Wally. He actually owns the airport."

"Good to know," Cole said dubiously, looking at the man.

"This is actually one of the filming locations. We negotiated two weeks where he'll close down the strip entirely."

"Unless we need to use it. For actual flights." It was a verification, but the blanched look on Ben's face was worrisome.

"Right. Of course," the man managed.

"Verify it," Cole said to Ben, and the car lightened as Don got out. He rolled down the window and shook Don's hand when it was extended. "See you in two weeks."

"I'll get casting and legal on the contracts. Start the PR department on Summer. Tell her to hold on tight, her life is about to change in a big way."

"I told her we'd pay five hundred thousand."

Don laughed. "Really? What'd her agent think about?"

Cole scoffed. "Come on, man. We're lucky she's not asking for payment in cornhusks. There's no agent. Tell legal we can be aggressive with the contract."

"Hey, as long as you're the one going over it with her." Don patted the hood of the car and stepped back.

"Fly safe." Cole waved and watched Don walk toward the plane. He shifted the car into drive and turned to Ben. "Okay. Let's go get some sleep."

CHAPTER 38

I sat on the floor, my mouth pressed against the window's trim, my eyes just above the sill, and watched Ben's car pull down the drive, its headlights filtered through acres of cotton. It was a child's pose, and I half expected Mama to flip on the overhead light and catch me. It was funny how that always happened. You behaved for ten years in an empty room, and then, the minute you reached for trouble, someone came in and saw.

I wasn't doing anything wrong—wasn't causing trouble—but I didn't want Mama, or anyone else, in that moment, to see me. I wanted a breath of quiet, to watch the men drive away and have a moment to reflect.

I thought I did well. It was hard to know what they had wanted. I'd read the book; I knew what Ida Pinkerton was like, but America's impression of a strong Southern woman often differed from reality. And I wasn't sure which version, truth or fiction, was stamped in the minds of Cole and the director. Cole. Funny how I was already thinking of him as that. For so long, he'd been Cole Masten—the last name part of the first—the entire package one surrounded in my mind by glitter and stars. I hadn't dropped his last name due to familiarity; he and I were still strangers, despite our few conversations. I dropped his name, when I sat and thought about it, because the glitter was gone, the stars were faded. The image I had of COLE MASTEN was gone. It was, from my spot against the window, disappointing.

Ben's car turned left, picking up speed, and if it'd been day, I'd have seen the plume of dirt road dust rising up behind it. But in the dark night, all I saw were faint beams of red and white, fading into specks, then into nothing.

I would not be my mother.

I would leave this town. I didn't know where I'd go, or what I'd do—but it would be somewhere other than this.

I closed my eyes and pulled my knees up to my chest. I looked at the empty plates stacked on the counter, bits of cobbler drying on their surface. I saw an abandoned glass of tea, its condensation leaving a ring on the wood that Mama would flip a biscuit over. I thought about the stack of dirty dishes that I had piled into an empty laundry basket and stuck in my closet. All things I should have stood up, right then, and attended to.

But I didn't. I hugged my knees to my chest and enjoyed this one, terrifying moment that might have just changed my life.

THREE DAYS LATER

Cole stood in a living room of chicken hell. Wallpaper with chickens on it. Chicken clock. Chicken pillows. Framed plates with chickens on it. Hands on his hips, Cole did a slow sweep of the living room, his shoulders twisting as he got full exposure of the disaster that was to be his home for the next four months.

"This is a joke," he finally managed. "Right? This isn't actually where I'm staying."

Ben paled, and Summer, damn her to hell, laughed. He glared at her, and she slapped a hand over her mouth, her shoulders shaking underneath the straps of a red sundress. A sundress. It was crazy how the knee-length hem was sexier than that of a minidress, crazier still how he couldn't keep his eyes off of her legs. The woman had no idea what appropriate attire was for… well… whatever this was. He looked toward the kitchen. "Please say it's just this room." He took a step toward the open doorway; Ben fretted, Summer's giggles increased, and Cole scowled at them both—pushing past them and into the kitchen, stopping short in the doorway.

More chickens. Ceramic ones, perched along the top of the cabinets, squatting alongside the coffee pot, a cookie tin made from an especially fat one. A chicken mat in front of the sink, curtains on either side of the window. He stepped closer and peered… yep.

"Chicken cabinet pulls," he said aloud. "Really?"

"They're roosters." Summer said, as if that made any difference. "Not chickens. Note the red comb and wattles."

"They're creepy," Cole retorted, turning to her. "It's like Dahmer's human organ decor."

"*That's* creepy," Summer responded, her brow raising. "Who thinks of *that* when they see roosters?" Her eyes on him… they were distracting. The mischievous glitter in them lit a spark, somewhere inside him. It wasn't a good spark. Not with this girl.

Cole looked away first. When he finally spoke, it was to the window. "I want this country shit out of here."

"It's cute," Summer interjected. "And homey."

That it was. Yet another reason to get it all out.

"We can't touch any of the décor," Ben spoke up. "That was a very firm stipulation of Cyndi Kirkland's. You can't move or change anything."

"And who agreed to that bullshit?" Cole exploded.

"We did," Summer said evenly, stepping forward as if she expected a confrontation. "And that *bullshit* is the only reason you're staying here as opposed to a hotel. Do you *know* how hard Ben has been working? Of course you don't! You're too busy in California, surrounded by your—"

Suddenly, the spark became a flame and his mouth was on her, her words swallowed as his hands found her waist and pushed, her feet stumbling, her back—that damn dress—hitting the counter. She tasted of sweet fucking rebellion, her tongue softening, accepting. Then both of her hands were on his chest, and her adorable, tiny knee came up *hard* between his legs.

The words of his defense didn't make it out. They were swallowed by the pain—his hand reaching out blindly, needing a support system, a shot of morphine, a gun to shoot this crazy bitch in the head, anything. He wheezed out a breath and cupped himself—distracted for a moment by the chub in his pants. What was he—thirteen? He hadn't gotten turned on by a kiss since high school. Sex after Nadia had proved it. A sexual three-ring circus was now required to get his cock to pay any attention at all. His eyes found Summer, and she glowered at him, her stiff arms ending in fists at her side, as if she was ready to follow up her knee with a punch. He staggered back. "What's wrong with you?" he gasped.

"What's wrong with *me*?" she hissed. "Are you kidding me? You just—"

"Kissed you. I just kissed you. Big fucking deal. You wouldn't shut up."

"You didn't ask me to shut up."

"People don't normally ask someone to shut up. They tell them to." His joke was accompanied by a smirk, both which came through lingering pain, his attempt to fully straighten painful.

She didn't appreciate the humor. "Kiss me like that again and I'll rip your eyes from their sockets."

He held up his hands with a hard smile. "No worries, princess. I have no desire to repeat that experience." He leaned forward slightly, enjoying watching her bristle. "And I'm not talking about the cheap shot. I'm talking about the kiss. I've had better. Much, much better."

It was a lie. That kiss, that brief moment before violence…

It might be worth losing sight over.

He held his eyes on her and saw the moment the girl of stone cracked, crumbled, and broke. He saw the quick inhale of breath, the loosening of defiance in her eyes, the tightening of her forehead, in between her eyebrows, her bottom lip curling slightly underneath a tooth. It was a small act, no burst of tears, no wail of drama. Another man might not have even noticed. But Cole saw it all and instantly wanted to take his cruel words back, to stuff them into his hollow shell and see if they'd blot up some of the pain there instead of cutting this innocent thing deep.

He looked away, collected himself, and looked back, but she was gone—the kitchen door flapping against the frame with a loud SMACK.

Ben cleared his throat, and the eye of every chicken stared, accusingly, in his direction.

CHAPTER 39

I hated that man; he was an asshole unlike I'd ever known. Why God deemed to gift men like him with looks like that was beyond me. Or maybe looks like that shaped men into assholes like him.

I stood in the Kirklands' back yard, on perfectly cut grass, the fingers of which tickled the edges of my feet—a birdbath beside me trickling, a patch of sunflowers swaying before me. Beauty, all around. And behind me, darkening that rooster-infested patch of square footage: The Beast.

I hadn't kissed someone in three years. The last person was Scott, and look how *that* turned out. For Cole to just grab me and *do* that, in front of Ben… I let out a hot breath of anger. And then, his laugh. Scornful and mean. As if it had been nothing. Worse than nothing. *Bad.*

I hadn't kissed a lot of men in my life, but for me, it hadn't been nothing. And it certainly hadn't been bad. He probably kissed a different girl every day. I'd seen him, onscreen, kissing women so beautiful they'd make your eyes hurt. He'd been married—or technically still was—to Nadia Smith. Why was I not surprised that my kiss didn't compare? I shouldn't have felt hurt; I should have felt mad. I had been. Mad enough to push him off and inflict pain while doing so. I was *not* Cole Masten's to take. I was certainly *not* Cole Masten's to ridicule and push aside with a laugh.

Tears burning the edge of my eyes, I stepped to the picket fence at the edge of the Kirklands' lawn, undid the latch, and stepped down into the first open lane of cotton. Crossing my hands over my chest, my flip-flops soft in the dirt, I headed home.

CHAPTER 40

Cole rested his hands on the sink and leaned forward, looking out the kitchen's window, watching Summer's hair picked up and pulled by the wind. "Where's she going?"

"Home," Ben said from behind him. He stepped forward, joining Cole at the sink and pointed, a manicured nail tapping on the glass. "That big house back there is the Holden plantation. Her house is the little one, to the right."

"That's her house? Right there?" Cole squinted, surprised. "It's so close."

"They're neighboring estates," Ben said with some importance.

"How pissed is she?" Cole nodded toward Summer, who was smaller now, her red dress barely visible, her steps quick.

"You should go after her," Ben said. "She's pissed… but I also think she's hurt."

Hurt. It had been a long time since Cole had cared whether anyone was hurt. He pushed off the sink and turned away, stepping toward the living room. "Show me the rest of this place, Ben," he called out, moving farther from the window, from her, from weakness. "And if I see a fucking chicken in the bedroom I will rip it apart myself."

He couldn't go after her. Even if it was the right thing to do. Even if it would make their relationship smoother, the movie better. Because he knew himself. And right now, if he chased her down that dirt row and pulled her around, apologizing would be the last thing on his mind.

CHAPTER 41

"What the fuck is wrong with you?" Brad DeLuca's voice boomed through the cell phone's speaker, Cole wincing and pulling it away from his ear. Cole hadn't had a clear call since he set foot in Quincy, yet DeLuca's voice was crystal. A crystal hammer.

"What?" Cole sat up in bed and looked for a clock, his eyes landing on a small silver timepiece, quite possibly the only thing in this damn house that didn't have a rooster on it. "It's eight in the morning," he mumbled.

"I'm well aware of that. And my wife has come three times so far this morning, so get your ass out of bed and be productive."

"I'm on California time," Cole mumbled, his eyes closing. Anything to break the view. If he saw one more rooster, he would go insane.

"I was very clear in my instructions to you. You were to go to Quincy and behave. Not run around grabbing the first single woman you find. And then you made her your costar?" The man growled out the last word, and Cole sat up.

"How do you know that? *Deadline*? Who reported it?" He kicked at the covers to get his legs free. It was probably Perez. That prick had informants coming out of his freshly bleached ass.

"It hasn't hit any press. But it will. And Nadia's attorneys will *crucify* you with it. You can't put your new girlfriend in the movie that we're—"

"She's not my new girlfriend," he interrupted.

"Sorry. Your new fuck—"

"No," Cole stopped him. "She's nothing. I didn't cast her because

I'm fucking her or dating her. I cast her because she *is* Ida Pinkerton. She's perfect for the movie; she was born for this role. And she's cheap. It's a good decision all around."

"Perfect for the movie or your cock?"

Cole closed his eyes. "The movie. I listened to you. I'm behaving and focusing on the movie. I haven't even thought about Nadia since I got here. Everything has been about the movie."

"Then why, with all of that said, did you kiss her?" DeLuca's voice was softer, a cushion ready for a confession, soothing undertones hiding the blades he held beneath.

"What?" Cole stood. "Who told you that?"

"That scout told me. We hired him." Of course they did. Nice to know he had a babysitter.

"The kiss was nothing." The lie fell easily, so authentic that he believed it himself.

There was enough silence, before DeLuca's response, that Cole almost doubted his performance. Then the man sighed. "Okay. Good. Keep it that way."

"Can I go back to bed now?"

The man chuckled. "Sure, pretty boy. At least when you're sleeping I don't have to worry about you. But check your email when you wake up. I sent over the response we filed against Nadia. It's brutal; I'm just going to warn you. We aren't a cupcake firm… we rip the throats out of our opponents and eat them for breakfast."

"I don't want to punish her, I just—"

"We're only being aggressive about *The Fortune Bottle*. The response rolls over on the other items, though I think you're being a fucking saint about it."

"No, that's good." Cole closed his eyes. "Thanks."

"No problem. Welcome to Team DeLuca."

Cole smiled. "Talk to you later."

The call ended, and he dropped the phone against the pillow. The man was the right fit, even if he was a freaking bulldozer. And he was right, Cole *shouldn't* have kissed Summer. But he didn't need DeLuca to tell him that. He'd jacked off three times since yesterday. Couldn't get the taste of her out of his mouth, no matter how many times he brushed his teeth. Couldn't get the feel of her waist, the cotton of her dress, off his hands. Last night he had wrapped a T-shirt around his cock and jerked off around it, his mind on the hug of the red fabric to her breasts, the float of the hem when she spun around. If he'd have run his hands up her thighs, it would have lifted up and shown him what she wore beneath.

He closed his eyes. He had to get her out of his mind. He had to stay away from her. At least until filming started and their union was forced. He rolled over on the sheets and vowed to avoid Summer Jenkins at all costs.

Tap.

He lifted a hand and dragged a pillow closer, hugged it to his chest.

Tap.

His eyes opened at the thin, metallic sound.

Tap.

He sat up and looked toward the window, his eyes squinting against the morning sun. The sound repeated, and he confirmed the source, his feet finding the floor and stepping to the window. He pulled aside the curtain and held up a hand against the glare. Another pebble hit the glass, and he fumbled with the latch.

She was throwing rocks at his window. What a cliché thing to do. He realized, in the split second before he opened the pane, that he was smiling, so he schooled his features into a scowl. Pulling the window open, he ducked out, his hands gripping the white sill, his eyes finding the one person he didn't want to see, standing on the green expanse of lawn, in a green top and white shorts, a wrapped towel held against her shirt. "What?" he called down, his voice coming out irritated and scratchy. Good. Let her know that she'd woken him up. Let her know that she had no positive effect on his mood or demeanor.

"I brought you something." She held up the towel, and he glared down at it. He couldn't think of anything he'd want in a towel.

Though… maybe it contained breakfast. He was hungry. He'd gone through the kitchen cabinets last night and hadn't found anything. Another example of how much he needed Justin.

"Is it breakfast?" he called out.

"Are you going to let me in, or are you just going to holler down at me?" she yelled back. A distinct non-answer. He debated, then pulled back, shutting the window, watching Summer as her head dropped, and she headed to the back porch. He reached down for his T-shirt from last night, then thought better of it, moving out the door and down the hall, toward the stairs. If she wanted to barge into a man's house at eight in the morning, she could suffer the consequences for it.

When he unlocked the kitchen door, he got the full impact of Summer in the morning. Her hair wild and long, curling around the top of her shoulders. The top straps of her bright green tank top had a scalloped edge, the neckline dipping behind the mound of towels in her arm. Her eyes shone playfully at him, her pink lips curved into a playful smile. It was such an unexpected and beautiful combination, so different from the injured girl who had run home yesterday after their kiss. He held open the door and tried to understand what was happening. Her eyes dropped down his bare chest and to the low hang of his boxer briefs, and she blushed, turning her head, her next words directed away from him. "I could have waited for you to get dressed."

"I don't think so," he chuckled, leaning against the doorway. "You were awfully persistent with those rocks."

She didn't respond, but the sun's shine on her flushed cheeks was beautiful.

"You have something for me?" he pushed, trying to see the toweled gift she cupped against her chest.

"Can you put on some pants?" she snapped, looking back at him, her eyebrows raised accusingly. "It's rude to waltz around with your junk out."

"Fine." Cole swung the door shut, the edge not quite sticking, his view of Summer a thin sliver as he grabbed for his jeans, tossed on the kitchen floor last night. He stepped into them and tried to remember why, of all places, the kitchen had been where his pants had come off. Oh. Right. This had been ground zero for the first jack-off session, his eyes on Summer's house, picturing her returning, catching him with his cock out, eyes closed, her soft gasp and then… he snapped the memory shut, twisting the fly of his jeans shut and returning to the door, swinging it open. God. Another minute of that and he'd have been hard again. "Come on in," he called.

Her eyes skipped over his body briefly and she stepped inside, apparently approving of his new level of dress. Funny, a fan had never yelled at him to put *on* clothes. Though Summer wasn't a fan. She'd made that abundantly clear.

She stopped in the middle of the kitchen and nodded to one of the bar stools. "Sit," she ordered, the gleam in her eyes back.

He sat, hesitantly, more scared of friendly Summer than he'd been of the hostile version.

"I know last night was a little… rough. So I wanted to come over and give you a housewarming present." She beamed, but didn't set the towel down.

"A housewarming present," he said slowly.

"Yes. To mend the fences. Between you and I," she clarified, like he was a complete idiot.

"You want to kiss and make up," he risked.

She glared at him, but he saw the laugh in her eyes. Oh… so many different pieces to this woman. "In a metaphorical sense. But what I said yesterday—"

"I got it," he interrupted. "No kisses. You don't like that."

Her forehead scrunched in an odd fashion. "Right."

"So what is it?" He gestured toward the wrapped bundle before he lost all patience and swept her onto the counter. The package, he meant. Before he swept the package on the counter.

"Oh, right!" She stepped forward and gently set down the towel on the counter, parting it in careful motions, as Cole leaned forward. When the head popped out, in one quick jerk, he jumped back with a curse, the stool flipping out from underneath him, his hands trying to grip the counter for balance, then he fell back, his ass hitting the tile floor hard, with a smack hard enough to make him yelp.

There was a quiet pause from behind the counter, then Summer's head came cautiously over its edge, mirroring the actions of the tiny baby chick that wobbled out from the towel's bed and looked down at Cole.

CHAPTER 42

A rooster. I thought he'd find it funny. We could laugh about it, in Cyndi Kirkland's ridiculous rooster house, and make amends. Get our friendship off on a better foot, one that didn't involve insults and barbs and impromptu kisses. I woke up that morning determined to get over my insecurity in regards to kissing and to get on the right side of the asshole that was Cole Masten. I needed this money, I needed this role, and if I happen to suck at kissing, so be it. A present was the most obvious solution to the problem. I would have made him something to eat, but he had curled his lip at my apple cobbler so I had to think outside the box. And when I thought of a rooster, it seemed perfect. Funny, light-hearted, a country gift for a city boy. I didn't expect the man to fall backward like I'd put a bomb on his doorstep. Didn't expect him to glare at me like he was, right then, my hands gently wrapped around his new pet.

"Are you crazy?" he gasped, pushing to his feet and brushing himself off. Not much to brush off. Cyndi Kirkland's floors were cleaner than a Holiday Inn room on inspection day. "Literally, I need to know this, for the future of the movie. Are you insane?"

The baby chick clucked nervously in my palms, and I slid him back a few steps, closer to the protection of my chest. Against my fingers, his heart beat a rapid patter.

"Well?" he demanded, and I blinked.

"That's a serious question?" I responded. "I thought you were just asking it to be a smart ass."

"No. It's a serious question. What normal person brings someone a fucking bird as a housewarming present?" He gestured to the baby chick, and I had the ridiculous urge to cover up its tiny ears to protect it against the swearing. I should have. Just to see the look on Cole's face.

"I am not insane," I responded. "And it's not a baby bird. It's a baby rooster." I nodded in the general direction of Cyndi Kirkland's decoration insanity. "I thought it'd be funny."

"Oh, it's hilarious." He raised his hands to his head and turned away. "This whole thing is fucking hilarious. I'm gonna have a nervous breakdown over how fucking hilarious this is. What am I supposed to do with that? Eat him?"

I started back, bringing the tiny body to my chest. "No! He's a pet!"

"I—" He pointed to me, then to the baby chick. "I can't have a pet. I don't have anywhere to keep a fucking rooster, Summer."

"Would you *please* stop cussing? It's so… unnecessary."

The man's eyes widened before rolling upward, and I turned away before I set down my heartfelt gift and meat-cleavered this man to pieces. I carefully cradled the chick against my chest, his little beak pecking at my shirt, and opened the pantry, then the kitchen cabinets, looking for different items, Cole's footsteps loud as he walked behind me and stopped.

"What are you doing?" he asked.

I didn't answer him. I found a large plastic bin in the back of the pantry, holding bags of dog kibble. I unloaded the bags and gently put the chick in it. Then I left it there, on the floor in the pantry, moving to the back door and opening it.

"Don't leave that thing here!" Cole shouted after me, panic edging the sides of his words.

"Chill," I grumbled, moving to the edge of the lawn and yanking at some taller pieces of grass, gathering several handfuls before I trotted back inside, dropping the grass in with the chick.

"I mean it," Cole rambled, following me as I opened cabinets, finding a small bowl, then a lamp from the living room. "I can't have a pet. I'm too busy. And I don't know a damn thing about chickens."

"It's a rooster," I repeated. "Or, well, he will be when he grows up. Fred sexed him for me. That's why he has those little spikes on the top of his head." I used the sink, filling the bowl half full of water and setting it in the corner of the plastic bin. Plugging in the lamp, I put it on the floor, next to opposite end. "You'll need newspaper to line the bottom. The lamp is for heat. Baby chickens need a lot of warmth. Keep it on, even at night."

"Summer!" His hands closed around my shoulders, and he turned me around, looking down at me, his face dark, our bodies close in the small space. "You are taking that thing with you."

"No," I said firmly, reaching down and pulling off his hand. "I'm *not.* It's a gift, and you don't refuse gifts. It's *rude.*"

I moved around him, snagging my towel from the floor, and walked to the door, glancing back as I opened it to find Cole, his hands on the edge of the plastic container, looking helplessly from me to it, the pose distractingly sexual given his lack of shirt.

"Newspaper. Find some and line the bottom. Oh, and Cole?" I smiled sweetly, and he looked at me. "You're welcome. And welcome to Quincy."

I shut the door and skipped down the back steps, moving through the yard and out the gate before he had a chance to respond.

Okay, maybe mending fences had been my goal. Or maybe, I just wanted to give the man a jab back. Kissing might not be my forte, but sparring… I could do that just fine.

CHAPTER 43

As God as his witness, if Cole knew a place in this small town to hide a body, Summer Jenkins would be dead.

He stood in his new kitchen and stared down at a tiny bird that stared right back up at him. And then scratched at the edge of the plastic. And then stared at him some more.

He left it, him, whatever, there and jogged up the stairs. Grabbed his cell off the bed and, damn the time change, called California.

The hospital was not very accommodating, the nurse hesitant to put the call through, her tone flipping when he said the two magic words that made all doors open: Cole Masten.

The phone rang six times, Cole pulling on his shirt, before Justin answered.

"Cole."

"Justin. How are you?"

"I'll live. Sorry I can't be kicking ass and taking names for you down there." His voice was weaker than normal, his words slower than standard, and Cole felt a moment of guilt for his early call.

"I'm sorry," he said quickly. "I'll let you get back to bed."

"Shut up, man. I'm surprised you've survived without me this long. What's it been, three days?"

Cole laughed. "Yeah. It's been hell. Literally. Satan would be comfortable in this heat. How long before you're back in my corner?"

"Doctors say four weeks. I'll be out of here in about a week, but I won't be able to travel until around the time filming starts."

Cole stood at the top of the stairs and looked down, swallowing his list of requests. "Get better. I need you back."

"You know it. And call me if I can do anything from here."

Cole only nodded, his feet trotting down the stairs and back to the kitchen. Back to the bird. He hung up the cell, eyed a thin telephone book that sat underneath a cordless phone, and headed toward it.

"Coach Ford and Buick, this is Bubba."

Cole glanced down at the ad and reaffirmed the number. "Yes, do you service the Quincy area?"

"Sure we do. Quincy, Tallahassee, Valdosta, Dothan. We'll service anybody that brings us business." The man's tone was hearty, a bellowing voice that probably couldn't whisper if it tried.

"I'd like to purchase a truck."

"Wonderful! We're open 'til seven. Do you need directions?"

"No. I'd like to buy one over the phone and have you deliver it."

There was a long silence. "We don't really do that. There's financing paperwork, an inspection check, the test drive…"

Cole let out a long, irritated sigh. Maybe he should have called American Express. Let them handle this shit. "I'm paying cash. I'll give you a credit card number and someone from your dealership can bring the paperwork with the truck. Okay?"

Another long pause. "I think I better let you talk to Mr. Coach." There was a muffled shout and the huff of breath, as the man seemed to, from all sound indicators, run. Cole stared at the chicken and wondered if he should name it. It was kind of, despite any level of common sense, exciting. He'd never had a pet before. His father had always said no, and Nadia was against anything that might, at any point in time, smell, make noise, or cause inconvenience.

Cole wandered over to the fridge and opened it up. Stared at empty shelves and wondered what to feed it. He needed a vehicle; that was the first step. Then he and the bird would get whatever they needed to survive.

Bubba came back on the line, this time with the dealership's owner. Cole introduced himself and, ten minutes later, had verbally chosen one of the six trucks they had on the lot. They promised delivery within the hour, and he hung up the phone with a newfound sense of accomplishment. Maybe a few weeks without Justin would be a good thing.

"Well," he said to the bird, "I guess it's just me and you."

Damn Summer. Damn her to hell.

CHAPTER 44

It took twenty minutes in his new truck—a red F250 Super Duty—to find Quincy's version of a pet store, a long white building with the words FEED AND TACKLE in big, red letters along its side. When Cole stepped in, Summer's tub under his arm, the store's lone inhabitant looked up from his counter at the back of the store and grunted a hello. Cole stepped gingerly forward, his new boots squeaking as he walked past horse collars, mud boots, bags of horse feed, and an enthusiastic display of rat traps. He got to the counter and set Cocky's tub on the worn wooden surface. The chick's name had come to him while driving, a humorous play on words but also wholly unoriginal. No biggie. There was only one Cole Masten; if he had a less than uniquely named rooster, so be it. He waited for a moment for the recognition, the traditional 'Hey, aren't you...' but the man just glanced at the tub, then at Cole, his mouth opened enough to roll his toothpick to the other side and then it closed.

"I just got a baby rooster," Cole started.

"I can see that," the man drawled. He leaned forward, his chair creaking, and peered through the thick plastic. "Why'd you bring it with you?"

"I don't know. I thought it might need to be checked out, or you might have questions, or it might not be able to be left alone…" Cole's voice trailed off, and he realized exactly how stupid he sounded.

"It's. A. Chicken." The toothpick in the man's mouth fell out as he spat out the words. "It's not a pet. You don't name the thing and give it a bedazzled collar."

"What does it eat?" Cole snarled, taking Cocky's tub down off the counter and setting it on the floor, his boot pushing it to a safer location, a little to the side.

"Corn."

Cole waited for more. And waited.

"Just corn? Nothing else?"

The man raised his eyebrows. "Its. A. Chicken. There ain't no Chef Boyardee prepackaged meals in nine different flavors. You want to get fancy, buy the FRM brand. It's twice as much and doesn't make squat shit bit of difference."

"Where's that?"

"Two rows left, at the end. It comes in fifty-pound bags. Think you can lift that?" Cole swallowed, his eyes on the man's, and wondered what his publicist's reaction would be if he cold-cocked this hick.

"I can lift it," he said evenly. "Anything else I'd need for it? Medicine or vitamins or shots?"

"It's. A.—"

"Chicken," Cole finished. "Got it. How much for the bag of feed?"

"Eighteen bucks."

He pulled out his wallet and tugged out a twenty. "Here. Keep the change."

He slapped down the bill and crouched, lifting Cocky's tub carefully and taking it out to the truck. He set it down on the passenger seat, buckling it in, then returned to the store, throwing the feed bag over his shoulder with ease while the man behind the counter looked away and spit into a red Solo cup.

CHAPTER 45

BATTLE LINES ARE DRAWN: CODIA IS OFFICIALLY DEAD

> The divorce between Cole Masten and Nadia Smith has moved into high gear, with each side lawyering up and court documents flying furiously back and forth between the pair. Nadia, who recently won her first Academy Award for *Heartbroken*, is allegedly going after an equity stake in *The Fortune Bottle*, Cole Masten's latest film, which begins filming in just two weeks.

I was engaged once. Three years ago. I thought I was in love. But love shouldn't hurt, shouldn't dig through your chest, carve out your heart, and serve it like a meal. Or maybe it only hurts when it's real. Maybe when breakups didn't hurt—that was when you knew the love was false.

I wondered if Cole and Nadia's love was real. I wondered how much he was hurting. I wondered how much of his asshole behavior was pain, and how much was just him.

I hadn't spoken to him since I dropped off the baby chick. Word around town was that he had a new truck and bought a mess of chicken feed. So I guessed he kept the chick; I guessed he was settling in. Ben met with him twice about locations, and brought me over a script. I shrugged when he delivered it, tossing it onto the table, and scurried about finishing the batch of chicken salad I was working on. But as soon as he left, I devoured it. Settled into the recliner and ran my fingers reverently over the top page. It wasn't bound, it wasn't protected, it was just a fat stack of pages, held together with one giant clip. I flipped over the top page and started reading.

Three hours later I took a break, standing up and stretching. I stood at the sink and filled up a glass, looking out the window, across the field, at the Kirklands'. I'd been doing that lately. Staring at the house. I had known before Brandi Cone had called, her voice all high-pitched and excited, that Cole had a new truck. I had watched it being delivered, had seen a barely-visible Cole jogging down the side steps and over to the trailer. I wouldn't have guessed him to be a truck guy. He seemed more the flashy convertible type.

Then I went back to the script. Read every line slowly, sometimes aloud. The role was manageable. Ida was an independent thinker, a secretary with a nest egg to invest. She often stood up to Cole's character, keeping him on his toes, and they had a respect/hate relationship that morphed into friendship by the end of the movie. The fights—and the script was full of them—would be easy. The respect, the eventual friendship… that would be more difficult. But not impossible. No, for a half a million dollars, I'd charm the spots off a frog.

Filming started in just two weeks. Before, I'd have been busy helping Ben get any final details in place. Now, as an actress, I had a different set of things to handle. Just one teensy problem: I didn't know what they were.

"I feel like I should be doing something," I spoke into the phone, the long cord twisted into a knot of epic proportions, my fingers busy in its coils, trying to make sense of it.

"The other actors are meeting with voice coaches, working on their dialect. You don't have to do any of that," Ben said, his voice scratchy, the sound of drilling loud and annoying in the background. He was at the Pit. Cole wanted it finished yesterday, and the crew was still working out some electrical kinks. Next Monday, starting early, our construction workers would move out, the crew would move in, and our sleepy little town would be taken over by Californians. I was terrified and excited, all in the same breath. Each day felt a hundred hours long and still passed too quickly.

"So what *should* I be doing?"

"Waiting. Next week you'll get an acting coach and have some media training. Have you signed the contract yet?"

I glanced over at the dining table, where the FedEx envelope lay, the hefty contract inside. "No."

"Why?" he challenged.

"It's eighty-two pages long. There can't be anything good to say in that many pages." I gave up on the knot and stretched the mess outta the exposed line, reaching over and snagging the envelope from the table. I studied the outside package, ENVISION STUDIOS printed in block on the return address form.

"Then get an agent like a good little actress and have them look it over."

"For fifteen percent?" I laughed. "No thank you."

"Then get a manager. That's what everyone in LA who can't get an agent does. Managers only take ten percent."

"Still too much." I pulled out the first of three contracts and skimmed over the initial paragraph, which was filled with enough *thereafters* and *heretos* to make my head hurt.

"Summer. Either quit bitching and sign the contract or pay someone to review it. Hell, pay a lawyer an hourly fee to review it. But do something. You're running out of time here."

I couldn't just sign it. Not without knowing what it said. Not without knowing what I was giving up or agreeing to. "I'll call my lawyer," I finally said, dropping the contract back into the pack.

"And then you'll sign it?"

"Depending on what he says, yes." I tossed the contracts back on the table and tried to smile at Ben's celebration on the other end of the phone.

"Okay, go. Call him right now." If I could see him, I'd bet a hundred dollars he was doing a little shooing motion in the midst of the construction area.

"I will," I promised, and hung up the phone, eyeing the mess of phone line. My next purchase: a new cord. Or better yet, a cordless phone. Really fancy stuff.

I needed to handle the contract; I knew that. I needed to have a professional review it; I knew that. It was worth paying an attorney; it was smart to pay an attorney. And I had one, one who had known me my entire life, one who would watch out for my best interests and do it for free.

I picked the phone back up off the base, took a deep breath, and called Scott Thompson. My attorney. My ex.

CHAPTER 46

Cocky seemed lonely. Cole sat next to the bathtub, in workout shorts and tennis shoes, and watched him. The baby rooster scratched at the Quincy newspaper and looked up at Cole. Tilted his head and opened his beak. Chirped out a tiny sound. Cole had turned the bathtub into his new home, the lamp plugged in and sitting at the left end, three layers of newspaper lining the bottom, the tub four times the size of Summer's pathetic creation. He was bigger this week, his legs long with giant knobby knees halfway up. Early that morning, he had puffed his chest, white down fluffing out and *strutted.* Cole had laughed, his toothbrush in his mouth, mid-brush, and pulled out his phone. Tried to catch video of the action but failed.

Now, he pushed off the floor and bent over the tub. Scooped up the bird and held him to his chest, the bird's feet kicking against his chest. Walking out the bathroom and thru the backdoor he set him carefully on the back porch. Stepping down the back steps, he looked back and saw the bird carefully follow 'til he got to the edge of the first step and stop, wobbling, his head tilting down at the fall, then back up at Cole.

"You can do it." Cole patted his leg for encouragement, then felt stupid. He crouched down and clucked. The chick squatted, then hopped.

It turned out Cocky couldn't do it. When he landed, his baby feet stumbled against the step, his head tipping down, hitting the step before he sat back, shaking himself out, his feathers poofing. Cole hurried to his side, lifting him up and whispering apologies, moving him safely down to the bottom, where the chicken ran into the grass.

100 pushups. His palms flat on the ground, the grass tickled his nose

with every down pause. Everything was in place, everything on time, ready for next week. This moment of cohesion would be ruined the moment the crew and cast set foot in town. From that moment on, it would be pure, expensive chaos. That was the nature of the beast. A beast he loved, a beast that fed him. This would be the first time it would be a beast he paid, and not the other way around. But that was a temporary situation. Because once it hit screens, then his financial future would be set. The stakes were always high, but this was truly the movie that would define him. Success or failure. Billionaire or just another LA rich guy.

He finished the set and took a deep breath, resting on one palm, then the other. He switched his weight to his fist, then started a second set. It felt so odd, being alone. Here in Quincy was one thing; it was a hundred transitions in itself. Back home would be different. Back home—he paused on his seventieth rep. He didn't even have a home anymore; Nadia had moved out of the hotel and was back, in their bed, no doubt with that prick beside her, on his sheets, in his shower, in her fucking arms. He finished the hundredth rep with a groan and rolled over, the grass warm and soft underneath his back.

He had to stop thinking. What was funny was that the one thing he wasn't really thinking about was Nadia. And when he *was* thinking of Nadia, it was only to distract himself from thinking about the blonde and her stupid chicken. He felt an unsteady weight against his shin and looked down to see Cocky, wobbling in his steps, walking along his shin. He laughed and dropped his head back against the grass.

He didn't have time for this. He should be on sit-ups now, then burpees, then a long run, preferably up and down some hills. He sat up, his hands quick to catch the bird's fall, and set him carefully to the side, taking a moment to scratch a spot just alongside his neck. He had read online that they liked that. Had felt a little proud when he'd found the fact himself. He'd gotten too dependent on others, on Justin.

Watching Cocky, the bird pecking at the ground in response, he started the first of two hundred sit-ups.

CHAPTER 47

I knew, my fingernails tapping against the side of the phone, that I was making a mistake. Dialing Scott was opening a door that I had taken great pains to superglue shut. But I did trust him. Even if I hated him.

"Summer." His voice was surprised, and that made me happy. At least I'd never been that desperate ex, the one who gets drunk and calls in the middle of the night, the one who leaves long and sad voicemails that only further cement the relationship's death. No, I hadn't been that ex; he'd been. I'd been the one to listen to his voicemails, tears streaming down my cheeks, his name a long and vile curse from my lips as I stabbed the button to delete his bullshit.

"Hey Scott." I played with the edge of the FedEx envelope. I didn't want to go see him. In the last three years, the only times that I felt regret over not marrying him was when I saw him. I'd spent countless hours since then carefully arranging my life to avoid as many Scott sightings as possible. And now, here I was. Chasing down the man to save a few dollars on legal fees.

He coughed into the phone, and I could picture him clear as day, pulling at the knot of his tie, his eyes dropping to the side as he tried to think of what to say. Maybe his eyes dropped to the framed picture on his desk of his new wife and their little baby. I'm not bitter. He was the hottest property in Quincy. I wasn't surprised then, and I'm not now, that he was forgiven quickly and snatched up. They bought the Lonner place when the old man passed. They were also one of the few families in Quincy that Ben and I didn't call. I just couldn't.

"I have a contract that I'd like you to review. It's all Greek to me. I just want to understand what I am signing and have you point out anything that looks bad."

"Okay. I can do that." He sounded eager, ready to please. Some things hadn't changed. "Send it to Shelley, my assistant. She'll make sure I get to it today."

"I know who Shelley is." My blood heated below my skin. Shelley had been a bridesmaid, one of the fateful seven. She hadn't ended up in the hospital that night. Lucky girl.

"Of course you do. I just—it's something I'm used to saying."

"Of course it is." I didn't want to mock him, but the words came out that way. Bitter. Sounding bitter hadn't been part of the plan, and I bit my lip.

He said nothing, and I said nothing. Next would come an excuse to get off the phone. He was never good in a fight. Preferred to sleep off the anger and pretend that everything was fine in the morning.

I spoke before he had a chance. "It's a talent contract. They want me to be in the new movie." I hadn't planned on telling him. I'd planned on the contract sideswiping him, his brow furrowing higher and higher as he sorted through the lines of the contract, his head snapping up at the figure—*$500,000.00*—and at the description: *a leading role in* The Fortune Bottle. His stomach would roll with a mixture of pride for me and regret at his loss.

"Really?" It was a mild question, just enough interest in the word to validate a response from me.

"Yes. Cole wants me for the lead." It was a foolish, prideful thing to say—completely unnecessary for our business relationship, yet completely necessary for my ego. I wanted to prance my success before him with the exuberance of the Quincy High marching band.

"Cole?" Scott didn't like my casual familiarity with his name. Not a surprise.

I mumbled out a sentence, covering the receiver with my hand, then moved it away and spoke into the receiver. "I've got to run Scott. I'll send the contract to Shelley." I hung up the receiver quickly, before I waited for a response, before my voice wavered, before I lost the ground I had just gained for the first time in a long time.

I rested my head in my hands and replayed the conversation. I did okay. He behaved. That made it easier. Though, ever since he got married, he'd been the picture-perfect husband. That shouldn't have made me mad; it should have made me happy.

It didn't.

CHAPTER 48

Cocky back in the tub, fresh corn sprinkled down. Cell phone on the counter, one Voss bottle drained and in the trash. Earbuds in, vintage Sublime playing, his feet rattled down the steps and hit the grass.

Cole hadn't run on solid footing in years. Not since *Four Songs of India*, when they'd been filming in the middle of nothing, in an area where, with sunglasses on, he was just another white face. And now, where he could run five miles and see only a handful of houses, it felt safe. If felt worth a try.

He started slow, taking a left out of the Kirklands' long drive and heading away from Summer, away from town. It was hot outside. Muggy hot. Different from California. But then again, everything was different from California. Dirt underfoot instead of pavers. Live oaks towering instead of palm trees. Summer instead of Nadia. He stopped, a puff of dust created, and put his hands on his knees, breathing hard. God, this girl was like a virus, attacking his weak immune system and making a home in his veins. He stood, his hands moving to his hips, and turned in one slow circle, noticing and appreciating everything that wasn't Summer. The breeze that cut through the heat. The sway of white cotton, stretched out beside him in a perfect row. No paparazzi, no cameras. No one to see him, watch him, judge him. He could have a breakdown, right here on this road, and no one would be the wiser.

He didn't have a breakdown. Instead he began to run again.
Harder.
Faster.
Farther away from her. Nadia, and that sick, deceitful world.
Farther away from her. Summer, and that distracting, judging, innocence.

Harder.
Faster.
Farther.
The dirt flew out from underneath as he ran.

Well… let's see. I think I first heard about Summer being in that movie from Jenny, she works at the post office. I don't know who Jenny heard it from, but I didn't believe it. I mean Summer? Our Summer? She's pretty, but she's no Minka Price. And she's not even from Quincy.

We have in our notes that she moved here when she was five.

Exactly. You can't play someone from Quincy unless you are actually from Quincy. Otherwise you just don't know the dynamics of the town.

Unless you're Minka Price.

Well, yes. Now my daughter, she would have been perfect for that role. Much better than Summer. Her name's Heather. You should write that down. Heather Robbins. She works at the local flower shop, but she could get time off if Summer doesn't work out.

CHAPTER 49

I wasn't exactly sure how Quincy found out about my role, but I could bet the leak came from Scott. Or, more specifically, from Shelley. I knew the minute I forwarded the email with my contract, her email address carefully typed in the upper field, that I was signing a death sentence to my life of anonymity in Quincy.

I'd watched movies; I knew how other places worked. How celebrities were fawned over and stampeded in public. That would never happen in Quincy. We liked to gush from the privacy of our homes, stalk through word of mouth and gossip. The more we pretended not to care, the more important something was.

I could feel the buzz roll through the town. I got the extra-long looks, the side glances from people whose children I grew up with, heard the whispers stop as I walked by the Benners' coffee shop. I knew Cole would find it strange. I didn't expect for me to also fall victim.

"Not one call!" I threw the ball of dough down on the wax paper and pushed my fists into it, being rougher than necessary with my kneading.

"Are you surprised? You know how people are in these parts." Mama looked up from the Sunday paper, scissors in hand, a coupon half cut.

"I know." I rolled the dough over and pressed my palm into it. "I just thought… somebody would call."

"You got a heap of calls a few weeks ago. That damn phone wouldn't stop ringing."

"About the movie. About Cole." I sprinkled a fresh bit of flour down.

"Ahh… you want them to call about you. To congratulate you." I heard the scissors when she put them down on the table, and I stared forward at the rose wallpaper. I couldn't see her face right then, the sympathy in it. "It's okay, Summer. To want some attention."

I pulled my hands from the dough and looked down, yanking a dishtowel from the ring and wiping off my hands. "It feels stupid. Weak."

"You've been alone in this town for a long time. Punished for something not your fault," she said quietly. "Everyone's licking their wounds right now. They don't want to be seen as a fair-weather friend—showing up just because you've had some excitement."

I'd take a fair-weather friend. In high school, I'd had plenty of friends, our social standings ignored in a united stand against growing up and taking on life. And as Scott's girlfriend, then fiancée, I'd had his friends. It's been a long, cold three years with only my mother to lean on. And right now, with Ben's imminent departure, I'd take anyone. Even if their friendship was opportunistic and fake.

Scratch that. Maybe it was for the best that my phone hadn't rang.

CHAPTER 50

Cole Masten came to call in the summer heat on a Tuesday afternoon. I was on my knees, halfway down the Holdens' drive, when his ridiculous truck pulled in.

I heard the engine and looked up, instantly recognizing the vehicle, and eased to my feet, wiping a hand across my forehead. I was covered in sweat; it had dampened my tank top, a drop of it running down the middle of my back as I stepped out of the drive and nodded an out-of-breath hello. His window rolled down, a whiff of cold air floating over, and I fought the urge to crawl face-first through the opening. Too bad that'd put me in his lap. A perfectly clean lap, from all appearances. His sparkly white V-neck shone from the inside of the cab, the neck leading to his gorgeous face, covered in a layer of unshaved stubble, past a scowl on those lips and up to the glare of his green eyes. I spied a water bottle in a center console's cup holder, and eyed it. Ice Cold. Frost on the outside of the glass. Cole's hand covered the label and he picked up the bottle, holding it out.

"Want it?"

I swallowed my pride and took the gift, looking at the bottle before twisting off the cap. Voss. Never heard of it. I tilted the bottle back and greedily chugged half of it before stopping, wiping off my mouth with the back of my hand and putting the cap back on. "Thanks." I nodded to the bottle. "Where'd you get this?"

"That grocery store on..." He waved in the general direction of the town. "In town."

"You went to Publix?" I raised my eyebrows, surprised.

"No. I paid Ben to get me a list of stuff." He eyed the half-full water bottle that I offered back. "You don't have any water?" He didn't reach for it, and I unscrewed the top again. No point in it going to waste now.

I shrugged. "And ruin your opportunity to help a damsel in distress?" I tilted back the bottle and finished it. "It's a fairy tale concept. You should be familiar with it."

"You're hardly in distress." He pointed to the Holdens' house. "How far's that? A hundred yards?"

I stared at his well-kept brows and wondered if he plucked them. "Did you have a reason to come here?"

"You're not answering your cell. I've been trying to call for three hours."

I tossed the bottle on the ground, next to a discarded tool belt. "I don't have a cell. That's the house phone number. And I've been out here."

"You don't have a cell phone." He said the words slowly, as if they might make more sense that way.

"Nope." I didn't feel the need to explain that I had no reason to be available or contacted twenty-four hours a day. Plus, I spent eighty percent of my time at home. Who would I chatter to while in line at the deli? Who would I need to call on my way home? It had also been the teensy matter of cost. I made five hundred bucks a month. A cell phone could have easily eaten up twenty percent of that. The home phone at our house was free, along with the internet, cable, and utilities, courtesy of the Holdens. No brainer.

"You need a cell phone. At least for the next four months. If you want to go back to your life of reclusion after that, be my guest."

"Fine. When I get my check, I'll get a cell phone."

He eyed my clothes, then nodded to his passenger seat. "Hop in. We can go get one right now. I'll pay for it."

I shook my head. "I've got one more post to put in. I can't leave this fence half fixed. The horses'll get out."

For the first time, he seemed to notice my surroundings, the hole digger leaning against the fence rail, the two-by-fours one rail down, the nail gun on the grass. "You're putting in this fence? Isn't there someone…?"

If he said more qualified, I swore to myself that I would use that nail gun on his beautiful arm.

"… else who can do that?" He looked around, like there was a team of handymen hanging out behind us.

"The guys are off today," I said tartly. "Why don't you run along to the Gap and let me work?"

He stared at me for a beat, then burst out laughing. I stepped closer and glared, and let's all pretend, for a moment, that my change in proximity had nothing to do with an increase of air conditioning access. "The Gap?" His laugh died down to a chuckle. "Summer, I stopped shopping at the Gap when I hit puberty."

"Well, wherever you idiots shop." I waved a hand in frustration and turned back to the broken fence. Last night we'd had a bad storm. It had washed out the ditch along this patch of fence line, and I'd woken to find the fence on its side. Thank God Hank had brought the horses in for the storm. Spots would have jumped the downed fence and teased half the horses in Thomas County before noon. I'd spent a day chasing her down with Hank before. It was a pain in the ass—excuse my language.

Cole surprised me by opening his door and stepping out, one tennis shoe hitting the dirt, then a second. He wore jeans that, I swear, if I squinted hard enough, had iron lines on them. "I'll help," he offered.

"Help me finish the fence?" Now I laughed. "Please, pretty boy. Get back in the truck before you get dirty."

He didn't like that. I could see it in the set of his face, the way his eyes changed. He turned away from me, walked to the back of the truck, and put down the tailgate. When he returned, his hands gripping either side of my hips, I jerked back. I pushed against his chest, preparing for another unwanted kiss, and squealed in surprise when instead he lifted me up, my hands suddenly holding on instead of pushing away, my struggle ending when he set me gently on the open tailgate. He leaned in, his hands moving from my waist to the truck, corralling me in, his mouth close to mine. "Stay," he whispered, and there was a moment of eye contact before he pushed off, brushing off his hand on the back pockets of his jeans as he walked to the truck and turned it off. I heard the back door open and got my second surprise when he returned with the baby chick in his arms. "Hold him for me," he said gruffly.

I took the chicken, which was really no longer a chick. It had grown in the last two weeks; it had long legs, big knees, and a comb that had become red and soft. The rooster peered up at me, then back at Cole, and shook out its feathers.

"Just set him on the tailgate and let him move around," Cole instructed, turning back and examining my handiwork on the new sections.

I found my words and used them. "You brought the chicken? With you?"

"I thought you might want to see him," he called out, pushing on the top of a new section, as if to test its strength.

"It's a split-rail fence," I called out. "You have the line posts and then—"

"I know how to build a fence," he interrupted, turning to me.

"Really? What fence have you ever built?" I challenged.

"Ever seen *Legends of Montana*?" he asked. "I spent six months on the ranch there. Bought the damn thing when I was done with it. I can build a fence, Summer." He stared me down, and I shrugged. It was a good answer.

"Then build the fence." I gently set the rooster next to me and tucked my hands underneath my thighs, swinging my feet out a little to get some space. The bird promptly put one gentle foot on my bare thigh and hopped up. Cole smiled at the bird, glared at me, and reached down, grabbing the pole diggers and walking to the last crooked pole. He tossed down the diggers and grabbed the pole, working it back and forth a little in the dirt before pulling up on it.

"You should take off your shirt," I called out. "It's gonna get dirty." He looked over his shoulder at me, his hands still on the post. I don't know why I said that, don't know where the flirtatious tone had come from, and why it had chosen then, right then, to come to life.

"You should take *your* shirt off," he called back. "I'm not going to be the object of your ogling."

I laughed. "Puh-lease. We've all seen what you've got." And we had. He went full frontal in *The Evidence Locker*. America swooned, and my vibrator got a fresh round of batteries. He turned back to his work, and I settled in. It was nice eye candy, even with his shirt on. And, after a few minutes of watching him, I relaxed. He did know what he was doing. Probably more than me. He was certainly quicker than me. His shirt was just beginning to stick to his back when he finished the job, grabbing the leftover wood and tossing it into the bed beside me, the chicken hopping to the end of my knee and looking up at him.

"Hey buddy," he said, scooping him up and setting him down on the ground.

"I can't believe you brought him with you."

He shrugged. "What else is he going to do? Sit at home and stare at nothing?" He sat next to me and the truck sagged a little under the additional weight. "You really don't have a cell phone?" he asked, turning to me.

"Nope." I watched the chicken run, quick and fast away from the truck. "Why were you trying to call?"

"Don wants to have a meeting. He's coming in tomorrow, wants us to run through some lines together. Why haven't you signed the talent agreement?"

"My lawyer has it. I'll call his office, find out where he's at on it." Scott had called twice, the first time leaving a message, the second time having the poor luck of getting Mama. It wasn't a pleasant experience for him. I had giggled into my bowl of cereal and mentally urged her on. I guess, seeing my job wasn't secured yet, I should probably call him back.

"You have an attorney?" He looked so surprised that I was almost offended.

"Yes, we country folk hire legal help just like you do."

"I didn't mean…" He looked down. "We need it signed. If there's any issues, we need to know that as soon as possible."

"Okay. I'll call him tonight."

"Wow." He looked over at me, and his arm brushed against mine. "Evening service? I need your attorney."

I laughed, thinking of his attorney. "I'd rather have yours."

"Oh, that's right." His voice darkened. "I forgot the fawning session on your front porch."

"What?" I pushed off the tailgate and faced him. It felt better, having some space between us. I could actually breathe.

"You were drooling over him. You have Cole Fucking Masten on your front porch, and you were staring at *him* like your damn panties were about to combust."

I tilted my head at him. "Oh. My. God. You're jealous." He was. I could see it in the pinch of his forehead. Jealousy I recognized, even if I hadn't seen it for a long time. Scott had had jealousy down to a science. "And who refers to himself with the F word as a middle name?"

"The F word?" he questioned. "Your country-girl mouth doesn't get dirty?"

With his words, the feel of the conversation changed, putting us in territory I felt uncomfortable with. Yes, my country girl mouth could get dirty.
Jackass.
Asshole.
Prick.
I had a whole list of words I could have screamed at him. Instead, I turned away and busied myself, chasing down his chicken, who ran from me and over to him. Cole carefully moved off the tailgate and picked the rooster up.

"When can you meet about the script?" The question came quick and businesslike from his mouth.

I shrugged and tried not to stare at the way his T-shirt sleeves had ridden up his arms, revealing more of his bicep. "Tomorrow? I'm open whenever."

"I'll call you tomorrow morning and set a time. We'll do it at my place. Don's shacked up at that tiny motel." He's lucky Ethel Raine wasn't in earshot. She wouldn't hesitate to cut off his balls and serve them for breakfast with grits and biscuits.

"Fine." I put my hands in my back pockets and watched him open up the truck's back door and carefully put the bird inside. Then, without a word of parting, he got in the front seat, slammed the door behind him, and pulled off, the recent rain softening the dirt, a wet sound of suction left behind as he floored it. I stepped to the side and watched him hit the end of the driveway, the red truck turning around in the yard and barreling back in my direction. I leaned against the new fence, arms resting on the rail, and watched him fly past, a quick glimpse of the chicken's head poking up along the bottom of the back seat window. I guess he had changed his mind about getting me a cell phone. I was glad. The last thing I wanted was to go anywhere with that man. It had been one thing to dislike him upon our first meeting. But now, as time passed and pieces of him came to light, I felt more and more off-balance around him. There were times when he seemed almost likeable, other times anything but. Right then, sitting next to me, the occasional brush of his arm or leg… it had been too much. Too much man, too close. Too much magnetism when he smiled, too tempting when he flirted, too big of a hole dug by him being nice. I couldn't let his charm, his temptation, drag me into that hole and push me down. For him, flirtation was nothing, a country girl finding him attractive normal. For me? Falling for the unattainable Cole Masten might just break all of my bones upon impact.

I couldn't break. Not for a man who didn't deserve it, not for a man who would split town even faster than me. We were both, when filming wrapped, getting out of here. There was no point in seeking out good in a man like that.

I watched his truck turn at the end of the drive and accelerate off, toward the Kirklands'.

CHAPTER 51

He was stupid. He should have never gone there. He should have sent Ben or Don or some other lackey. He certainly shouldn't have showered and shaved and put on fuckin' cologne, like he was a teenager heading on a first date.

He hadn't expected her to be outside, and certainly hadn't expected her to be working. Really working, her shirt sticking to her, chest heaving, arms dirty and strong and beautiful. And she *had* been beautiful, her hair wild, barely contained in a ponytail—her shorts showing off the full length of those legs. It was all he could do, when picking her up and putting her on that tailgate, not to crush his lips to hers, to pull off her shorts and wrap her legs around his waist.

And that was the problem. He *wanted* her. In some primal way that didn't make sense. He'd never been tempted—not in the years with Nadia—to look at another woman. Had spent the two weeks before Quincy sampling every type of woman out there. None had reduced the sting of Nadia's actions. Now he'd spent a handful of moments with Summer, in the one situation where he shouldn't touch anyone, should be behaving and celibate and focused on work, and he couldn't stop thinking about her. Figured it would happen with a woman who didn't seem the slightest bit interested in him. Worse, who seemed to *dislike* him.

It was ridiculous. The whole situation, from start to finish. He took the curve out of her driveway too hard and the truck bounced, Cocky squawking from the back, Cole's head hitting the window with a smack. He glanced back at Cocky and slowed down, pushing thoughts of her away as he reached for his phone and for a distraction.

"Don," he spoke into the phone. "Where are you at?"

CHAPTER 52

If Media Training was my first hint at what being an actress was all about, I was toast. Toast charred past the point of edibility, brittle and crumbly on a plate destined for the trash.

Brecken Nichols came down from Atlanta, her blue suit strolling through the humidity like she had all the time in the world though, by my watch, she was already fifteen minutes late. I waited, impatiently, next to Ben, watching her approach and summing up everything I needed to know about the woman.

She had one of those monogrammed bags slung over one arm – the big floppy kind, packed with enough items to keep me alive in the desert for weeks. Bright red lipstick, the kind Ben would have shot me dead over, her dark hair up in one of those poufed ponytails that Heidi Klum pulled off but I looked ridiculous wearing. Brecken didn't look ridiculous. She looked pulled together. Perfect. Her brows, one which raised critically as she approached, were thick, her eyes sharp and well framed in makeup that must have taken her all morning to apply. This was not a woman who hit the snooze button and picked up after her pets. This was a woman who lunched in fancy restaurants, filtered suitors based on their bank balances, and who looked at women like me as snacks. I slid one hand in the back pocket of my new jeans, and felt, before she even opened her mouth, the scorn.

"God please tell me Wardrobe didn't dress you in *that*." The words huffed out of her as she stopped before me, her head slowly tilting down as her eyes trailed from my head to my shoes, a long moment passing as she scrutinized my sneakers. They were Nikes. Brand new. She didn't seem impressed.

"I dressed myself." I offered the obvious fact in a friendly tone, while my inner thoughts imagined an additional dozen cruder responses. "I'm Summer Jenkins." I stuck out my hand, and she stared at it.

"Never introduce yourself," she finally snapped, moving past my hand and tugging open one of the wide double doors. "They should know who you are, they will know who you are. Understand?" She didn't wait around for a response, her heels clipping down the hall before us, and I grabbed Ben's arm, squeezing it so tightly that he yelped.

"Be nice," he whispered. "And come find me when it's over." He darted away, my grip on him lost in some twist of his arm, his skinny legs skittering across the parking lot without a backward glance.

I turned just in time to see Brenda dip into a room on the right. Letting out a breath, I stepped into the building and trudged after her. *Never introduce yourself.* Of all of the pompous, ridiculous behavior… I stepped into the room and watched Brecken flip on a row of switches, lights illuminating in quick succession, all shining down at one empty chair. Mine.

"Sit," she said brightly and wheeled out a camera, lining it up into place, her hands quick and efficient. "Let's begin."

Media training was a fairly simple, if not painful, process. I sat on a chair, then a stool, then a couch, and answered questions that Brecken threw at me. Sometimes she sat across from me and had me face her. Other times she was behind the camera and had me look into it. She said ridiculous things and then scolded me when I giggled. She asked off the wall questions and then picked at my stumbles. She knocked over a lamp and then lectured me over flinching. And after every take, she'd pull me around and we'd watch the video and she'd pick out my mistakes.

From Brecken's expressions and my own ears… I was bad. Really bad. And I didn't even have a speech impediment to blame.

"Relaxxxx," Brecken intoned. "You look like you, literally, have a stick up your ass."

I rolled my shoulders, let out a deep breath.

"Nope," she called out. "No change."

"How can I relax when you pick apart every single thing I do?" I glared into the camera.

"I wouldn't pick apart everything you do, *dahling*… if you actually did something right." She drawled out the words in a ridiculous manner, clearly imitating me, my accent something she'd criticized for the last three hours.

"Did anyone ever teach you manners?" I stood up from the stool. "Or niceties?"

"Niceties will get you screwed in this business." She came out from behind the camera and crossed her arms. Stared at me without flinching.

"Glad to know I'm not the only one she hates."

Both of us turned at the voice, a low one, thick and masculine. Cole. Of course. The last thing this equation needed if Brecken wanted me to relax. He stepped into the room and pulled the door shut. Walked up to the monitor and looked at the still image. I did one of the Brecken UnAllowed Actions and chewed on my fingernail. She cleared her throat and he did what I hoped he wouldn't do. Reached down and pressed a key on the board, my hesitant voice coming through the speakers and I winced as I stumbled through Brecken's question, my response filled with enough *Ums* to drown a cat. He hit another button and the carnage stopped. "How long have you been working?"

"Three hours," Brecken oh-so-helpfully supplied.

"Grab some lunch." He nodded toward the door. Brecken didn't move. "Go. I'll work with her for a while."

Oh no. No no no nononono. I pushed off the stool and onto my feet. "I haven't eaten either."

"We're making some progress," Brecken jumped in. "You should have seen the first takes." She didn't move from her spot and I felt the immature desire to hide behind the woman I'd cursed all morning. Even she was better than him. His eyes laughing at me, a hundred opportunities for him to pick at me later.

"Not enough progress." His voice had taken a hard turn, and she yielded, giving a tight nod and walking past the camera, her frame stooping as she reached for her purse. Then the door opened, she walked out, and it was just the two of us.

"Do you need a sandwich?" His eyes were level and steady on mine, his features quiet, giving no sign to the psyche underneath.

"No. I'm fine." Despite my failed attempt to join Brecken for lunch, I couldn't imagine eating, not right now, with the current state of my stomach—one rolling ball of knots.

He reached over and flicked off a panel of switches, and half the lights on me went dark. I was still standing, before my stool, and I stepped back a pace, my heel hitting the leg, and I pushed myself back onto the metal seat.

"I'm going to turn off the camera." He reached up and pressed a handful of buttons, his hands sure, familiarity showing as he moved aside the cart and then grabbed an extra stool, sitting down in front of me, the front of his jeans tight as his knees spread, his posture relaxed, and his hands hung loose and clasped before him. "What have you guys worked on so far?"

"Just answering questions and then reviewing it on…" I pointed to the monitors and tried to think of how Brecken had referred to them. "The screen," I finally said.

"Did she go over jargon, wordage and abstractions?" His voice was mild and I rubbed my hands on the front of my jeans. I should have washed them prior to wearing them. They were too stiff, too scratchy.

"Umm ... probably. It's all starting to run together."

"You don't have to worry about jargon. You're Southern, that's okay. We don't need you to sound like something you're not."

"She said I can't say y'all." One rule I could remember, only because I seemed to break it frequently.

He shrugged. "You can say y'all. Maybe not when you're promoting a sci-fi thriller, but right now, that's fine."

"Okay."

"Wordiness, though, for you, might be a problem." He leaned forward. "Rambling. Don't ramble."

"Yeah." I winced. "I do that."

"That's okay. We'll work on it."

"You don't need to. I mean—you're busy. I can work with Brecken on it." I nodded enthusiastically, like she was my new best friend.

He ignored the comment. "Abstractions are another thing you don't have to worry about right now. But the verbal fillers, the 'you knows' and 'uhhs'—"

"I know. And the fidgeting and the touching of my hair and blinking too much—" I stopped talking before my voice showed the thin ledge of hysteria where I sat. I looked away, focusing on a sweater that hung off a lighting rig. It was cold in there, without the additional lights. Maybe I could borrow it. Another layer between Cole and I seemed like a good idea.

He stood up and reached between his legs, grabbing the stool and dragging it closer. When he sat back down, there were only a few feet between us. "Summer. Look at me."

I did. It was hard not to, when he was that close. And God, he was gorgeous. So much so that it hurt, like staring at the sun, the pull of attraction so sharp and dangerous that it physically hurt my heart. It was staring at something you could never have but desperately wanted, despite any sense to the contrary, despite any danger that accompanied the attraction.

"Forget the rules and ask me a question."

That distracted me from his beauty and I lifted my eyes off the perfect curve of his jaw and to his eyes. "A question from the list?" After three hours, I knew Brecken's twenty questions by heart.

He shrugged. "Any question. Anything you want."

"Are you in pain?" Any question. I had any question in the world and where that one came from, I had no idea. If I'd expected it, I might have looked away, might have given him a chance to react privately.

But I wasn't expecting the words to leave my lips and so I was there, staring at him, when the blow hit. There wasn't much of an impact. His eyes dimmed a little, green irises going a little dark, his neck contracting as he swallowed. "From her leaving… I mean. I just…" I finally was able to look away. "You don't seem that upset."

"Don't ramble. Be concise." He touched the edge of my knee to catch my attention. "And don't look away. That indicates shame."

Shame. No joke. I *was* ashamed. It was way too personal of a question for me to ask.

"Nadia and I were together for a long time. Anytime you lose someone who has been a part of your life for that long, it hurts. But I think that this was for the best. She's happier in her new relationship and that's what I want. Her to be happy." He gave a small smile, lifting one shoulder in a shrug of resignation. I felt a sudden urge to comfort him, was about to reach forward when he straightened, his posture changing. "That's what I would say, if a reporter asked. It puts me on the high road and subtly turns everyone against her."

"Is it true?" Another personal question. It was like I had to chase down this dog until it died.

"No." Now he looked away. "I feel very… odd about Nadia." His words came out slowly, as if he was weighing each word and recording its worth. "I feel… stupid. I feel taken advantage of. I feel very, very off balance." His head lifted, and his eyes returned to me. "I don't know if pain would be the word I would use."

I swallowed. "I like that answer better."

His mouth curved. "So would the press. The truth is always more interesting. It's also much more dangerous." He didn't move, but I swear, from just the way he looked at me, that he'd gotten closer. "Did you feel like you are closer to me now? Knowing that?"

"Yes."

"If the public knows you, Summer, they will destroy you. They can't help themselves. They love our weaknesses so much, it causes them to latch on, to dig deeper, to feast and pillage on our exposures until the moment when we, as people—me as Cole, you as Summer—are gone. And the only thing left is what they want to see."

It sounded terrible. I had been worried about looking stupid. Not losing myself. I swallowed, his next words pushing my anxiety even higher.

"My turn." He rubbed his bottom lip, his other hand tucked under his elbow and looked at me. *His turn. I'd been so personal with my question.* What would he ask me? Probably how many men I'd slept with.
My bra size.
My favorite sexual position.
My—

"Who is your favorite actor?"

My mind stuttered. "My favorite actor?"

"Yes."

"Like… to date? Or who I respect?"

He shrugged. "Both."

Five months ago I'd have rattled off his name without hesitation. Not as the actor I respected the most, that honor would have to go to an older man. But as the actor I found the most attractive… Cole Masten had always held that spot in my mind. Always. He was everyone's gold standard, the photo first in Google Results when you keyed in 'heartthrob.'

"Ummm…" His eyes sharpened and I cleared my throat. "As far as actors I respect…" I swallowed. Brecken had told me, whenever I felt the urge to say a filler word, to swallow. Take a breath. Or a sip of water. "Jake Gyllenhaal. He was really strong in Nightcrawler. And Christoph Waltz. And… Tom Hanks."

"Interesting list." He nodded at me to go on.

"As far as actors I find attractive… maybe Chris Pratt?" I don't know why I gave my answer in the form of a question.

Cole's brow furrowed. "Chris Pratt?" he repeated.

"Yes. The guy from *Parks and Recreation*? He… he was really hot in Jurassic World."

Cole's mouth twitched. "Anyone else?"

I tried to think of someone, anyone who was as opposite from Cole as possible. "Jonah Hill," I blurted out.

Cole tilted his head, my explanation rushing out before his question came. "He's very talented. And smart. I like that in a man."

"And he's fat," Cole said flatly. "You have all of Hollywood to choose from, and Jonah Hill is your choice."

"He's not… he's cuddly."

"And that's what you want? A cuddly guy?"

I raised my chin. "I answered your question."

"Yes, you did." He got off the stool and walked back to the wall, flipping back on the lights. Halogen and hot, their glare unsettling. "With only one 'umm.' Let's go through a few more with the lights, then we'll turn the camera back on."

"Don't you have other stuff to do? This doesn't exactly seem to be something you need to waste your time on." I needed him out of there. He was too close, too casual. Just the two of us, now brightly lit by lights… it was too much.

"Is that your next question?" He settled down on the stool and kicked out a leg, resting the sole of his shoe on my stool and just like that, we were connected. I looked up from his leg.

"No." I had another question, one waiting in the wings, one that had been pushing at my brain for three weeks and now, in this empty room, with his smart mouth quiet, his eyes on me… now was the only time I might ever be able to ask it. "I have a different question."

"So ask it." His voice had deepened, like he knew what was coming, all humor out of it, and I braced myself for his answer, my hands together, in between my thighs and gripping at the edge of the stool.

"Were you telling the truth? When you said I was a bad kisser?"

CHAPTER 53

Oh, what an innocent, naïve question. Someone shouldn't put themselves out there like that. Show their insecurities. Show that you cared enough about a man's opinion to ask a question like that. She had showed up, the morning after that kiss, all bubbly energy and friendliness. He'd been convinced, right then, that she had gotten over his snipe. Had been certain that he'd been the only one to carry that moment around. Dwell on it. Fester on it.

But here, in the hunch of her shoulders, the gentle drop of her vowels, the hurt was still present, the moment not forgotten.

"Do you want the industry answer or the truth?" He asked the question to buy time, valuable seconds needed because he had no idea how to answer. No idea what to say that didn't lay him bare or give her an opening. She couldn't have an opening. Right now, he needed his heart packaged in bubble wrap and locked behind six feet of steel. Half because it was a condition of DeLuca's representation. Half because DeLuca's reasoning was right.

"The truth." She said the words simply and he could see her spine when it found its strength, steeling against whatever was to come, her shoulders sliding back, chin coming up. She was such a paradox. In some ways, the strongest woman he'd ever met, her fire and spite and self-sufficiency clear and defined. In other ways, she was the softest, most vulnerable. She put herself too far out there, felt too strongly, would love too fiercely, give too freely, her actions a roadmap to destruction that would one day kill that spirit. His instinct to protect that spirit, to strengthen her defenses… he both wanted to throw her to the wolves and lock her away in a castle, all at the same time. It was an inner struggle that would drive any man mad. It was an inner struggle that, right then, he didn't need to be dealing with.

He let his foot drop from her stool, and its impact with the floor was loud but she didn't jump. Maybe because Brecken had actually taught her something. Or maybe because she'd been expecting it all along. He stood and fought the urge to lean forward, to rest his hands on her thighs and kiss her, right there, in a way that left no doubt as to her effect on him.

Instead, he picked up the stool and gave her the only thing he could manage. Two letters. "No."

"No?" She shot back the word quickly, her brow rising, the word a challenge between them.

"Don't ramble. Be concise," he reminded her.

"Is be evasive also a rule?" She was on her feet, coming after him, and damn, she wasn't going to let this go.

"Actually yes. Anytime you can be evasive, you should." He set the stool against the wall where he had gotten it and she stared at it, her eyes narrowing when she turned back.

"You always run when put in the corner, City Boy?"

"I'm not running. I have other things to do. As you just pointed out." He flicked off the lights and reached for the handle, her grip tight when it grabbed his forearm.

"Wait."

He stopped, turning to her despite his better judgment, his features masked, any emotion hidden behind two decades of practice. "Yes?"

"Thank you." She blushed, her hands pushing into her back pockets. "It sounds really stupid but I needed to know that. It's just… you know. Been a while."

"Since you were kissed?" No, no. She hadn't meant that. She had been referring to the compliment. Only… the moment his incredulous words fell out, he knew that they were right. It had been *a while* since she had been kissed.

How was that possible? Didn't everyone in these small towns just fuck and farm? How, with her looking like that, with her being like she was, had she not been kissed every day, multiple times, suitors lining up around the block like dominoes waiting to be knocked over? And how long was a while?

Her eyes flicked up, and there was a moment of petulance in her face before it smoothed over. "Thanks for helping," she said stiffly.

"I'll talk to Casey, Brecken's boss. See if we can keep you away from the press."

"Because I'm terrible." She said the insult almost cheerfully.

"Without sugar coating, yes. You're too rough right now."

She nodded, stepping back from him, and he almost followed her. "So… I can go. No more media training?"

"For now. Have you met with your acting coach?"

"He comes in next week. I thought it was this week, but—"

Cole waved off the explanation. "That's fine. Don't worry about the acting. It won't be like the media bits. Those are live, so you only get one shot. The acting we can do over a hundred times. And the lines, your role… you just have to be yourself."

"But that's all media training is. Being myself." There was a thread of panic in her voice and he looked back over his shoulder, his escape interrupted, this last sentence too valuable to ignore.

"No Country. In Hollywood, off camera, you can't be yourself. You can't be weak, you can't be honest, and you can't be genuine. Not if you want to survive."

"So what does that make you?"

Her eyes were on him when she asked the question, her tone quiet, unaccusing, the words hanging in the space between them. Then he turned, stepping into the hall and pulling the door firmly shut behind him.

He had a million answers to that question, yet even he couldn't sort the bullshit from the truth.

CHAPTER 54

ONE WEEK LATER

That day, on that driveway, he should've gotten Summer the cell phone. Thrown her over his shoulder and then into the passenger seat of his truck. Buckled her in and driven into town. He shouldn't have let her get him worked up and mad; he shouldn't have let that moment of possible productivity pass. Now, that error was raising its head, her line ringing busy. Cole stood at his kitchen counter, the cordless phone in hand, and tried the line again.
And again.
And again.

"Did you get her?" Don walked into the kitchen, a pen stuck behind his ear, a stack of pages in hand.

Cole turned, suddenly reminded of the real reason for his call to her. To get her over there. They needed to go over these script changes, to get her on the same page so that she would be ready to film. "No," he muttered. "Her line isn't working." He hung the phone on its cradle. "I'll just run over there and grab her."

Don glanced at his watch. "Fine. But I'm about to hop on a call with Eileen to go over the latest budget. You want to wait, join us on that call, and then head over there?"

"No." Cole bent down and held out a cracker, trying to get Cocky to grab it. "You take the call, I'll go get her."

Cocky ignored him, strutting toward the living room, half the skin on his back exposed, pink showing between the white feathers. Cole had been panicked at first, heading to the local vet before he pulled over and consulted google. Turns out it is normal, the loss of chick fuzz while the real feathers came in. But even half-bald and gangly, he was a beautiful bird, and would be even more so once his plumage came in. According to Google, that would start to happen in the next few weeks.

He looked to Don, but the man was back at the dining room table, his cell against his ear. Cole grabbed his tennis shoes and worked the first one on. No point in taking the truck, not when they were so close. He yanked off his shirt. He'd run over there and knock on the door. Give her some grief about her phone, then bring her over to meet with Don. Assuming she didn't have an afghan to crochet or a well to dig, what else could she have to do at nine-thirty in the morning?

Sleep. That was apparently what Summer Jenkins had to do at nine-thirty on Wednesday mornings. Cole stood, his hands on his hips, and stared down at her. Correction: Sleep hard.

He'd been almost panicked when he'd come in. Her truck was in the drive, unlocked, the keys in the ignition. He'd glanced at it, then climbed the front steps, knocked on the door and waited, leaning on one hand against the wall. There had been no answer, no doorbell to press, the curtains on the front closed tight. He'd knocked again, harder. Walked around the house and then returned to the front. After the third round of knocking, he'd tried the door. Unlocked. Like the truck. This was a town of people waiting to be killed.

He had cracked the door, calling out her name, the quiet house open before him, lights off, no response made. Then, with mounting unease, he stepped in. The first door he'd opened had been to her room. And there, stretched out on the bed, had been her.

Red underwear. Between that and her dress, she was on her way to ruining the color for him. She lay on her stomach, arms up by her head, one knee higher than the other, her beautiful ass on full, uninterrupted display before him. He could stare without being caught; his eyes could travel over the lines of her body without a glare; he could have one, continuous moment of Summer worship. And he did, right there in her bedroom, noticing everything he could and cementing it into his mind. The freckle on the back of her right arm. The tan on her legs that faded to white the higher it went on the back of her thighs. The dimples on her back, barely seen—a thin white tank top almost covering them up.

He wanted to wake her up.
He wanted to stand there and stare at her forever.
He wanted to turn around and leave because she was obviously safe and this was behavior that would put him in jail.

He never was good at making decisions.

CHAPTER 55

Our house was always hot in the morning. It was built in 1904, a sharecropper's cabin to the Holdens' plantation and was put on the dirt facing west, in order to capture the morning sun. That might have been great for cotton pickers who rose at five, but for Mama and me it was a pain in the ass. More for me than Mama. She was out of bed by seven, in her car by eight, and at work by eight-fifteen. Me, I liked my sleep. When our house phone jangled sometime around nine o'clock, I kicked off my hot sheet, rolled over on the bed, and shoved a hand in the general direction of my bedside table and the telephone. There was a crash, my wandering hand a little too energetic, and the phone stopped ringing. I went back to sleep.

A throat clearing awakened me. A man's throat. I opened my eyes, my yellow sheets coming into focus, and slowly rolled over. Cole stood at the foot of my bed. Shirtless. In black running shorts. Staring at me. I closed my eyes and tried to remember what I had gone to bed wearing. I felt something hit my foot and reopened my eyes.

Cole was leaning forward, his hand on my foot. He straightened when our eyes met. "Summer," he said quietly—a stupid thing to say as we were looking right at each other.

"Why are you in my bedroom?" I had to look down, just to see if… oh God. I was only wearing underwear and a wife beater. I looked back at Cole, and he was staring, his eyes following the path mine just took, his jaw tightening, one finger twitching against the top of his hip.

"You didn't answer your door, your front door was unlocked, and your phone line is busy." He clipped out the sentences without looking at my face, his eyes still on my body, and I shifted a little on the bed when I realized that the front of his loose shorts was *tenting*. Tenting. I hadn't been touched, hadn't been kissed—other than that kitchen disaster—in three years, and this man, this sex god who'd had Nadia Smith, was *aroused* by me. My inner mention of his wife shut down my sex drive, and I rolled over, trying to block out the image of the arousal on his face, the push against his pants, the roll over preventing my legs from opening up for him. And holy crap, I'd been about to do that. Invite Cole Masten, my costar, into my bed. I reached out for a sheet, something to cover me up because my butt was now right *there* in front of his eyes. My hands found nothing, and I stopped moving, stopped breathing because I could hear his breath, hard and loud in the room, and *ohmyword* it was sexy. The bed sank beside my right knee, then beside my left, and I felt the brush of soft fabric against the bottom of my feet—his shorts—and it was so erotic I almost moaned.

"What are you doing?" I gasped, a set of fingertips moving slowly, from my right knee up, along the side of my thigh and drifting gently over the curve of my butt.

"Shh…" he whispered. "For once, Summer. Just shut up."

I didn't respond because his hand fully settled on my skin, sliding under my cotton panties, and palming my bare skin, squeezing the flesh so hard that I gasped, my shoulders lifting, his other hand pushing, holding me back down.

"Don't move. Don't think. Please. I need this."

"Nadia," I gasped out her name, my only protest, and his hand instantly stilled on my ass.

"Summer." He leaned forward, the change in position pushing his pelvis, his hard-on, against my feet, his hand harder on my butt, and his breath was suddenly hot on the nape of my neck as he softly spoke. "If I never hear that name again, I will die happy. There is nothing about her that needs to be in this moment."

"But—" My protest died when his lips settled on the back of my neck, his teeth following up the kiss with a scrape against my skin.

"For the love of God, Summer. If you want me to stop you need to tell me *right now*."

Tell him to stop? I couldn't. He ground his hips and my feet lifted, apart from my brain, and brushed against one large, hard item. "Yes…" he hissed, sitting back, his mouth leaving my neck, his hand running slowly down my back. The other slid from my thigh up, underneath my panties, both of them palming my ass. The man appeared to have all of the time in the world, and I swallowed a moan as he squeezed, rolling his hands up and out, in small circles, the place between my legs affected by the movement, the cotton of my panties pulled tight by his big hands, the friction just one more piece in the unraveling of my sanity in this moment.

How would I ever recover from this? How would any man ever be able to compete?

He spoke, his words gruff and barely controlled, and I lost all reason with the next words out of his mouth.

"Summer, what will happen when my hands move lower? When I slide my fingers in between your legs?" I felt the pressure as one of his hands moved, teased me, fingers sliding over my ass and almost lower, almost there. I hoped his question wasn't a literal one because I couldn't form words, or thoughts, or anything right then. "I'm about to find out exactly how much you've been wanting my cock." He growled the last word, and I almost bucked under his touch, my need burning, crying out, my legs scrabbling underneath him, crawling up the bed, a feral desire deep inside me wanting to be on all fours, my butt in the air, ready for him, frantic for him.

"No," he said, holding me down, his knees tight against me as he held me in place, prevented my climb, one hard finger sliding back down the crack of my ass and further, in between my legs, and he swore in the silent room, my low groan joining his curse. "Do you get this wet for all of these country boys?" His fingers played with the soaked material between my legs, my thighs fighting to part, and he gave me a little room, my knees urgent in their spread, my feet clamping around his arousal, and he groaned, the sound deep and needy, pouring fuel on my need and pushing it further, more intense, my initial shock at how hard he was replaced with a constant hammering in my brain to have it now, right now, because I swore I would die without it.

He didn't push aside my panties; he didn't rip them off; he just moved, with slow and patient strokes, from my ass to my taint, back and forth, and I pushed my hips higher in the air, my face buried against my fitted sheet, any composure lost as I begged him to go lower, begged him for more.

"Jesus, Summer, I want to taste you so badly," he whispered, his head dropping, his teeth softly biting into my left butt cheek. "I want to flip you over and bury my face in between your legs and fuck you with my mouth. I want to make you scream my name and come underneath my mouth and taste the moment you fall apart for me."

"Then do it," I challenged. "Shut up and do it." I may have told him to shut up, but I had coveted every word, every sentence—words uttered to me, about me, from *him*. I could hate this man, curse him to hell, but there had never been a question on this earth that the man was beautiful, that his body was sin, that his sexuality was addicting. And now he was here, in my bed, his hands on my skin. Skin that hadn't been touched in so long. Skin that begged for more, raw need pulsing through me.

"I can't." His voice broke on the two words, his fingers frantic as they pulled at my hips, pulled them up, his fingers skimming my soaked panties down, and I was suddenly bare before him, bent over, the hum of the fan brushing air over my most sensitive place. "Where's your condoms?" he rasped, and I tried to find reason and came up short. Condoms weren't an item I had ever stocked, and I couldn't think of anything right then but having him.

"I don't… please. Just please…"

He didn't ask questions; he didn't do anything but yank at his shorts, and push, bare and beautiful, inside of me. In that moment, that push, I lost every hold I had on myself and became his. He shuddered out my name, pressed himself fully inside, and waited for one long breath.

"Are you okay?" His words were painful and tight, gritted out between his teeth, and I nodded, unable to form words, unable to do anything but worship at the altar of Cole Masten from that moment forth.

"Good," he moaned. "Because I'm about to unleash hell."

He was wrong. It wasn't hell. It wasn't anything close to hell. It was beautiful, fucking heaven, his hands tight on my ass, his pumps fast and quick and barely controlled, the perfect, rapid rhythm pushing me to a place I had never been from just sex, a completion that took me completely by surprise and caused my body to tighten, my breath to gasp out, my fingers to dig into the mattress, and my world broke, around his heaven and to my hell. I came, screamed his name as I did it, and his arms came around me, pulling me up against his chest, his final thrusts done with his mouth on my neck and his hands up my shirt and tight on my breasts.

He pulled out at the last moment, his hand fast, his body rolling, taking me onto my back against him, his orgasm hot and wet against my back, and he moaned my name as if he was breaking. I rolled over, for no sane reason, straddling his body, and pushed down, taking him in me, my mouth covering his as I filled myself with his cock and rode out the last tingles of my orgasm, his hands gripping me down, hugging me to his hard chest as he gasped against my mouth, his kiss desperate, hard and needy, his hands moving with manic need, squeezing, gripping, sliding over me as he feasted on my mouth.

He was hell. But his body, his cock, what he did to me? It was heaven. And I wasn't sure, in the moment that I finally pulled away from his mouth and rolled off him, how I would handle that. I wrapped the sheet around me, stared at the ceiling, and felt the push of a thousand questions welling in my throat. Why was he there? Why had he touched me? Had it been anything other than a basic need fulfillment? What did he think of me now and how would this change our dynamic?

I was a Southern girl. We were all born to go to heaven. Even if it was the last place I belonged.

CHAPTER 56

Brad DeLuca would kill him. Of that, Cole was certain. He would fly up there, wrap those big hands around Cole's over-privileged neck, and strangle him.

And Cole would die with a smile. A second fact he was certain of. Because what just happened made his prior obsession with Summer look like an adolescent crush. What just happened was a game changer and one that'd be worth going to the chopping block for. What just happened validated any curiosity he'd had about Summer and increased it tenfold. Being inside her had been completely different than Nadia… than anyone else. He looked up to the ceiling and tried to put his finger on what had made it so different. Tried to figure out how a woman so frustrating could have a body that felt so perfectly in tune with his.

She rolled off him and sat up on the bed, the worn, white undershirt riding up her back, and he reached over, pulling it down carefully, his fingers caressing the skin of her back, missing the touch when she pulled away and stood.

"That was a mistake." She found her panties—those damn red panties—and bent over to pull them on, his eyes dropping to her skin, her ass, the arch of her back.

"You need fresh ones." He reached down for his shorts, feeling suddenly naked on the bed. "Those are a little wet." He smiled, and she seemed to miss the joke, standing up and turning to him, her arms crossing over her beautiful breasts. He suddenly realized the comment that he'd ignored. "It wasn't a mistake."

"It was. It was—" She threw up her hands. "Stupid."

He followed her lead, getting off the bed and stepping toward her, her hands coming up as if to hold him off, and he stopped. "Is this something you do? Go psycho after you fuck someone?"

She flinched as if she'd been slapped, and he wished, in a heartbeat, he'd kept his mouth shut, his brain-to-mouth function around her permanently broken. Maybe he'd had others speaking for him for too long. Or maybe she was the type of woman who drove a man insane. "I don't… fuck people," she seethed, her face darkening, the strength he lov—respected coming through. "And I'm not psycho. Forgive me if I don't want to cuddle with my costar afterward."

"Costar?" He laughed away the jab he felt hit his gut. He couldn't take rejection, not right now, not with Nadia so close, so recent. Maybe DeLuca was right. Maybe his rules of celibacy were about more than Cole's reputation. Maybe Summer was right, and this was a mistake. "High on yourself, aren't you?"

She stepped to a dresser, white and sagging, set against the wall. "Wow. You really are an asshole." She pulled open a bottom drawer and bent over, pulling out a pair of shorts, and he didn't know how this had turned so wrong. Maybe his after-sex social skills needed work. He hadn't needed those skills during the last six years with Nadia. And the experiences since… those girls had been too interested in taking a selfie with him to have a conversation. Especially not a conversation like this.

"Summer…"

She yanked up her shorts, and her nipples were visible through the thin top. He stared, she caught him staring, and her cheeks flushed pink, her arms stiff as she jerked open another drawer and pulled out a T-shirt.

"Did I miss something?" he asked, trying to chase down the root of this problem. "Did I do something to piss you off?"

"You're *married*." She spat out the words and pulled the shirt over her head, his eyes getting one last feast of her torso before it was covered by a bright pink celebration of the Class of 2002.

"My wife was married when she fucked half of Hollywood." The response came out hard and sour and she turned to him, her eyes blazing, and he knew, before her mouth opened, that she'd taken it the wrong way.

"Is that how your marriages are over there? She cheats so you cheat? Everyone goes home happy and even?"

She suddenly wasn't the only angry one in the room and he stood up slowly, taking a deep breath, trying to control his anger. "I never, from the moment I met Nadia, kissed another woman, slept with another woman. Not until she served me divorce papers. That might have been how she operated, but not me." He turned to face her, his voice level. "You're concerned about me being married? I'm as ready to be out of that as anyone. And trust me, my activities are the last thing on my *wife's* mind."

"I'm sorry that you got hurt. And I'm sorry for jumping to conclusions. But you are still married. And it seems like you're awfully quick to just jump in the sack to look for another." She moved out of the bedroom, her bare feet quiet as she burned a path to the kitchen, her hands still angry despite her apology, her movements quick as she pulled the coffee maker out from the wall, ran water into a pitcher, and opened and slammed more cabinets than seemed necessary for a cup of coffee.

He followed her, his words trying to catch up with her thought process, and find the place where she got such a wrong impression of him. "Look for another wife? Babe, that's not what this is—"

"I am not your *babe*." She pulled a lime green mug out and slammed the cabinet door so hard it broke, falling crooked off one hinge, and she stared at it, blinking rapidly, her mouth pursed tight. "I don't even *like* you."

"I—" Everything he said was coming out wrong, the emotion radiating from her body nerve-wracking, and he stepped back, putting his hands on his head. *I don't even like you.* That didn't hurt when it came from a stranger, from critics, from fans who didn't get autographs signed. When it came from her, it was different; it stung. Stung so much that he stepped back, needing the distance.

"Please leave, Cole." Her words were broken and took his heart along with them, a jumbled mess of regret rolling down a hill iced with dislike. That was the problem with what they had just done. Because no matter how great it had been, it hadn't been done on a bedrock of friendship or compatibility or respect. It had happened between two people who didn't even like each other.

He followed her wishes, for one of the first times in their clusterfuck since meeting, and turned away, walking through the small living room, out the front door, and off her porch.

When his tennis shoes hit the dirt, he began to run. And it wasn't lost on him, as he moved farther from Summer and closer to home, that running seemed to be the only thing that he had mastered. Running from any hints that he missed in his marriage with Nadia. Running to Quincy, away from the temptations that LA held. Running from the blonde behind him, in her warm and cozy home, from her eyes that saw through him and didn't like what she saw.

CHAPTER 57

My bright future in Quincy ended the night of my rehearsal dinner. It was being held at the Chart House, which, in Quincy talk, means More Money Than Brains. But Scott's family was the Thompsons, who were one of Coca-Cola 67, so special events required a certain amount of fanfare, and the wedding of their only son was one of those Events. The rehearsal dinner, along with all of our wedding bills, were being quietly paid for by the Thompsons. They didn't have to be quietly paid for; everyone in town knew that Mama and I had nothing, and they had everything, but it was still one of those things that nobody talked about.

I found out about Scott and Bobbi Jo two nights before the rehearsal dinner. I should have just cancelled it, sat down with Scott like a rational adult and broken it off. But I wasn't rational. I wanted to teach them a lesson. All of them.

I still remembered late in the evening, the dinner's ruination well underway, the sound of running steps, clipping along the Chart House's wood floors, the thirty-some people running for the exit. At that time, I had stayed in my seat, my hand on my champagne stem, and smiled. I had toasted my future, or lack thereof, and taken a final sip.

I thought of that as I watched, from the living room window, Cole Masten run down the long drive, his stride never hesitating. And unlike Scott, his head never turned to look back.

This time, I didn't smile. Had I had champagne, I would have spit it out.

CHAPTER 58

"Where's Summer?" Don Waschoniz looked up from the dining room table, papers spread out before him, the dark walnut barely visible.

"Not coming," Cole said, breathing hard, his hand on his knees. He'd sprinted the quarter-mile from Summer's, his legs not moving fast enough, the pain in his chest and lungs welcomed, the burn in his muscles appreciated.

"Not coming?" Don stood up, pushing his reading glasses up on his forehead. "Did you go there?"

Cole ignored the question, walking to the fridge and opening it up. He stared at the options before him, damn the early hour, grabbing a beer. He swung by the bathroom and found Cocky, standing on the edge of the tub, jumping off when Cole stared at him. Maybe it was time to move him outside and build him a coop. He wasn't a chick anymore, his head already reached almost to Cole's knee. He whistled and stepped back, Cocky following. Turning around, Cole bumped into Don.

"Why isn't Summer coming?" Don demanded. "We need her to see these changes."

"Why?" Cole said curtly, holding the bottle to the edge of the counter and hitting the top of it, the cap popping loose.

"Why?" Don repeated. "*You're* the one who insisted we have her here. You're the one who sold me on a no-experience actress sitting in on this."

"I was wrong." Cole opened the kitchen door and ushered Cocky out, bringing the beer to his lips for a sip. "We don't need her."

"You sure about that?" Don rested his hands on the counter and tried to meet Cole's eyes. "Did something just happen? Because if there's an issue between you two, I need to know about it. I can't direct what I don't understand."

Cole chuckled around the next sip of beer. "Well, good luck with that, Don. I don't think anyone could understand that woman."

"So there *is* a problem."

"Nope," Cole said flatly. "No problem whatsoever." He finished off the beer and put it down, with a loud chink, onto the counter. "Let's get started. I want to be done with this shit before the sun sets."

No problem whatsoever. It was a bit of a lie. There was a problem between he and Summer; he just didn't know what it was. *I don't even like you.* Her statement stuck in his head, a record playing on repeat. She had seemed to like it enough, her body responsive, the sounds from her, words from her… but there was a difference between liking a touch and liking a person. And he didn't know if he wanted her to like him. He hadn't exactly given her the keys to make that happen, had hidden away anything good behind a wall of hostility and sarcasm. There was his current level of attraction toward her and then there was what would happen between them if she did like him—a man who wasn't at a place worthy of a relationship, a man who had his own shit to figure out before he could figure out another person, a man who… if he pushed his best parts forward and was rejected, might not recover from the snub.

Don said nothing, and Cole turned, walking back to the dining room and away from the conversation.

CHAPTER 59

"Tell me I'm an idiot." I leaned back in the rocking chair and rested my feet on the railing, a beer clutched in my hand, half the label already picked off.

"You're not an idiot." Ben sat, dainty in his rocker, beside me. He sipped at ice water and adjusted his sunglasses on his nose.

"I *am* an idiot. I—" I closed my eyes. "I'm not even going to tell you the things I said to him. It's embarrassing."

"He's Cole Masten, Summer. Don't worry about it. He's probably heard things your sweet little mind couldn't even think up."

I scowled and brought my beer to my lips, the ice-cold alcohol the only good thing about this moment. His comment didn't make me feel better. It made me feel worse. Like I was one of thousands, just another stupid girl who fell victim to his sex appeal.

"When do you leave?" I took another sip and looked out across the fields, toward his house, his stupid red truck out front, Don's rental beside it. I couldn't wait for filming to start, for him to spend his days somewhere other than right *there*. Another stupid thought. Filming would put us face-to-face, words-to-words.

"Not 'til next week. Your trailer comes this afternoon. Take it easy on those beers, and we can run over there in a few hours."

I rolled my eyes and finished off the bottle, leaning down and setting it on the porch, next to the first empty. I sat back and slid my palms in between my thighs, closing my eyes. My trailer. What a foreign concept. Ben had laughed when I had asked if I'd have a director-style chair with my name on the back of it. Apparently those don't exist in the real world of Hollywood. Apparently a trailer is where it's at—a place where I can shut the door and be alone in the midst of madness. It sounds like a lonely place. It makes me wish, for the first time in forever, that I had a friend, someone other than my mom, to show it off to, to giggle inside of. Someone to experience this journey with. Someone other than a gay man who was going to abandon me very shortly.

"You're not going to get pregnant, are you?" He peered over at me. "Because that *would* make you an idiot."

"No," I said quickly. That was one thing I had already arranged. Driven all the way over to Tallahassee to grab a morning-after pill just so I wouldn't start half the town talking. I didn't mention to Ben the box of condoms I also purchased. I was still working over that impulse buy myself.

"Shit," Ben remarked from beside me. "Maybe you *should* have another." I glanced over at him and raised my eyebrows in question. "You're moping," he pointed out.

"I'm *not* moping," I grumbled, further proving his point.

"You bagged a movie star. You should be throwing a fucking party and bragging on Twitter. What you shouldn't be doing is moping, not when you threw him out of your house like a baller."

I sighed. "I don't think it came across as baller. I think it came across as a little psychotic."

"No offense, but all women are a little psychotic."

I glared at him. "No offense, but all gays are judgmental."

"Guilty as charged." He grinned at me, and I couldn't help but grin back. I laid my head back on the chair.

"Seriously, Ben, how much did I mess up?"

"By screwing your costar?" He laughed and pulled at the bottom of his shirt, fanning it against his chest. "Honey, you wouldn't *be* Hollywood if you didn't bang a costar at some point. It's nothing. Just don't let it affect the performance."

The performance. A stress point in itself, without adding this on. And as far as being Hollywood? From what I could gather of it so far, I was anything but. I wanted another beer but already felt woozy.

I reached out and asked for a sip of Ben's water with an impatient wave of my hand. He passed it over, and I took a big sip, reluctantly returning it to him.

"It's nothing," I repeated his words and tried to find solace in them.

"Right. Just don't let it affect the performance," he said again.

"Yeah," I mumbled. Good thing my performance was of a woman who didn't like Cole's character. That should make it a hell of a lot easier.

I closed my eyes and tried to breathe normally, to let the stress melt off me in the hot summer air. Couldn't, no matter what I tried, get the image of Cole out of my head. It wasn't the shirtless Cole who'd stood at the end of my bed, his hand reaching out for my ankle. It was the man in my kitchen, his eyes vulnerable and weak, his voice catching… that was the image I was stuck on. And I had told him to leave. Had picked a fight and yelled and done everything I could to get him out the door so I wouldn't crack and give the poor guy a hug.

I understood cheating, understood the betrayal that you went through when you found out. Understood the lows that your self-esteem struggled with, the validation that you tried to find, the loneliness that haunted your nights as you mourned a future that, in an instant, disappeared.

I'd kissed Tim Jeffries the night after I'd found out about Scott. I'd never told anyone that before, not Mama, not even Hope Lewis—the one friend who had stuck around after the Rehearsal Dinner from Hell. I'd thought about telling her, but then her boyfriend got a job offer in Atlanta, and, just like that, Hope was gone. I'd kissed Tim Jeffries with my princess-cut diamond twinkling out from its platinum setting, Tim's sweaty hand brushed it when he grabbed my hand and pushed it to the crotch of his jeans. We'd been sitting in the front seat of his truck, behind the Circle K, his smoke break turned illicit, my gas station stop turned disastrous. Tim had been a high-school flame that had petered out after only one date, and he had smiled at me in just the right way, and I'd been weak and vulnerable and when he'd asked if I wanted a smoke. I'd said yes, even though I didn't smoke, and I'd smelled trouble. He must have smelled something on me, the scent of desperation, of insecurity. I wasn't sure. I just knew that he felt bold enough to try, and I felt low enough to accept.

And now, I couldn't help but feel like I was Tim Jeffries. Slightly chubby, I'll-take-him-cause-he's-there, and toss-him-out-later Tim Jeffries. And Cole was me, spinning out of control, the sting of betrayal hot and consuming, on his way to a Rehearsal Dinner from Hell of his own.

My Rehearsal Dinner had haunted me for three years. His might implode more quietly, on a small-town stretch of Georgia dirt, the only casualty a Southern girl's heart.

CHAPTER 60

With filming about to start, I signed the damn contract, revised three times between Scott and Cole. My half-million dollars ended up actually being four hundred thousand dollars with a hundred thousand dollar bonus when the film hit a certain gross threshold. Scott assured me that it would hit that threshold, not that he knew jack shit about movies, but so did Ben, and I trusted him so I signed the papers. I hadn't heard a word from Cole and hadn't seen him in the three trips Ben and I made to the Pit, the old supermarket's lot now packed with empty trailers, tents, and signage. Everyone would arrive early next week. That was when the madness would begin.

I was ready; I was anxious for it to get here, for filming to begin. Because the sooner that happened, the sooner this would all be done. Then I could take my fat bank account and leave this place. Give Mama a chunk of change and start somewhere fresh. I was twenty-nine years old. It was time, way past time, to leave this old rotting nest.

I parked my truck on the outside of the Pit, in a spot marked for CAST, a bit of excitement passing through me. Cole's red monstrosity was in his personal spot, his name labeling the parking lot so that anyone with a vendetta against him would know exactly where to go. So stupid. So egotistic. I climbed out, my new flip-flops hitting the hard asphalt, newly redone because Hollywood can't park on cracked pavement, swinging the door shut and pushing my new cell phone into the back pocket of my shorts.

"Nice of you to dress up, Country."

I looked over my shoulder. Cole stepped out of the door of the closest trailer—Don's—and trotted down the steps in a white button-down and slacks, polished black dress shoes carrying him in my direction.

I swallowed, looking down at my khaki shorts and the loose blouse I had pulled the tags off just that morning. "Ben said—I thought…" A meeting, that was what I was coming in for. To run over the schedule and introduce me to my acting coach. Ben had promised me that it didn't matter what I wore. I had still shopped for the occasion, my newly padded bank account causing me to swipe my debit card at JC Penny with ease.

"Ignore him," Don called from the open door. "He's been doing press in that monkey suit. Let him sweat like an asshole for it." He waved an arm to me and flashed a friendly smile. "Come on in."

Cole laughed, undoing the cufflinks on his sleeve. "Easy there, Summer. Someone might figure out that you don't belong here."

I ignored him, my shoulder bumping his as I moved past, toward Don, smiling brightly up at the man who had saved me. "The air-conditioning working in there?" I asked.

"You know it." He smiled at me and held open the door. "You ready for next week?"

I nodded, stepping into his trailer, which was set up entirely different than mine. His was a workspace, a conference room on one end, a secretary's desk and separate office on the other end. Ben had already showed me the place where they reviewed daily footage and did the real work. I had reached out to touch a dial and had about four people jump to stop me. Now, in Don's space, I kept my hands to myself, just to be safe.

"Head on into the conference room," he directed. "Pam and Dennis are already in there, they'll introduce themselves."

Pam ended up being in PR; she ran me through a calendar of media training that would be happening in between filming. I smiled and nodded and took everything she passed to me, enough reading material to choke a horse. Dennis was introduced as my acting coach; he stood up from the table and gave me a hearty hug. I gripped his large girth and immediately felt at ease. "I'll take care of you," he promised.

"We both will," Pam joined in. "Think of us as part of your team." She smiled, and I felt ten times better. They informed me that my assistant, Mary, would arrive on Monday. I did another round of nodding and wondered what on Earth I would do with an assistant.

My back was to the door when Cole walked in, but I could tell you the moment his foot hit the carpet. My nails dug into my thighs, and I nodded at whatever words were coming out of Pam's mouth—something about YouTube and a trailer—every sense focused on the man who was moving closer. Pressure hit the top of my chair, and I glanced over to see his hands gripping the back, his knuckles white as he leaned on the plastic.

His hands tight on my ass, his pumps fast and quick and barely controlled, the perfect rapid rhythm pushing me to a place—

"Excuse me," Cole said warmly. "But I need to borrow Ms. Jenkins."

"Of course, Mr. Masten." Pam stalled her YouTube plans and stood, her hands quick as she gathered up her materials, Dennis following suit, his retreat slower, his heft out of the chair more cumbersome. I smiled weakly at him, waiting for the door to close behind him before I was out of my chair and away from Cole.

"Easy, Country." He smiled, still in place, his weight still resting on the back of my chair.

"Stop calling me that." I kept my voice low, well aware of the cheap construction of these trailers.

"What, you can call me City Boy, but I can't call you Country?"

I said nothing. It was ridiculous to try and have a logical conversation with this man.

"Are you ready for next week?"

I met his eyes. "Of course I am." Of course I wasn't. I would never be ready to step in front of a camera with him.

"You know that we won't film in chronological order." The statement was said without a dose of asshole, and I shifted my weight to my other hip, my hands sweaty on Pam's pages.

"No, I didn't know that." But it made sense. I had a flashback to Ben's and my preparations, how we would book a week at one plantation or location. Of course. They'd film all of the spots at those points at once. It made sense.

"We're working on a shooting schedule today. I'll have a courier bring it over to you tonight."

"Thank you." I rubbed my bare arms, the room suddenly cold. The air conditioner really *did* work.

"Cocky tried to crow this morning." His voice was sheepish and held a hint of pride.

"Who?"

"Cocky. That's his name. Our rooster."

Our. That hit hard, in a strange place in my heart. "He's yours," I blurted out. "I gave him to you." *Cocky*. I would have asked who names a rooster, but I had names for every one of the Holdens'. Cocky's mama was named Matilda, even if I was the only person who called her that.

"I was in the kitchen when I heard him out in the yard. I thought he was hurt, or getting attacked. He…" He made a hand gesture of sorts with his hands, and I laughed despite myself.

"I know." I smiled. "I've seen when they learn. It takes them some time to figure it out."

"It was pathetic," Cole admitted, tucking his hands into the pockets of his suit pants. "I was embarrassed for him."

"He'll figure it out," I said. "And he'll do it at all hours of the day. It only happens at dawn in the movies."

Cole's eyes smiled at me. "Gotta love Hollywood, right?"

I swallowed my smile. I had to. The warmth pushing through my veins right then… it was a dangerous thing. And this beautiful man before me, smiling at me like I was his? That was my downfall, wrapped in an expensive suit and cufflinks. I could smell my demise in his cologne and charm. And that was what he was doing. Turning on the charm and using every tool in his belt to do it, including cute little Cocky. The question was *why*? Why turn on the charm now? Or was this his normal magnetism, no effort required, that showed when he dropped the asshole bit? I studied his smile and tried to understand it. "Did you need me for something?"

He coughed, looking down. "No. That was it. I can drop off the shooting schedule myself, if that'd make it easier…"

"It wouldn't."

His shoulders rolled back. "Right. Then I'll see you on Monday. Check the schedule to see where to be. I'm sure your assistant will help you find it."

"I know the locations, but thank you for your concern, Mr. Masten," I said stiffly, and he stepped forward, into my personal space, his face somber as he looked down on me, his eyes searching mine.

"Are we good?" he asked. I tried to step away but hit the table.

"Stay out of my way, and we'll be just fine," I snapped.

He coughed out a laugh and shook his head. "I don't chase, Summer. I get tired of that real fast."

"This isn't a game." I spoke louder, damn the doors, and his eyes flicked back to mine. "I'm not saying one thing and meaning another. Stay away from me."

He stared at me for a long moment before shaking his head. "I was wrong about you." He took the two steps to the door slowly, and I knew, before he turned back, his hand pulling open the door, that he'd have at least one parting shot. "You're a terrible actress."

I couldn't think of a comeback, of a retort, of anything. I watched the white door close and felt a wave of nausea.

He was wrong on one thing: I was telling the truth; this wasn't a game for me. The stakes were too high, and I didn't know the rules enough to play. But he was also right; I *was* a terrible actress. He looked into my eyes and saw right through my lies, exactly how much I wanted him.

CHAPTER 61

I thought the Pit had been interesting before. Then, Sunday arrived. The Sunday before filming. I hadn't been expecting it, had been at church when they arrived: the crew, the cast, the rest of everything. *Hundreds* of people. After my lunch, courtesy of the First Baptist Church potluck, I wandered over. Watched a swarm of bodies fill the empty spaces between trailers, everyone busy, everyone working. Ben found me and latched on, introducing me to actors and actresses whose names I could have rattled off with quick efficiency. The supporting cast. Playing under Cole and me. Such an upside down situation. I smiled and shook hands. Fought the urge to ask for autographs, smiled apologetically to members of the crew whom Ben pulled me away from.

It was an absolute zoo—the air thick with importance and money, every item unpacked expensive and complex, each new body striding out of vehicles stuffed with arrogance and energy. I found a corner and leaned against a wall. Let Ben run off to tend to things, and I just watched it all. Devoured it all. Was terrified but excited by it all.

CHAPTER 62

It's my money; I think I know what I want to spend it on. A complicated sentence. I read it three times, my mind tripping over easy vowels, then raised my head and looked at Dennis.

He smiled encouragingly, and I read the line. "It's my money, I think I know what I want to spend it on."

"You sound like you're concentrating."

I huffed out a breath. "I *am* concentrating. That's an obstacle course of words. Why can't she just say, "I'll spend my money however I damn well please"?

"You don't have to stick to the script exactly, but don't be wandering too far outside of the lines or else you'll mess up the other actors. Remember, you'll be listening for cues to say certain lines. So are the other actors. For example, if Mr. Masten doesn't say the line you are expecting, it could cause you to miss your cue."

Great. One more thing to stress over. I tossed the script down and leaned forward, rubbing my temples.

"Would you like me to have Mary call in the masseuse?" From behind him, my assistant started, coming to her feet and stepping forward, her notepad and pen at the ready.

I looked from her into Dennis's face. "What? Is that a joke?"

"No. You look stressed."

"I'm fine." A masseuse. I've never even had a massage. And right in the middle of a training session seemed like an odd place to start. Mary deflated, as if she was disappointed, and slinked back to her seat. I don't know what I had expected in terms of an assistant, but the mousy brunette with the stern face wasn't it. I had pictured a tattooed smartass, one who I could lean on in times of stress and learn all of the secrets of the set. If I leaned on Mary, she'd probably hand me a sterilized box of tissues and a self-help novel on independence. Anyone who had a Post-It dispenser attached to her belt wasn't a candidate for friendship.

"Okay, let's roll with this line a few more times, then we'll move on." Dennis leaned forward and nodded at me.

I didn't argue. At the rate we were going, picking apart every word, every nuance… we'd never get through the script. I swallowed and sat back, looking down at the script and staring at the damn sentence whose words kept jumbling in my mind.

It's my money; I think I know what I want to spend it on.

I wet my lips and spoke.

CHAPTER 63

"It's my money; I think I know what I want to spend it on." My hands found their way to my hips and rested there, on top of a tweed skirt, the back of which—hidden from the camera—was held together with jumbo clips.

"Honey," Cole drawled, lifting a glass to his lips, the ice clinking as he tilted it back. "You don't want to invest in refreshments. Let the boys downtown find a Certificate of Deposit for that money. Or bonds. Bonds are a great, safe place for your inheritance to sit."

My lips tightened, and all I had to think about was Cole's feet running off my porch for my eyes to flare. "Don't talk down to me. If I want to light my money and smoke it like your cheap cigars, I'll do so. I believe in this product, just the same as you, or Mr. Eggleston, or any of the other investors. And I want in."

I bent, the saddle shoes I wore sticking slightly to the floor, and pulled at my briefcase, hefting it to the desk, and pressed the side latches, the locks popping out. *So far so good.* This was the thirteenth take, and I was sweating underneath the scratchy skirt. Don had turned up the thermostat, wanting an 'authentic feel' to the set, and my hairline was damp with perspiration. We were in one of the created sets in the old supermarket—this one of Royce Mitchell's office, a drafty space with dingy cream walls, wood floors, a big desk, which Cole reclined behind, his leather chair tilted back. I stood across the desk from him, three cameras all pointing my way. Cole had nailed his lines already. These retakes were all for me, Don or Cole unhappy for one reason or another, each new criticism a rattle to my already shaky confidence. I pulled open the briefcase lid, ready to grab at the small stack of worn dollar bills and toss them onto the desk. My hand reached out and froze, my eyes widening at the contents.

Condoms. A hundred of them, the first one that snagged my eye advertising its LEMON FLAVORED! ability in big, proud font. I pushed my hand into the pile of packages and found the stack of money. I pulled it out and threw it on the desk, my eyes finding Cole's, who smirked at me before leaning forward and picking up the cash.

"Some of the investors aren't wild about having a woman on board, Ms. Pinkerton." Cole was still amused by the condoms; I saw the curve of his mouth as he bit back a smile, his eyes beaming at me. I looked down and saw a bright green one that had fallen out of the briefcase during my dramatic throw of the money. I left it on the desk and shut the lid, praying it wasn't in sight of a camera.

"And what's your opinion?" I practically snarled the words, a detailed plan forming in my head, one that involved my hands around his neck as soon as the AD yelled "Cut!"

He shrugged and opened his desk drawer, setting the cash in it. "I love women. But then again, you already know that, don't you, Ms. Pinkerton?"

It was off script—way off script—and I stiffened, my fingers tightening in their press on the briefcase. "I don't know what you mean, Mr. Mitchell." I glared at him and felt the uneasy shift in the room. I didn't know what to do. Whether to play along with his ad lib or to turn to Don and ask what in the blue blazes was going on. I saw Dennis along the edge of the set, and he gave me a 'keep going' gesture with his hands. I looked back to Cole, who pushed the drawer closed and stood up, setting his drink down on the desk.

The room, which was hot before, was suddenly boiling, the lighting hanging from all sides of the ceiling blaring down, the thirty people in the room contributing to the pressure, too many eyes watching this one terrible moment. I felt, for a horrific second, like I would faint, too many takes, too much pressure, the condom stash still under my palms, Cole stepping closer, around his desk, toward me. I had no idea what he was going to say, would have no idea how to react, how Ida Pinkerton—what a horrible name—would react, and then he was right *there*, his hand reaching out, running along the outside of the starched white shirt, caressing the curve of my—

I slapped him, the sound loud, like the crack of a whip in the quiet room, thirty-some people hearing the sound of my palm, a collective intake moving through the room.

"Don't you dare touch me," I seethed, my finger moving on its own accord and jabbing into his chest. It was a mistake, his chest muscles hard and firm, and it made me think of *my mouth covering his ... his hands gripping me, hugging me to his chest.* I shouldn't have rolled over, shouldn't have made that last move, putting him inside me, my mouth on his. It made that moment in my bedroom, that mistake, even more personal.

He stepped back, his cheek red from my slap, and my hand smarted when it brushed against my side.

"I'm sorry, Country," he said, so low I had to strain to hear the words. "I thought you liked it when I touched you." He flashed me a cocky smile, and my palm itched to reconnect with his face. He was lucky it was only a slap.

"Cut!" Don yelled, and his body was suddenly between us, his hand on Cole's chest and my arm. "What the fuck was that?" The comment was directed at us both, and I snapped, yanking my arm away from him.

"Ask your golden boy." I nodded at Cole. "He's the one who filled my briefcase with *condoms*."

"Oh, I'm sorry," he mocked. "Is that too racy for you Southern belles?" He laughed away my glare. "Jesus, Summer, it's a prank. Think of it as your initiation."

"It's an expensive prank," Don said with a hard look at Cole. "Don't forget that you're footing the bills for every take now."

"And it was worth it to see her face. Never seen a condom before, Summer?"

I *hate* that we didn't use a condom. I *hate* that I let him push inside of me without any barrier. Forget pregnancy, how many women had he been with? And how little did it say of me that protection was the last thought in my mind? It had been too long since I'd been touched, my only sexual experiences prior to him with Scott, and we'd never used *anything*. My on-camera dig through Condom Mountain to reach the cash was the first time I'd ever *touched* one of the damn things, my recent purchase still sitting inside their box. But I'd be damned if Cole knew that. I stared at his perfect nose and pictured it cracking beneath my fist.

Don let out a barely controlled breath, followed up by a curse. "You two, stop it. I didn't sign on to referee. Summer, let's get you back in Hair and Makeup to freshen up, then we'll shoot scene twelve right back here. Cole, you're off for a bit. I'll have Jack send you a new call schedule in fifteen."

My eyes moved from Cole's untouched nose to his eyes, which held mine. I could see, in my peripheral vision, his smile. I hated that smile. I hated his ease in this environment. I hated his confidence.

I hated, most of all, that I wanted his hand back, his brush against my shirt to dip underneath the waist. I wanted him to lift me up onto this desk, for his hands to push up my skirt, and for his fingers to discover that these pantyhose only reached my upper thighs. I hated that, right there, with Don in between us, I was *wet* for him. And I was terrified, glaring in his eyes, that he knew it.

"Summer," Don said, gently tapping my arm. "Hair and Makeup."

I met Don's eyes and smiled. "Of course. Thank you, Don." I turned away from the two of them and headed for the exit, the crowd parting before me without a word.

CHAPTER 64

Cole sat in a screening room, his tennis shoes propped against the edge of the board, an expensive array of buttons and sliders spread out before them, underneath the three television screens. A different video played on each, his and Summer's faces presented at different angles.

"Did we get it or not?" Cole rolled his neck and glanced at his watch. 11:15 p.m. He looked for the closest PA and snapped his fingers. "Find a catering truck and get me a sandwich. Ham and swiss on wheat."

"Catering trucks closed up at ten," Don said dismissively, skimming through a reel.

"Then find me one somewhere else," Cole snapped. "Why the hell are the catering trucks closing up early?"

"Look around. Everyone's gone." Don glanced up at the production assistant. "Ignore him, he'll be fine."

"Fuck that." Cole fished in his pocket and pulled out a wad of cash. "Sandwich. Find one or make one, I don't give a damn. And a Pepsi."

"Coke," Don corrected.

"Right. Whatever. Anyone else need something?" Cole glanced over at the other bodies in the booth, a collection of sound and video mixers. No one spoke, and Cole passed the cash to the PA, then dropped his leg, sitting forward. "So show me. Did we get it?"

"I think so, despite your best efforts."

"She needed her feathers ruffled a little. She was getting too tense."

Cole grinned at the memory of her face, the widening of her eyes, the way they had burned at him across the room. He probably shouldn't have done it, but she'd handled it well, not stopping, not reacting. It'd been a test of sorts, but also pure entertainment on his part. Ever since they'd had sex, Summer had more or less ignored him, her attitude increasingly more indifferent as time went on. He had needed that fire, that attention from her, that spark that seemed to grow stronger the more anger that blew between them. So he'd lit a match. And he'd enjoyed every bit of the result.

Don mumbled something in response, pressed a button, and the short clip played seamlessly, the transition between Cole and Summer spliced from over a dozen takes. Less than a moment of footage, everything from Cole's ad lib deleted.

"It's good," Cole said, nodding, his eyes trained on Summer's face, the defiance in every part of her features. Her beauty changed when she was mad. Just another reason to push her buttons.

"I agree," Don said, and one of the mixers, two bodies over, spoke up.

"Do you want to show him the other cut?"

Don ran a hand over the back of his head and said nothing.

"What cut?" Cole asked, looking over at the director. "Don?" he pushed.

"Yeah," Don said, the word clipped. "Roll it." He lifted his hands to his face and rubbed his forehead.

Cole glanced at the screen, a new clip playing. It was from after the prank. When he'd stood up and walked over to Summer. Someone had spliced the scenes together, layering the camera angles to record the moment in one concise, smooth take. He shifted in his seat and watched a close up of his hand running, slower than possible, down her shirt. Saw in high definition the swallow of her throat, the burn of her cheeks, the slight curve of her back as she, in the moment before her slap, arched into his touch. A hundred details he had missed, his mind too focused on one thing, the burning need to have her white button-down ripped off, his hands exploring the skin underneath. There was the slap, the violence of it more pronounced on screen, the darkening of Cole's eyes, his start forward… Cole looked into his own eyes, on screen, and saw what anyone would be able to see. Lust. Raw animal lust. The clip ended, and the room went dark for a moment before the next screen came on.

"So," Don said quietly.

"What was the purpose of that mix?" Cole asked tightly.

"It's hot," one of the overpaid guys said, swiveling his seat around and facing Cole. "I've got a hard-on just from watching it, Mr. Masten. I mean, the other stuff is good, but this has emotion, it has *heat*. You guys look like you were moments away from banging on the desk." He stared Cole down through his horn-rimmed glasses as if he had a say in anything.

"He's right," Don tilted back in his chair and looked at the ceiling. "I hate like hell to say it, but he's right. The other clip looks like chicken shit compared to this."

"That?" Cole sputtered, pointing to the frozen image of Summer, her cheeks flushed. "You can't use that. It's too…"

"Real?" Don asked, turning to him.

"No," Cole said quickly. "It's not that. I just don't see a plot scenario where—"

"Ida and Royce hate each other," Don said. "That's already in there. Hell, it was reality. But if we use that hatred… and make it sexual tension…" He glanced at Cole. "It could add another element to the film. And it would bring in the female viewers who, right now, we have no draw on, other than your pretty mug."

"She won't go for it," Cole said flatly.

"Since when does that matter?" Don said with a laugh. "She doesn't have script approval!"

"She'll hate it." He glanced at the screens. "Play it again."

"I'm not crazy about the idea either, Cole, but the more I think about it…" Don tapped his fingers against the arm of his chair.

"Play it again," Cole repeated, leaning back in his chair, his arms across his chest, his eyes on her face.

A button was hit, and the clip restarted.

The mixer was right. It was hot. And Don was right; a romantic element, or hell, just a *sexual* element between Ida and Royce would draw in the female audience.

Summer would hate it. But Don was right on that card, too. But Summer wouldn't have a choice. She'd have to go with whatever Cole said. And that, despite any moral ramifications that should have existed, made him smile.

The clip finished, and Cole sat forward, turning to Don, the director's eyes wary.

"Let's do it," Cole said. "Call the writers. Get them in here now."

CHAPTER 65

"How was it?" Mama's question came from her bedroom, her voice's edges slurred with sleep.

"It was fine," I said quietly, sticking my head in. "Long, but fine. I did good."

"Of course you did," she mumbled, her form rolling over in the bed. "Love you."

"Love you too." I flipped off the hall light, and she disappeared, a blanket of black swallowing the room. I stepped back to the living room and dropped onto the couch, pulling the afghan off its back and over my chest. The day hadn't been fine. It had been stressful and long and hot and horrible. I thought I could work with him. I thought I could spit out lines and be in character and be fine. I thought, because the set was on Georgian soil, that it'd be my turf. I didn't realize how foreign that world would be. So many terms I didn't know, tossed effortlessly between hundreds of strangers, no attempt made to clue in the new girl. The Southerners they brought in from Atlanta were all in the movie business there, so they waltzed around with ease, taking their cues, their places, without a stumble. I was the odd girl out, looking like an idiot. I saw the looks, the side glances and raised eyebrows, saying, *What is she doing here?* clear as day. By lunch, my confidence was shot. By afternoon, I'd used up every pep talk I had. And by the time Cole Masten introduced me to condoms, my defenses had crumbled to nothing. I'm gonna blame that fatigue on my weakness when he had come around the desk and touched me.

After that touch, on my way to hair and makeup, I had ditched Mary and ducked into a restroom. Called Ben's cell and left a teary voicemail. He'd flown to Vancouver that morning for his next gig. I'd begged him to stay just one more week, offered him money, dumplings, freedom to use my makeup… but he'd had to go. We'd hugged it out in front of the Raine House at seven AM before he'd all but pushed me in the direction of the Pit. A half-hour after my pathetic voicemail, I got a text from him.

I'm in the air. Toughen up. Where's the Summer I know?

I had smiled at his text. Blotted my eyes before the makeup artist had my hide, and reached down deep. He was right. Screw all of the side looks and whispers. Cole and Don had wanted me for a reason. I would learn the things I needed to. And in the meantime, I couldn't show any weakness—not to any of them, but especially not to Cole. I was stronger than that. I was better than that.

By the time I had pushed out of the makeup chair, I was ready for battle. And now, five hours later, I was bone tired.

The next day would be better. I knew that. The first day was always the hardest.

I reached up to rub my eyes, but my hand didn't even reach my head before I fell asleep.

"Summer's lucky she could round up six bridesmaids. Really, Scott was the only reason those girls were even doing it. They were saints! And then for Summer to go and do that to them. White trash, that's what she is. I told my Bridget. I told her not to associate herself with that girl, but my daughter's too nice, always has been. And look, I was right."

"Bridget is your daughter?"

"Oh yes. She's Bridget Anderson now. She married a doctor. I'll give you his card in case you ever have any feet issues."

CHAPTER 66

The first thing I saw my second day on set was Cole's rooster. It stood on a fenced-in patch of grass that hadn't been there yesterday. I stepped from the truck, shutting the door with my butt, and walked over to the pen. Pat and Gus from Colton's Construction were there, in the midst of construction on what looked to be an open coop.

"Hey Summer," Pat greeted me, Gus looking up with a nod.

"Hey guys." I stared at their creation, the grass still pieced out in sod squares. "Did you jackhammer up the concrete?"

"Yep. Started at seven. Sheriff Pratt already showed up about the noise."

"I bet he did." I stepped over the knee-high fence and bent down, the rooster suddenly at my side, pecking at the sparkles on my bag, which hung over one arm. "Stop that," I chided him, running a hand over his back. He was bigger, his red comb developing, his eyes alert and proud as he tried to step on my knee, while I held him off.

"Friendly thing," Pat remarked, putting a bit on the drill and tightening it into place.

"He should be," Gus scoffed. "I heard Cole Masten keeps him in the house."

I raised my eyebrows. "Where'd you hear that?"

"Around. He brought him here this morning in his truck. *Inside* the truck," he clarified.

"The Kirklands are gonna blow a gasket," Pat added in.

"You making the coop open?" I nodded to the half-built house.

"Yep. We told him it would just fly over this little fence, and he told us to cover the whole thing with chicken wire."

"The whole thing?" I looked at the piece of grass, which covered three parking spots. *Valuable* parking spots on a piece of land as crammed as Walmart on Black Friday.

"Yep." The look that passed between the two men clearly communicated their opinion of Cole Masten, and I laughed, giving the rooster one final pet before standing.

"I've gotta go." I waved to them and stepped over the fence, the rooster squawking at me.

I was smiling to myself when I entered the madness, weaving in between the tight cluster of trailers, bee-lining for mine. My baby was about halfway into the lot, wedged in between a sound trailer and a coffee truck, the latter causing a long line, which I skirted around on my way in. When I pulled on the door, Mary was already inside, her head snapping to me, a polite smile stretching over it.

"Good morning," I greeted brightly. My resolution for today was to be cheerful and strong. My sub-resolution was to avoid anything that affected that mindset. Mainly Cole. I'd received the call sheets yesterday for the day's scenes, and none of them involved Cole, so my outlook was bright.

"Good morning. I'd like to put in your breakfast order. Do you know what you'd like?"

"Breakfast?" I dropped my bag on the floor and moved to the table, thinking of the leftover biscuits I'd slathered with jelly and choked down on my drive in. "What do they have?"

"They can make anything." She gripped a silver pen over her always-present notebook, and waited.

"Umm… I guess an omelet? Ham, peppers, and cheese. With grits and bacon. Please."

Her pen didn't move, and I waited. Finally, she looked away from me and down at the page. "Okay. A ham, cheese, and pepper omelet with grits and bacon. What would you like to drink?"

"Milk. Whole if they have it."

Another scribble on the page, then she looked up, passing me a folder. "I've put the Sides and the updated Call Sheet in here. If there are any Day-Out-Of-Days I'll bring them to you as needed."

"Sides?" I asked.

"Those are the scripts for today's scenes only. There are some new scenes, so you'll want to review those before your call times." *New scenes. New scripts.* My cheery outlook took a sharp turn toward PanicVille.

"What are days out of whatever?"

Her smile became less patient. "Day-Out-Of-Days. We typically call it DOOD. It's a general schedule for all of the crew. Just don't worry about that; I'll make sure you are where you need to be."

I sat down at the table and opened the folder, pulling out the new call sheet and reviewing it. My newly manicured nail ran down the shooting schedule, over a list of familiar scenes, before stopping at SCENE #14: ROYCE AND IDA: OFFICE KISS. My breath stopped, and my fingers scrambled for the accompanying script, Mary's post-it clearly marking #14 in neat, bright orange fashion. It was a long scene, and I flipped through it, my stomach twisting as I skimmed the lines, my feet moving before I reached the end, Mary's placement of my breakfast order interrupted by the slam of the trailer door on my departure.

I think I might have bulldozed someone on my storm through the coffee line.

CHAPTER 67

When the door to the production trailer burst open, it brought with it a wave of heat and beauty. Cole looked up from the storyboards and locked eyes with Summer, who blew across the room like a tornado on tilt.

"There's no love story between Ida and Royce," Summer snapped, throwing down the script, pages fluttering between them. In the small trailer, conversations stalled, and he could feel the attention turn their way. "I've read the book. Three times!"

It was good to know *someone* had read the damn book. Cole glanced down at her temper tantrum of a mess and back up, raising his eyebrows mildly. "It's a movie," he said, turning back to the storyboards. "The writers are adding some excitement. It's *normal.* You'd know that if you were in this business." The dig was unnecessary, but he couldn't help it. This woman turned him into the devil.

"I read the first script. The one you sent over with my contract. Ida and Royce *hated* each other. Why would Royce…" she snatched up a page from the ground and read a line. "*pushes Ida against the file cabinet and kisses her passionately.*" She balled up the page and threw it down to the ground, and he could see, in her eyes, the panic. *Panic.* An unexpected reaction.

"We'll use that here." Don made the dangerous move of stepping in, putting a soft hand on her shoulder. "You don't understand. The passion from their hatred will make it hotter."

"No," Summer said, her face hard, her eyes on Cole. "It doesn't make it hotter. It makes it stupid."

"Aww… come on, Summer," Cole chided, moving closer, his hand reaching out to pull at her wrist. She fought him, yanking it back, the meeting of their bodies not happening. He leaned down and whispered, right against her ear, the smell of her apple-scented lotion enough to make him want to empty out the production trailer right that moment. "Sure it does."

She jerked back and twisted away. "If he kisses me on camera, I'm going to lose it," she shot at Don, pointing an accusatory finger in Cole's direction.

"I know you will," Cole laughed, crossing his arms to restrain them. "You'll fall apart under my mouth, baby."

Summer screamed in response, her hands thrown up in frustration, and spun to leave, her script left behind, the slam of the door loud in the full production trailer.

"That went well," Cole mused. He linked his hands and rested them on his head, rolling his shoulders back. *Panic.* She'd had panic in her eyes. *Fuck.*

"What do you expect?" Don said. "You threw this on her without warning. I told you we should have met with her this morning, gone over the changes to prepare her. But no, you just wanted to dump it on her via call sheets and sides."

"Dump it on her? I was *People*'s Sexiest Man last year. She's not mentally adjusting to a war camp for God's sake. How hard is it to kiss me?"

"It's actually three kisses," a dark-haired PA to his left pointed out. "And a grope."

He gave her a hard look, and she withered a little.

"I'll go talk to her," Don said. "Eileen, you shoot number four, and I'll talk to Summer. I want to try to get fourteen shot at eleven, so let's get our asses in gear and get this *done*."

"I'll talk to her," Cole stepped in. "You shoot four, and I'll talk to her."

"No," Don snapped. "With my luck, you two would make up and any authenticity to the scene would disappear. Just stay away from her, and be ready at eleven."

Cole chewed on his cheek, then nodded. “Fine.” Don was right. He should stay away from her. Because right now, the only thing he could picture was the panic on her face. And that look, that vulnerability? It made him want to comfort her, to protect her. And those urges were dangerous, they turned things between them a different way. A way that made him more vulnerable too.

CHAPTER 68

SCENE 14: ROYCE AND IDA: OFFICE KISS

"I want blue. Something cool and refreshing." Cole pushed the ad copy toward me, and I fidgeted, scratching the back of my stocking with the toe of the vintage Mary Jane heels.

"The focus groups liked red better." I avoided his eyes when I spoke, running my finger over the edge of a stack of cards, lining them up against each other. I was supposed to be hesitant in this scene, uncomfortable. It was an easy role to play. I felt so lost. On the set, in the role of actress, in the lust/hate relationship that Cole and I seemed to have.

"Red means stop." Cole's voice was tired, one hand rubbing at his eyes, the other pulling at his tie. I wish we didn't have to do this scene today. I had asked Don, *begged* Don, when he had come to my trailer—begged him to push this scene—for us to do it in a few weeks, once I had the acting thing down, my kinks worked out. What I didn't say to Don was that I needed more separation from my sex with Cole to this kissing scene. Twelve days. That was all it had been so far. Twelve days, which still seemed like only twelve hours. When would I forget how his fingers felt on my skin? The tone of his voice as he had gasped my name? When would I forget how he felt inside of me? When would I forget the incredible sensation that had shaken my body? Part of me wanted that answer to be never. Another part of me just wished it had never happened. You can't miss something that you didn't know existed.

"You don't use a color that means *stop* when you want someone to buy something." His voice hardened. "It's common sense, Ida. Use your brain."

"I don't care if your literature says that red means stop. The blue… when combined with the dark cola, looks weak. The red has more punch, looks more iconic." I hold up the card, the cursive script of the logo standing out against the red mockup. "It looks patriotic."

"Blue is patriotic, too."

"Yankees wear blue," I pointed out, and this was easy, the lines falling into place and coming easily.

"We're not doing red," he said flatly.

"Let's ask the other investors."

He stopped messing with his tie and looked up at me. "Let's not." My finger, which had been picking at an itch on my arm, stilled. This was it; it was coming. He twisted in his chair, turning it to the side, then slowly to the front, considering me.

I waited for the next line, my lungs tightening, the simple act of breathing in and out in a normal fashion a chore.

"Come here," he said softly, pushing on the edge of his desk with one smooth-soled dress shoe, his heavy chair rolling back. He waited, his hands on each arm, his knees spread, the dress pants stretched tight over his frame.

"What?" I breathed out the question in a mild state of panic. This was off script. He was supposed to ask about my husband, or lack of.

"Come here." He nodded to a place before him.

"I'm fine right here." I set down the ad cards.

"I'm not gonna bite you, Ida. Come *here*."

I shouldn't have moved. Ida wouldn't have. Ida would have primly told Mr. Mitchell where he could stick it.

I moved. I walked on uneven floors in unsteady heels over to him and stopped, five feet or so away, my hands clasped before me. I could feel the soft hum of the camera beside me, could hear the shift of our audience behind me, the loud click of someone's walkie. Cole's eyes never left mine, his stare burned up the path between us, and he rotated his chair slightly, 'til he faced me. "Closer." The word came out a little hoarse, and he cleared his throat. "Closer," he repeated.

I moved closer, one slow step at a time, my heels loud in their clicks against the wood, then I was before him, and he rested his head back against the chair and looked up at me. "Sit. On the edge of the desk."

My hands reached behind, found the ledge of the desk, and I leaned back, grateful for the support.

"No," he corrected. "Sit on it. Or I will put you on it." The order in his voice, the image of his threat… it stirred a feminine place in me that shouldn't, in this moment, surrounded by onlookers, be touched. I pushed up on my toes and worked my way onto the desk, my skirt pushed up by the action. I pulled at it, crossing my legs and covering myself as best I could. Surely, Don would call for us to cut. Surely, someone would stop this waste of valuable film time.

"Do you know why I hired you, Ida?"

I lifted my eyes from the tassels on his shoes. "No."

"No, *sir*," he corrected.

I pursed my lips and said nothing.

"Do you want to know why I hired you, Ida?"

"Not particularly," I said tartly. "*Sir*."

He pushed off the arms of the chair, standing up in one fluid motion. I tensed, waiting for him to step forward, but he didn't. He stayed in place, his hands slow and deliberate as they rolled up one white shirtsleeve to the elbow, then moved to the other. "I hired you," he said quietly, stepping forward and stopping before me, his eyes dropping to my legs. I lost a breath when his hand settled on my knee, and I uncrossed my legs, pinning them together, my hand pulling down my skirt. "I hired you because you walked into my office in your cheap little dress, and I thought 'I bet that woman will be one hell of a lay.'" His hand moved higher, up under my skirt, and I stiffened, my hand falling on his forearm and pushing, resisting. He chuckled, his second hand pulling my legs apart, and, with a sudden jerk, he slid me to the edge of the desk, my knees spread, my skirt pushed high enough to expose the ridiculous garter straps. His eyes met mine for a moment, his fingers light and slow as they drew lines across the bare skin of my upper thighs, tracing the edge of the garter straps to the place where they crossed my panties, a lace set that matched. "I hired you because I pictured you *right* here, *on* my desk, *moaning* my name."

My hands closed hard on his in the moment before his fingers moved again, the edge of my panties too close, my need too great, my composure a tiny step away from begging. I told him no with my grip, and he listened, pulling his hands away, back to my stockings, then my knees. When he looked at me, his hands were already back to his tie, tightening the silk back into place. "What I didn't do was hire you because I cared about your opinion or your advice. You make a fairly decent cup of coffee and look good in a skirt. That's why you're here. Don't forget that."

"You're an *ass*." The rough words scraped through my mouth but barely hid the tears at their formation, and Cole *smiled* at their receipt.

"Oh yes, my dear." He leaned forward and yanked at the edge of my skirt, covering me up with one hard motion. "That just might be the smartest thing you've said all day." The response hit the script, the familiar line the only thing I could hold on to, and I did, biting back a hundred stupid feminine words. I pushed off the desk, my heels shaky when they hit the floor.

"Thank you for making your position on this point so clear, Mr. Mitchell. I'll keep my opinions to myself from this point forth."

"Good to hear." He settled back into the chair, and I turned away, moving to the door, looking past the camera which focused on my face and caught the tear moving down my cheek.

Later, Don would tell me I was brilliant, that the scene was perfect—one of the few in his career that had been captured in a single take. Later, I would nod and laugh and accept his praise as if I hadn't been breaking, as if Ida and Royce had no correlation with Cole and me, as if I had been acting and not living through the skin of Ida Pinkerton.

CHAPTER 69

Three years ago, I should have known. When I called Scott and he didn't answer. When I went by his office and he wasn't there. I should have known that something was wrong, I should have seen the signs and put them together. But I didn't. I was twenty-five years old and naïve and in love, and I thought that best friends and fiancés didn't mix.

I didn't even pick up on it when I saw Bobbie Jo's car parked behind the barn at his house. I thought, with a week before the wedding, they were planning a surprise for me—thought I was going to walk in and catch them red-handed with a honeymoon itinerary to Amelia Island spread out on the kitchen table. I almost left. Almost got back in my truck and drove home… to let them plan my surprise, to let them have their moment of AHA! where I would act surprised, and they would be clever, and I'd get the honeymoon of my dreams after all.

I would have done exactly that were it not for Scott's mother. That was why I was hunting him down to begin with. She'd called me from home, needing her medication, and he was supposed to have picked it up that morning. She was in pain, and I was the future daughter-in-law, swooping in to her aid. I was feeling pretty good about myself, about my surprise, about my loving fiancé and doting best friend. I was all but bursting with happiness when I walked around the side of the house and toward the front porch. I was so busy in my personal positivity party I almost didn't hear Bobbie Jo moan.

But I did. I heard her moan, and I heard him groan, and I realized, in the moment before my foot hit the first step, everything that I had overlooked.

CHAPTER 70

When Cole's phone rang at six fifteen in the morning, he contemplated ignoring it. Glancing down at his watch, he kept pace, his feet quiet on the soft dirt, the fields stretching out before him, the sun low behind the trees, the sky pale pink and peaceful. He didn't want to talk to his attorney right now, not when he was breathing clearly for the first time in days, his mind working through things that it had stumbled over for the last week.

Like Summer. There was a problem there, between him and her. A problem that had only disappeared during the twenty minutes in her bed. Too short of a time. Embarrassing, really. Nadia would have laughed at him and pushed him off. Then again, he'd never come that quickly with Nadia. He tried to put his finger on what was different with Summer, what had set her apart. He was just starting to work through that when DeLuca's call came through. He declined the call.

He'd miss this when he went back to California. Running outside, the give of the soil beneath his feet, the breeze devoid of pollution and competitive fight. Maybe he'd try the Observatory when he got home. Run those hills and bring Carlos and Bart with him. Be aware, with every step, of the paps documenting his trip.

The call came through again, and he slowed to a walk, answering the phone. "Hello."

The man's voice came through a wall of static and missed vowels.

"I can't hear you," Cole said with a smile. "The service here sucks."

There was another staccato string of words, *asshole* and *summons* coming through clear.

"I'll call you from a landline when I get home." Cole ended the call and turned off the phone, killing his music at the same time. It didn't matter; he'd think more clearly without it.

It had been a mistake, changing the scripts. Infusing sexuality into *The Fortune Bottle* might work well for the movie, but it was raining hell on him. It'd taken every bit of his self-control to stand before Summer, her skirt around her waist, her lace panties, the contrast of her skin against the dark stockings, the dainty garter… his fingers had twitched against her skin, his common sense on a thin ledge, his lines forgotten, the set and crew forgotten, everything fading but the tremble of her and the images of everything he wanted to do to her. He'd been rock hard when he had yanked her skirt back into place and stepped away, had walked to the viewing room bathroom and found pre-come coming out of his dick. "We didn't get the kiss," he had griped to Don. It had been easy to feign irritability, to scowl, to call her a rookie. It had been easy to argue with Don when he'd said that the kiss didn't matter, that the scene was even hotter from the lack of kiss. Foreplay, Don reminded him, can be the hottest thing. And wasn't that the damn truth.

But today, they would need to get the kiss, would need to document that transition in Ida and Royce's relationship, to properly build for the sex scene that would eventually come. Jesus. He would kill himself on that day. There was no way, without some release, that he'd last.

A truck approached from the opposite direction, and he jogged right, to the side of the road, his hand mimicking the driver's and lifting in a wave. The truck rumbled by slowly. Another thing that would never happen in Los Angeles—a friendly wave to a stranger. Especially not from him. A wave would prompt the car to stop, then others, a crowd mobbing him for autographs and selfies, a start that wouldn't have a finish until he was called an asshole and documented on every gossip rag and Twitter feed as such. He hadn't been approached once in Quincy. It was odd. Almost scary. He'd wanted to ask Summer about it, had set it aside as a safe topic for the next time they were cordial. That'd been three weeks ago. Cordial just didn't seem to be in the cards for them.

Before his six years with Nadia, he'd screwed plenty of costars, most of them. It was normal, with four months together, socializing with the crew a non-possibility, for the leads to gravitate toward each other. Lines were often run late at night over drinks. And lines and drinks typically led to drunk kisses and drunker sex. Costar sex had often been good but never great. Then he had met Nadia, fallen for Nadia, and never looked back, never been tempted, never yielded to a costar's pathetic play at an affair.

And sex with Nadia had always been good, it had been the basis of their relationship, now that he stepped back and examined it. But sex with Summer… that experience had been another league entirely. He had lost his mind in those moments in her bedroom. Touching her, the feel of being inside her, her kiss, her sounds… he had let himself, in her bedroom, enjoy her, want her, worship her. He'd been, in that moment, completely hers. And that, more than their tension, more than Brad DeLuca and his threats, is what scared the absolute hell out of Cole.

He rounded the bend and headed home, extending his stride and pushing the last half-mile hard. He needed to shower. Jack off. Get in some type of a reasonable mind-set before he called DeLuca back and then headed into town.

SCENE #22. That was on the docket today. Rewritten to incorporate the kiss that didn't happen yesterday. He kept his eyes straight ahead, on the narrow strip of clay, and didn't look to Summer's house. A kiss. Child's play.

Between the swing of his stride, he felt himself grow hard at the thought, and he groaned in protest.

He was fucked. Absolutely, unequivocally, fucked.

CHAPTER 71

"I need you in California this afternoon." Brad DeLuca didn't mince words, his greeting skipping straight to the point. Cole stuck the end of the hose in the kiddie pool and twisted the nozzle. Cocky liked the kiddie pool, especially on a day like today, where it was gearing up to be in the high nineties.

"I can't go to California today." He watched the pool fill and lifted the towel from his neck, drying off his head, still wet from the shower.

"Yes, you can, and you will. I spoke to your director, and he's shifting the shooting schedule, said it will be no big deal."

"You spoke to my director." Cole mused, spraying a burst of water in Cocky's direction, wondering when DeLuca had time to sleep.

"I wasn't going to waste your time by calling you for something that couldn't be done. I verified that it can be done, and now you're going. Justin has already set up a flight for you at eleven."

Eleven. Cole breathed a little easier. Plenty of time to shoot twenty-two and then hit the airport. Worst-case scenario, if Don wasn't happy, they could reshoot it later in the week. "Why do you need me there?"

"You've been summoned. It's an initial play at mediation. Nadia's team is trying to look good; though, I can tell you from the tone of our communication, they are anything but cooperating."

"So it's a waste of time."

"Not at all. I spoke to them this morning and gave them an ultimatum. Told them tomorrow is their last chance to stay out of court. They gave us three options on dates for the mediation, and this is our best shot. If we could knock out *The Fortune Bottle* issue now, especially since you're clean as a fucking whistle, then the rest is easy. You could be fully divorced by Christmas."

Clean as a whistle. He didn't feel clean. With everything happening with Summer, he felt dirty as fuck. He said nothing and opened the back door, Cocky perking up his head. *Divorced by Christmas.* That would be good. And Nadia would definitely want to avoid court. Maybe this mediation could be it, one giant stress removed from his life.

"How are you handling things?"

Cole looked at Cocky and contemplated bringing him to the set. He'd have to ask Summer to watch him while he was gone. There wasn't really anyone else.

"Cole?" DeLuca prodded. "I don't want you drinking your feelings away. Nadia's not worth it. You'll know that one day."

"I'm fine," Cole snapped, leaving Cocky in place and pulling the back door shut and heading for the front, grabbing his keys off the counter.

"Don't give me that. You want to play tough on the set, fine, but be upfront with me. I have a shrink that is brilliant. Why don't you talk to him? Just vent, or break down, or do whatever it is that you Californians do when you have a broken heart."

Cole laughed, his hand on the front door, the cordless phone pinning him to the house when he really wanted to get to the Pit. "Brad. I'm fine. I swear to you on God's green Earth that I am *not* pining over Nadia."

"So you're over Nadia." Brad's voice was skeptical, and it ate up valuable time. Cole glanced at the rooster clock by the door and tried to calculate how many takes they'd have time to fit in.

"Yep," he said shortly.

"I thought I told you to stay away from pussy."

Cole's attention returned to the call. "What?"

"You can't get into a relationship right now. *Absolutely* not. We're walking into our first round of mediation, and we need you to look wounded and struggling. If you're in a new relationship it's going to paint Nadia's affair in a different light." The man's words rolled out focused and deadly.

"I'm not in a relationship." It was true. Summer and whatever their *thing* was wasn't a relationship. It was an obsession at a convenient time. If it helped him to get over Nadia, even better. It, like his obsession over racehorses and *The Fortune Bottle*, would fade. Probably before this movie even wrapped.

"I swear to you, Cole, if the media catches wind of this, you will be crucified. Right now, you have all of America in your corner. You are Jennifer Fucking Aniston and she is Angelina Jolie covered in shit. Don't join her in the shit, Cole. Not until we have your movie in front of a judge, and I have it in your name, wrapped up in enough legal tape to make sure that Nadia never touches it. Then, if you want to take this girl to the premiere and roll her around in the millions this will bring you, go for it. But not before then. You know better than anyone how these bloodhounds will sniff out stories, Cole. Don't hand them one on a silver platter."

"I'm *not* in a relationship, I'm *not* seeing anyone, and I'm *not* fucking anyone." He bit out the last line in easy concert with the truths and rested his forehead on the door, willing the man on the other end to buy his words. It wasn't really a lie. He wasn't *fucking* Summer, he had *fucked* her. Past tense. Wasn't going to happen again. Probably. "If you want me on a plane by eleven, I have to go."

DeLuca sighed into the receiver. "Fine. I'll see you in LA. Justin's arranging a driver for you at the airport."

"Okay." Cole ended the call and straightened, tossing the phone onto the couch and pulling open the door, the sky full of morning light, a sparrow flying off the porch railing at first sight of him. Cole jogged toward the truck, squinting in the direction of Summer's house and was pleased to see her truck wasn't out front.

He climbed into the cab, starting the big diesel and heading toward town. It would be a busy morning. SCENE #22. The first kiss between Royce and Ida.

He'd knock that out, then he'd fly to Los Angeles, and rejoin the demons.

CHAPTER 72

I was halfway through a plate of Belgian waffles when Mary popped her head in. "May I come in?" she chirped.

I nodded through a mouthful of strawberries and syrup, glancing up from the script I was reviewing. I was about to ask if she could run some lines with me when she held up a new call sheet. "Bad news," she said, placing it before me. "Mr. Masten has to leave for California so they've shifted some scenes around."

Cole leaving for California sounded like great news to me. I put a regretful look on my face and picked up the call sheet. "Scene twenty-two?" I started to flip through my master script, but she stopped me.

"I'll get you a new script. Twenty-two was revised after your, ugh…" she glanced down at her clipboard and made a notation of sorts, "… after your ad lib yesterday. Or rather, Mr. Masten's ad lib."

Revised. That didn't sound good. I flipped through the sides she passed me and looked up. "A kiss? That's what this scene is?"

"Yes." She tapped the side of her pen on the clipboard. "They want you camera-ready in fifteen."

Fifteen. Fifteen minutes wasn't enough to get me into hair and makeup and camera-ready. Five years wasn't enough to get ready to kiss Cole Masten.

SCENE 22: OFFICE PARKING LOT. ROYCE GIVES IDA CAR.

"This is stupid." I balled up the top page of the script and walked over to Don. We stood in the middle of a fake parking lot, in front of a fake office front, the vintage Coca-Cola sign hanging above the building's door the only authentic thing on the set. Well, it and a vintage Cadillac Phaeton that sat before us, a big bow wrapped around her middle.

Don sighed, resting his hand on the top of a camera and looking at me. "What's the problem, Summer?"

"Royce, out of the blue, gives Ida a car, and she's supposed to kiss him for it?"

"It's a peace offering," Cole chimed in, coming around Don with a cup of coffee in hand. He was already dressed in a brown suit, his face shaved, green eyes blazing. I ignored him.

"Ida's not going to accept a car, and she's not going to jump up and down and do this whole pathetic routine you have her doing." I waved the script in the air, and one of the writers looked up from his chair, his brows pinching.

"It's not pathetic. It's how women in the fifties acted. You have to realize that she is a divorced woman looking for a man. Royce is giving her a very generous gift and, when she hugs him in gratitude, he goes in for the kiss…" The man, a tiny bit of a man with bright red hair and a Grateful Dead shirt, shrugged. "It's logical."

I stared at him, and, by the look on my face, hopefully communicated how much of a sexist idiot I considered him to be. "It's logical if we are talking about a woman who sits at home and knits all day. It's not logical if we are talking about Ida Pinkerton, one of the Original 67." I looked at Don, then Cole, in disgust. "Did *anyone* read this book other than me?"

"Scripts aren't the book. It's an adaptation." Now Grateful Dead boy was rising to his feet.

"You—shut up," Cole snapped, pointing at the writer and walking toward me. He glanced at his watch and stopped in front of me, so close that I could see the tiny green lines inset in his brown suit. "Summer, I've got to get on a plane in two hours. Please don't fight me on this. Just say your lines, and let's wrap this baby up." He cupped the side of my arms with his hands, and I looked down at them in surprise.

"It's not her," I hissed at him. "This whole hero-worship bit is bull crap. It's completely out of character."

"Then ad lib it," Don interrupted. "Like you guys did in the office. I can't get either of you to stick to the damn script anyway."

I turned to Don, distinctly aware that Cole's hands still were on my arms. I jerked my shoulders, and he let go. "Ad lib it?" I asked.

"Sure. Say whatever you think Ida would say. But in return I need a kiss." He pointed at me and held my contact. "Deal?"

"A kiss," I repeated with dread.

"Yes," Cole said. "I know. Painful. Trust me, Country. I'm not looking forward to it any more than you are."

I whipped my head to him, his mouth curving a little bit when he took in my glare.

"Liar," I accused.

He laughed and leaned in, close enough for only me to hear his response. "Yes, baby. And so are you."

I closed my eyes and tried to mentally prepare for the scene. Tried to picture how I'd react if I walked out of my front door tomorrow and my truck was gone, a flashy new car in its place. I don't think I'd handle it well.

Beside me, Cole waited. "It's not rocket science, Summer," he said in a low voice. "It's a fight. Something we do well."

"Lock it down!" I heard the AD yell, and the building fell silent. *Showtime.* I squared my shoulders and pushed on the door, my skirt tight around my legs as I stepped into false sunshine, a giant, artificial sun shining down from the rafters. Cole bumped into the back of me as I stopped short, my eyes scanning over the cars in the small lot. When I saw the bright red car, its white top down, the bow stretched across its windshield, I stared. I stared and tried to think of an Ida Pinkerton-plausible response.

"Well?" Cole boomed out the question, walking around me, his hands extended, his face proud and happy. "What do you think?"

"Do you often wrap up new cars for yourself?" I asked the question primly, tilting my head to the side and scratching at a tight place on my bun. The girl in Hair had gone way overboard with her bobby pins, a hundred pokes lying in wait for one wrong turn of my head.

His smile fell, and he looked at me. "It's for you."

My hand dropped from my bun. "Me?"

"Yes. It's red."

"I can see that, Mr. Mitchell. I'm a woman, not colorblind."

"You're also not very appreciative." He stepped forward with a scowl, and I saw, for the first time, the key chain in his hand. "It's Coca-Cola red," he said, turning to the car. "The dealership mixed up the color just for you. Since I agreed to change the branding." He smiled like I should be grateful.

"How generous of you," I said tightly. "Where's my car?"

"This." He extended both hands as if it made it clearer. "This is your new car."

"I'm not deaf, colorblind, or stupid. I understand that this car is red, and that you are of some misunderstanding that I should be happy to have you give it to me."

"Yes. Exactly. That is exactly my misunderstanding, Ms. Pinkerton. I'm so glad that, for once today, we are on the same page." He stopped before me and held out the key. I tilted my head up at him and smiled sweetly.

"Where is my car?" I repeated. "The black Ford."

He threw up his hands. "I'm not sure. Can you focus for one moment on this?"

"Get it back."

"You don't want it back." He stepped closer, and his hand fell to my lower back, softly pushing, ushering me toward the car.

"You don't know what I want," I sputtered.

"I know you want this," he all but dragged me to the car, my heels digging into the dirt, a puff of dust following the rough journey to the shiny red side, my hip knocking against the door handle as he pushed me up against its side.

"I have a car, you bullheaded—"

"Not the car," he cut in. "This." Then, with his hand firmly planted on the back of my neck, he pulled me up and hard into his kiss.

There should be laws against men who could kiss like that. With a mouth that dominated yet begged. Tongue that teased yet delivered. Tastes that dipped into an addiction stream and hooked a woman after just the first hit. I had kissed him before. In his kitchen. In my bed. Both times I was distracted. This was a different experience entirely.

I sank in his arms, my knees buckling, my body supported by him and the car, everything lost but the action between our lips. My fight left after the first break, his lips coming immediately back, the second kiss softer and sweeter in its coupling. His hand on my neck yielded, less of a grip and more of a caress, his other sliding down and pinning me to his body, our connection firm and complete as we explored each other's mouths. I grew greedy, my tongue meeting his, and his yielded under my direction, letting me lead, our cadence perfectly coordinated. As my hair fell around my shoulder, his hand quick with the pins, diving into and gentle on my scalp, I wondered how it was so easy, how our mouths matched so well when our personalities clashed so strongly. I wondered how my mouth could crave this man when my mind hated him. He pulled gently on my hair, and I resisted, our kiss breaking, my breath hard in the gap. He stared down at me, his eyes on my mouth for a long moment, then his gaze lifted to mine. He stared at me, and I closed my eyes, pulling forward, back to his lips. I couldn't have him look at me right then. In that moment, my legs wobbly from his kiss… there was no telling what he would see. I pressed my lips against his mouth, and it opened for me, his hand tightening on the back of my head.

He was the one to pull off the second time, his hand keeping my head in place, and he placed a soft kiss on the top of my head before stepping away. I felt the press of his hand in mine before he stepped away and looked down, seeing the silver key lying in my palm. He stepped toward the building, his hands in his pockets, his head down.

"I meant what I said, Mr. Mitchell," I called out, and his stride stopped, his head turning my way.

"About what?" he called back.

"The car. I don't want it."

"And us?" He turned to me, his hands in his pant pockets, like he didn't care about my answer. I stared at his face and said, for a long period, nothing.

"I don't want the car," I finally responded. "I'd appreciate it if you got mine back."

He nodded his head toward me. "Understood, Ms. Pinkerton. Enjoy your long walk home."

My mouth fell open, and I stepped forward, my hand reaching out, a protest on my lips, a trio of actions ignored by the man who pushed through the office's faux door, the screen door smacking shut behind him with a loud crack.

I let out a strangled yelp of fury and turned to the car, looking at the key in my hand and then back at the vehicle. My hand closed around the key, and I threw it down into the front seat of the car. I tucked my clutch under my arm and pulled one heel off a stocking foot, then the other. With my heels clutched in my free hand, I squared Ida Pinkerton's shoulders and headed home through the dust.

When my stocking foot hit the edge of the set, reaching mat instead of dust, I stopped, turned back and waited for Don's voice to boom through the set. It didn't, and I watched him zoom in a cam, manually circling the car before zooming in on the front seat, most likely the keys that had landed in the front seats. After a long moment, Don looked up from the camera's monitor. "Cut. I think we got it."

Cole cracked open the door of the office building. "We good, Don?"

"Got enough. Go catch your plane." Don nodded at Cole. "Good work."

Cole nodded at him and grabbed a baseball hat off the back of one of the director's chairs, pulling it onto his head and walking toward the exit. I watched him leave, my eyes narrowed. The least he could do, after kissing me senseless, was acknowledge me. I felt a general nudge against my elbow and looked left, a mic'd man gesturing toward Don.

"Great work, Summer," Don said. "That wasn't so bad, was it?"

I smiled weakly. "Am I done?"

"For now, yes." He walked over and flipped through a clipboard. "I'm gonna work with the guys to review this and splice and dice it before Cole gets back. We're not shooting anything else with you until tomorrow, so feel free to get out of here if you feel like it."

If I feel like it? I reached up and fished the remaining bobby pins out of my ruined bun. "Sounds good." I smiled at Don. "Thanks."

"Hey, thank *you*! Not many can ad lib, so great work, really. You guys work well together." A compliment paired with insanity. But this time, when he smiled at me, my return smile was genuine.

I had done a good job.
We had kissed and I had survived.
I had the rest of the day off.

Things could definitely be worse.

CHAPTER 73

Cole sat alone in the cabin on the plane. One of his feet rested on the empty chair before him, his chair slightly reclined and a drink untouched before him. He watched the ice settle in the glass, and wondered what in the hell was wrong with him. The plane dipped slightly, and he glanced forward, the flight attendant smiling brightly at him. He looked back at the glass.

The kiss had been different, so different, from the kitchen. It had been more like the kiss in her bedroom, and that was probably what was nagging at him. When he had been in her bed, and she had rolled over, climbing on his body and kissing him, he had been half-conscious, drugged out of his mind by the experience, his body on autopilot, their kiss just one more ingredient in a decadent dessert. But on that set, by that car, he hadn't been drugged. He had experienced every sense, every taste, every movement of her tongue. He had relished it, dammit.

Shifting in his seat, he closed his eyes and wondered why he was beating himself up so much over her. He hadn't thought twice about banging the twins in the hotel room, or the Brazilian on Dillon's yacht three days after catching Nadia in the act. It wasn't cheating. Nadia had been photographed a hundred times since with that director; his cock was probably tattooed on her body by now. So what was the problem?

Maybe it was Summer. Maybe it was some ingrained part of him that saw something he didn't and wanted him to stay away from it. Maybe it was DeLuca and his threats. A piece of ass wasn't worth losing half of *The Fortune Bottle.* And that's all she was—temptation. That was what he needed to remember.

He suddenly thought of Cocky and reached for his phone.

When she answered, she was out of breath, her huffs into the phone completely innocent and completely erotic. He lost his mind for a minute, then found it. "Am I interrupting something?"

"Interrupting something?" she pounced. "You left set an hour ago. I just walked in the door. How could you already be interrupting something?"

He ignored the question. "I forgot to ask you if you'd watch Cocky. While I'm gone."

"Before I forget, I meant to talk to you about his name."

"You gonna give me hell for naming him?" He closed his eyes for a minute and massaged the bridge of his nose.

"Cole, I cried like a baby when my first chicken died. I'm not going to make fun of you for naming him. I just think you could have been a little more creative than Cocky."

He dropped his hand and smiled. "Next pet chicken I get, I'll let you name it." He regretted the statement as soon as it fell out. It was too much, pushing their shaky ground too far. But she ignored it, breezing on to a new topic.

"Where *are* you going?" The question had a naive curiosity about it, and he enjoyed, for a brief moment, their lack of sparring. Enjoyed and also hated it. There was so much familiarity in their battles that he almost felt uncomfortable with cordiality.

"Home. Or, rather, Los Angeles. My home there is now under the control of my ex."

"So where will you stay?" She stopped him before he could answer. "Nevermind. That sounded… that came out wrong. Yes, I'm happy to watch Cocky."

"I'm staying at a hotel." He didn't know why he felt the need to tell her. He wanted her to know, wanted to follow up the detail with the word 'alone.' *I'm staying at the hotel alone.* She wouldn't care. The insecurity in her voice had been imagined. Why would she care? She wouldn't.

"Fancy stuff."

"Lonely stuff." Another stupid thing to say.

"Right." She snorted out a laugh. "Likely."

He stopped the runaway of his mouth by filling it with whiskey, tipping back the glass and finishing it off, the flight attendant at his side instantly, her fingers lingering over the back of his hand when she reached for his empty glass. She'd come back to the hotel with him if he wanted it. She already had, after the first flight when he'd gotten the divorce papers. Her hips were double-jointed. He looked away.

"Where's Cocky's feed?"

"It's by the kitchen door, in a clear container, there's a scoop inside. I'll have Justin send you more info." He cleared his throat, well aware that the next sentence would make him sound like a pansy. "He's used to me being around a lot… I don't know how he'll do at night, I've never left him in the yard all night…"

"Do you want me to bring him to my house? Or want me to stay at your place with him?"

The image of Summer at his house, in his bed… his hand trembled slightly when he took the tumbler back from the flight attendant. "Yes," he choked out. "Stay at the house. If you don't mind."

"I don't mind." She laughed a little, and he heard water start to run in the background, heard the sound of metal banging. Pots and pans, probably in the sink. He could picture her easily, her shoes kicked off, her sleeves rolled up, her house phone resting against her shoulder. "Did you leave it unlocked?"

Shit. "No. I—"

"Ben had an extra key from when he signed the lease. I'll find out what he did with it. Anything else?"

He tried to think of something, a way to extend the conversation, but came up blank. "No. Call me if there's any issues."

"When are you getting back?"

"Tomorrow night. Early." He should invite her to dinner. Any other costar he would. Especially if they'd pet sat. Though, when he flipped through his last dozen costars, none of them were the type to pet sit.

They all had people for that, or a pet nanny on salary.

"I'll be sure to be back home before you land. Call me if you need anything."

"Will do. Thanks." The word sounded odd when it came out and he tried to think of the last time he'd used it. Scary that he couldn't remember.

"You're welcome," she said soberly, then laughed. He hung up before he laughed back, then smiled at the ridiculousness of it all. A chicken. He had a pet chicken. What the hell would he do with Cocky once filming wrapped? He couldn't leave him behind. He'd have to—he dialed Justin's number before he got sidetracked and forgot.

"Hey boss." Justin sounded good, his voice clear and healthy.

"Hey. How's the healing going?"

"Good. I'll be flying back with you tomorrow night. Can't wait, man. I'm going stir-crazy over here."

"Did DeLuca tell you about the mediation?"

"Yep. I got a car ready for you at the airport. You eaten? I can have him grab something on his way."

"No, I'm good." Cole pulled down on the window shade and closed his eyes, half listening, his purpose for calling already forgotten.

"You're at the Avalon tonight, and I put your Ferrari in one of their private garages. I'll have a full details sheet for you in the car. And for dinner, I have Dan Tana's, the Prawn House, and Morton's all reserved, if—"

"Justin." When he said the man's name, his assistant stopped. It was one of Cole's favorite qualities, his ability to run a thousand miles an hour and then stop on a dime.

"Yes?"

"I'll be fine. Cancel the dinner reservations; I'll fend for myself. Can you join me for breakfast in the morning?"

"Breakfast?"

"Yeah."

"Since when do you eat breakfast?"

Cole laughed. "You got time for me or not?"

"Of course I do. I'm just surprised."

"I've missed you, man."

The man laughed in response. "Who are you, and what have you done with Cole Masten?"

"Seven at that restaurant in the Avalon lobby. Get us one of those pool cabanas, something with some fucking privacy."

"There's the man I know. Consider it done. See you then."

Cole suddenly remembered the reason for his call. "Any luck finding me a house?"

"I have four or five that are up your alley. I'll bring sheets on them tomorrow."

"Make sure you get one with a yard. And find out the city code on owning a chicken."

There was a long silence on the other end. The man had organized sex parties, bribed paparazzi, and given Cole his pee for a studio drug test, yet *this* is what gave him pause.

"A *live* chicken?" Justin finally asked.

"Yes. A rooster."

"I'll find out," Justin managed.

Cole said goodbye and hung up. He had lost a wife and gained a pet chicken. Yep. Sounded about right.

CHAPTER 74

At the end of a very long day, Cole walked into the hotel suite, tossing his wallet on the counter, while he scrolled through his phone. He found the Kirklands' home phone number and pressed SEND, trying to do the math in his head. It was… midnight there? Eleven?

"Hello?" her voice was thick, almost drugged.

"Summer?" He removed his watch and dropped it on the granite, holding on to the edge of the island as he worked off his first dress boot. "It's Cole."

"I know." She yawned. "It's late. Are you just now getting home?"

"Yeah. But it's not that late here."

"Still a long day." There was a rustle of something and then quiet.

He got his second boot off and walked to the first chair in the living room, collapsing into it. Why had he called her? He tried to think of a reason. To check on Cocky? That was flimsy. "Summer?" The line had been quiet too long. "Summer?" he repeated, more urgency in his tone. This woman's refusal to lock doors was ridiculous. What if someone had come in, snuck into her room?

"Hmm?" More rustling.

"Did you just fall asleep?"

"Uh-huh." A response completely lacking in apology.

"Do you know how many girls would kill for me to call them? The studio runs giveaways for shit like this all the time, with millions of entries."

"Girls," she mumbled. "Not women. I used to want a belly button ring too, once."

"I'm not a belly button ring." That was a statement he never thought he'd say aloud.

"Uh-huh." The word was muffled, as if she had a pillow over the receiver.

"Where are you? Which bedroom?" He tried to think of which bedrooms had phones. Tried to remember if they were cordless or not.

"Yours. I tried to sleep in the downstairs bedroom, but it was too hot." She suddenly sounded a little more awake. "Is that okay?"

Good Lord. Her voice wasn't the only thing that just woke up. His cock suddenly needed an adjustment, and he undid his belt, his hands busy, purely for comfort reasons, unzipping his pants just to give his cock room to breathe.

"What are you wearing?" the words came out much more sexual than he had intended.

"What?" she giggled against the phone. "Cole Masten, I am *not* doing this with you."

A *giggle*. That was new. He liked it. He ran his fingers down the length of himself, then wrapped his hand around it, squeezing his cock firmly. "I'm asking purely out of concern for Cocky. He's never seen a naked woman before. I worry about his poultry hormones."

"His poultry hormones?" her words were no longer muffled. She had probably rolled over. On her back. Her eyes staring up at him. "You don't have to worry about Cocky. I'm not naked."

"Oh." He dragged his fist from the base of his dick to the head, his grip firm, an exhale of frustration over the day escaping. He should hang up the phone. Jack off and go to bed.

"I'm wearing underwear."

His grip tightened, his cock now fully hard, sticking up and out of his hand. "Summer," he groaned. He thought of her, stretched out in his bed, the covers kicked off, how she had looked in those tiny cotton panties. "And a tank top?" he asked.

"No." she sighed out the response, hesitation in her next words. "I was hot."

He pushed on the base of his dick, worried for an adolescent moment that he might nut right there. Was this actually happening? This conversation? This direction?

"I should go to bed," she whispered out the sentence.

"No." He closed his eyes and slid deeper in the chair, his feet spreading, his head falling back on the chair. "You shouldn't."

"This is wrong."

"Summer." The words were a painful distraction from the ache in his hand, and he slid his thumb over the head, a stream of pre-come leaking out, his eyes watching it. "My cock is rock hard, and all I can think of is you in my bed right now. Please don't torture me by hanging up the phone."

Her breath catching was the most beautiful sound in the world. "You're thinking about me?"

"I've been thinking about you all day. I wish I were next to you. I wish you could reach over and feel me right now."

"I've never done this, Cole. I don't even know what to say."

"You don't have to say anything. Just… touch yourself." He closed his eyes and pushed against the floor, tightening his legs and working his hand up and down. "Have you ever touched yourself?"

"I've been single for three years," she said tartly. "Bringing myself to orgasm is not a new thing."

He laughed despite himself. "God, I'd love to fill up that smart mouth with my cock."

"I wish… that morning…" He held his breath while he waited on her to complete the sentence.

"I wish you had done it. Had flipped me over and put your mouth on me." There was the sound of sheets, and then her voice was clear again. "I've thought about that so much."

Put your mouth on me. I've thought about that so much. Cole had been with countless women, Nadia one of the dirtiest talkers on the planet, but there was nothing as erotic as when this woman opened her mouth and spoke. Each shy admission was another bullet into the tissue paper of his self-control, and he cursed her name as his hips ground into the leather seat. "Tomorrow night," he groaned, holding onto the chair with one hand while he jerked himself off with the other. "Stay at my house. The minute I get off that plane I will drive there, pin you down on my bed, and worship your pussy. I won't stop until my mouth is imprinted on your mind and your taste is my fucking middle name."

There was a small sound, a whimper that came from her mouth and found its way to his cock, and he yanked his hand away, gripping the chair's arm and trying to stop, trying not to…

It didn't stop. His cock twitched on its own, erect and fully upright, his come squirting once, twice, six fucking times before it settled down, his breath huffing out, the phone, held against his shoulder, falling down to his lap. His hands fumbled as he grabbed it, holding it back to his ear, gasping her name as the final shudders of his orgasm tingled through him.

His heart broke when he listened to her, her orgasm following so close behind his, her breath hard, his name soft, and he could picture her, twisting against the sheets, back arching, and he was almost hard again by the time she quieted, a long stretch of nothing on the phone line between them. He didn't mind. He couldn't move, couldn't think, couldn't consider what just happened and what it meant for everything else.

"Goodnight, Cole." Her voice was quiet, and he needed a lifetime more of Summer to know what it meant—if this was post-orgasm sleepy Summer or weirded-out, awkward Summer or upset-about-to-cry Summer. He didn't just need it. He wanted it. And that didn't make sense.

He frowned into the phone and worked over the right thing to say, the right question to ask but the line clicked off and she was gone.

CHAPTER 75

His sheets smelled like him. I pushed the phone's cradle over, to the far edge of the walnut side table, and considered lifting it back off the receiver. Letting the dial tone die and suffering through the *beep beep beep* madness until it ended. But that was a little egotistic, thinking he'd call back. And if I took the phone off the hook, then I'd never know if he did try to call back. I left the ticking time bomb on the edge of the table and rolled back into place, his sheets hot against my sweaty skin. Having orgasms did that to me. Amped up my personal temperature, the blood thrumming through my veins, making me hot—and not in the sexual sense, but in the literal, I-have-to-rip-off-these-clothes-before-I-die, sense.

I blinked up at the ceiling and sorted through my feelings. I already regretted what had just happened. *I've been thinking about you all day.* That was what he had said. He hadn't meant it; it had been a tool in his belt—one he had used to perfection. I had taken that line and let it untie every loose knot of resistance. I rolled onto my stomach with an aggravated huff of air. So stupid of me. I didn't need Cole to have an orgasm. I should have hung up with the first sign of flirtation and brought myself there without showing him my cards. Because that was what I'd done, right? Let him see how deeply, despite my hatred, he affected me? I skipped back through and tried to remember the things I had said in the weak moments of my surrender.

"I wish you had done it. Had flipped me over and put your mouth on me."

Oh, right. That landmine. Why did I say that? And then… his response… had he actually meant that? That he wanted me to wait for him to arrive back in Quincy and he would… oh God. I covered my face with my hands, my legs twisting together in a wasted attempt at non-arousal.

I couldn't do it. Absolutely not. That… that had been a mistake. One weak moment in the middle of the night. I would tell him that when he returned. But not at his house. On set, in a safe location, where there was no chance whatsoever that temptation might hit.

Yes. A plan. I burrowed my face into his pillow and—like a crazy stalker—inhaled deeply. I had lied to him on the phone; I didn't try the downstairs bedroom first. I went in there, messed up the sheets a little bit, then scampered up the stairs, anxious to explore whatever secrets his bedroom might hold. I'd been disappointed. No secret love letters tucked under his mattress, no porn stacked by the DVD player. His clothes were neatly hung in the closet and folded in the drawers. It was almost boring. I had undressed and slid under his sheets, the dark gray set different than the Kirklands', the material thick and expensive. I'd hugged one of his pillows to my chest and fallen asleep thinking of our kiss. Of the way he had tasted, of his fingers in my hair.

His smell. I could make potpourri out of it and become a millionaire.

CHAPTER 76

'Most of the successful people in Hollywood are failures as human beings."
~ Marlon Brando

"Something's different." Justin tapped his fingers on the arm of his chair and tilted his head at Cole.

"Yeah, you look like a chemo patient," Cole snapped, nodding to Justin's head. "Couldn't they have left you a little bit of hair to cover that ugly head?"

"No… not different with me." Justin leaned forward. "With you."

"My wife left me. I've been stuck in bumfuck Georgia. After you're in Quincy a month, let's see if you don't look a little crazy."

"I expected you to look crazy. Or be strung out on some sort of backwoods drug. But you look… good." His brow furrowed like it was a bad thing.

"I'm not," Cole said flatly. And he wasn't. He'd jacked off twice that morning and was still horny, just thinking about his call with Summer. He should have just let her bring Cocky to her house. Maybe then he'd be able to eat eggs benedict without needing to adjust himself.

Justin eyed him. "I got to be honest, I wasn't sure you'd survive out there without me."

"Your job security has definitely taken a nose dive now that I have become more self-sufficient." Cole waved off the waiter's offer for more juice.

Justin looked at his watch—one that Cole had given him for Christmas. "All right, I've been patient for fifteen minutes."

Cole looked up, mid-chew, his eyebrows furrowed in question.

Justin laughed and spread his hands, as if waiting for Cole to spill his soul.

Cole swallowed. "You've got to give me more than that."

"Summer."

One word that perfectly described her hot fucking deliciousness. "What about her?" He'd ask how Justin knew about her, but that was a waste of a question. In Hollywood, an assistant's worth was primarily composed of three things: organization, ability to keep secrets, and ability to find out secrets. Justin had ninja skills in all three.

"How serious are you about her?"

"Serious?" Cole coughed out a strangled attempt at a laugh. "She's my costar. I got Nadia's team breathing down my neck, and that Rottweiler of an attorney you tied me to threatening my nuts in a jar if I so much as unzip my pants. The only thing I'm serious about is staying as far away from that country beauty queen as possible."

Justin said nothing, sitting back in his chair and staring at him.

"Once," Cole mumbled. "I fucked her once. It's not happening again."

"Is that why you're calling for script changes every day? You know this business, Cole. Your production budget is climbing faster than Lindsay Lohan's chance of a crack baby pregnancy."

"I'm calling for script changes because they're making the movie better. You'll see when you come. The new scenes work, and they add a different element to the movie."

"Porn. That's the element you're adding to the movie. This was a standard biopic. According to the crew, you two are all but fucking on camera."

Cole scowled. "That's bullshit. We've kissed on camera once."

"Well, that's what they're telling me. And if they're talking to me, you know they're telling their families. The tabloids will be all over this shit within the week. I won't be surprised if they get dailies and blast that shit primetime."

"It's on camera. I can bend her over and screw on screen if it's for the movie. And there's nothing that you or DeLuca or Nadia or the fucking *Hollywood Reporter* can say about it." Cole pushed back his seat in irritation.

Justin's eyes narrowed. "Fuck me. You in *love* with this girl?"

Cole threw up his hands. "Oh my God. That's not what this is about. This is about the movie. This is about me not being bored off my ass in the middle of nowhere."

"No." Justin shook his head. "This is different. I've known you for thirteen years. Something's off. You think it's a rebound?"

Cole looked away. "It's not a rebound. I wouldn't do that to her."

"To Summer? Or to Nadia?"

His eyes hardened. "Nadia can fuck herself."

"So you're not wanting to hook up with Summer because you're worried about *hurting* her?" Justin looked to the ceiling and chuckled. "Who the fuck are you, and what have you done with my best friend?" He grinned at Cole. "Seriously. This is the same guy who was healing his pride with a pussy buffet, just… oh… seven, eight weeks ago?"

Cole sighed. "Let's go. The mediation is soon."

Justin stood, his eyes on Cole's as he finished off his water. "Just talk to me. I know you're not talking to anyone else."

"Nothing to talk about." Cole pulled out his wallet and peeled off a couple of bills. "It happened. It's over. Everything else is about the movie."

"If you say so." Justin slapped him on the back as they moved around the table. "Now let's go nail this bitch to the wall."

Justin pulled back the private curtain, and they came face to face with pure fury in the form of a six-foot-two Italian.

Brad Fucking DeLuca.

CHAPTER 77

"Jesus…" Cole stepped back, the man glowering at them like he was ready to pull them apart.

"How did you get back here?" Justin snapped back the rest of the curtain, oblivious to their impending demise, and glared toward the restaurant. "We rented out the pool deck."

"My wife just became best friends with the manager. And a thousand bucks got me a first class ticket to your cuddle session." Justin started to speak, and DeLuca turned to him, holding up a hand. "Get the fuck out of my face and let me talk to my client alone."

Justin blanched, his eyes moving to Cole, who nodded. "Stand outside and make sure no one comes around." This was bad. He ticked through his conversation with Justin, his eyes closing in dread. There was the pull of curtains, and then they were alone.

"What I just did to get here any paparazzi could have done," Brad spoke quietly, his eyes on Cole's.

"Justin's never gotten me in trouble. He cleared the place, I thought we were—"

"Sit down and shut up for a moment." Brad pointed to a chair, and he fell into it.

"I can't deal with your lectures this morning," Cole said wearily, rubbing his eyes and wishing he had ordered a drink with breakfast instead of juice.

"Is your assistant correct?" Brad sat down, across from him, leaning forward in the chair, and the lowered stature caused the tight knot in Cole's back to lessen a little. "If this is something else, then just tell me and we can attack it from a different side."

"What?" Cole cracked open an eye and looked at Brad.

"I've been told to stay away from someone before. It made me chase her down like she was a wounded gazelle. Now, *she* ended up being my soulmate." Brad sat back in his chair. "Chances are that this woman isn't yours. But I'm not gonna fuel any sexual tension between the two of you by telling you to stay away from her."

Cole tried to understand. "So… you're telling me I *can* date her?"

"I'm telling you that I need to know what is going on so that I can control the media and—more importantly—the judge and Nadia's take on it. I can't do my job if you are keeping things from me."

Cole sighed. "I don't know what's up with this girl." He spread his hands. "That's the truth of it. I don't think she even likes me."

"But you like her."

Cole closed his eyes. "I don't know. Yes, I like her as a person. She's different than… well, any of the women around here." And she was. She was tough and strong but also soft. Soft in all of the ways that pulled on his heart and his dick. "I like her as a person," he repeated. "But I can't see us together. It'd never work."

She'd never want him. That was the truth of the matter. It wasn't insecurity talking. He just wasn't the type of man that she would go for. She'd laugh in his face if he ever tried. And the reality was, when you pushed all of the attraction and chemistry bullshit aside, he wasn't at a place in his life where he could take that. Not right now. And definitely not from her.

"So that's it?" Brad pushed. "You like her, but you guys aren't compatible. How was the sex?"

"What?"

"How was the sex?" Brad repeated the question slowly and clearly. The man had no shame.

"Does it matter?"

"Yes. It absolutely matters. I don't want to know the placement of your dick; I just want to know if it was dreary or life-shattering."

"It was great." Cole looked away. "And disappointing."

The big man waited, in no apparent rush to make their mediation on time. When Cole didn't elaborate, he pushed. "Explain."

"I'll sound like a pussy." Cole exhaled, regretting this path of honesty.

"It's just you and me here. And I love pussy. Give it to me."

Cole winced. "She was on her stomach. It felt disconnected."

"Are you a typically a 'make love' type of guy?"

"No." Cole rubbed his thighs and wished in that moment to be anywhere else. "I fuck." And he did. That was the name of the Cole Masten Bedroom Show: Fucking. Even with Nadia, *especially* with Nadia. That was what they did. That was really all they ever did. Just another relationship realization a half-decade too late.

"So…" Brad mused. "You had sex with her, and it was great, but you wanted to have more of a connection with her. You like her, but blah-blah-blah you two are too different for it to work. Do you hear the giant holes in this?"

Cole met his eyes. "What do you want from me? Are you trying to convince me to date the girl?" He shook his head. "I'm a little confused over here."

"I want you to be happy. I want to do my job so that you can move past this divorce and have a chance at normality."

"Normality?" Cole laughed, raising his hands in exasperation. "I'm in a roped off room with my assistant standing bodyguard, in a town I don't even fit into anymore, late to a conversation with my wife and her attorneys who—six *fucking* weeks ago were my attorneys—to discuss division of a life that I was pretty happy with. Normality in Hollywood is as twisted as our deals."

"You live here, you work in the industry. You don't have to *be* it."

"Is this still about Summer? Or is this a fucking psych session about my life now?" Cole stood, his voice rising.

When Brad rose, squaring off against him, the dynamic changed. Cole stepped a pace back.

"Let's go to mediation. Keep your mouth shut in there, and let me do my job. When you get back to Quincy, I want you to get your head straight about Summer. Either date, or befriend, or stay the fuck away from her. But you need to make a decision one way or the other because otherwise you're going to drive her and yourself crazy and ruin the movie in the process." Brad put sunglasses on and nodded to the door. "Let's go."

Cole waited like an obedient dog for Brad to pass, then he followed. When they stepped into the sun, he saw Justin. And beside him, her head tilted back in a laugh, was a strange brunette. He tensed, then saw Brad approach her, his hand wrapping around her waist. This must be the soulmate. So glad to know she was present to witness this train wreck.

"Julia," Brad said. "This is—"

"Cole Masten," she interrupted with a smile. "I'm aware. And I'm sorry for aiding my husband in his evil plot to destroy your breakfast." She gripped DeLuca's arm with affection, and Cole tersely nodded. The woman was obviously insane. Any woman who chose to spend a life with that man had a death wish. A vision of Summer on her porch flashed in his mind, how her eyes stuck to Brad, her warm smile at him, and Cole's mood darkened further.

"Are we leaving?"

Brad shot him a warning look and kissed his wife, a kiss that lasted a breath too long, in Cole's opinion. "There's a driver up front in an S-Class. Do you want to use him, or would you prefer to drive?"

"I'll use the driver. Get some shopping in while you boys work." She hugged Justin, and Cole wondered, at what point in crazy time, she'd managed to break his shell. She turned to Cole, and he stiffened, not ready for a third pep talk this morning. "It was nice to meet you." She stuck out a hand, and he breathed a sigh of relief, shaking her hand, his eyes catching the details. The rock on her finger. The tan skin, peeking out from a slouchy tee and capris. Her barely present makeup and long, natural hair. She released his hand, and he stopped himself from wondering if she'd be friends with Summer. This was ridiculous. The girl was stalking his thoughts.

His feet moved, following Brad and Justin to the front, a mini traffic jam caused by the crowd of hotel guests waiting in the lobby, their camera phones out. He swallowed. This place had only thirty suites, and every single resident must be there, on their toes, hands waving excitedly for his attention. He smiled, big and beautiful, his eyes dead behind his shades. Out front, steps away, his car. His retreat. He ducked into it, waiting for Justin, watching Brad step into an adjacent Mercedes, his wife taking an identical one. "You know where we're going?" he growled to Justin, hitting the gas before the man's door had safely shut.

"It was one mistake. I'll have the manager fired. Don't be an asshole about it." Justin pointed to the outside lane. "Four lights down, take a right. It'll be a block down."

Cole's tires squealed on their exit from the hotel, and it was the only sound until he pulled to a stop at their destination.

Either date, or befriend, or stay the fuck away from her. Those had been the options offered by DeLuca.

But how could he choose between three impossibilities?

CHAPTER 78

"In Hollywood, brides keep the bouquets and throw away the groom."
~ Groucho Marx

Nadia was, as always, flawless. Cole studied her face, the perfect lines of her makeup, and wondered, as he often had, why she bothered with the team that arrived every morning, equipped with makeup brushes and extensions, their home's dressing room turned into a circus for a valuable hour in the morning that'd be better served sleeping. She didn't need all of it; she was beautiful without it. And for a day like today, for her to know she'd be sitting across from him, her jilted husband, the extra effort seemed cruel. But that was Nadia. She'd always wanted everyone to want her, especially those who she rejected. She looked up from the document and met his eyes.

"You have beautiful eyes." The first line after their first screw, which had happened minutes after he'd walked into his trailer and found her stretched out on his bed. She'd said the word shyly, her feet sliding to the edge of the bed and off, and he'd shrugged.

"Thank you." That had been his unimaginative response. He hadn't needed imagination.

"They distract from your nose." She had wrinkled her own and raised to her tiptoes, the movement pushing out her bare breasts. From her new height she had peered at his nose, then dropped to her heels again. Her breasts had bounced back into place; he had stared. *"I have a guy, if you want a referral. He did my roommate's nose. Really great work."*

"My nose?" It had drawn his attention away from her breasts and to

her eyes. *"Are you joking?"* Even then, he'd been a superstar, one Oscar already in the bag. And his nose, broken twice—once from a fight and once from a snowboarding injury—was one of his trademarks. It took the polish off his pretty boy features and made him rugged. Now, looking back, he could see how calculated she'd been. Playing the part of the cool girl who wasn't impressed by the big star. She'd played him hot and cold, didn't fuck him again until a third date, and had him tie her up on the fifth. She'd been a porn star in the bedroom and used every bit of his money, power, and name to fuel her own star. She'd been an unscripted extra on that first movie. On his second, she'd played a minor role with lines. Then graduated to supporting roles. Five days after their wedding—a gaudy affair that had made every magazine cover—she got her first big-budget, starring role. From nothing to famous in a year.

He hadn't been stupid; he'd known her ambition. It had been one of the things that had attracted him to her. And he'd been happy to help. But now, glancing down at the agreement, red pen marks all over the page, he wondered if there had ever been any love between them at all. Had he just been a mark, perfectly played?

"Okay, so we've worked through all of the assets. Cole will get the boat, plane, and the Montana ranch; Nadia will get the California and Hawaii real estate. All bank accounts will go to their respective owners with the joint account split, leaving five hundred thousand for any outstanding items and attorneys' fees. Attorneys' fees will also be split. Nadia's future earnings will be hers, as will Cole's." The mediator stopped and looked to DeLuca, a stumble in her voice before continuing, "Nadia has agreed to forfeit all ownership or claims on *The Fortune Bottle* in exchange for five percent of recurring royalties on Cole's current backlist of movies and endorsement deals." She took a deep breath. "Do we all agree on the basics of this agreement?"

Cole looked at Nadia, who nodded, her mouth tight. She was pissed; he could see it in the small wrinkles around her mouth, in the glower of her eyes. He should have been happy about that, but he wasn't. He was sick—over the day's worth of arguments, over the reduction of their relationship to insignificant line items and who gets the fucking Picassos. Thank God for DeLuca, who'd been worth his weight in gold, and the mediator, a beady-eyed woman who was actually competent.

"Cole?" the mediator pushed. "Do you agree on the basics of this agreement?"

"Yes." He kept his eyes on hers. If she backed out now, if she dragged this into court and further, he would let DeLuca off his leash to do everything the man had been fighting to do since he was hired.

"Nadia?"

The gap in between the question and her reply lasted years. Cole held his breath, his eyes on hers, the defiance in them ending in the moment that they fell to the table. "Yes," she said in a wounded fashion, like she wasn't walking out of there rich. At least she wasn't getting *The Fortune Bottle*. At least he had one untainted thing in his life.

Summer came to mind and then left, a page pushed in front of him for his signature. "This is legally binding," the mediator reminded them. "It will let the court know of your decision and will stand in place until your attorneys can draw up all of the corresponding paperwork."

Cole scrawled his name and wondered how long it would take for the messy signature to show up online, the details of their separation spread open for anyone with an internet connection. Nadia understood, same as he did, the damage that this could do to their reputations – the hidden skeletons that mud slinging would bring out. It was why they had stayed relatively cordial during this process. It was also the only reason that they'd managed to reach an agreement during mediation, both of them opposed to court.

DeLuca waited until Nadia signed, her signature neat and perfect, then spoke, "We'll be in touch with initial drafts of our agreements next week."

"In a hurry, aren't we?" Nadia spoke from her seat at the table, her eyes on Cole. Interesting words from a woman who served him divorce papers so quickly. He didn't respond, just stood, grabbing his sunglasses off the table and putting them on.

"Nadia?" He smiled when she turned, her hand tugging on the handle of her Hermes. "It's been an absolute pleasure."

She smiled brightly, and the sum of their entire relationship could be condensed into that exchange: two actors playing their parts to perfection.

Sad that it took so long for him to finally see that.

CHAPTER 79

Cocky was freaking adorable. Entitled and adorable. Cole, apparently, didn't think that a chicken could spend the night outside. He'd set up the downstairs bathroom for him, and I could pretty much guarantee you that Cyndi Kirkland would castrate him herself when she saw the state of it. I stood in the door and eyed the floor (covered in newspaper), the walls (pecked to bits), and the chicken poo, which had managed to paint the toilet, sink, tissue holder, and windowsill. The troublemaker stood on the toilet seat and tilted his head at me.

I had received, from some organizational freak of nature named Justin, a detailed list of items concerning Cocky's care. The list included such ridiculousness as:

#8 Cocky gets scared by loud noises (dogs barking and the dryer). Please sit with him in this event and do not run a load of clothes in the dryer.

As well as:

#17 Cocky is accustomed to being taken out once during the night. Please take him into the backyard between the hours of midnight and six AM and allow him fifteen minutes to roam the yard. Make SURE that the fence is locked and do not allow him to jump or fly over the fence.

How does someone keep a chicken inside a fence? I had closed my eyes at that one, picturing Cocky running off into the cotton fields, and me, standing at the edge of the fence, hollering the rooster's name like a crazy woman.

Cole's lucky that it's me chicken-sitting. Anyone else and his reputation in this town would be ruined. The locals, especially the men, would crucify him over this. I closed the door. According to Justin's directions, Cocky's bedtime is at nine. The previous night, I was a wild and cool babysitter and let him run around the backyard until ten. This night, with Cole coming home, I had him in his bathroom early. I couldn't think straight with his baby wattle jiggling at me. I shut the door to his squawk and flipped off the hall light, heading up the stairs and toward Cole's bedroom.

This was so stupid. Sitting here, waiting for him to come back. I didn't want to be at Cole Masten's beck and call. He'd made that comment in the heat of phone sex passion. He probably didn't mean it. He'd probably walk in the door and scoff at me to get out of his house. I stepped into his room and smoothed the edge of the bedspread. I'd made the bed; I couldn't help myself. Made it and thought, with every tuck, smooth, and tug, about him messing it back up with my body.

My fingers itched for activity. If I'd been in my house, I'd have cooked. Made some chocolate chip cookies and bagged up the extras for the crew. Even though Mary said that isn't done, her eyebrows rising in alarm when I brought a carrot cake in for the prop master's birthday. Apparently there was some bullshit line drawn between 'talent' and 'crew,' and we'd all burst into flames if any cordiality existed between the two. I was supposed to treat them like hired help, and they were supposed to like it.

I didn't want to cook in his house. I already felt like some fifties housewife. I walked to the window and looked out over the dark field and toward the airport. I should go outside. I'd be able to see his plane from there.

When I stepped outside I realized I forgot my shoes. I think they were by Cocky's bathroom, where I had slipped them off. I considered going back, but stepped out onto the front porch and to the steps. I sat on the first big step, the wood damp from the afternoon rain, and wrapped my arms around my knees, my head lifted toward the sky. It was cloudy, the moon brightly illuminating the clouds and shadows, bright points of stars dotting the black canvas beneath. I read in a magazine once about light pollution. It is a real thing, our millions of artificial lights eating away at our world's darkness and ruining our ability to see the galaxies beyond us. Like smog, but instead of eating clean air, our lights eat pitch black, and leave us all in a haze of dusk. I could see it when I looked south to Tallahassee. The entire horizon glowed in that direction; the city lights diluting the big city residents their chance at perfect star gazing.

I didn't think we'd ever have that problem in Quincy. Even with the Pit's kliegs that ran constantly, crews working until late setting up for each next day… our sky was still perfect, its stars clearly defined.

I wondered, not for the first time since cashing my movie paycheck, where I would go from here. With more money than I'd ever had, I had no excuse to stay. I could buy Mama a house and move along with my life. I could move anywhere, do anything. Go to college, take art lessons, buy a horse.

Anything.

A terrifying concept.

Above me, a plane approached.

"Well, sure, Scott cheated. He's a man… they make mistakes. But you know, the Bible says that you should forgive them. Not bring the wrath of hell. That's for God to do, not us. Our job is to forgive and forget."

"Has your family forgiven Summer?

"Well, no. Some things are just unforgiveable, and what she did was one of them. If we all just forgave her, then she wouldn't learn her lesson."

CHAPTER 80

"Congrats man." Justin walked from the back of the plane, his hand patting Cole's shoulder as he passed. Taking the seat across from him, he popped the cap off a beer and held it out.

"I'm good." Cole waved it off. "You sleep well?"

"I did 'til we hit that turbulence." He shrugged. "It'll be fine. My painkillers put me under, so I'll pop a few of those when we get to your place."

Cole shook his head. "No. You're not staying with me."

Justin's beer stopped at his lips, his eyebrows raised. "I'm not?"

"No. Sorry. There's a bed and breakfast in town. You can stay there." Cole moved the curtain and glanced out the window.

Justin chuckled. "Anxious to get there?"

"I'm just tired of traveling. Plus, I can't wait to see your reaction to Quincy."

"It can't be as bad as Bismarck. At least there's no snow."

Cole smiled. "It's not Bismarck. Tomorrow, after filming, I'll give you the tour."

Justin glanced at his watch. "You're really not letting me stay with you? I had my hopes set on seeing Casa Rooster."

"Sorry." Cole sat back in the seat. His fingers tapped against his leg, and he looked out, anxious for the small lights of Quincy.

He dropped Justin off at the Raine House and pulled off, the streets quiet, streetlights dim, the clock on the courthouse glowing in the dark. He hadn't realized, with the time change, how late he would be getting back. Rubbing at an ache on the back of his neck, he contemplated calling Summer. It had been an inner debate that had lasted all day. He'd been holding back itchy fingers ever since she had hung up on him. *Goodbye Cole.* He shifted in his seat.

When he pulled down the drive, a light was on in the back of the house, the glow hitting a few rooms, and he sat in the truck for a minute, the engine off, and watched it. Was she in there? He hadn't been thinking when he had said that—putting into words what he had wanted to do since the day she opened her front door.

The minute I get off that plane I will drive there, pin you down on my bed, and worship your pussy. I won't stop until my mouth is imprinted on your mind and your taste is my fucking middle name."

He winced at the memory. Maybe she didn't hear it. Maybe she put up Cocky and was sitting at her own house, not even thinking about the possibility of a night full of fucking. He pushed on the front of his jeans, willing his cock to soften. Yeah, she was probably at home, doing her own thing, oblivious to the thoughts that Cole had been having all day.

He opened the door and got out, grabbing his leather duffel from the backseat and walking up the front stairs. When he opened the front door, he knew instantly that she wasn't there.

CHAPTER 81

I couldn't do it. I couldn't wait there and be his sex toy, no matter how much I'd enjoy it. Cole Masten was dangerous to my heart, to my self-worth, to my future self.

I would film this movie with him.
I would cash my check.
And then I would get out of Quincy.

CHAPTER 82

The next morning, I studied my bagel with particular interest when Cole walked in. We were in one of the conference rooms, one of those random meetings scheduled for no clear purpose. I'd been dreading it since I woke up that morning, unsure how to interact with the man who I had just had phone sex with. I mean, I thought it was phone sex. I always thought phone sex would be more complex, detailed descriptions needed from both parties, more directions involved, the entire thing lasting longer than our quick encounter had been. But I came. And I thought he came. And we'd been on the phone. So… yeah. I was pretty sure that was what phone sex was all about.

My bagel was wheat. I hated wheat. Unless it had blueberries. But Mary said they didn't have blueberry, even though two seats down, one of the ADs was going to town on one, and I could see the blue dots on it. She smeared strawberry cream cheese on the top in an attempt to make up for it, but I didn't like flavored cream cheese, a preference that, if I pointed it out now, would only make me look difficult. So I was stuck with this bastard of a breakfast creation, her beady eyes glued to me, just waiting for me to take a bite so that she could cross one neatly-written item off her list: Feed Summer. I took a small bite. Yep. Nasty.

I could feel when he sat down in the seat next to mine, his long legs stretching out under the table, one bumping against me, and I shifted, pulling my feet under my chair, his shoulder coming into my peripheral vision as he leaned over. I ignored him, my study of the top of the bagel unwavering in its intensity.

"Morning." His voice was rough, like he'd recently woken up and hadn't yet spoken.

I smiled politely and took a bite of the bagel, my eyes moving to the left, away from Cole, looking for something, anything, to focus on. I hadn't prepared for this, had hoped he would be as uninterested as I was in conversation. My eyes found Becky, one of the producers, the one who was leading this meeting, and willed her to begin. I shouldn't have arrived early. I should have ducked in at the last minute, and would have, had Mary not been a freakin' drill sergeant, her schedule worked down to the minute, any hope of my lagging disappearing with the first tap of her Timex.

"How late were you at the house last night?" Oh my word. He wasn't letting this go.

"Shhh…" I hushed, glancing around, worried about who might hear. It was the wrong thing to do, him shuffling up in his seat and leaning closer, his head close to my ear.

"It's an innocent question. How late were you there?"

I shrugged. "I'm not sure. You're welcome, by the way. For watching Cocky." I turned my head slightly to him, not too far to touch him, but enough that I saw the curve of his mouth when he grinned.

"Thank you."

"You're welcome." I took the last, painful bite of the bagel and pushed the rest aside. It was a calculated amount of nibbles. Enough not to offend, not too much for Mary to think I actually liked it.

"I wish you'd stayed."

My heart lost a beat in those words. I tried to recover it, tried to breathe normally, to *act* normally. *I wish you'd stayed.* A simple grouping of four ordinary words. But they were like peanut butter cookies. Four simple ingredients: peanut butter, sugar, flour, and egg. Together, they created something most women loved.

I hated peanut butter cookies. And I hated that sentence out of his mouth.

Because no matter how much it would have complicated everything, no matter how much of a mistake it would have been—

I wish I'd stayed too.

Becky cleared her throat and began the meeting, and I, for a little longer, was saved.

CHAPTER 83

Summer was acting weird. Weird even for her. Jumpy. Skittish. Avoiding eye contact. Avoiding conversation at all costs. Cole stared at the wall in his trailer and tried to think of the last time they'd had a direct conversation with each other. In the conference room? Right after he'd returned from LA to an empty house. That had been it. And that hadn't been much of a conversation at all. And that'd been a week ago.

He'd tried pissing her off, and she hadn't bitten. He'd tried being friendly and she'd cut him off. He was running out of options, other than dragging her into his trailer and forcing her to talk.

"You there?"

He flinched at the voice and turned to Justin, who sat opposite him, script pages spread out between them. "What?"

"You zoned out. Did you hear anything I just said? About Tokyo?"

"No."

"Rentho's Tokyo premiere is next week. We need to shift your shooting schedule to accommodate it, so Don wants to know how many days you'll be out." He arched an eyebrow, pen in hand, twitching above a calendar. "Five?"

"The Japan premiere is now? I thought we were waiting."

"They bumped it up, back in July." Probably around the time of Justin's accident.

Cole nodded. "I'm not going."

"Why?"

"We're getting stuff done here; this is more important. When are we filming thirty-eight?" Thirty-eight. The sex scene between Royce and Ida.

"We were going to push it 'til after the Japanese premiere. Don wants to give Summer some more time to—"

"No," Cole interrupted. "We can't wait." He couldn't wait. Not an extra minute, much less a week. The sex scene had been another add-on, one he'd pushed the writers for. One that Summer had fought tooth and nail. "We'll do it next week, and I'll skip the premiere. Send Charlize instead, she loves those things."

"When are you just going to admit to yourself that you like her?" Justin put down the pen, and Cole looked away.

"I do like her. That's not an issue. I like you, too; though I hate admitting that even more." He grinned, but Justin didn't grin back.

"Stop fucking around."

Cole's grin dropped, and his gaze hardened. "I'm not fucking around. She's hot; I'm hot. There's a flirtation there. If I want to fuck her, I'll fuck her. If I want to like her, I'll like her. If I want to hate her, I'll do that too. The movie is most important, and everything that I've been doing with her is for that end game. *The Fortune Bottle* is killing it in those cuts. You know, you've seen it."

"So that's what this is? You're playing the little Georgian's heartstrings to get your movie a statuette?" Justin's gaze never left Cole's, the strength never left his shoulder, his voice didn't back down, and Cole respected that. Even when he hated it.

"Nobody's playing that girl's heart. She won't give me the time of day."

Justin laughed, pushing away from the table, to standing, his hands resting on the glass top of it as he leaned forward. "She's protecting herself, Cole. The best she can. Hell, if I had a snatch I'd put a steel trap on it before I stepped in the same room as you."

"She's not protecting herself," Cole said, his head tilting up to look at Justin, his hands tightening on the edge of the chair arms. That wasn't what Summer's frostiness was all about. It was because she didn't like Cole, despite the attraction between them.

But as he said the words, worked through the thought process, there was, in the back of his mind, doubt.

CHAPTER 84

SCENE 38: ROYCE AND IDA: LOVE SCENE AT ROYCE'S HOUSE

When Mary banged on my door, I ignored it, my arms wrapped around my knees, my thumb pressing at buttons on the remote without thought. I used to wonder why they put a TV in my trailer; it wasn't like I had time to lounge around and watch cable. But now I knew. It was for moments of panic, the last line of defense against skittish actresses whose toes were itching to leave. Mary banged again, her delicate little fists doing an impressive number on my locked door. The phone on the kitchenette rang, the third time that had happened in the last fifteen minutes.

I had understood the scene, I had known the need for it, I had finally stopped my complaining and been a big girl about it but now time had run out. It was time for the scene. And every pep talk I'd given myself had run out of gas. I couldn't do it. I wouldn't do it. No.

A new voice joined the chorus outside my door, and I tightened my grip on my knees. *Him.* I turned up the volume, Judge Judy giving it to some redneck who had promised to babysit a dog, then didn't. I murmured support and almost missed the jiggle of my trailer's handle, the door swinging open, the glare of incoming sunshine sliced by one muscular male form. My eyes dropped to the giant key ring now dangling from my lock. Figured. It was only a matter of time. I had hoped for Don. Or Eileen. Or anyone but him.

"I'm not doing it," I repeated, my eyes back on the TV, and there was still hope, in all of this madness, that I wouldn't cry.

"You have to do it. You signed a contract." He spoke from the middle of the room, the door settling shut behind him, his legs slightly spread, hands hanging at his side. This was his first time in my trailer, and it was too small of a space for both of us.

"The contract didn't say anything about me being naked on camera."

"Correction. The contract didn't say anything about you *not* being naked on camera. That is a very important distinction, and it's not my fault your dimwit ex missed that."

There was a horrific moment of weakness when my bottom lip trembled, nerves inside of me breaking, one by one. "Please go away." My voice cracked on the first word, and out of the edge of blurry eyes I saw him move closer, his knees hitting the floor beside the couch.

"Summer." His voice was quiet, softer, but I didn't look over, wouldn't give him the satisfaction of seeing my weakness.

"I'm not doing it. I haven't…" I stared at the top of Judge Judy's head and blinked quickly. "I haven't been naked in front of anyone in a long time. Other than… you know." *Other than you.* A stupid disclosure to have to add. I ran a backwards palm across my cheek, my pinky catching the moisture of a stack of unshed tears. "And I'm not doing it now, not in front of all of those people—" My words almost hiccupped, and I stopped. Pulled up my T-shirt, over my chin, and pressed the material into my wet eyes. Those lights. God, when he and I were being filmed, you could stand in Thomasville and see the details of our faces, we were lit so strongly. What would it be like to be naked under those lights?

"You're not really naked—" Cole started, and I snorted against my shirt. The outfit that Wardrobe had dropped off was a set of pasties—two nude ones for my breasts and then one long panty-liner looking one, which I was supposed to stick in between my legs. I had tried it, had peeled off the backing and gently, then more firmly, pressed the cold stickers against my flesh, my reflection in the mirror too much for me to look at. That was when you knew you were doing something wrong, when you couldn't look at yourself in the mirror to face it. Now, under my T-shirt, the pasties pulled a little on my skin when I shifted, a constant reminder of the disaster looming before me.

"Summer…" His voice was calming and sweet, a plea for something, and it made me madder than a branded bull, my hands dropping from my face, the T-shirt falling, my head turning to him. He was still on his knees, and I caught him mid-motion, his hand moving back to his thighs. He'd been checking his watch. Any weakness in me vanished, and I gripped onto my anger and held it like a shield. *He'd been checking his watch.* Screw the concerned face, the friendly and caring position, Cole Masten, kneeling beside his injured costar, his voice tugging at her to behave. Screw my contract; if I didn't want to do it, I didn't have to do it. We'd filmed too many scenes, it'd be too expensive for them to start over with a new Ida.

"Get off my floor." My tone was a knife, solid and sharp, and Cole looked up in surprise. I swung my feet off the couch and stood, the sticker between my legs pulling painfully at little hairs, the entire ensemble covered by a pair of sweatpants.

Cole didn't move. Of course. The man couldn't—wouldn't—do what anyone told him. He just watched me, and I stopped before the front window of the trailer and peeked through the blinds. There was a group still out there. Don was there, as was Eileen, as were the requisite PAs and Mary, her pen moving furiously over a new Post-It, and I could imagine it stuck to her bathroom mirror at her hotel, her frantic message bright and red on the yellow. *Find A New Job.*

I dropped my hand from the blinds, and they fell back into place. "The movie doesn't need the sex scene."

"It's the climax of the relationship arc. Of course it does." Cole finally stood, easing up slowly, and he met my eyes when he spoke, the authority back in his voice, his coddling tone from earlier gone.

"A body double." The idea was sudden and brilliant, and I hated that I hadn't thought of it before. It happened all the time, I remembered watching *Pretty Woman* after reading that Julia Roberts had used one. I'd stared at every single clip of their love scenes and could never see anything that gave it away. "There's got to be some clause I can sign, and you can use a double. Easy!" My hand trembled against the top of my air conditioning unit, and I squeezed it into a fist to stop the shake. This would be fine; this could be fixed. I moved to the door, Cole stepping forward as if to stop me, and I yanked it open. "Don!" I called, the director turning from the crowd, his head tilting up at me. I waved him in, and Cole groaned, lifting his hands, his fingers finding each other, linking, and settling onto the top of his head. Don ducked in the trailer, the door shut, and now it was really crowded.

"I want a body double." I chirped out my new idea, standing close to Don, my arms crossed around my chest, and I watched closely as Don glanced at Cole.

Cole shrugged his shoulders, his face impassive and stubborn. "Isn't happening. We don't have a five-foot-six blonde in your body type just lying around the set, waiting to strip off her clothes and get in front of the camera. And we don't have time to go through casting. That could take a week, or longer, which we can't afford."

I focused on Don. "Florida State is forty-five minutes away." I gestured in the general direction of Tallahassee. "You have twenty thousand college girls there. Trust me, you'll find someone who would be more than happy to strip naked and hop into bed with *him*." I felt an odd burn of something dark, the image too clear in my mind, and I pushed it aside.

"Glad to know that our Pecan Queen knows casting so well."

I glared at Cole. "I know that if we put up a tent on Landis Green you'll have two hundred girls stripping naked for a casting camera within two hours. If you can't find one who looks like me before dinner time, I'll—"

"What?" Cole cut in. "You'll do the shoot?" He stepped forward, his hands dropping from his head, a smile curving over his face. "Let's make a bet, Country." He glanced back at his watch as if he couldn't remember the time. "It's eight-thirty. Right now, let's pack up some cameras and a team, and do it. Take your ridiculous suggestion and see. But if we don't find a girl by six o'clock tonight, then *you're* filming this, first thing tomorrow morning, and I don't want to hear shit about it. No tears, no woe is me bullshit. You're gonna man up, and be a professional about it."

I rolled my bottom lip against my teeth, and glanced at Don who looked back and forth between Cole and me like we were insane. "Okay." I nodded. "But I'm coming, so are Don and Eileen. If three of the four of us agree that a girl will work, then I win, and I don't have to do the scene at all."

Don stepped in, holding up a hand. "This is the stupidest thing I've ever heard, but if this has any chance of working, I'd need you to do some close up stuff. Kissing, gasping, et cetera."

"But you could do that with a strapless bra on," Cole interjected. "And shorts." He stuck out his hand. "Deal?"

I shook it without pausing to think, without pausing to examine the details or require more stipulations. I shook and felt an enormous wave of relief.

The man, I was certain, had never been to Florida State. It was where God vomited all of his beauties. We wouldn't need until six o'clock. We'd have a dozen options by lunch.

CHAPTER 85

"If you weren't financing this movie, I'd have you fired. An impromptu public casting call? On a film day?" Don stood in the middle of activity, his arms waving in the air like an inflatable tube man, his face a dark shade of red, sweat streaking down his temples. Behind him, one of the set trailers was being packed up, a dozen people moving in concert—lights, rigs, cables, and signage flowing in one smooth sea of motion.

"It'll be fine," Cole said with a smile, slapping the director on the back, his hand snagging the shirt of a passing PA. "You. What's your name?"

"Ugh…" The kid's eyes darted to Don, then back to Cole. "Tim Myers."

"Tim, find Justin and get him here."

Don's mouth tightened into a thin line, and he ran a hand over the top of his bald head. "Do you know how much this will cost—this stupid bet between you two?"

"We need the scene, and she's not doing it without it." Cole smiled. "Relax, Don. It's not your money, it's mine."

"And it's my career if this movie tanks. Or runs out of funding. Or if my costars kill each other before the last shot is wrapped. We could have just covered her with a sheet and filmed it. All this…" Don watched a man run by, his arms full of clipboards, "is ridiculous."

"I don't want to film some fucking Nicholas Sparks love scene. I want raw, sexy footage. I told you that; you know that. We can't build up to something and then leave the audience hanging."

"Sure." Don looked up at him. "Let's pretend that's what it's about." He stepped closer to Cole and lowered his voice. "But we both know that it's not."

Cole shrugged. "Just get me the scene I want. If I need a therapist, I'll have…" He snapped his fingers in the direction of the departing PA.

"Tim Myers," Don supplied.

"Yeah. Tim Myers will get me one." He threw an arm over the director's shoulder. "Now. Let's get on the road."

CHAPTER 86

I wanted to drive. It made sense for me to drive. I knew my way around Tallahassee, could get our two SUVs, plus the trailing semi, in the general area of where we needed to go without it becoming the circus act that it seemed destined to be. But I wasn't on the insurance, and I was a woman, and between those two gigantic hurdles, I got stuck in the backseat, staring at the freshly cut hairline of Cole Masten, dark hair meeting in a straight union with tan skin. I'd bet his neck was shaved with a straight blade. Probably on set, the team all but trying to give me a bikini wax every time I set foot into the Hair & Makeup trailer.

I noticed, staring at that freshly cut hairline, that my bet with myself, made that first night in my kitchen, had never been won, his skin a golden hue of tan. Of course, he hadn't burnt. Instead he'd bronzed, because gods like Cole Masten didn't suffer from mortal problems like the rest of us. I looked away from the bane of my existence and out the window, the car slowing as we got deeper into the traffic disaster that was the capital city.

On Florida State's campus, Landis Green stretched from one ugly traffic circle to the Strozier Library, a gorgeous building where—just a few years or so ago—a student brought in a gun and went crazy one late night during finals. Mama and I had sat in front of the TV, slices of lemon pie uneaten before us, and watched the live action unfold. *Right there*, Momma kept saying. *Remember when I used to take you right there*? I had remembered. Sunday afternoons, after church, we used to go into Tallahassee. We'd eat a late lunch at Momo's, then head to the library. I'd sit down against a wall and read novels inappropriate for my age, and Momma would read their papers. She'd start with the *New Yorker* and work through three rows of publications before we'd pack up, walk back to our car, and head home for dinner. I could still remember the smell of the building, the green plaid print of their carpet, the look of pinched student faces, their books spread out over long tables like they were claiming spots, knees jumping, pens tapping. When I started high school, I stopped going, old enough to stay at home alone. A few years later, Momma also stopped going. Maybe she needed me with her to make it stick. Maybe, without me, it lost its fun. I looked out the window, at the big library, and felt a moment of sad nostalgia. When I moved away, would she stop making biscuits on Sunday morning? Would she stop taking walks on nice evenings? How much of her life would slowly stop?

"Summer."

I heard my name and looked up to the front of the car, Cole's eyes on mine in the rearview mirror. "What?"

"You gonna get out?"

I swallowed a smart response and reached for the handle, stopping when I saw the man at my door, his hand on the handle. I hesitated, my eyes catching everything that I had missed in my walk down memory lane. Three suits on this side of the car. A line of cops behind them, facing out. I turned to the front seat, to ask a question, but the doors were all being opened, mine included, and the men were stepping out. I grabbed my bag, and took the hand offered, stepping into the summer sun. A cheer broke out and I turned in the direction of the sound, my eyebrows raising, and saw Cole raise his hand, a bright white smile beaming out from that famous face, his index finger pushing his sunglasses on, the crowd on the other side of the cops surging forward, then pushed back, a living beast that seemed to have no decorum whatsoever. I suddenly appreciated the stoic pride that Quincy held, their refusal to fawn or fangirl. I couldn't imagine if every day, every experience required this level of ridiculousness. I followed the trio of men, security following me closely, a stranger with an earpiece putting a protective hand on my shoulder. I glared at him, and he removed it.

Before us, a staked out orange safety fence led to the trailer, which was parked next to a fountain on the far end of the lawn. A second crowd had formed there, and it turned as one as we approached, hands and cell phones filling the air, an excited hum floating through the crowd. We were stopped halfway to the trailer, Eileen pulling a cell phone away from her ear long enough to dictate information.

"We'll have a tent set up in fifteen minutes for the signups and age verifications. I'll be there and will narrow down the pool as they register. If I see a possible candidate, I'll have them escorted to the trailer. Cole, we'll put you and Don in the viewing end. Summer, you stay with me."

I swallowed my objection, the woman already moving, our group pushing after her. Cole slowed his steps, slinging an arm around my shoulders. "You look irritated, Country."

"What happens in the trailer?" I nodded toward it, watching as a group of orange-vested men rolled a large tent out on the grass. The speed at which all of this had come together was impressive.

"We'll take some test shots. See how the girl looks on camera."

"Naked." I looked up at him and he laughed.

"Well, yes. That's what we need."

"Rough afternoon for you." I could feel my lips tighten, and I hated the reaction. It was the objectification of the women that bothered me. Nothing else.

"I'd rather be looking at someone else."

I shrugged off his arm and squashed the bit of joy that came from the flirtatious remark. "Just focus on your bet. I'd hate for you to lose to a girl."

"We need this out now, before those jackasses at THR scoop this."

"Envision is going to have our ass. You know that, right? Putting this out without giving them a heads up."

"Just let legal know to be ready. But this is it. The cover. You've got three days before it goes to print. Make it happen."

CHAPTER 87

Live events were always a pain in the ass. Cole smiled, his side aching from a sharply-timed Summer elbow, and stopped, taking the pen from the closest girl and scribbling his name. Then again. Then again. He glanced at the closest suits, and they swarmed, pulling him away, Cole pretending to argue before signing one last notebook and stepping off. Summer snorted, and he glanced in her direction, her hands wrapped around a snow cone, her eyes meeting his before she looked away. Where the hell had she gotten a snow cone? He slapped at a bug on the back of his neck and ducked under the shade of the tent. From the far end of the road, the boom of a radio station satellite van started up. All this bullshit. But all necessary, all good. There'd be photos of this across every Seminole's social media feed within the hour. #FortuneBottleCasting would be trending on Twitter, if it weren't already. Every class would be skipped, and every hot coed would be here, Tweeting and Instagramming their hot pink nails off. The best advertising a day off filming could provide. And if it could get Summer Jenkins practically naked and on top of him? Hey, even better.

He climbed the steps into the air-conditioned trailer, and nodded to Don and Justin, taking the available seat and scooting it forward slightly. Before them, the west end of the trailer held a white backdrop, two photographers at work with cameras and lights. Behind them, a changing room and single chair, for the girl on deck.

"Eileen got the release forms?" Cole asked, twisting the top off a water bottle and taking a sip.

"Yep. Anyone walking in this door will be cleared and will have signed a non-disclosure. Not that any of this, with that circus outside, will be kept quiet." He sighed, the seventh or eight non-verbal indicator of how he felt about this event.

It wasn't smart. Not for the budget. What was smart was to have shot a different scene and had someone flown in from Central Casting. But Summer had challenged him, he'd called her bluff, and now they were here. Playing a game. And hell, it was fun. He glanced at the trailer window and saw Summer, seated at the table next to Eileen, her smile big as she laughed at something. See she was enjoying it too. And she only had a few months of obscurity left. Then the trailers would start, then the release would come, and overnight she'd be a household name. Poof. Everything, in an instant, different. She'd no longer be his secret; she'd belong to the world.

The trailer door opened, and a girl, blonde hair, the right height, the right build, stepped in. Tim handed her a robe, led her to the bathroom, and they all waited, a silent hum of anticipation in the room. A few minutes later, Cole heard the door open and the girl walked by, onto the set, her robe pulled tight, her smile gone, face nervous. Cole looked at her and saw Summer, her hunch against the couch, hands tight on her knees, her voice shaking.

"Next," Cole said, Don turning to look at him, his eyebrows raising.

"What?" the girl said quickly, her hands suddenly moving, jerking on her sash. "I'm ready."

"No." Cole looked down at the page before him and prayed that she hadn't already opened the robe. "Thank you for your time. There are signed movie posters by the exit. Justin?" Justin stepped up from his seat and to her side, his hand cupping her elbow as they moved past.

"What the fuck was that?" Don spoke out of the corner of his mouth, waiting for the door to shut before turning to Cole.

"She was nervous. Skittish. I don't need another Summer, who will require a pep talk. I want a girl who wants to be seen." He reclined in the seat and rested his boot on the table's axle. "Half the girls on this campus dance topless at house parties on the weekend. Let's find them and get this done." There was a large whoop from outside the trailer, and Justin stepped back inside, a smile on his face.

"Girls are doing body shots off the radio station van."

"See?" Cole spread his hands and leaned back in the chair. "Easy."

Maybe Summer was right. Maybe he would lose the bet after all. Maybe it would be for the best. Maybe, with a different girl under his hands, he'd finally get her out from under his skin.

The door opened, a fresh blonde walking in, and he turned, his eyes locking with hers. She grinned, and confidence, with this one, wouldn't be a problem.

CHAPTER 88

This was a stupid stupid stupid idea of mine. Especially because, riding back to Quincy, I was stuck in the far back of the truck, listening to a twenty-two-year-old girl prattle on about Emma Stone as if anyone gave two craps. Apparently Emma Stone was Carly's favorite actress. And she saw that movie that Emma and Cole were in together—you know, the one with the theme park killer? And she *loved* it. And she really really really thought that Emma Stone and Cole should do something else together. A love story. And she wanted to know if Emma Stone was as sweet in person—KILL ME NOW. Seriously. I just wanted them to pull this car over, let me hop out into the street, and then just plow me down. Cole would probably enjoy it. And I could finally end the torture of listening to this woman.

She had a tattoo on the back of her neck. I would have pointed it out to someone, but that would have lost me my bet and—thirty minutes earlier—I was so excited about winning that I overlooked the little discrepancies that made her different than me. Like her chest, which was definitely bigger. And the belly button ring, sparkling out from the bottom edge of her shirt. Ida Pinkerton would not have a tattoo or a belly button ring. The tattoo was of a dove. Why would someone want a *dove* permanently etched on the back of their neck? Or anywhere else for that matter.

When I was fourteen, I'd wanted a tattoo. Had big plans for my eighteenth birthday: the Chinese symbol for *grace* tattooed along my ribs. Because, yeah, what was more graceful than a country hillbilly with a rib tattoo? Thank God that I outgrew *that* phase. Otherwise I'd have nothing to sit back here and mentally trash talk about. I sighed and settled deeper into the tiny third row. Tattoo and belly ring aside, the girl was perfect. Ridiculously perfect. I peeked at the photos they shot of her. Photos where she was butt naked and smiling sunnily into the camera, not an ounce of insecurity on that face. Nothing like me, my sniffling, baby self, curled into a ball on my trailer's couch. Lord, I must have looked dumb. I was surprised that Cole did all this, allowed all this. I was surprised he didn't just laugh at me and tell me to toughen up. That was probably what I would have done to a girl wasting everyone's time and money.

I looked up front and saw him watching me. He glanced away, and I looked down. I felt sick. It was probably from riding in the back.

CHAPTER 89

It turned out that sex scenes have rehearsals just like a traditional scene. That would have been a good thing to know when I was in a stage three panic. It might have calmed my nerves to understand that Cole and I would walk through the scene fully clothed, just to understand what was happening, which cameras would be where, what would be said when. Also, instead of the camera operator right there by the bed, they were using the remotely operated cameraheads. Meaning there was some illusion of privacy. Unlike our kissing and office scenes, there wouldn't be someone *right there* looking between my legs.

We were on the fourth set, which was supposed to be Royce's bedroom. It was the ugliest bedroom I'd ever seen, but I guess, back in the thirties, that was what you got. Dark green carpet, horribly wallpapered walls, and a plaid bedspread: that was the décor a bachelor had. Not exactly the sleek *Mad Men* look I was expecting, but that was why these guys made the big bucks, and I watched YouTube videos on scrapbooking.

I'd also been wrong about the lights. I'd pictured the huge bright spotlights that we'd filmed under. But here, on this set, it seemed almost dim. And instead of five cameras, there were only two. Much more manageable. There was also no crowd of people. The grips and caterers and production assistants upon production assistants all gone, there were only six of us and—in the big room—it felt almost empty. It felt almost, with the dim lights, intimate. And that, for some reason, bugged me. It shouldn't have. I wasn't the one on the bed. Carly was. She was the one who'd been giggling like a banshee, even though Don had asked her twice to be serious. And she was the one on her back, naked as the day she was born—no pasties for her—her back arched off the mattress as Cole ran his lips down the center line of her stomach, one of his hands moving up one thigh. My stomach flipped in an unnatural way and I turned away from the bed, my hands shaking as I pushed my hair away from my face.

I felt a silent hand at my back and turned my head, careful not to look at the bed, wanting to cover my ears and drown out the sounds of Carly. "It's not that bad," Eileen whispered, her mouth close to my ear. "I promise, your part will be easy."

I closed my eyes and nodded, pretending, for both her sake and mine, that my performance is what I had been stressing over.

CHAPTER 90

"This part is easy." Cole rested his hands on either side of Summer's head, and she nodded. Looked away. He could feel her leg bouncing against the bed. "Congratulations," he added. "You won." He smiled, and her eyes moved to his, absolutely no reaction on her face. He shifted a little, uncomfortable, and wondered if he'd missed something. "Are you nervous?"

"No."

That had to be a lie. First, the evasion eye contact in the car. And now, her mouth was tight, eyes unmoving, her fingers tapped against the side of her legs, an unending rhythm, and he wanted to grab ahold of them. And her legs. Hold her still and make her look into his eyes and tell him what was wrong. Because it didn't seem like just nerves. It seemed like she was also mad. And over what? She'd won her bet, gotten her way. She should be happy.

"Okay, guys, we're ready to begin in five. Summer? Cole? You guys set?" She nodded, and he nodded, and then, silence fell, and it was just the two of them. No initial lines. No choreography. They were just supposed to kiss and caress, and she was supposed to give them all of the reactions that would replace the ones that the college chick had done. The sheet between them was thin, but she'd insisted on having it there, as well as her shorts and the strapless bra. He, on the other hand, hadn't changed from the first shoot, was still wearing the cock sock that had made Summer's eyes widen, her cheeks turn pink when he'd dropped the robe.

Silence fell on the set, and he stared down at her. There were so few times when he could really stare at her. She often caught him when he did, as if she could feel the weight of it. But in this moment, on camera, he was allowed, and he drank his fill, his eyes dragging from the light brown of her eyebrows to the thick fur of her lashes. Her golden eyes flicked to his, and he said nothing, did nothing, just watched the minute jumping of her pupils, their twitch as they settled. He rested his weight on his knees and one hand, lifting the other to her face. She didn't look, didn't react, just stared at him. His fingers soft, he ran the tips of them across her cheekbones and down to her lips, a dark red lipstick on them, typical Ida and nothing like Summer. He suddenly wanted it gone, and opened his mouth, sticking his thumb in and closing his lips around it. Her eyes dropped and she watched as he dragged the digit out, his teeth scraping at the pad. When he gripped her face, his fingertips rough against her cheekbone, earlobe, and jaw, she tensed beneath him. When his wet finger smeared across her mouth, taking the red with it, she opened her lips, and a hard sigh fell from him when she caught his thumb in her teeth, her eyes on him, then sucked it, going deep and then slowly pulling off. His thumb felt a hundred sensations that his cock wanted and—in that moment—there was no one else in the room, everything disappearing but the two of them.

The minute his thumb left her mouth, he dropped down atop her, his hand gripping the back of her head, his mouth crashing onto hers, and he kissed her like he'd wanted to from the start, rough and wild, her tongue fighting back, their kisses missing their mouths as much as they hit them.

Cole grabbed her, rolling onto his back and putting her above him, his hand yanking the sheet down, pulling the clasp of her bra, and the piece was suddenly gone, and her breasts were tumbling free onto him, and he groaned, pulling her down, the soft weight of them against his chest so beautiful, so incredible that he lost his fucking mind. He bit her ear, wrapped his hand deep in her hair, and pulled it tight, his mouth going to her throat, and then he was back to her mouth, and her hands were covering her chest and he remembered the scene, *the fucking scene*, and rolled back over, shielding her from the camera, his mouth softening as he pulled the sheet back up, his whisper at her ear almost silent. "I'm sorry. I didn't think."

She tugged on his hair and brought his mouth back to hers, and he didn't apologize again.

What happened between them when they touched… it was nothing like Nadia and nothing like the blonde and nothing like every other woman he'd ever had.

And that difference scared the hell out of him.

CHAPTER 91

"This is bullshit! Learn your marks and stay on them!" Cole threw up his hands and glared at me, and *sohelpmeGod* if there weren't a hundred people staring at us, I would have his nuts in a vice. A steel one. With teeth.

"You've moved the marks five times in the last two hours. Make up your mind and there won't be a problem!" I pushed on his chest with both hands, and the damn man barely wobbled. This was what I got for neglecting my chores and spending my days prancing around a movie set. Cole stepped closer to me, and his voice dropped.

"Touch me again, and I'll put you on your damn mark and hold you there."

I stepped back. When he was that close, something in my body lost control. I thought it would fade. It hadn't. We'd shot four scenes since our fake bedroom scene. None of them had been sexual in nature, yet I still wanted to hump this man like a dog in heat whenever we were in arms' reach. It was getting ridiculous.

"Cole, Summer," Don's voice rang out. "Let's take five. Summer, you're looking a little shiny." Makeup ran forward, a powder brush in hand, and I looked away from Cole and smiled a polite greeting. We were in the front room of the Frank plantation, lighting crews angled up the grand staircase, beaming a thousand watts of hot light down on us. Mary stuck a Tervis tumbler in front of me with iced tea. I took a sip, careful not to mess up my lipstick. We were on our nineteenth take, hours spent on a simple scene that should have been knocked out easily. Interesting that the quickest scenes we did were the ones that had heat. I didn't know what that said about us.

When the front door swung open, it was lost, no one looking up, our mid-shooting break taking center stage. But when the door shut, the wind caused a suction, its slam a little too strong, and the sound caught my ears. I turned my head and there, in the doorway, stood a tall woman with white hair, blood-red lipstick, a pencil skirt, and sky-high heels. She was looking right at me, a cell phone to her ear, briefcase in hand, and my stomach twisted. Brecken's boss. I knew who she was, had seen the senior publicist meet with Cole countless times, the clip of her heels always causing a scowl to come over his face. But this time, her steps effortless despite the heels, her face hard and stressed, I knew she wasn't coming for Cole. I knew, this time, this was about me.

Don intercepted her, his hand held up, his headphones pulled off. "Casey, we're filming. Not now."

Cole waved his hand, frustrated, a growl in his throat. "Make it quick, Casey."

"We're rolling in two," Don said, squaring off with Cole. "Whether you're done or not."

"I'm not here about Cole." I think I was the only one who heard her perfectly modulated tones.

"Don, run through Summer's marks with her; that'll eat up another ten minutes, easy." Cole's jab was tossed out with a glance in my direction, to make sure I was listening. I wasn't. I was pushing to my feet, off the folding chair, the makeup applicator chasing me down with a big fluffy brush. I knew I couldn't run from this, a part of me, in the gut, had known since the day Ben mentioned this job, that this was a side effect.

The Rehearsal Dinner wouldn't go quietly into the night. Not now that I was a celebrity or was going to be a celebrity. Casey skirted by Don, and I stepped forward, and we met like enemies on the Persian rug in the middle of the Frank parlor.

"Summer."

"Yes?"

"We have something we need to talk about."

CHAPTER 92

It had been a simple enough prank. And that was really all it was meant to be: a prank. Something to smack my wedding party on the back of the head and punish them for their betrayal.

Because they'd all known. I'd left Scott's house that day and had driven to Corrine's house. Walked into a houseful of my bridesmaids, their hands busy with net, lace, and rice, their bubbly chatter stopping when I'd walked in. Stacey, Scott's secretary, had been the first to speak. "Hey," she'd said, and my sensitive ears heard the red flag in her cautious tone. "I thought you were in Tallahassee today."

"That was this morning." I'd breezed through the girls and into the kitchen, ripping a paper towel from the roll and dabbing at my eyes, grabbing the wine bottle, freshly opened on the counter, and taking a generous swig. I'd pasted a smile on my face and stepped back into the doorway. "Where's Bobbie Jo?"

Four girls didn't lie well as a group. There was an uncomfortable stammer, someone saying 'Working' at the same time as Bridget said, "She isn't feeling well." With another swig of wine, I'd turned back to the kitchen.

"I'm gonna head home," I'd called over my shoulder. "I don't feel well."

The girls had chimed in a chorus of regrets, their vocal cords suddenly working just fine. I'd stuck their extra, unopened bottle into my purse and pasted a smile on my face. Wiggled my fingers at them and heaped out my thanks for their tireless bridesmaid efforts as I walked back through and out the door.

It was what I had deserved, befriending the cool crowd of women in

Quincy. They hadn't really ever been my friends. They'd ignored me in high school and only buddied up when I'd started dating Scott. Scott's friends had been their boyfriends, husbands, and brothers, our three-year relationship the only grounds that our friendship had been built on.

I had driven home to Momma, tears dripping down the stupid purple mascara that Avril Lavigne looked good in, and Bridget had raised her eyebrows at. And that night, one pruned toe playing with our bathtub drain, I had devised My Plan.

My Plan had been simple. My Plan had been foolproof. My Plan had been, according to *Variety Magazine* in that fateful issue that changed my life, diabolical.

I thought diabolical had been a strong adjective, used by a magazine editor who had clearly never read stories of Herodias or Jezebel. I mean, let's face it. Nobody *died.*

CHAPTER 93

"How did I not know this?" Cole exploded, throwing a Coke can against the wall, the contents splattering on some poor PA. "How did *we* not know this?" He held up a magazine and waved it wildly, the flap of its pages loud in the quiet room. I couldn't see the cover from my seat, his motions too fast, but I had seen him reading it, had seen *everyone* reading it, copies passed out like candy. I hadn't taken one. I had simply taken my seat at the end of the table and waited for punishment.

"We didn't think we *needed* to do a full work up on her." Some man I'd never seen spoke up, his hands nervously adjusting the bridge of his glasses. "I mean, look at her." He gestured in my direction, and I looked down at the table, the chastised child. "We ran criminal, background, and porn searches—did the blood work. Everything came back clean."

Porn searches? They talked about me like I was a prop in the scene, one without feelings or emotions or explanations. Though, as far as explanations went, I had none. What I had done was terrible. And whatever was printed in that magazine… it probably painted it exactly in that light.

"It wasn't *that* big of a deal," I spoke up from my corner of the table. "And it was years ago."

"So you already know what this is about?" Casey rested her weight on the table, her long red nails matching her lips.

"My rehearsal dinner?" I guessed.

"The *Rehearsal Dinner From Hell*," she read loudly, her words over enunciated, her fingers shoving a glossy cover in my direction. It skidded halfway down the table and stopped. No one furthered its journey, but I could see the cover picture from where I sat. It was Scott's and my engagement photo. Some creative mind at the magazine had drawn horns on my head and given me a tail. I looked away and saw Cole, staring at me, his weight against the wall. Our eyes met, and I couldn't look away. I tried. I failed.

"Why didn't you tell us about this?" Her voice rang out across the room, and I felt like I was eight years old, in Mrs. Wilson's class, fessing up to forgetting to feed Sparky the Goldfish. I wanted to look at Casey, wanted to look at the floor, wanted to look anywhere but couldn't pull away from Cole's stare.

"Clear the room," Cole spoke, a copy of the magazine crumpling in his fist. "I need to speak to Summer. Alone."

No one moved, save for that Coca-Cola-drenched PA who started to stand, then realized no one else was, and plopped back down.

"I mean it." Cole turned to Don, who sat next to Casey, his hands pressed to his temples. "Film the entry scenes. Have extras stand in for us. I want a chance to talk to her alone."

Don looked at Cole for a long moment, then stood. No one, out of the ten who left, looked at me. It was three years ago, all over again.

When the door shut, I spoke. "Cole…" I didn't even know what I had planned to say. I just knew I had to speak; we had to have something between us other than empty space.

"You should have told us. We can control something that we know about. This…" he set the crumpled magazine down on the table and tapped at its surface, "this we can't control. Not now. Right now every tabloid and entertainment publication has someone, as we speak, getting on a plane and coming to Quincy. And they will talk to every one of your friends, and every Chatty Cathy they can find, and you will be a Trivial Pursuit answer before the end of the week."

Every one of your friends. Ha. Good luck finding those.

"I don't care." I looked down at the table when I spoke, a dried glob of something… was it ketchup?… on its surface. With all of the Franks' money, you'd think someone here would have cleaned that.

There was the sound of slickness on wood, and I turned my head,

watching him walk down the long length of the table, his fingers braced on the wrinkly magazine, sliding it down.
Closer to me.
Three places away.
Closer to me.
Two places away.

He stopped. "Repeat that?"

I looked up into his face, and forgot, for a moment, how much I hated him. "I don't care."

"You will. Maybe you don't right this second, but you will."

I shrugged. "I don't think so. I've been an outcast in this town for three years. I can't imagine caring if some soccer mom in Nebraska also thinks I'm psycho."

"It's not just moms in Nebraska. It's *everyone* in this industry."

"No offense, but I hate your industry. This is a one-shot thing for me. Then I'm taking my money and running."

"Really." He laughed. "You get a lead role in a feature film, and then you are going to just disappear?"

I didn't smile, I didn't smirk, I just stared at him and made sure that he understood the words out of my mouth. "Yes."

He slid the magazine the last seat length toward me and stopped. My thigh jiggled against the seat, and I wanted to stand, wanted to change this dynamic of him looking down on me, but I didn't. I sat in my chair like a good little girl and tried not to look at the front of his pants. He half-sat against the edge of the table, pulling the magazine around and before me, and his new position was even worse. There, one leg cocked up, the other one on the floor, I could see the outline of him. He was not hard, but I… in this horrible situation, was turned on. I couldn't help myself. It was a chemical reaction between us that didn't understand anything else.

He moved his hand from the magazine, and I forced myself to look at that instead, at the glossy photo from a time when I thought that teasing my hair made me look sexier. It didn't. It made me look trashier. I see that now, and I have no doubt the observation will be so helpfully pointed out by someone like Nancy Grace or Kelly

Osbourne or… I swallowed hard. I told him I didn't care, but part of me did. Part of me had just recovered from being ignored. I didn't know if I had the strength to now be ridiculed.

When he said my name, it was an exasperated sigh, and I looked up to see him rubbing at his neck, his eyes closed, his features tight. "Summer…" he let my name fall and stretched his head back. "You are so different from every other woman I know."

"Thanks." I said the word without the slightest bit of sarcasm, and he laughed.

"Whether you value your reputation or not, we need you to meet with Casey. Let her do her thing. You may have to go on a couple of talk shows and tell your side of it."

I frowned. I had a hang nail on my left thumb, and I picked at it, my hand twitching when my nail dug too deep. "I don't really want to talk about it." It was none of anyone's freaking business; that was the truth of it. And plus, dragging out my drama with Scott now… when he had a wife and baby… it seemed dirty. Rotten. Whether or not I had forgiven him was secondary to the life he was currently living. A life, which was most likely already being rocked by this article.

"You don't want to talk about it on camera? Or with me?"

I choked out a laugh. "With you? Why would you care?"

"I need to know if I should keep ambulances on speed dial for the crew."

I twisted my mouth and tried to hide a smile. He was too close, sitting there. I could smell a hint of his cologne, and I wanted to lean forward and get more of it. "The crew? I'd be much more worried about you, Mr. Masten."

"Don't do that." His words were husky, and I looked up in surprise, my hangnail forgotten and saw his eyes on mine, and in them… I have seen that look before. In my bedroom. Right before… well…

"Don't do what?" I shouldn't have asked the question. I should have looked back down and changed the subject. But I didn't. I pressed.

"Call me that. Not here anyway." He sat back in his chair, his stare still on me, that feral, dominant stare that told me exactly what he had on his mind.

"Then where, Mr. Masten?" I dragged out his last name, and his eyes darkened, the left edge of his mouth curving up. It was official. I was going to hell.

He chuckled. "I'm not playing that game with you. Last time I walked into my house with an erection the size of Texas and you weren't there."

"I'm here right now." A woman I didn't know, one who had hidden inside of me for a long time, stood up, emboldened by the look in his eyes, by his words. I reached up and undid the top button of my shirt, then the second, his eyes closing for a minute before he reached forward.

"Stop." His hands closed on mine, and they were so warm, so strong. I looked up into his face, which was tight with regret. "Not here. I did a half-ass job with you last time. I'm not making that mistake again."

I digested the words, then slowly nodded. "It was pretty half-ass."

He laughed. "Easy, Country. You're dealing with a movie star. We're known to have fragile egos."

I pulled my hands free and reached for my buttons, but he brushed my hands aside, his fingers doing the job, the simple act of a man buttoning up my shirt causing something in me to weaken. "Why are you suddenly being nice to me?" I didn't look at him when I asked the question. I couldn't.

His hands lifted from my top button and cupped my face, turning it up, forcing the connection of our eyes. "I broke something over a man's head when I caught him fucking my wife." He shrugged. "Maybe you and I are more similar than I thought."

"Not likely."

He pulled forward with his hands and brought my mouth to his in a kiss completely different than the others—a quiet and soft kiss, one that tasted me and then let go, my eyes still closed when his hands left my face. "Don't push me away, Summer," he said. "Right now, you need a friend."

"A friend." I opened my eyes, and he was right there, those famous green eyes on mine. I laughed to take away any relationship reference he might infer. "You?"

"Yeah."

"I have to like someone for them to be my friend." I stepped back and hit the chair, stumbled. Of course I did. I couldn't have *one* well-executed semi-witty comeback.

"Do you have to like someone to fuck them? Tonight?" My attention turned from the execution of my dramatic exit and back to him. He sat, hunched forward, against the side of the table, his hands now gripping its edge, his eyes tight to mine.

"Tonight?" I stalled, and I could literally feel the stick of my panties to me.

"Yes." If eye contact had a leash, his would have been wrapped tightly around my heart.

I had a plethora of options in my response:
Oh… sorry. The Bachelor's *on tonight.*
I have to run lines due to your incessant script changes.
Yes, I do have to like someone to fuck them, so no, tonight is not good.

I said none of those. When it came to him, I could only nod. Just off the cliff that I was going to eventually trip down anyway. "I'll see you tonight, Mr. Masten."

His mouth twitched, and his shoulders loosened a little. "Good."

I had absolutely nothing intelligent to say to that. I swallowed, reached for my bottle of water, and headed for the door.

When I opened it, Casey stood there, her arms folded, nails rapping. "Let's go, Summer. Right now. We need a game plan."

I let out a deep sigh and let her take me. Through the kitchen and into the office. I let her walk me through containment and recovery process, one that would involve little on my part other than to behave. I nodded politely, tried to listen but all I could think about was my face on that cover, the words in those pages, what they'd say and how they'd paint me.

And, for the first time since he landed on this spit of country soil, I appreciated Cole's magnetic sexuality, the obsession my skin seemed to have for his touch. Because the only thing I could focus on—the only light at the end of my tunnel, through Casey's lectures and pen taps and gripes of dismay—was the fact that in just hours, I'd be at his house. I'd have his hands and his mouth on me. And I knew, in that moment, I wouldn't be thinking about Scott, or The Rehearsal Dinner From Hell, or the article at all.

He would be my distraction. He would be, for this one night, my salvation.

CHAPTER 94

This was the second time in four weeks that I was shaving for this man. Like, *really* shaving, in places that a good girl didn't allow to see the light of day.

My giant epiphany from earlier, the one where Sex With Cole Masten would heal all of my problems? That thought process had lost steam, sputtered out and was hovering on the brink of death. I shouldn't go over there. I should bail. Sit on my couch with my mother, eat banana pudding, and watch sweet little Jacob give his last rose to that skank who jerked him off on their Mystery Date even though ex-nun Anita was obviously *so* much better for him. Yep, I could definitely bail. I mean, what would be the consequences? He'd think poorly of me? That box was already checked. And now that I sat my butt down and thought about it, why was I primping for a night with a man I didn't like? And who didn't really like me?

Oh, right. Because he was Cole Masten. Because he'd poured gasoline on the fire of my arousal with his last performance, and there wasn't another man alive who would be able to recreate that. Because, even though I liked to pretend I hadn't seen it, pieces of the real Cole had peeked at me. Moments with Cocky. Moments with me. Moments where I saw a man better than the myth. And I wanted, before he hopped on his big jet and returned to California, before he moved on with his life and forgot all about Summer Jenkins, another taste of *that* man. Even if it ruined me for life. It *had* to be incredible to be my damnation. Otherwise it would just be another lay, easily forgettable, easily moved on from. Funny how that worked. Sex with him was my drug, and the better the high, the more I would crave it when it was gone. That night, I was succumbing to my addiction, and would take the hit despite the consequences.

So there would not be banana pudding, or *The Bachelor*, or a crossword puzzle with Mama. Nope. I rinsed the razor out under the bathtub's tap and fully committed, in my mind, to the decision.

"I need your help." I spoke rapidly into the house phone, my nerves at a level that couldn't possibly be good for my mental health.

"I knew it!" Ben chirped. "You're finally taking my advice and taking those waves straight. Please tell me you are spending all that movie star cash and flying me down there to use the straightener myself."

I paused, my hand on a duffel bag, stuffed in the back of my closet, that I hadn't used since high school. "No."

"Shit," he said glumly. "Needing fashion advice?" His voice took on a more hopeful lilt.

"Sort of…" I yanked at the bag's handle, and half the items in the closet fell out. "I'm going over to Cole's house tonight for sex, and I don't know whether I should pack an overnight bag."

Total silence. Quite possibly the quietest my adorable little Ben has been all year. "Repeat that?" he finally asked.

"Shut up and help me," I groaned, pulling a pair of vintage Nikes out of the bag and examining them dubiously.

There was a long pause, then he spoke, "Is this a relationship hookup or just sex? In other words, are there feelings behind this?"

"No. I mean, intense dislike. If you count that as a feeling."

"Ooh… hate sex." He sighed dramatically. "I'd give my right nut for hate sex with that man."

I grimaced. "Focus Ben."

"Can you leave a bag in the car and grab it if he invited you to stay the night?"

"No." There was no way on God's Green Earth that I was driving my truck to Cole's and leaving it parked out front all evening or—worse—all night long. If I did, every soul in Quincy would hear about our activities by tomorrow morning's coffee brew.

"Then don't pack a bag. Stick a toothbrush and change of underwear in your purse. Everything else you can wing until tomorrow." He paused. "What are you telling Mama Jenkins?"

I laughed. "Mama Jenkins has all but pushed my butt out the door in his direction. She seems to think Cole is her only shot at grandchildren. She found the condoms I bought and threw them in the trash." I'd been so embarrassed when I'd opened the lid and saw the small gold box. I didn't have the heart to tell her that condoms did more than stop pregnancy. Instead, I gingerly removed the box, wiped it off, and hid it in my rain boots. Apparently my underwear drawer no longer counted as an acceptable hiding place.

"What happened to virginal vaginas being one of her requisites for marriage?"

I sat on the edge of the bed, kicking off my flip-flops and laughed. "I think she gave up on that scenario when she walked into the house and heard Scott's hyena orgasm."

"Who?"

I had forgotten, for a moment, that I hadn't ever told Ben about Scott. Also forgotten, until right then, about the magazine article. "My ex. Have you been online today?" I hadn't. Casey had made me swear to stay off all social media and websites. Before I left the Franks', I read the article. It made me sick, my anticipation of each word giving it extra weight, the worst part being the quotes from local 'anonymous sources.' It made me hate every inch of Quincy, their low opinion of me so much harsher when printed in black and white and broadcasted to the entire nation. Don sent me home early, Cole's head turned my way when I walked out, but I didn't pause, didn't meet his eyes, didn't want to do anything but get into my truck, drive home, and crawl into my bed.

Momma met me at the door, and I didn't ask why she wasn't at work. I just dove into her open arms and sobbed. Sobbed like a little girl. She sat with me in bed, handed me tissues, and listened to my incoherent ramblings while rubbing my back. At some point, while her hand smoothed back my hair, I fell asleep. And when I woke up to the smell of chicken and vegetable soup, I wasn't upset any more. Instead, I was pissed. At Scott, at Bobbie Jo, at *Variety Freaking Magazine*. I wanted to chop down ten trees, run fifty miles, take my gun to the big oak out back and empty a hundred clips. I wanted to screw and be screwed ten ways from Sunday by Cole Masten, and I wanted it immediately.

I had gone into the kitchen and kissed Momma on the cheek. Had a bite or two of soup, then excused myself into the bathroom. Used two razors and half a can of shaving cream. Stuck my box-o-condoms in my purse and dressed, pulling on the only sexy panties I owned, then a blue Tommy Hilfiger sundress that Ross had had on discount. It was then that I got stuck, my brain catching up with my libido, the simple logistics of the hookup foreign to me. That was when I'd called Ben. Ben, still in Vancouver, hadn't yet heard my news. Either Canada didn't give two craps about a no-name actress in Georgia, or he'd been too busy, but either way, I didn't chase down the subject. Instead, I made excuses and hopped off the call as soon as possible, telling him I'd call him tomorrow.

Ben was right. Me showing up with an overnight bag would be weird. Really weird. As we clearly worked through in the Franks' dining room—this was not a date. This was for one thing. One thing that I badly needed to work out the funk that was collecting in my system. My earlier thought process had merit. He would be my distraction. An earth-shattering, toe-curling distraction.

I grabbed my purse and kissed Mama goodbye. Then I opened the back door and jogged down the steps, heading to the fields, his home visible in the setting sun, lights on inside, his truck parked in front. Behind me, at the end of the Holdens' long drive, a cluster of strange cars squatted outside the locked entry fence. We'd never locked that fence, not in the six years I'd been on the plantation. But Casey had called during my nap and warned Mama. Told her to tell me to stay put, to not talk to anyone, to avoid them. I took a deep breath and entered the fields, pushing everything out of my mind with each step farther away from the vultures.

A distraction. That was all this was.

Maybe an entire box of condoms was a little intimidating. I should have opened it and just pulled out one or two. Or three. Was this a one-sex visit? Scott and I had never had sex more than once per twenty-four hour period. But I read books, I watched Showtime, I knew that other couples were not the prudes that Scott and I were.

Not that Cole and I were a couple. It was a figurative reference.

It was stupid for me to wear flip-flops to walk there. My toes were already covered in dust, and I was only halfway there. Cole was not going to want to have sex with a girl with dirty feet. And it wasn't like I could invite myself in and then ask to wash them off.

Rainboots. That would have matched this sundress and still kept my feet clean. Though the whole boot-removal process was a pain. And super unsexy, my hands gripping one boot while I grunted and wheezed through the contortions required to get a rubber object off a sweaty foot.

I should have eaten more. I was already hungry and those two bites of soup were tiny. When I was chicken-sitting at Cole's, I raided his kitchen, and it was pathetic. The man appeared to live off milk, beer, and ham sandwiches.

I came to the end of the field and stopped. Before me, the Kirklands' backyard, green grass stretching fifty yards in either direction, the white fence keeping the wildflowers at bay, the large home looming up and breaking the canvas of the night sky. And in the middle of the yard stood Cole, his hands on his hips, his white T-shirt stretched tight over a muscular chest, workout shorts on, his eyes on me. My dirty feet and I waited, stuck in place, and tried to think of something to say.

CHAPTER 95

He had been so worried she wouldn't show. When she'd stepped out of the Franks' house, her head had been down, her eyes not meeting his. He was sure that she'd change her mind, would leave him hanging. But now, coming to a stop outside the fence, she was here. He skirted around Cocky and walked over to the gate, resting his weight on it and looking at her.

"You came," he said.

"Yeah." She shifted her purse higher on her shoulder. "I brought condoms. Or..." She blushed. "A condom. You know. If..." She brought a hand to her mouth and giggled. "Oh my Lord. I'm an idiot."

He laughed. "I have condoms but thank you." The dusk light made her hair look pink, the wind picked up wisps of it and took it across her face, and she suddenly looked vulnerable. It was a new look on her and stirred some alpha male instinct deep within him, one he didn't recognize. He put one foot up on the fence. "Before you come in, I wanted to propose something."

"I don't want to talk about the night of the dinner," she said quickly. "If we could just, right now, ignore that."

He shrugged. "Fine by me. It's your thing. You change your mind, I'm here."

"What's the proposal?" She narrowed her eyes in suspicion, and he wondered, for an insane moment, if a child of theirs would have hazel or green eyes.

"Twenty-four hour truce." He gestured between the two of them. "You and I have some aversion to civility. It's a Friday night. We don't have to work tomorrow. For the next twenty-four hours, no fighting."

She folded her arms over her chest. "What about when you act like an asshole?"

"I won't." He smiled. "Promise." It'd be hard not to push her buttons, especially when he enjoyed seeing her worked up. But he'd behave for twenty-four hours. He wanted to explore more of the girl who hid behind all of that fire.

"I don't know if I trust your promises." She stepped closer, dropping her arms and resting them on the gate.

He shrugged. "Then you can call me an asshole and storm out. Which is pretty much what you were already planning on doing after you got your use out of those condoms. Or condom. Or…" His grin widened. "Whatever."

"That is true…" she mused, a wicked gleam in those hazel eyes. "I practiced my dramatic exit and everything."

"I often fail at behaving." Cole leaned forward, against the rail, his voice conspiratorial. "So don't worry. I'm sure you'll get to use that at some point."

He pulled at the gate, then stopped. "Deal?"

"Are you going to turn me away if I don't agree?"

"Ummm… yes." He held the gate in place, half open, his body blocking the entrance.

"You're a terrible liar," she teased, stepping closer.

"Well, you know. I haven't had much practice." He smirked. "Deal?" He held out his hand.

"Deal." She reached forward and shook it, her handshake strong despite such a tiny palm.

"Where's your bag?" he eyed her purse, which was too small to hold much of anything.

"I didn't bring one. I thought… you know. This was just sex." She pulled at the bottom of her sundress.

God, she was adorable. "You're staying the night."

"Maybe." Her eyes narrowed.

"You are." He smiled and stepped aside, swinging the door open, Cocky squawking from the far end of the yard, his wings flapping as he half bounced, half flew, half ran over to her. She met Cocky halfway, dropping to her knees before the rooster, her hands light as they skimmed over his back and his comb. Cole watched her, a foreign lump in his throat. He cleared it with a hard cough and shut the gate, turning back to Summer. "You eaten? I was just about to grill some steaks."

"Steaks?" she looked up, surprised.

"We don't have to eat." God, this was awkward.

"No." she pushed to her feet. "Steak sounds great. Want me to whip up some sides?"

"Uh… sure."

She brushed off her hands and grabbed her purse, setting off for the back porch with purpose. On the ground, Cocky squawked his indignation at being left.

"Hush," Cole chided him. "You've already gotten more play than me." He looked up at the house, the light windows giving him an uninterrupted view of Summer's entry to the kitchen, her hands twisting up her hair then hitting the faucet, her head down as she washed her hands.

Twenty-four hours. The truce had been nothing but an excuse to spend more time with her. A dangerous gamble, but one he needed to take. There was something about her, something that had tugged on him since the moment they had met. A tug that had become an addiction. An addiction that he needed to cure. Twenty-four hours without the distraction of fighting would be his fix. Without the lure of unattainability, the hours would wear the shiny sparkle off her. She'd lose her mystery, would lose her charm. Then, with just one month left of filming, he'd have her out of his system and be ready to return to LA.

Leaving the rooster on the porch, he climbed up the stairs and pulled open the back door.

They cooked in silence, Summer finding some frozen okra and corn in the outside freezer, her hands quick as she riffled through the Kirklands' kitchen, setting up skillets, grabbing items, cracking open the window above the sink. Cole watched her from his spot on the back porch, the grill on low, his back against one of the big porch posts. Nadia had never cooked. She'd had other things to do, more interested in eating at a place that would get her seen rather than a meal at home. And their chef knew what they both liked, so it never seemed necessary. To Nadia's credit, Cole had never cooked either. Putting meat on a grill and taking it off before it burned. That was the extent of his talent.

She finished just after him, scooping out fried corn and an okra-tomato-corn medley on his plate. They ate on the back porch, the fan keeping the heat off, Cocky in the yard.

"He's a good chicken," Cole mused, putting a piece of his steak in his mouth.

"He comes from good stock. His mama is beautiful."

"You know his mom?" Cole looked surprised, and she laughed.

"I don't know if *knowing* her is the right word, but yes. She lives on our plantation. She's produced about twenty Cockys for us. Want to meet her?"

He surprised her by nodding. "Would she recognize him?"

"I don't know how much thought process there is in a chicken's head. She recognizes me. Knows I bring them treats. She won't recognize him, or won't care. They aren't the most nurturing mothers once their chicks are grown."

"I understand that," he murmured and was grateful when she didn't press it. "Treats?" he said, tilting his head. "I asked the feed store for treats and got laughed out of there.

She laughed, sucking some steak juice off the side of one finger, and his thought process went dormant for a moment. "Scraps. Boiled eggs, pasta, corn cobs… they love that stuff. Oh, and string cheese."

Cole stared at Cocky and felt like the worst parent in the world.

Cole had been discovered at seventeen, standing outside a club on Sunset Boulevard when, his fake ID in pocket, he had smiled shyly at some women in line. Walked closer and asked their names. They were older than him but attractive. Had seemed friendly. Laughed off his flirtations but one of them handed him her card. Told him to go home and to call her on Monday morning. That woman had been Traci Washington, and she'd been casting a teenage rom-com. Cole had carried her card in his wallet for a week before he called. The moment he did, everything changed. He had 'it,' and that teenage movie turned into a string of movies, which turned into the Cole Masten Empire. Washing dishes was not a thing that he had ever done. He pushed his hands into the soapy water and looked over at Summer. "We can just leave these. That girl comes on Monday."

"Monday?" Summer repeated. "It's Friday night. You're not gonna have a sinkful of dirty dishes for three days. The place will smell." She leaned over and ran the water, her body brushing against his, and when she dug into the sink for a sponge, he enjoyed the view down her dress. She caught his stare and elbowed him. "Focus. Just get the food off and stack them on the counter. I'll load them after I get everything put away."

For purely peace-keeping purposes, he obeyed, his head down, eyes on the plates, the food coming off cleanly, the chore quick given that there were only two of them. He heard the clang of a pot and glanced over, seeing two dirty skillets stacked with quick precision next to him. Finishing those, he drained the sink and grabbed a hand towel from the hook, drying his hands. He stepped back, to give her room, and watched her work.

"So… how do you think it's going?" she glanced over at him as she yanked out the trash can, snatching items from the counter and tossing them in, her movements fluid and unrehearsed, this act one she'd done a thousand times. He thought suddenly of her audition, on the porch, and made a mental note to add a cooking scene with Ida into the movie. Somehow. Though he could think of no clear fit. He had to be careful. This movie wasn't his personal memory box with which to store pieces of Summer. She stopped before him and waited. He focused on her questions.

"Well. We're behind. Script changes always push us behind."

"I'm not talking about the timeline," she snapped. "I mean us. The flow. The scenes." She turned away from him and bent over, opening the dishwasher, and he suddenly realized why Doing Dishes With Summer was always a good idea. And it had nothing to do with caked-on food and everything to do with the fact that there was nothing more beautiful than Summer loading the dishes in a sundress. When she bent over, her skirt lifted, and he wanted to drop to his knees and more properly enjoy the view. When she straightened, pulling her hair back and into a ponytail, he stared at the lines of her arms, the curve of her waist, the cut of her calves. She was barefoot now, her feet dusty, and when she reached up for a hand towel she went on her tiptoes, and he almost groaned.

"Cole?" Her feet had turned, and he looked up, to her sweet beautiful face, her eyebrows raised because, oh right, she must have asked another question. The woman never shut up with her questions.

"Come here." He had meant the request to sound friendly, but it ripped from his throat with a growl. He gripped the edge of the counter that he leaned against and willed himself not to let go.

She stepped forward, her movements slow as she ran the towel across the backs of her hands. Then she stopped, and he smelled just a hint of her soap and couldn't stop himself anymore. He reached forward, pulling her the rest of the way toward him and against his body.

CHAPTER 96

I had wondered when it would happen. Had been surprised when I had first gotten there and he had proposed eating. Had been on guard during our meal, my condoms at the ready, no more dumb mistakes for this girl.

Washing the dishes… I had thought that was a safe activity. But when I turned from the sink, the way he looked at me… maybe cleanliness was a turn-on for him. I'd been nervous walking over to him, my mind flipping through what I had eaten, wondering if there was pepper in my teeth, wondering if I should reach for my box full o'condoms now or—

He took all of that away when the bite of his fingers cupped against my back and pulled me forward. His kiss was frantic and needy, his tongue tasting me as if wanting the flavors from dinner, his hands sliding down my waist and over my hips and gripping my butt through the dress. It was so rough I almost gasped, his grip holding me against his body, and I could feel everything this man was thinking through those shorts, and God did I want it. I reached down, I couldn't help myself, my fingers dragging over his T-shirt and down to his mesh shorts, pushing at the top hem and then *under*. Under. God. I haven't touched these parts of a man in so long. And Scott—Scott was soft and a little doughy, his skin yielding if I pressed on it. My fingers slid right down the hard lines of Cole, under his underwear and he tilted up his pelvis as if he wanted it, and then my fingers brushed against it, and he groaned in my mouth, and I just about combusted, right there in his kitchen.

"Grab it," he choked out against my mouth, his hands now both in my hair, hard against my neck, and he kissed me as if we would never kiss again, desperate and needy, his tongue against mine. I did grab it, wrapped my hands around his shaft, and he literally shuddered, my body pushing harder against his and when I squeezed it, it twitched. "Jack it. Please." I don't know how he managed to say the words, his kisses so close together, his lips on mine, on the side of my mouth, on my bottom lip. I felt his teeth for a minute, then they were gone, and my eyes closed as I tightened my hand and stroked it all the way up, then down, my confidence growing as the man freaking *whimpered* my name against my mouth. "Faster." He panted and my hand moved faster.

One of his hands moved to the back of my dress and there was the rip of a zipper and then my dress was falling, his hands pushing the straps down my arms, my bra undone with talented fingers, his hand tugging it off, and I heard the sound of its clasp as it hit the kitchen floor. "Don't stop."

I wouldn't stop, I couldn't, because the feel of him in my hand was so beautiful, so perfect, his hips now thrusting, my hand doing nothing but holding tight and still as he jacked himself off in my grip. It was as if he couldn't get enough, of me, of my mouth, of my touch. My dress was now around my waist, bunched up and stopped by the connection of my hand and him, his shorts still on, my hand still under, and I pulled at the fabric with my other hand, Cole and I fighting over space, both of us too anxious to be polite. I got his shorts over his hips, and they dropped to the floor. Cole pushed me off, and I stumbled back, my hand releasing him, my eyes opening, half-glazed with arousal, but I could see his chest heaving. My eyes focused on his, and he was as affected, maybe even more, than me. He yanked at the bottom of his shirt, pulling it over his head, and I got a brief moment, when his head was covered, to stare at his beauty. Then his shirt was off, his feet were moving, and he was back on me, his hands settling on my bare waist, and he picked me up easily, swinging me to the counter. He yanked at my panties and then they were off and he pushed my knees apart. I reached for him again and he pushed away my hand, looking up at my face.

"I'm gonna come if you keep that up, and I've been waiting for this, fucking *dreaming* of this for two months." He dropped to his knees and lifted my knees, pulling me to the edge of the counter, pulling my legs over his shoulders and leaning forward with his mouth.

Thank God I shaved. That was my first thought as I watched his mouth come closer, his eyes right *there* on my most private place, a place that Scott had only seen once or twice, his interest more focused on—I lost thought, literally lost the ability to think when he ran his mouth softly over the space between my legs and then inhaled. *Inhaled.* The way you would to a peach, when you can't get enough of the smell and you want more. I'd done it, countless times. I knew the look that crossed over your face, knew the way your eyes closed. I never, not in a million years, thought that a man would have that look at the way I smelled. It made me want to open my legs wider, made me want to grab at the back of his head and say *it's yours* and *take it please.*

I must have made some sort of a sound because he looked up at me, and I couldn't stop my eyes from begging, couldn't stop my hands from pulling slightly on his shoulders, couldn't stop one of my legs from slowly dragging up his shoulder, my foot finding a resting place, my body opening even more. He held my eyes for one, long second, his tongue dipping into and out of me. Then he closed his eyes, as if in bliss, and leaned forward, his head dropping, his hands sliding up my thighs and under my butt cheeks, lifting me up into his mouth.

I couldn't tell you the things I said. The things I screamed so loudly that my lungs hurt. The man shouldn't be allowed to have a mouth. Shouldn't be allowed to use that thing like a weapon, to cut open a woman's soul, her secrets, her control, and rip them all to shreds. I lost myself, in those minutes with his head between my legs. He took all the pieces that made me Summer and swallowed them whole, made them his. I screamed his name and laid myself bare, and when I came I think I told him I loved him. I didn't really know. I didn't know who that woman, naked on a kitchen counter, was. I didn't know who that man, that heartbreakingly beautiful, sexual freak of nature, was. I just knew that right then, in that instance, I loved him.

And at that moment, in that breakthrough, he stood up in the midst of my orgasm, yanked me back to the edge of the counter, and he pushed himself inside of me. Pumped his hips quick and fast—deep, furious strokes that made my orgasm never stop, never slow; it just stretched further and further until I lost it, somewhere along the line, and it just became gorgeous, beautiful sex. I wrapped my arms around his neck and his lips found mine. He kissed me, then moved to my neck, his teeth grabbing, then his tongue, and I held on to his shoulders and wrapped my feet around his back and I held on to him with all of my strength and what little control I had left. And when he came, I felt his break, felt his mind fall apart, heard him gasp my name, over and over, over and over, a stream of incoherent mumblings as he lost everything and found it in me, his arms locked around me, hugging me to him, and then I was off the counter and on the floor and against his chest, and the kitchen was finally quiet, save our shaky breaths.

CHAPTER 97

He loved her. He did. He fucking loved this woman. He loved her giggle when she couldn't control it. He loved the mischief in her eyes when she was playful. He loved how her body stiffened and hands balled up and her gaze could eat through a grown man when she was mad. But none of that compared to how much he loved her sighs, the sound of his name when she screamed it, the way her mouth responded to his kisses, her scent—God he could bottle her juices and become a billionaire, but he would never because he couldn't, in that moment, ever imagine another man with her. He would kill to keep her his, pay every cent of his fortune, destroy his career and never have another if it would keep her his. This was not a rebound, this was not infatuation, this was the end of his life as he knew it, and the realization hit that even if she didn't want him, he would never ever find another woman like her, he would never ever get over her. He closed his eyes, felt her leg move against his, her chest heaving against his, her mouth by his neck, and he had never been so terrified.

CHAPTER 98

The decision was made, after I finally rolled off him, my shoulders hitting the cold tile, my legs trembling when I stood, a moment of awkward silence between us before I giggled and he smiled, that we needed dessert. Ice cream, preferably. On that we agreed. I went to the bathroom and felt a moment of panic when the evidence of his orgasm came out. Right. Another unprotected experience. Good thing I had just finished my period, my window of fertility not open yet. Still, I should probably go back to Tallahassee. I should also have my head cut open and examined because I had lost something, somewhere, that kept me intelligent.

Quincy had no ice cream shops, at least not that were open on a Friday night past ten. We debated over our problem, but there was really only one solution.

"Walmart?" Cole looked at me as if I had suggested we stage a coup and overtake the Quincy government.

"Yes. You know, giant superstore, has everything at every moment of the day?"

"I can't go in a Walmart."

"Because…"

"Not to sound like a pompous prick, but because of who I am. There will be crowds. Paparazzi. And DeLuca will have my ass if I am photographed with you. Especially with…" He made some general hand gesture that I'm pretty sure was meant to encompass my magazine article.

"It's Quincy. At ten-thirty at night. There will be, like, three people there. And look—" I opened the curtain and pointed. "All the photographers are camped out at my house. Waiting for me to go batshit crazy." It was true, they were still there, a line of six of their cars, stretched out politely to the left of the Holdens' gate. Mama was going to turn the lights on and off through the night and keep the blinds drawn, television on. She'd wanted to get more creative with the ruse, but I shut that down. Mama, when she got creative, could go a little overboard. "We could get treats for Cocky there!" I added.

"There are still security cameras in Walmart." He shook his head at me. "No."

I twisted my mouth, then got an idea.

CHAPTER 99

"We'll look like robbers."

Summer looked at the two bags laid out on the dining room table, with a serious face. "You're right." Her forehead wrinkled, and then she looked back at him, an excited look on her face. "We should decorate them."

He scowled in response, a grin pushing at the corners of his mouth. She clapped her hands in excitement, and it was official: he'd never be able to tell her no.

"This is stupid." He pulled at the bottom of his paper bag and scratched an itch the paper was causing against his neck.

"Shut up," Summer chirped, leaning over the gearshift and adjusting it, his eyes suddenly better lined up with the holes. They were face to face, her own paper bag covering her features, her eyes the only thing visible, shining through two oval circles, her holes much more 'feminine,' according to her, than Cole's basic circles. She'd added blue eye shadow, giant lashes, and carefully drawn eyebrows, courtesy of a thirty-pack of markers they'd found in the study. "Your eye makeup looks fantastic," he whispered and became suddenly aware of her hand, on his thigh, where she was resting her weight.

"Thank you," she whispered back and giggled. "Though you should get that mole looked at. It's worrisome." Oh yes, the mole that she'd felt the need to add, drawn on his cartoon cheek. She'd added a thin hair coming out of the top of it, and just like that, his paper bag self was suddenly ugly. He'd compounded the issue, drawing worry lines on the forehead and bags under his 'eyes.' "He looks stressed," she had said, then added a cigarette, limply hanging from his mouth. "There," she said triumphantly. "Now he has a reason."

"Lung cancer?" Cole had guessed.

"No!" When she'd shoved at his shoulder, he'd wanted to sweep the bags off the table and take her, right there, the markers pushed to the end of the table, her hair spreading out on the walnut surface. He hadn't. He'd let her finish. "Bad breath and teeth staining," she'd said somberly. "They are very serious side effects."

"And that makes my bag man worry."

"YES," she'd stressed, picking up a watermelon pink marker and filling in the lips of her woman.

Now, he stared at those lips, then impulsively leaned forward, the paper bag crinkling as he pushed his lips against hers through two layers of brown papers. Her hand tightened on his thigh, then it was over. Her eyes laughed at him. "Are you done romancing? I want to get inside before you smear this super-expensive Crayola lipstick."

"I'm done."

"Then let's do this." She fist-pumped and opened his door, opting to crawl over his lap and out rather than return to her side. He didn't mind, helping her on her way out, his hands friendly, and she shrieked out a protest before both feet landed on the ground.

At almost eleven at night, they were the fifth vehicle in the lot, if you ignored the line of employee cars parked on the far side of the building. Cole's steps slowed as Summer strode toward the entrance, her feet hopping over a parking curb. Her head turned to him, and she saw his lag, her hand reaching out and grabbing him. "Come on, chicken. Grow some balls." She tilted her head at him, the giant bag making her look like a bobblehead, and he grinned behind his mask.

It was stupid.
It was ridiculous.
It was also her idea, and she was laughing, and he would be damned

if he interfered with that. He let her pull him forward and they stepped up to the front door. Wearing paper bags pulled over their heads. The greeter, a short older man with a belly, turned, a smile on his face, and paused, the unlit cigar hanging from his mouth drooping.

"Hey Bob," Summer chirped, snagging a cart from his hand and pushing it forward.

"Hey Summer," the old man drawled, the cigar fully dropping from his lips as he watched her pass, his nod in Cole's direction slow and cautious. "Hey Mr. Masten."

Cole smiled out of habit, then realized the man couldn't see his mouth, and nodded. "Good evening." He jogged a few steps, catching up with his paper bag girlfriend, and lowered his head to her. "He knows it's us," he murmured.

"Of course he does," she said, her giant head turning to look up at him, her hazel eyes shining. "Now, Mr. Masten, let me properly welcome you to the beauty that is Walmart."

She stopped, in the middle of the wide, main aisle, and spread her arms. Spun around a little and stopped. Did a curtsy for no apparent reason and then laughed.

"The list," he reminded her.

"Oh yes." She dug in her purse, her head tilted down, hand holding her mask in place against her mouth. "Here." She shook it out and, from a register halfway down, a blue-aproned employee walked to the end of her aisle and stared at them. "Corn, string cheese, pasta, spaghetti, cabbage, berries, dried peas, plastic bottles, ice cream and whipped cream." Her words ran together in a line, the last set as one long mashed together word.

"Whipped cream?" he repeated the last one, confused.

She tugged at the bottom of her bag as if to make sure that it was still on. "I always wanted a guy to lick whipped cream off me. Scott was never that adventurous." She shrugged her shoulders, and the bag moved slightly as she shook her head. "You might be my last chance."

The woman thought that whipped cream was adventurous.

"Okay…" he said slowly. "Whipped cream."

She tilted her head. "Your face is so sad, I can't tell if you think that is a good idea or a bad one."

He stepped closer and looked down at her big-eyed, bright-lipped face. "Woman, I think it's an incredible idea. I will buy every single can they have in stock."

Laughter bubbled out of her, and this truce was the best idea he'd ever had. "I like when you call me woman. And don't be so eager. This is Walmart. They will have a gazillion cans in stock."

He looked down at her and was glad that she couldn't see his face. *I like when you call me woman.* He wanted to call her a lot more than that. *Only one month of filming left.* The sudden thought was sobering. Not enough time to figure out if his post-sex epiphany was true. Not enough time to properly win her heart.

CHAPTER 100

I wanted to split up. Divide and conquer, that was the best strategy when dealing with the enormity that was a superstore. But Cole said no, that we needed to stick together, and when his old man bag face said something, I couldn't seem to say no. We should wear these all the time. Behind mine I felt fearless, like the words coming out of me weren't mine at all, but those of some other, braver, more confident individual. Whipped cream? Where did that come from? And did I actually tell him I wanted him to *lick* it off? I should have been mortified, but I wasn't. I felt free.

We took the scenic route through the store, stopping at the sunglass stand—our bag heads too big for proper modeling—then the toys section, a heated discussion erupting over a wall of board games and puzzles. We decided on Taboo and Scrabble, then got distracted with a cartwheel competition: Cole bet me a *hundred* dollars that I couldn't do three cartwheels in a row without my bag falling off (I won, my hair is fluffy) and then I bet, double or nothing, that he couldn't do three cartwheels in a row without falling over. Needless to say, I left two hundred bucks richer.

It was in the pet section when it happened. We were arguing over the toy selection, Cole insisting, his mouth muffled through the bag, that Cocky was a chicken—a distinction that he seemed to think removed any chance of him enjoying a cat toy—and I was arguing that if Cocky was a chicken then maybe he didn't need any toys. That's when he dropped the ridiculous tiny dog collar he'd been considering, and pinned me to the cart, his arms on the handle, my body in between.

I squirmed, and he wrapped a leg around me, holding me against him. "Kiss me," he said, and I stopped squirming, my hands softening their push against his chest.

"Now?" I squeaked, and turned my head to look down the aisle, my paper bag getting crooked in the process, my right eye losing all sight.

He let go of the handles and pulled at my bag, my hair floating up with it, and he tossed it into the cart, his hands coming down to smooth the erratic pieces. "Cole," I whispered. "The cameras."

"I don't care about the cameras," he said gruffly, his bag pulled off and joining mine, and there was a moment of nothing, then he pulled with rough hands at the back of my head, and there was a moment of everything.

I knew I was supposed to hate this man, but I kissed him in that pet aisle and somewhere, in the months since he moved here, I lost that objective. I let him kiss me and couldn't, no matter how deep I reached, find any hate at all.

CHAPTER 101

Our covers were blown, everyone in the store knew who we were anyway, but we still put the bags back on and continued shopping. The kiss had changed things, his hands constantly on me, resting on my lower back, playing with the ends of my hair, his fingers sliding through my fingers when we'd stop at a display. I found him a giant cowboy hat that I was able to squash on his head, the worried old man face now looking eerily similar to a country version of Robert DeNiro. He returned the favor with big hot pink earrings that he pierced the side of my bag with. "We're so sexy," I mused, striking a pose in front of a dressing room mirror. I had a sudden thought and wheeled around, facing him. "Photo booth!"

"What?" He adjusted his hat in the mirror. "God, this hat makes me look ridiculous." His hands stalled as his statement sank in, and we both burst out laughing.

I chased down my original idea. "Let's take a picture in the photo booth."

"They have a photo booth?" I couldn't see them, but I was pretty sure his eyebrows were raised in skepticism.

"The photo lab machine takes selfies. Come on." I grabbed his hand and tugged at it, pulling him and our cart in the direction of the electronics department. I hadn't been entirely sure of myself, but when we parked in front of the standalone machine, it turned out that I was right. It took pics in bursts of three. We took ten. The electronics girl popped her gum and stared at us like we were idiots.

We *were* idiots. Something about this man, whether it was having sex with him, or kissing him on camera, or running up a nine hundred dollar bill in the middle of the night at Walmart, made me act like an idiot. The cashier, a pixie brunette who I'd attended high school with, bagged our items, handing Cole his credit card and nodded at me. I smiled at her and wondered, for the first dark moment since entering the store, if she'd been one of Quincy's 'anonymous sources.'

When we pushed the buggies out the front door, the parking lot was dark, the ten thousand watts of parking bulbs out. And around us, as far as I could see, was pitch dark. We stopped, the carts squeaking, and stared.

CHAPTER 102

Ten minutes later, our new items in the backseat of the truck, we found out that the power outage was caused by a trip at the power station. I would go into greater detail except that verbiage meant diddle squat to me. It was Carl at the gas station who told me. I nodded intelligently and asked him if the two for two-dollar candy bar deal included Rolos. They didn't.

On the way back to Cole's we drove by the Pit. He spoke to the security officers there, who assured him that they would be diligent in watching for any vandals who appeared on the heels of the blackout.

I snorted when he drove off. Vandals? This was Quincy. Those guys were going to have a long night of waiting ahead of them if they expected trouble. We did one final loop of the town, then drove slowly back, his brights on, our eyes peeled for deer.

When we pulled down the long drive, the white house lit by the moonlight, I looked to my house and thought of Mama. This time of night, she'd be asleep. She wouldn't even know about the blackout but it felt odd for me to think of her, in that house, alone. Once I moved away she would always be alone. That idea, like every time before it, felt odd too. I would get used to it. I'd have to. It was only natural for the young to grow up and leave the nest.

We set up camp in the Kirklands' living room. I found candles and lit them, the large room glowing in flickering light, and I had the sudden vision of flames licking up the wall, the wallpaper bubbling, and hurried to blow out a few. There. Four candles lit. Enough to see by, just not in high definition. We unpacked in the living room, the floor strewn with our gear, Cocky picking his way gingerly through the pile. I saw some of his poo on the floor behind Cole and nodded toward it, passing him a can of wipes. I put on Cole's new cowboy hat and ripped open a Nerds rope, chewing on one end of it as I shifted through our haul. Cole returned, scooping up the rooster and I plucked out the bag of peas, holding them up to him. "Sprinkle some of these in his tub. He'll like digging through the bedding for them." My words came out garbled, through a mouthful of Nerds goodness, but Cole nodded, grabbing the bag and heading to the bathroom. We'd have to build an outside pen for Cocky. He was too big to be inside, despite whatever notions Cole had for making him a house chicken. I frowned around the piece of candy. *He'd. He'd* have to build an outside pen. It was silly for me to think that we'd continue hanging out. Just because the sex had destroyed my world and rebuilt it in an entirely new way. Just because we'd had fun and been reckless and kissed in a Walmart aisle. Whatever heartbreak I had coming when Cole Masten left town was my thing, not his. That was what I needed to remember.

"His light doesn't work."

I looked up to see Cole standing in the dim corner of the living room, by the bathroom. I shrugged. "So? He doesn't need the warmth anymore. That was just when he was a chick."

"Do you mind if we hang out on the back porch? Just 'til the power comes back on?" He held Cocky under his right arm, like a football. A football he now scratched the chest of.

I grabbed the newly purchased bottle of wine, hefting to my feet. "Sure. I'll grab some glasses."

After my third glass, our bare feet hanging off the edge of the porch, my head on his shoulder, I decided to tell him about that night. Rehearsal Dinner Night. We'd lost Cocky to the darkness, his cluck occasionally heard from somewhere far in the yard. Every once in a while, Cole would dig his hand into the peas and toss them out into the grass. Sometime next summer, Cyndi Kirkland would be pulling out pea sprouts and cursing his name. At some point, around the second glass, his right hand had slid into mine, our fingers linking, and stayed there. It was on the third glass that my head had rested on his shoulder and my mouth had opened.

"It was crazy," I said out of nowhere. "What I did that night. The article had it right, what happened."

"Crazy isn't always a bad thing." That was all he said, and I was glad. I let out a big breath and then told, for the first time ever, the whole story.

CHAPTER 103

On a farm, things happened. Hospitals were not close by, and Tallahassee was too far away if there was a problem. So we had things. Ipecac syrup was one of those things. If a kid, or a stupid adult, or an animal ate something they shouldn't, Ipecac caused a violent vomiting spell that got out all of the nasty. And Ipecac was what I reached for in The Plan.

It was easy to set up. The restaurant was serving crème brulee for dessert, topped with a medley of berries. I put the syrup in a flask, in a thigh holster. After the first round of toasts, I excused myself, walking right past the bathrooms and into the kitchen. I hugged Rita, the chef, and held up the flask. "Mind if I give the head table some extra flavor?" That was all it took. We were a dry county, liquor scant except in our private homes. She smiled. "Just pretend I didn't see you. The platters are numbered, your table is number one."

I'd like to say that I hesitated, my fingers twisting at the flask's silver neck, but that'd be a lie. Two days of pent up anger, an hour of polite dinner conversation with false friends… it all pushed my actions, and I left the kitchen a minute later with all twelve of my table's desserts tainted.

After that, there was nothing left to do but sit, sip my champagne, and watch.

When Ipecac hit, it was sudden. Explosive. If you gave someone too much, you could hurt them. I didn't give my victims too much; there was about a half cup in each dessert. Scott was, brilliantly enough, the first victim. I saw him take his first bite, and I stood up, moving a few steps back and leaning against the wall, my champagne glass hanging from my recently manicured (professionally!) fingertips.

Bridget saw me move and shot me a strange look, her elbow moving, out of sheer habit, to notify Corrine. Corrine glanced over, shrugged, and took her first bite of dessert. I stared point-blank at Bridget until she looked away, focusing on her dessert as if it was the most important thing in her life. Which, right then, it would be. Our table was up front, a long piece that cut the room in half, three couples on each side, Scott and I crammed on the end because weddings have this obsession with putting the bride and groom front and center, damn their need for elbow room to cut a steak.

My shoulders against the rose wallpapered wall, I watched the clock, a big silver piece that looked like it'd been around since the Civil War. Four minutes after Scott stuck that first bite into his deceitful mouth, it happened. He was speaking to Bobbie Jo at the moment, her sitting to his left, and there was no warning, no clutch of his stomach, holding of his mouth, no running to the bathroom. He just opened his mouth and vomit spewed out, soaking her lavender cardigan, unbuttoned low over those ridiculous breasts, her scream loud enough to make every head in the room turn. I giggled, watching Bobbie Jo's date, her cousin Frank, as he tried to move away, his hands frantic in their push against the table, but Scott wasn't done, his second attack came while trying to stand. Scott got his chair pushed back, got his feet under him, his hands on the table, and then it came again. We'd had fried green tomatoes with dinner. A piece of poorly chewed tomato caught the ear of Scott's Best Man, Bubba, and hung there for a moment, the big guy flailing at the piece, then he was the next victim, and Tara and Scott got coated by his wretch.

It was a horrific unfolding, the medicine hitting everyone within the same three minutes, every head in the room turned, mouths opened, and murmurs gaining volume as it kept getting worse. Stacey was the first to hit the floor, vomit already covering her lips and chin, her hand over her face, her heels loud on the floor as she ran down our table's side, then hit a pool of stench and slipped. I heard the splat as her dress, a Calvin Klein she had bragged over, hit the puddle. She screamed, her cry joining the sea, and tried to stand, her skinny legs flailing, slipped, tried again, and failed. It was hard to stand up when you wouldn't put your hands on the floor. It was hard to put your hands on the floor when the floor was covered in stomach contents.

One bystander had told *Variety Magazine* that it had been 'almost like a circus, with so many things happening you didn't know where to look.' I agreed with that statement. The week after the disaster, the cinematographer had asked, her voice tight with disdain, if I wanted the video from the event. I had already paid for it, after all. I had taken the video and sat on my living room floor, popped it in the DVD player, and watched it. That was the first time I felt guilt. I felt sick. I saw in high definition the moment that the poor sweet boyfriend of Tara's bent over. I saw my first grade teacher, old Mrs. Maddox, trying to hobble for the exit among the masses, clean guests infected by screaming, puking bridesmaids, innocent victims caught along the way in the bottleneck that was the sole exit.

"It was evil," I said quietly. "Doing it there. In front of everyone. Especially in a town where appearances and decorum are so important." It was hard to respect someone when you'd seen them vomit all over their grandmother, then run for the exit. That had been Corrine. Her ninety-two year old Grammie had chosen that unfortunate moment to come over and say hello, her frail hands gripping Corrine's chair for support when disaster hit.

"Isn't that why you did it there? To punish them?"

"Yeah but… I went too far." I didn't feel bad about the wedding party. It was all of the others whose night had been ruined. Mr. and Mrs. Thompson. I cringe at their faces, so much of their money wasted, their perfect son's perfect night destroyed…

Everyone had known it was me from the beginning. Maybe it was my manic laughter as I stood at the front of the room and watched the stampede. It was certainly confirmed by Rita, who pointed a flour-covered finger straight in my direction. I had shrugged, accepted the blame. It wasn't like I'd ever thought about discretion. I'd *wanted* them to know. I'd wanted them to realize what they had caused, what Bobbie Jo and Scott had caused. I wanted them to know that you didn't screw with Summer Jenkins and get away with it.

I'd been young, rebellious, and self-centered. And the town had, as a result, made me pay. My hour of glory had been the last moment in the Quincy sun. After that, the chill from Quincy's elite had been solid and unyielding, a layer of impermeable frost.

"You don't need them." Cole pulled my hand up and kissed it.

I turned to him. "I know that. I just wanted you to know. The—" *type of person I am.* That was what I wanted to say. I wanted him to stop this thing he'd been doing all night, looking at me like I was made of fairy dust. I didn't finish the sentence. Probably because I liked the way he had been looking at me. And I didn't want it to all break apart. I had told him what I had done. The magazine had gotten it pretty much right, even if it had been horrible to read. But I'd wanted to fill him in on my motivations. He could make his own decisions from that point on.

"I just won't ever cheat on you." He turned to me and patted his leg. "Come here."

I didn't question him, just crawled over, 'til my butt was on his thigh, my legs stretched over his lap, one of his hands holding me in place, the other tucking a bit of my hair behind my ear. "No man in his right mind would cheat on you."

If you had asked me, before that moment, if I'd had any self-doubt due to Scott's affair, I'd have said no. I'd have said that he was an idiot, and Bobbie Jo was a *ho*, and that it had nothing to do with me. But his simple sentence, stated with such resolution… it opened a crack in me that I hadn't known existed, a deep fissure that ran all the way to my bones.

He opened that crack, and a dark black tidal wave of insecurity and sadness rushed out.
Pretending that I didn't care if Quincy loved me.
Pretending that I didn't want the picket fence and the kid on my hip and the Thompson that followed my name.
Pretending that those girls were all bitches and I'd had real friends, but they'd just grown up and moved away or gotten lives, and that was fine because I had my books and my mama and lazy summer afternoons in the sunshine.

A pile of *pretends* and *ignores* and *feelings* that had been stuffed inside the dark marrow of my bones, and Cole Masten pulled them all out with just that sentence and that look and the pull on my neck and his kiss, soft and sweet, on my mouth.

No man in his right mind would cheat on you.
But a man in his right mind had cheated on me and it stung.

"You are incredible, Summer. I think you scared him with your beauty and your strength and that fucking incredible mouth. I think he felt insecure about it and found a woman who he felt superior to." He kissed me again, harder this time, and I pulled at his hair, clutched at his arm, and felt a part of me, a part of that crack, close, all of the yuck leaked out. I wanted to ask if he meant it, if that was a line of Hollywood bullshit or his real thoughts, but when I pulled back to ask, when I came off his lips and saw the look on his face, I knew. I knew that he wasn't full of it. And I realized, in that moment, in that look, that every feeling I had bottled up… my inner conflict of self-preservation—the push of hatred, the pull of attraction? He had it too. In his eyes searching mine, the emotion on his face, I saw more. More than just fairy dust attraction. Something deeper and fuller and more real.

I moved on his lap, repositioning myself to face him, straddling him, and I crossed my bare ankles behind him, on the porch floor, our faces close, his eyes closing when I trailed a finger across his lips. "I see you," I whispered, and those green eyes reemerged, looking at me, his brow furrowing, and I traced the lines of it as well. "God, you put up a lot of layers of asshole to keep people out."

"It's not asshole," he breathed, his mouth moving forward, burrowing into my neck, nuzzling at the skin, and he took a gentle bite, his hands cupping my ass and pulling me tighter to him. "It's me."

"No." I shook my head slightly and lifted his face with my hands, pulling him in for one kiss and then pushing him away. "*This* is you. And you are perfect. I love *this* you."

His breath stopped against my mouth, and he didn't move, didn't pull back. He thought that I was incredible and beautiful and strong but probably didn't want *this*, and it took every bit of my strength to keep talking. "And I love your asshole self too. I think I'm addicted."

"You?" he responded, his words coming out in a rush of air. "I haven't stopped thinking about this." He moved one hand lower on my butt and ran his fingers across the silk barrier of my panties, between my spread legs. That was what I got for straddling this man with a dress on. He did it again, his fingers pushing at the silk, pulling it against me, and he stared at me, his eyes hungry. "I haven't stopped thinking about that, or this…" He pressed his lips to mine, his mouth eager and rough. "Or these…" His hands pulled my dress down and came back up my bare front, lifting my breasts, the image of them, in his strong hands, enough to make me grind a little against him, and he was hard, and I could feel it, and I wanted it but it wasn't enough. "But most of all I am addicted to *you.*" He said the words softly and stared down at my breasts in his hands, my legs wrapped around his waist, my dress bunched at my hips. "I can't stop. I don't think I can ever stop."

It wasn't *I love you.* But when he wrapped his hands around my back and lifted me up, his butt pushing off the porch and onto the grass, his hands gentle when they lowered me to the ground… when he pulled down his shorts and lifted my dress, his body settling over me, his lips on my skin, his name a gasp from my lips when he pushed himself inside… it was, in that moment, enough. Having Cole Masten addicted to me was enough. Having him tell me that Scott was wrong and I wasn't broken… that was more than enough.

CHAPTER 104

The power came on, at some point during the night. I heard Cole stand, heard the slide of wood as he shut the windows, then he was back in bed, with his hand sliding around my waist as he pulled me against him. I was naked, and his chest against my back was warm and comforting, his hand, cupping my breast strong and possessive. He gently kissed the back of my neck, and I smiled. He said something, but I didn't hear it, sleep pulling me back under.

In the morning, I woke first, his arm hot and heavy against my chest. Sunlight was streaming through the curtains, and I blinked a few times at the alarm clock, trying to see the time. Ten fifteen. We'd slept late. I slid carefully out from underneath his arm and walked downstairs. Pulled on Cole's T-shirt, abandoned on the living room floor, and my panties, which had somehow ended up on the stairs, then put Cocky in the backyard and laughed as he chased a squirrel, his chest puffed, wings flapping. Our leftover steaks were in the fridge so I tossed them in a skillet, heating them on low while I got out eggs and milk, stepping over Nerf bullets as I moved, my grin widening as I remembered our late night battle. I'd claimed the kitchen as my base, Cole had taken the dining room, and we'd played capture the rooster handkerchief. Afterward, when I'd run around, picking up bullets while swigging wine, Cole had mentioned a maid. Now, in the light of day, my eyes skipped over the carnage with a wince. I cracked the final egg in the skillet and heard Cole's voice holler from upstairs.

"What?" I yelled back, spatula in hand, the egg popping in the hot skillet.

"Come back to bed!" His voice sounded groggy.

"Come down to breakfast!" I tossed my yell up the stairs, then moved quickly back to the skillet, stirring the eggs before they browned. I heard a response, some words bellowed out, and ignored them, a smile eating at the corner of my mouth. A few seconds later, feet hit the floor, and I heard the stumble of him out of the bedroom and down the stairs.

"Morning." His voice still held cobwebs, and I turned with a smile, one hand holding the skillet, the other spooning scrambled eggs onto a plate. I almost dropped the iron skillet when I saw him.

He was naked, his right hand unsuccessfully over his junk, half of it peeking out from said hand. His abs were on full display, his body beautiful, the lines and cuts of his shoulders, the hard plane of his chest, the clench of his forearm as he adjusted his grip and still didn't wrangle it all. "Morning." I grinned.

"You can't cook breakfast in my shirt unless you want a fucking." He growled out the words and pulled at himself, his eyes doing a full sweep of me.

"You can't eat my breakfast if you don't put on some pants." I pointed with a spatula at his shorts, which lay in a pile by the fridge. Ah… yes. The whipped cream. He was worried it would spoil due to the lack of refrigeration. I had suggested we stick it in the outside freezer. He had popped off the cap with his teeth and grinned at me, turning his head and spitting it out, and if that hadn't been the sexiest thing ever, I didn't know what was. Possibly what happened next, his slow wander behind me, his mouth dropping to my neck, his teeth gentle when they closed on my shoulder, his hands dropping from Summer's Favorite Organ Ever and running up my hips, under his big shirt and settling on my waist, his head tilting as he looked under the shirt. "Oh… Summer…" he tsked his tongue, his fingers sliding under the edges of my underwear. "These are going to get in the way."

"No they're not," I warned, setting down the spatula and turning to face him, fixing to tell him off for interrupting my cooking. But when I turned around, he bumped against my thighs, and my eyes dropped and stared and when I looked back up, at his cocky face, his hands pulling me forward, his mouth dropping for a kiss… Well, a woman could only be so concerned with eggs when a man was that naked and hard for her. I reached back and flipped off the burner.

CHAPTER 105

Cole was done for. He'd kept thinking, after sex, that it'd fade. That he'd come to his senses and find his footing. Realize that she was a normal girl and that they'd had one night of fun and now filming should be smoother, his life in Quincy less antagonistic. But he was still crazy in the middle of the night, when he fought sleep just so that he could enjoy holding her just a little bit longer. And he was definitely still crazy when he woke up, a morning chub out of control, and craved her. Smelling food, finding her in his shirt, in his kitchen, a spatula in hand, had made it even worse. He'd been attracted to women before, had loved fucking Nadia, but had never had someone crawl under his skin like this. He looked at this woman and saw her bouncing his child on her hip, saw her running through the field on his Montana ranch, saw her sitting in a velvet seat at the Academy Awards, her hand light on his arm, her mouth warm against his ear. And all of those images scared the hell out of him.

Now, sex in the kitchen completed, breakfast eaten, dishes washed, he watched her. She stood in the living room, her hands on adorable hips, frustration in her stance when he rounded the couch and faced her. "What's wrong?"

"I can't carry all of this stuff home." She gestured to her haul from last night, a pile that included a popcorn machine (she'd never had one), iPad (he'd insisted on it), and minion pajamas, among four bags of other things. She had been planning to wear the pajamas to bed, thank God she hadn't.

"I can drop you off." He didn't want to drop her off. He wanted to drive over to her house, pick up all of her cheap shit, and move it in. He wanted to sit down and work out their shooting schedule, their next fifty years, find out every dream she'd ever had and then make them realities. He wanted to fly Brad DeLuca up here and personally hug the man for putting him in Quincy early, for putting him on her doorstep, for saving the rest of his life.

"The reporters," she reminded him, chewing on a thumbnail as she reached down and shifted through the closest bag.

"Fuck the reporters."

"Ha." She pulled out a pack of gum, Bubblicious, and ripped it open, holding it up before shaking one out. "Want one?"

"No." He watched her unwrap it and pop the pink cube in her mouth. A children's gum. She chewed children's gum. Her jaw worked, and she glanced up at him, popping a bubble before speaking. "What?"

"Can we talk about this?" A stupid question. He should have kept his mouth shut. Taken her home. Let everything play out properly. Or not play out properly. And in that risk laid his worry.

"About us?" She popped her gum again, and he fought the urge to kiss it out of her mouth.

"Yes."

"Are you freaked out by what I said last night?" She tossed down the gum and turned to fully face him, her arms crossing in front of her chest. Not defiantly, her arms were tight, as if she was giving herself a hug, her hands under her armpits. Nervous Summer. A new side. Nadia would never have responded in this manner. She would have played games, been cool, skirted direct conversation while he chased her down with questions and insinuations. Their fights were exhausting, which is probably why they both avoided them—him working out his anger on their gym's punching bag, her on, apparently, other men.

"No." It was the truth. Her weak declarations that could be analyzed a hundred different ways depending on how long a man wanted to stay awake… those didn't freak him out. Not when they were so pale compared to his feelings, live and vivid in a thousand different hues. He looked down, at the pile of shopping bags, and wished he'd picked a different location for this. It'd be too serious if he invited her to sit down, yet standing here, in this dim room, the fan above them off balance and ticking, wasn't exactly how he imagined this going. Not that he had thought this through. If he had, he'd have duct taped his mouth shut. Bringing this up now could only lead to disaster.

"So talk." Her shoulders had loosened a little, and her chewing quieted.

He took a deep breath and jumped off the cliff. "I meant what I said last night. A man would be crazy to cheat on you. A man would be crazy to want something else, when he could have you. I've had you—the real you—for these last eighteen hours, and I don't want anything else. I don't think I'll ever want anything else." He stepped closer and looked down at her. "Tell me we aren't great together."

She looked away, into a far corner of the room, then back up at him. "We aren't, Cole. This…" she gestured between the two of them, her hand a floppy wave of heartbreak, "… this doesn't even *compare* to what I had with Scott." She lifted one of her shoulders in a tiny shrug of indifference. "I'm sorry."

"But… you told me you loved me. I thought…" He stepped away from her and pressed his palms to his eyes, everything in his life spiraling down in one hellacious drain of WTF.

"You thought I was a terrible actress." There was a smile in her response, and he looked up, confused. She blew a giant bubble and popped it.

"So you were acting? With me?" His mind started shuttering through their night, and she rolled her eyes, stepping forward and wrapping her arms around his neck, her mouth sugary when she pressed it to his lips.

"God, you are dense," she whispered against his mouth. "Yes, we are great together. Yes, I don't want anyone else either. Yes, you big stupid man who can't say the words that every woman wants to hear, I love you too." She leaned back to say more, but he didn't let her go. He crushed her into his arms and somewhere, in the course of their kiss, he got her gum and swallowed it and then threw her over his shoulder and carried her upstairs.

CHAPTER 106

When we pulled into the Holden's driveway, the gate was open, the string of stranger's cars now in a neat line in front of my house. At our approach heads moved in the cars, doors opened, rigs were grabbed, and feet stepped quickly out, flashbulbs popping in the brightest sun that God could provide.

"Are you sure we don't need to call Casey?" I asked nervously, Cole's hand tightening on mine.

"First rule of Hollywood, babe. The gods don't ask permission. Own your shit and don't forget to smile." He put the truck into park and leaned over, waiting for a kiss, his smile widening when I leaned over, and our skin was lit when the paps went crazy.

I giggled, and he smiled, taking one more kiss before he grabbed the handle. "Let's go raise some hell." I grabbed my handle and cracked the door, a stranger before me wearing a Lakers hat, his black shirt a poor choice in this heat, a camera in his hand one that probably cost more than my truck. I smiled politely and he lifted his camera in response. We met at the front of the truck, Cole's hand reaching out for me. When I grabbed it, he pulled me all the way in, his arms supporting me as he dipped me low, my shriek in response captured by every camera present. He smiled down at me, and I scowled. Then he kissed me long enough that I blushed.

"Enough," I murmured. "I think they got it."

Cole pulled me up with a smirk. "Not yet." He kept his hand on my lower back, and we stepped toward the house, the curtain moving in the front window, and I wondered what on Earth Mama was thinking of this. On the front steps, Cole turned, hugging me to his side and facing the group, seven or eight bodies scattered across the lawn without any concern over my planting. I glared at the closest one, and he moved away from my butterfly garden, his hands raising in apology.

"I'm assuming, since you've squatted yourself on this personal property, that you know this beautiful woman beside me. But what you don't know is that she is mine. You fuck with her, you fuck with my team and—more importantly—you fuck with me. If I ever convince her to marry me, you all are invited to our wedding. We'll be serving crème brulee, be sure to eat up." I smacked his stomach hard enough to make him wince, and he pulled me against him, his head dropping for another kiss. "Just a joke, babe. Except for the marriage part. Too early?" He pulled off, his eyes on mine, a cautious smile on his features.

"Too early," I said sternly. "Especially since, Mr. Masten, you're still a married man."

"Ouch." He winced. "And you know better than to call me that."

"Mr. Masten?" I said playfully and wheeled out of his arms, reaching for the door handle, his hand too slow when it tried to catch me.

"Damn woman." He hooked a finger in the back tie of my sundress, pulling me back before I could twist the knob. "Have I told you that I love you?"

I didn't respond to him, I just smiled, and then the door opened and Momma was there, and her smile was stretched bigger than I'd ever seen it.

CHAPTER 107

TWO DAYS LATER

The bang on the trailer's front door was so hard that the walls shook. I rolled over and poked, with one lazy finger, Cole's side. He groaned. "I can't move, woman. You've destroyed me."

I laughed, my own muscles too weak to move, much less to stand, dress, and get to the door. "I thought we had two hours before the next shoot," I whispered to him. It couldn't have been two hours; there was no way. It'd been… I looked for the clock, but it was in the trailer's main room and that was a good eight feet away. I laid my head against Cole's chest instead. The person at the door pounded again, a series of raps that showed no patience or timidity whatsoever.

"Just pretend we aren't here," Cole stage-whispered, his hand tightening around me when I started to get up.

Our view on the bed afforded a door's width glimpse into the living room of the trailer. Enough of a glimpse that, when the front door was kicked in, we saw the edge of it swing, the man stomping up the steps appearing in our doorway a second later. I gripped the sheet to my chest and tried to place the man… Cole's attorney. DeRico or something like that. *Here.* With Cole's trailer door now lying on its side, cockeyed on the floor.

"Shit," Cole grumbled and pulled the sheet higher on me, his legs swinging off the bed, and he grabbed a pillow, covering himself as he glowered at the man. "What the fuck, DeLuca. Your phone doesn't work?"

"Don't bitch at me about communication. Not when you two go and play that stunt on national television without calling me first. Nadia is *pissed.* Beyond pissed. I had to listen to that bitch personally; she left me an eight-minute voicemail explaining her detailed plans for your castration."

Cole shrugged. "Want to give Summer some respect and get the fuck out of this room?"

The man glanced at me, then nodded. "I'm sorry." He made eye contact with the apology, and I shrugged my forgiveness. He turned his back to me and hovered at the door, looking to Cole.

"I'm coming," Cole barked. "Give me a minute."

DeLuca closed the bedroom's door, and Cole was on the bed and above me in a second. "Sorry babe." He kissed my neck and hopped off the bed, grabbing a pair of jeans off the floor and pulling them on.

"Will everything be okay? With Nadia?" We had conveniently forgotten her in this whirlwind of change, Cole solidly on the Obsessed with Me bus, oblivious to any of the side effects that seemed to plague Don and Casey's view of our new union.

He shrugged into a shirt. "We already came to an agreement. We're good. She's just pissed. It's normal." He squeezed my foot, the closest thing to him, and winked at me. "I'll be back."

CHAPTER 108

The chair, a leather straight back that sat by the door, was in serious danger of joining Cole's door on its trip to the set dumpster. DeLuca leaned on the back of it with both hands, his knuckles white, his face dark.

Cole sat down on the couch, his hand waving at DeLuca to proceed. "Okay, give it to me."

"Nadia is contesting the mediation document, saying that your good faith actions in the mediation were false, and that you were in love with Summer the entire time."

Cole tilted his head, trying to connect the dots. "But… she's in love with the director prick. Has been the whole time. Why the fuck does it matter who I've been doing what with?"

DeLuca let out a long, exasperated sigh. "Because you *knew* she was doing the director prick. It was a shared understanding. See, from Nadia's side, she was under the impression, when agreeing to our terms, that there was a chance that you two could rekindle things."

"What the fuck?" he exploded. "*She* was the one who filed for divorce. And rekindle things?" He laughed and felt almost delirious, this a situation happening to someone else. "Getting back with Nadia hasn't been part of the equation since before I even left LA." He looked to the bedroom door and wanted Summer out there. Hated her shut away like she wasn't part of this. He looked back at DeLuca, exasperated. "You're the one who told me, if I loved Summer, that it was okay."

"Is that what this is? It wasn't that damn long ago that I asked you and you didn't know."

"I love her." Cole nodded tightly and met the attorney's eyes. "Without a doubt."

"Right now, you have two options. Stay with Summer and split *The Fortune Bottle* with Nadia, or push this fling aside, we'll repair things with Nadia and the press, and the movie will be yours. All yours."

There wasn't a moment of hesitation in Cole's response. "Fuck no. Give her half if that's what it will take."

"You *sure* about that?" DeLuca let go of the chair and stepped closer, his head tilting as he examined Cole's face. "You're willing to walk away from half of this? Over *her*?" He nodded toward the closed bedroom door.

"You told me once that you had your soulmate. Would you have given half of a movie away for a lifetime with her?"

Brad's eyes narrowed. "You're not permanently walking away from her in my scenario. All I'm asking is for you to put this relationship on hold. Give it six months, then you can reunite, try it again."

"Would you risk your relationship with your wife?" Cole repeated, and it wasn't a question at all. It was a point, and Brad stared at him for a long moment before nodding in understanding.

"She must be special," he said quietly.

"She is." Cole grinned. "Now get the fuck out of here so that I can get back to her."

"No second thoughts?" DeLuca said. "It's half of your baby."

"No." Cole shook his head. "It's a movie. That's it." A statement he would never have made a few months ago. Back when his entire life was *The Fortune Bottle*, and he was ready to tear apart his soul if it meant keeping it from Nadia. But now, with just a flicker of risk to his new relationship, it had lost all of its value. He wanted to be done with Nadia, done with the press, done with everything but the feisty blonde behind that bedroom door. Maybe it'd been the months in this town, a place where pretense and competition didn't exist. Maybe it was the way that, through Summer, he had taken the first hard look at himself and wanted to change.

"Wow." DeLuca clapped him on the back, walking past the broken door and out, the summer heat pushing through the opening.

"Anything you need from me?" Cole called.

"Oh, no. Please." DeLuca waved his hand. "Less is more, Cole. Less is more." He moved into the crowd, and Cole stood in the doorway and caught Justin's eye.

"We're on it," Justin called, and Cole saw two engineers jogging over, tool bags in hand. Cole waved his thanks, nodded to the men, and stepped back, into the bedroom, closing the door behind him.

She sat on the edge of the bed, her pantyhose back on, her hands busy on the clasps of her shoes. "Everything okay?"

He leaned against the wall. "My door might disagree, but everything's great otherwise."

She stood and zipped up the back of her skirt. "You sure? I want to know if I'm causing problems."

He stepped forward and looked down at her. "I love telling you when you're causing problems. But no, right now, sadly, you are behaving entirely too much."

She grinned. "I'll brainstorm tonight over ways to cause you more grief."

"I'd appreciate that immensely."

"Yeah, yeah, yeah. You guys are in love, we get it," Justin called loudly from the living room. "Are you dressed? Because I need to get Mr. Loverboy over to Don."

"That's you," she whispered, her eyes mischievous, and his fingers itched to push her onto the bed, just for a moment, just long enough to make those hazel eyes roll back in pleasure.

Justin coughed from the living room, and she pushed Cole to the door. "He's coming," she called out, and he frowned down at her. "I'll see you on set," she promised and shut the door, his door, on his face.

Cole turned with a scowl, and Justin laughed. "Give Don ten minutes. Then you can come back to her."

CHAPTER 109

The movie wrapped on a Tuesday. It felt weird, the short week. Like the last days of school where you just watched movies and signed yearbooks, we all kind of milled around like lost children, Don barking at everyone constantly, the few scenes filmed were short redos that he hadn't been in love with the first time.

It was so much easier to film with Cole after that night. I didn't realize how much I'd been pushing him off, how much I'd fought my heart. When I stopped that fight, the surge of affection was scary, the feeling heady, the risk exhilarating. Now I knew why they said you *fell* in love. I plummeted with no parachute, and hoped like hell he would catch me when I hit the bottom. Only, there hadn't been a bottom. There was just him, his cocky grin grabbing me from the moment I woke up to the moment our bedroom light turned out. His hand sliding up my thigh in the midst of a production meeting, his sexual touch turning sweet as he found my hand and grabbed it. His chuckle, the one that used to light my anger—I was addicted to it. I understood his laughter now; I knew his smiles and his glares and everything between them.

A week earlier, we camped out on the edge of the Holdens' plantation, down by the lake. Ate s'mores and drank wine, and he told me about his mom, and how much he loved mine. And then we talked about Life After the Movie and what would happen to her. Cole wanted to bring her to California. I told him that Mama would make up her own mind about where she wanted to be. I'd never been to California, but I couldn't see her there. Not with everything Cole had described it to be. I wasn't even sure I saw myself there.

He was the first person I ever told about my Departure From Quincy. I think it hurt him a little. Not in a feelings sense, but more like the idea physically pained him. I had spent a lot of nights thinking, in my bed at night, staring up at my ceiling. My Departure From Quincy plans had been quite glamorous. I'd give Mama a budget and let her pick her poison—there were new homes going up on the edge of town, and eighty thousand dollars would get her a brick three-bedroom, two-bath with everything she never had. Or, if she'd rather, she could take that money and find something else. Maybe an older house on some land, farther out, on one of our hundreds of dirt roads. And I'd trade in the truck and get an SUV, something with air conditioning and low mileage. And then I was going to go someplace cooler. Maybe North Carolina. Find a town big enough to disappear in. Buy a house, find a job, maybe go to college.

That'd been the gist of it all, my fantasies lining up into place in the dark of my room. Before Cole. I told him the plan and watched his throat as he swallowed. He turned his head away, and the moon lit the line of his profile. We had joked about marriage, in front of the reporters. Had been connected at the hip since that night at his house. But we hadn't discussed the future. He'd tried, I'd evaded, and then, beside that fire, overlooking the lake, I stopped. I stopped running and turned and faced our future.

"What do you want? For us?" I asked the question and he turned, pulling me onto his lap so we faced each other.

"It's not about what I want. I want you to be happy. So I need to know what you want."

"I think I want to go back with you. To California."

"It's not a city you can get lost in, Summer. Not tied to me." His voice was guarded, tinged in worry.

"That's okay. I'm a big girl. I can tough it out." I had smiled up at him and saw the turn in his eyes, knew—before he'd even reached for me—what was coming. When Cole Masten loves, it is scary. The man puts his entire heart out with the expectation that it will be crushed. Sometimes I worry at the way he looks at me, at the way I feel for him. It seems too precious, too rare—our combination of souls. If I ever lose this man, I will never recover. If he ever loses me, I fear for the man that he will become.

I could take on California for him. I knew that already, but decided it there, by that fire, his push of me back onto the blanket, his hands frantic as they pulled at my clothes.

Together, we could take on anything.

CHAPTER 110

The aftermath of the magazine article was big. Bigger than I ever expected, bigger than even Casey and Cole had expected. Bigger… but different. The public, the big scary monster that I had been told to expect… *loved* me. Embraced my act of rebellion with a protective fury that scared the news outlets into submission. I avoided interviews, declined requests for comment, and with each retreat from the spotlight, my lore grew. Fan pages popped up in my name. A jilted ex in Chicago pulled a Summer Jenkins of her own at a bachelorette party. The hype also helped *The Fortune Bottle*, award nominations rumored before the premiere, the foreign distribution deals pouring in. I was happy for the movie but didn't want the fame, the attention claustrophobic in its unending continuity. The fame I may not have wanted but I loved the support. I didn't realize how much I needed it, didn't realize how the positive feedback, the love of strangers, would be inhaled by my greedy soul. The circus of support washed away the three years of scorn, the hundreds of dirty looks, upturned noses, and whispers. It made me feel, for the first time since that night, that I wasn't in the wrong. *They were.* That *I* wasn't the one broken but that *they* were.

I hadn't gone back to Quincy since the movie wrapped. I packed up my things that last week of filming, Mama and I staying up late, my belongings scant when put into cardboard boxes and weeded through. I threw out a lot. The purge was good for me.

And when I boarded Cole's jet for California, I felt like a new woman. One with a future. One whose past had made me stronger, better.

CHAPTER 111

The last time Cole saw Nadia, he was in his old attorney's office. He sat in the conference room's crocodile chairs, feet stretched out on the slate floor, and stared at a Harvard diploma with the prick's name in gold ink. DeLuca hadn't wanted him here. He'd wanted this to be done on neutral ground, but Cole wanted this last visit. Plus, with the bloodbath that they were wading through, it was a little victory that Cole felt they needed.

DeLuca's giant ultimatum turned out to be bullshit, a test of sorts. He was telling the truth about Nadia contesting the mediation agreements. He wasn't telling the truth about rolling over to them. Cole should have known better. This man had probably tied down his wife and forced the wedding ring on her hand. He certainly ripped the neck out of Nadia's response, and the paperwork got put in line and filed per their original mediation agreement.

But Cole was still only getting half of *The Fortune Bottle.* No one knew that except for Justin, DeLuca, and Cole. He was going to give the other half to Summer. Without her, the movie would have been flat. Without her, he'd have flayed around Quincy mourning the end of his life and probably drinking himself into rehab. Without her… he just couldn't imagine life without her anymore.

He wasn't gonna tell Summer about the movie just yet. He knew her, and the conversation wasn't going to go well. She wouldn't be a normal girl and go misty-eyed and cheer at the thought of eternal wealth. Her brow would tighten, her hands would clench, and Cole had full confidence that there would be a fight over the gift. But he looked forward to that fight, loved when they fought. And when the fight ended, his hands in her hair, her eyes wild, her body crawling up his, her lips… God. He'd never get his fill of kissing her.

He'd tell her after Sundance. When she was high on all of the critics' praise and was in a good mood. Maybe the carnage would be less then. The movie was wrapped, sealed in tins with the code name *Hey Harry* printed on them. It was the best work Cole had ever done. It was the best work Don had ever done. And, according to Summer, it was the only work she would ever do. With another woman, Cole would doubt that statement. But not her. She didn't want the attention, was convinced she didn't need the money, and had turned her full focus on nesting. Today, they were going to see an estate in Brentwood. It had eight and a half acres so she wasn't allowed to bitch about being crowded. The realtor promised Summer that, despite its twelve thousand square foot size, that it was 'cozy,' so it would be his head on the chopping block if it weren't.

Something bumped against Cole's elbow, and he looked up, past the death glare from Nadia and to the source of the tap: Brad DeLuca. "Sign where it's flagged." He pushed a stack of papers toward Cole, who signed as quickly as possible without appearing rushed, each turned page one less tie between he and Nadia. And at the end, his last signature slow and purposeful, Cole Masten was officially divorced.

CHAPTER 112

I have officially become a homeowner. Well… not just me. A big lug of man meat named Cole Masten… oh, you've heard of him? Yeah, I think he did a Doublemint gum ad or something. Anyway, Cole Masten and I now own a four-bedroom home over in Newberry. It's on twenty acres with a barn, paddocks and enough room for Cocky to hunt peas on till his legs fall off. It's also two hours from LA, which Cole likes to gripe about but I'm getting him a helicopter for his birthday, so *shhh* he can find something else to complain about. I'm also getting us lessons, so hopefully, one of us will be able to use the thing. I have no doubt that I will master it first, despite Cole being intimidatingly talented at everything he attempts. Okay, I'll confess. I already know how to fly it. Justin's been sneaking me over to Van Nuys when Cole's been working. But he's sworn to keep the secret, and I'm sure as sugar not going to say anything so there. Instead, I will look like a natural and will *finally* beat my future husband at something.

Oh, right. We're getting married. That's another secret. Not the engagement—that was plastered on every news channel in town before Cole even got off his knee. But the wedding date and location is still a secret. It's in six weeks, at the ranch in Montana. I swear, Heaven is hidden at that ranch. I understand why Cole bought it. It's perfection, wrapped in dewy sunrises and the huff of horses and the smell of wildflowers. *Heaven.* Until winter strikes, then it's *brutal.* Miserable, freezing… I kissed goodbye to any thoughts of living there full-time that first December visit. Turns out that I become a bit of a tenderfoot when temperatures drop below freezing. But it doesn't seem to bother Mama. She claimed one of the cabins and settled in, happy as could be. She wanted a job so Cole put her in charge of the grounds. She rides a four-wheeler around and makes sure that the plantings are as they should be, and spends the warmer months on her knees, in the dirt, planting. I think—now I may be wrong—but I think that she and Robert, one of the workers there, have a flirtation kicking. Mama and flirtation. Two things I never thought I'd see in the same sentence. Cole and I are laying bets on their behavior at the wedding. I'll win of course. Nobody knows that woman better than me.

So Mama's happy in Montana and we've settled in the Newberry house full-time. The property was a teensy bit out of my original price range but since the rest of my Departure From Quincy plan went to hell, so did my budget. And apparently I'm going to be rich the rest of my life on *The Fortune Bottle* money so I can afford to splurge a little. Did you know that Cole was *surprised* when he gave me half the movie and I accepted? Surprised. Shocked is actually a better descriptor. He kind of cringed a little when he delivered the news, his posture stiff, leaning away from me, as if he expected me to hit him. I accepted the gift, of course. Very graciously, I might add. Who wouldn't? Granted… I didn't realize exactly how much half of a movie was worth. Now that I know, it was a little greedy, me just accepting the gift without at least a half-hearted attempt to refuse the kindness. But the man was right; our chemistry is what made the movie a success. And it has been successful. A hundred million dollar opening weekend. Five hundred million so far worldwide. I don't know exactly what that means to the bottom line but it made Cole whoop and holler and spin me around until I got dizzy and forced him to take me to bed.

Before Cole, I had never been half of a whole, a pair of two joined so closely that it was hard to see where one personality ended and the other began. With Scott, I was always just *there*, occasionally stuck to his side, trying to chime into his conversations, waiting for the wedding that would put everything in its proper place. Now, I am half of *us*, Cole and I so in tune, so connected, that I don't know how I ever functioned alone.

America has also merged us, our two names too cumbersome so we are simply Sole. They call us Solemates, and I roll my eyes whenever it is said but secretly, I love it.

They say that love is finding your soul's match in another. I found my match. I found him, let him wrestle me to the ground, and then turned around and made him mine. I'm so glad that I didn't scare him off, I'm so glad that he didn't stop chasing. I'm so glad that Bobbie Jo screwed Scott and I found out about it. I'm so glad that Hollywood and dirt roads met in the uniqueness of Quincy. And I'm so glad that I was there, in that faded one-piece, when that damaged, beautiful man landed in our town.

EPILOGUE

Cole looked over at her, her long legs stretched into the floorboard of his Maserati, her short red shorts ones that he couldn't wait to rip off. Before them, in all of its grandeur, Walmart, the parking lot full, busy Californians rushing forward with personalized shopping bags, cell phones to their ears, importance thick in the smog of the city.

"You ready for this?" Cole asked, a grin on his face.

She reached up, pulling with both hands on the edges of her brown paper bag, her hands adjusting until her eyes were on his, gleaming out from a face with a teardrop tattoo, a blood-red pout, and a nose ring. "Do you even *have* to ask?"

Cole laughed, tugging down on his own bag, Summer working on it all morning, his dramatic mustache one that twisted and curled, bushy eyebrows on top that would cause his stylist to fall over dead.

"Can someone please, for the love of God, remind me again why we are doing this?" they turned at the muffled voice, twin faces staring at them from the backseat. There had been long deliberation last night, their brains fueled by Summer's fruit pizza and margaritas, over Ben and Justin's bag people identities. Cole turned to the shorter head of the two, Justin's Elvis face slumping back in his seat while Ben, who had wanted, for once in his flamboyant life, to be a girl, clapped his hands excitedly. He was supposed to be Marilyn Monroe, had spent over four hours on a brown paper masterpiece that would have a life of less than twenty minutes.

"We're doing this," Summer said patiently, "because Cocky needs a tether ball and we need the supplies to build it."

"They are going to think we are robbing the place and will shoot us,"

Ben said, his hands excitedly clapping. Cole stared at him and wondered why, of all things, *that* would be said in a gleeful tone. But Marilyn Monroe did have a point. Which is why, unbeknownst to Ben and Summer, Justin had already called the store. Spoken to a manager. Used Cole's name and black AMEX and celebrity status to convince the man to let them shop in ridiculous disguise. Inside the Walmart were already ten of his security, in plainclothes, ready to keep any crazies at bay. Still, there was no doubt that this field trip would probably end within five minutes of beginning.

"This is *California*," Summer said, in a tone that put Cole's fine state somewhere on the level of a kiddie park. "No guns, remember? You all love running around unprotected. Plus, no one's going to shoot a pregnant woman, so push me in front if you feel scared. Everyone in the backseat, stop being babies and get out of the car."

They opened the doors and stepped out of the car, and if he thought he loved her before, that was nothing compared to this.

AUTHOR'S NOTE

Quincy is a real town and its seventy-six Coca-Cola millionaires exist. It is located in north Florida (not Georgia), but besides that small detail, I tried to stay true to its roots. A local banker by the name of Pat Munroe convinced over seventy Quincy residents to invest in original Coca-Cola shares, even writing loans for their purchase. Those original shares were as low as nineteen dollars and are *each* now valued at over ten million dollars. What I said about Coke loyalty is true. Order a Pepsi in Quincy and you may get shown the door.

My chicken's name was Knobby. Knobby Knees but that was a bit of a mouthful so we called him Knobby. He was a horrible crower, never mastered that art, but he was fluffy and white and came inside our home on frequent occasions, despite what my mother believes to the contrary. My hometown was very similar to Quincy, only we didn't have millionaires, we only had good people who looked out for each other and would give you the shirt off of their back. I walked down memory lane a lot when writing this book, and it was one of my favorite things about writing it. Honestly, I don't know if I've *ever* had as much fun writing a book as I did with this one. I fell in love with the town, and the story and with Summer and Cole. I hope you did too.

If you *did* enjoy this book, there are a number of ways that you can support it:

First, please call or email a friend and tell them about this book. If you *really* want them to read it, consider lending or gifting it to them.

Also, please consider leaving a review for this book on websites like Amazon or Goodreads. Research has showed that reviews and friend recommendations are the strongest catalyst for readers' purchase decisions!

If you'd like to read more of my books, below is a list of my other titles. I'd also suggest signing up for my Newsletter or my New Release eBlast to be notified when my next book releases. You can sign up for either or both of those lists at www.nextnovel.com.

Thank you so much for your support! And please come visit me on Facebook or Instagram, where you can find out more about my writing process and personal life. Warning, my Twitter feed is extremely X-rated. J

Sincerely yours,

Alessandra

OTHER BOOKS BY ALESSANDRA TORRE

Black Lies

When socialite Layana Fairmont meets Brant Sharp, a billionaire genius, she falls hard. Too bad that Brant holds a secret… and another man is pulling her away. This 3X New York Times Bestseller has over 5,000 5-star reviews from readers!

Sex. Love. Repeat.

Madison is a SoCal beach bum with two men in her life: Stewart, a businessman with an addiction to his job and Paul, a professional surfer. Both men are in love with her, both men are aware that she has a second boyfriend. How will this twisted love triangle end? Find out in this USA Today Bestseller that was nominated for Book of the Year seven times and voted Best Twist by readers!

Blindfolded Innocence

The first book in the Innocence Trilogy, Julia Campbell is a feisty college student with no plans to settle down. Then she meets Brad DeLuca, a divorce attorney who had bedded half of the town, including his own clients. Sparks fly in this #1 Erotica bestselling series about forbidden love and breaking society's sexual norms.

The Girl in 6E

Awarded 'Suspense of the Year' by RT Book Reviews, this erotic suspense is also in production to be a movie! Deanna Madden was a normal seventeen-year-old girl when her mother killed her entire family. Now, Deanna struggles with her own demons, locking herself away in her apartment to keep herself from killing others. Working online as a sex cam operator, Deanna meets a stranger online and debates leaving her apartment to save a kidnapped girl.

The Dumont Diaries

Candace Tapers was a stripper, desperate for something better. Nathan Dumont was a stranger looking for a wife. But being a trophy wife isn't what Candy expected when she entered his life. And it turns out that Nathan is hiding a lot of secrets behind that sexy glare…

Tight

A girl kept prisoner. A woman falling in love with a man who is hiding something. This USA Today Bestseller explores the two worlds and the moment when they collide.

CPSIA information can be obtained
at www.ICGtesting.com
Printed in the USA
LVOW04s0330161215
466795LV00026B/2209/P